JAYNE ANN KRENTZ

WILDEST HEARTS

POCKET BOOKS

New York   London   Toronto   Sydney   Singapore

and adventures, which we don't want to end. Read, absorb, and enjoy."

Now available...Look for *Grand Passion* and *Absolutely, Positively*, collected in one stunning new volume from Pocket Books!

GRAND PASSION

"Filled with the kind of intelligent, offbeat characters...[who] are so fun to get to know that it's hard to close the book on them."

"Krentz at her best...with the snappy dialogue that has become her trademark and a cast of characters you want to know personally."

ABSOLUTELY, POSITIVELY

"[A] cheerful escapist package combining sex and mystery...."

"A suspenseful and satisfying story that strikes a deep, human chord."

—Patricia Matthews

SILVER LININGS

"The Krentz mark of excellence is more than evident in the snappy dialogue, steamy sensuality, and vivid characterization. Don't miss this outstanding romantic adventure."

—*Romantic Times*

"Jayne Ann Krentz entertains to the hilt in *Silver Linings*.... The excitement and adventure don't stop."

—Catherine Coulter

"Wonderful characters, a great plot with lots of action, and a fine romance with lots of spark—what more could you ask for?"

—*Rendezvous*

Also by Jayne Ann Krentz

Absolutely, Positively
Deep Waters
Eye of the Beholder
Family Man
Flash
The Golden Chance
Grand Passion
Hidden Talents
Perfect Partners
Sharp Edges
Silver Linings
Sweet Fortune
Trust Me
Wildest Hearts

Written under the name Jayne Castle
Amaryllis
Orchid
Zinnia

Published by POCKET BOOKS

JAYNE ANN KRENTZ

WILDEST HEARTS

POCKET BOOKS

New York   London   Toronto   Sydney   Singapore

An *Original* Publication of POCKET BOOKS

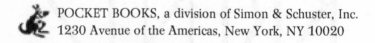 POCKET BOOKS, a division of Simon & Schuster, Inc.
1230 Avenue of the Americas, New York, NY 10020

ISBN: 978-1-4767-5272-3

POCKET BOOKS and colophon are registered trademarks of Simon & Schuster, Inc.

Visit us on the World Wide Web:
http://www.SimonSays.com

For my sister-in-law, Wendy Born,
who understood Oliver's passion for ferns.

With love and gratitude.

1

I don't think the elephant is going to work," Oliver Rain finally said. His soft, dark voice was shaded with polite regret.

"I was afraid you wouldn't like him." Annie Lyncroft gazed morosely at the beast and wondered how to broach the real subject she wanted to discuss with the inscrutable Oliver Rain.

"I'll admit he's unusual," Rain acknowledged.

"You're probably asking yourself the same question that a lot of my clients ask. You're wondering, Is it art or is it just plain tacky?"

"An interesting question," Rain conceded.

"Keep in mind that the elephant is functional as well as ornamental," Annie said in an instinctive, last-ditch effort to salvage the sale. "There's a little hidden drawer in the base. Very useful for small objects."

"I don't think he fits into this room," Rain said diplomatically.

Annie wondered privately if anything except Oliver Rain himself would look at home in the ebony, gold, and gray study.

She had been almost certain Rain wouldn't like the elephant. The two-foot-high cloisonné figure with its scarlet toenails and purple trunk looked cheerfully ridiculous standing next to Rain's Zen rock garden.

The garden, which occupied a large corner of the

1

study, was not a true garden, at least not to Annie's way of thinking. It contained no hint of green. Not a single leaf, let alone any colorful blooms, married the pristine perfection of the pearl gray sand.

The sand was encased in a low black wooden frame. It had been meticulously raked into abstract designs around five rocks. Annie suspected Rain had spent hours contemplating exactly where to put the rocks on the sand. It was undoubtedly just the sort of emotionless problem in aesthetics that would appeal to him.

The designer whom Rain had hired to do the interiors of the spacious new twenty-sixth-floor suite had sized up her client with unerring accuracy. All the rooms afforded seemingly endless views of Seattle, Elliott Bay, and the Olympics, and they were all done in the same forbidding tones of ebony, gold, and gray that dominated the study.

The end result was an austere, elegant lair perfectly suited to a man whom many people considered to be a dangerous predator.

No, Annie decided, the elephant was a handsome creature, but he certainly didn't fit into the disciplined, restrained decor of Rain's newly completed suite. She could not imagine anything from her boutique full of wildly whimsical one-of-a-kind items that would look right here.

Oliver Rain was clearly not much given to whimsy of any kind.

"I'm sorry the elephant isn't quite right," Rain murmured.

"Don't worry about it. I didn't think it would work. To tell you the truth, I haven't been able to interest any of my clients in him." Annie frowned. "Something about that elephant seems to put people off. I wonder if it's the toenails."

"Quite possibly."

"Well, it's not a big deal." So much for unloading the elephant on Oliver Rain. "You insisted I bring something else by, so I decided to try him out in here."

"Very kind of you. I appreciate your perseverance. Let me pour you some more tea." Rain reached for the black-and-gold-enameled teapot that sat on the nearby black lacquer tray.

Annie watched, fascinated, as he refilled her cup. The bright white cone of light from the halogen lamp on his desk revealed the sinewy strength of his hands. Rain's hands were not those of an ordinary business executive. They were rough, even calloused in places, as if he made his fortune working in rich soil rather than in gilt-edged investments.

He managed to imbue the delicate act of pouring tea with a riveting masculinity. Each motion was one of disciplined strength and grace.

Annie had learned that any movement Rain made, no matter how small, captured her full attention. Perhaps it was because each ripple of restrained power stood in such stark contrast to the vast, deep stillness that emanated from him when he was not moving. Annie had never met a man who was so completely in control of himself.

She eyed him warily as she accepted the teacup from him. "To be perfectly honest, I don't think I have anything in Wildest Dreams that will suit you."

Rain contemplated her as if she presented a curious but not unsolvable dilemma. "Just because the elephant doesn't work, I don't think we should assume that nothing else from your shop will work, either."

3

"You didn't like the carousel I brought on Monday," Annie reminded him.

"Ah, yes, the carousel. I'll admit it had a certain charm, but somehow the rather bizarre creatures on it seemed wrong in here."

"Depends on your point of view, I suppose," Annie muttered. Personally, she thought the beautifully gilded carousel with its collection of strange mythological animals had been a nice touch in a room that already contained the eminently unusual, near-mythic Oliver Rain.

No one knew much about Rain. But that tended to be the case with most legends, she reflected. The fewer facts available, the more legendary the man became in the eyes of the world.

She had first met him six weeks ago at her brother Daniel's engagement party. She had known of his existence, of course, because Daniel had once worked for him. But she and Rain had never been introduced.

Daniel Lyncroft was an acknowledged genius in the field of electronics. Five years ago he had been hired by Rain to set up several high-tech security systems for Rain's extensive business empire. Later, when Daniel had left to start his own electronics firm, Rain had invested heavily in the start-up operation, thus becoming Daniel's single biggest financial backer.

Daniel had warned Annie that, although Rain had been invited to attend the engagement party, he was unlikely to appear. Oliver Rain was almost never seen in public, let alone at social affairs. Furthermore, if he ever did decide to move in society, it would almost certainly be at a much higher level than the one the Lyncrofts occupied. The Rain fortune, which Oliver Rain had rebuilt from scratch after the mysterious disappearance of his father, was as much the stuff of legend as the man himself.

But to Daniel's obvious surprise and pleasure, Rain had turned up at the engagement party in the back of a black limousine. He had been dressed in stark black and white evening wear. The formal clothes had emphasized the dark, fierce stillness in him.

Annie had been enthralled by Rain from the moment she first saw him. He was unlike any other man she had ever known. There was a haunting aura of power, passion, and pride about him, but overlaying it all was an iron-clad self-control.

It was intriguing to watch the way people slipped unobtrusively out of Rain's way as he moved through the chic restaurant Daniel had rented for the occasion. She understood the impulse. There was no doubt but that the man radiated a potential for danger. He prowled through the throng of well-wishers like a leopard gliding through a flock of sheep.

Only a very small part of Annie wanted to flee to safer ground. A much larger, louder part urged her to get closer to Oliver Rain regardless of the risks.

Annie had concluded that Rain held the same sort of attraction for her as did the unusual objects she sold in her boutique, Wildest Dreams. He was not handsome in the conventional sense, but she found him utterly compelling. Something deep within her reacted to his presence with an acute sense of awareness. When he looked at her the fine hair on the nape of her neck stirred.

That night at Daniel's party, Annie had secretly memorized everything about Oliver Rain from the color of his eyes, which were an illusive, indescribable shade of gray, to the controlled impassivity of his features.

He wore his black hair much too long for a business executive. It would have brushed his shoulders if he had not tied it back in a low ponytail. His grim, harsh face betrayed an implacable, unbending willpower. The icy hint of silver in his hair together with the cold, calculating intelligence in his gaze led Annie to conclude that Rain was very close to forty.

This was a man who would never rely on his looks or his charm to get what he wanted in life, she decided. He would simply reach out and take it.

Rain had stayed at the party for less than half an hour. Except for the brief time that he spent with Daniel and the few minutes it had taken to introduce him to Daniel's fiancée, Joanna, and to Annie, he had held himself apart from the crowd. He had stood alone, occupying a space that no one else dared violate and sipped champagne while the guests ebbed and flowed around him.

Annie had been intensely aware of his eyes following her when she danced with some of Daniel's friends, but Rain had not asked her to join him on the floor. He had not danced with anyone at all.

When Oliver Rain quietly left the party, Annie experienced a strange disappointment. The small ember of unfamiliar sensual excitement that had flared to life within her when he had arrived flickered out when he departed.

She surreptitiously watched from a window as Daniel escorted Rain out to the waiting limousine. The two men spent a few minutes talking quietly in the drive. When the conversation ended, Rain glanced at the window where Annie stood as if he had known all along she was watching. He acknowledged her with a small, almost courtly inclination of his head. Then he got into the limousine and vanished into the rain-streaked night.

"He's an interesting but rather dangerous man," Daniel said to Annie later. "You never know for certain what he's thinking. I don't believe he trusts anyone. When I worked for him, he was almost obsessive about maintaining files on all key employees and the people with whom he did business."

"Files?"

"More like security dossiers." Daniel's mouth curved wryly. "He always claimed that personal inside information on people was what he relied on to give him the edge."

"I would imagine having an edge would be very important to a man like that," Annie said thoughtfully. "He would want to be in control at all times."

"The thing to remember about Oliver Rain is that he's always got his own agenda, and he never lets anyone else know what that agenda is until he's ready. He's a lone wolf, not a team player."

"Is he a gangster?" Annie asked, horrified at the possibility that her brother might be in debt to a criminal.

Daniel grinned. "If he is, he's smart enough to bury the bodies so deep that no one will ever find them."

"Why on earth did you let him back you if you don't trust him?"

Daniel looked at her in surprise. "I never said I didn't trust him. I just said he was dangerous."

"There's a difference?"

"A big difference?"

Annie hugged herself against the small shiver that

went through her. "What else do you know about him?"

"Not much, even though I worked for him. The man's a legend."

"Why?" Annie asked.

"Fifteen years ago his father walked out on the family. Just vanished. I don't know the whole story, but I do know that a few months before he disappeared, Edward Rain had persuaded some of his friends to invest in one of his development projects."

"Let me guess," Annie said. "The investors' money vanished along with Rain?"

"Right. Not only that, but Edward Rain had liquidated most of his own personal assets. He took that cash with him, too. The family was left with virtually nothing except a mountain of debts."

"I've heard tales of that kind of thing happening. There was a story in the papers just the other day about a prominent banker who simply got on a plane with several million dollars and was never seen again. He left his family and his whole life behind."

"That's what Edward Rain did," Daniel said.

Annie stared at her brother. "What happened?"

"Oliver paid off all of his father's debts within two years," Daniel said. There was cool admiration in his voice. "He rebuilt his father's fortune from scratch. It's now far larger than it was before Edward Rain disappeared, which should tell you something about Oliver."

"Poor Oliver," Annie whispered. "He must have been emotionally devastated when his father vanished."

Daniel frowned in alarm. "Now, Annie..."

"The shame and humiliation would have been intol-

8

erable to a man like that," Annie continued thoughtfully. "He's obviously been scarred for life. No wonder he's not very outgoing."

"Hold it right there," Daniel ordered. "Don't even think about it."

"About what?" Annie asked innocently.

"About trying to rescue Oliver Rain. He is definitely not another wounded stray male you can add to your collection. Believe me, Rain doesn't need rescuing."

"Everyone needs to be rescued at one time or another, Daniel."

"Not Rain," Daniel said flatly. "That man can take care of himself. Trust me."

Annie did not see or hear from Rain again until two weeks later. He had called the day after Daniel's private plane went down in the ocean on a flight to Alaska. That had been a month ago in October. Rain had asked her very gently if she needed help of any kind.

Caught up in the chaos of the situation, struggling to deal with reporters and the authorities who were conducting the search-and-rescue operation, as well as trying to console Joanna, Annie had been tense and distracted. She had brusquely told Oliver Rain that she did not need his assistance.

It was only as she hung up the phone that she belatedly recalled the fact that Rain was her brother's chief creditor. Now that Daniel had disappeared, Rain was a potential threat. If he chose to call in the huge loan on the grounds that Daniel's fledgling company lacked leadership, Lyncroft Unlimited would go under. There was simply no way to pay off Oliver Rain at this point.

But it wasn't Rain who had turned out to be the

immediate threat. It was a coalition of suppliers and the other investors, all of whom panicked when they realized that Daniel was no longer at the helm of his company. Barry Cork, Daniel's trusted assistant, did the best he could to reassure everyone that business was going on as usual, but no one believed him.

A few days later Rain had called again.

"Perhaps we had better talk," he said quietly.

"About what?" Annie demanded, knowing full well what he wanted to discuss.

"Lyncroft's future."

"Lyncroft is doing just fine, thank you. Barry Cork has everything under control. My brother will be rescued any day now, and everything will go back to normal."

"I'm sorry, Ms. Lyncroft, but you must face the fact that Daniel is very probably dead."

"I don't believe that and neither does his fiancée. We're going to hold Lyncroft together until he returns." Annie gripped the phone cord and tried to keep her voice calm and confident. "I appreciate your concern, but nothing has changed at the company. Everything's under control."

"I see." There was a long silence on the line. "I hear rumors that some of your brother's other creditors are starting to press for a sale or merger."

"Nonsense. Strictly rumors. I've explained to all of them that things are fine and that we expect Daniel to return soon."

There was another thoughtful silence. "As you wish. Please feel free to call me if the other investors become difficult. I might be able to help you."

Annie had hung up the phone feeling more uneasy than ever. Lyncroft Unlimited was a family-owned corporation. No one except family members could hold stock in the firm. Daniel had been intent on keeping full control of his company.

At the moment there were only two members of the Lyncroft family, Annie and her brother. That made Annie Daniel's sole inheritor.

Two weeks ago Rain had again contacted her. Instead of talking about the fate of Lyncroft Unlimited, he had explained that he was requesting her services in a professional capacity. He wanted her to provide the finishing touches for the rooms in his new penthouse.

Annie was still not quite sure why she had accepted the job. She certainly had more than enough to do without taking time out of her frantic days to provide personal consultation to a client.

But today was her fourth visit to the twenty-sixth floor of the downtown Seattle high rise. Thus far it had followed the same pattern as the previous visits.

It wasn't easy getting to Oliver Rain. First, she had to get past the doorman in the lobby of the building. There was a special code that had to be punched into the elevator control panel in order to get to the twenty-sixth floor. When she arrived at the penthouse door, she was greeted by a robot of a man known only as Bolt. He appeared to be a combination of butler and chauffeur. Annie wondered if he was also a bodyguard.

In his own way, Bolt was almost as interesting as his employer. He looked to be somewhere in his early fifties. Every time Annie had seen him he had been wearing a formal dark suit. His pale blue eyes betrayed no emotion of any kind. His thinning hair was razored to within a quarter of an inch all over his head.

There was a mechanical quality about Bolt that made Annie wonder if he was part machine. She had visions of him plugging himself into an electrical outlet each night to recharge his batteries. She got the distinct impression he did not approve of her.

On that first visit, Bolt had shown her into the study with a minimum of words. Tea had been brought in on a tray.

Annie had waited nervously for Rain to bring up the subject of her missing brother, but he had proceeded to discuss nothing except the appropriate finishing pieces for the penthouse.

After the first consultation Annie had begun to look forward to these quiet, serene interludes. During the time she was safely secluded here in Rain's study, drinking his exotic, aromatic tea and talking of unimportant things such as cloisonné elephants and gilded carousels, she could put aside her fears and problems. It was a relief because those fears and problems were rapidly turning into nightmares.

She had not forgotten what Daniel had said about Rain being dangerous, but she was finding it increasingly impossible to be afraid of him. There was something oddly reassuring about his strength. She found herself consciously trying to absorb some of it during these afternoon sessions in his study.

"It's obviously going to take some time to come up with just the right additional element for this room," Rain said with one last glance at the elephant. "But I'm a patient man. I'm certain we'll find something sooner or later."

"I doubt it," Annie said. Her eyes swept the austere,

elegant room. "Your taste obviously doesn't run to the kind of stuff I sell. My philosophy is that every room needs a jarring note. A beautiful interior needs a colorful touch of ugliness. A serene interior needs an object that clashes. A cluttered interior needs an element of order."

Rain didn't smile, which was hardly surprising, but a subtle change in his mist-colored eyes told her he was amused. She had only spent a few afternoons with him, but she was getting quite good at reading the small signals that indicated his moods. He was not an unemotional man, she realized, but somewhere along the line he had learned to exert an astounding degree of control over his emotions.

"I'm not concerned about the differences in our taste when it comes to elephants and carousels," Rain said softly. He fell silent, sipping his tea with a reflective air.

Silences were common around Oliver Rain. They did not appear to bother him, but Annie found them unnerving. She herself was rarely given to long silences in the middle of a conversation.

She swallowed tea and wondered if this was the moment to bring up the topic she wanted to discuss. Perhaps she should wait another week or so, but she was afraid she could not put it off much longer. Time was running out. If she could not get Rain to go along with her wild plan to save Lyncroft Unlimited, she would have to regroup and come up with another idea.

Unfortunately she didn't think there were any other ideas. She was at the end of the line.

Annie's stomach tightened as she steeled herself.

Very carefully she replaced her teacup on its black and gold saucer. "Mr. Rain..."

"Oliver. Please. I want you to think of me as a friend of the family."

"Oliver." Annie took a deep breath. "A month ago, right after my brother disappeared, you said something about giving us, Joanna and me, that is, a hand."

"I assume there is still no word on your brother's fate?"

"No," Annie admitted. The search-and-rescue operation had been called off three days after Daniel's plane had vanished. There had been no sign of either the wreckage or of her brother's body to date. The official verdict was that Daniel had been lost at sea.

"And now, at last, you're beginning to understand the difficulties you'll face if you continue to try to run Lyncroft Unlimited on your own," Oliver said calmly.

Annie met his cool gaze. "It's going to be impossible, isn't it?"

"Yes."

"You knew that all along, didn't you?"

Oliver shrugged slightly. "It was inevitable that there would be serious problems. Your brother was the driving force behind Lyncroft Unlimited. Everyone knows that. With him gone, the investors were bound to get restless."

Annie gripped the arm of the black lacquer chair. "The other investors and creditors invited me to a meeting two days ago. They gave me an ultimatum. If I don't agree to sell or merge Lyncroft with a major firm very soon, they're going to call in the outstanding debt."

"I'm aware of the meeting."

Annie wrinkled her nose. "I'm not surprised." She paused. "You weren't at it, though."

"No."

"Does that mean you don't think I should agree to a buyout or a merger?" Annie held her breath waiting for the answer.

"I didn't say that. A buyout may be for the best. It will keep the company alive so that it will have a chance to get your brother's new wireless technology to market. When that happens, everyone involved will recover his initial investment along with a considerable profit."

Daniel's inventions were in the hot new area of electronics that was revolutionizing everything from computerized inventory control systems to medical procedures. Daniel had often told Annie the office of the future would be "wireless." The electrical cords that currently chained machines to a wall outlet or a power source would vanish.

"I can't sell Daniel's firm." Annie curled her hands into small determined fists. "He's worked too hard to get it started. He's invested everything he has in it, not just his money but his sweat and his genius. The future in electronics is in this new wireless stuff, and he's going to be in on the ground floor. Don't you understand? I can't give it away."

Oliver's black lashes veiled his eyes. "You won't be giving it away. You can demand a very good price. There are a lot of firms in the industry that would give a great deal to get their hands on the new technology your brother was developing."

"I won't sell Daniel's company," Annie repeated. "Not as long as Joanna and I believe there's a possibility he may still be alive."

"One of these days you will have to take a more realistic view of the situation," Oliver said. "The odds are that Daniel is gone. You know that as well as I do."

Annie lifted her chin. "I would know if Daniel were dead."

"Would you?"

"Yes, I would, damn it. Daniel is the only family I've got, the only family I've had since Aunt Madeline died. I'd know if he were really gone forever." She stabbed her fingers through her wild thick bob of sherry-colored curls. "I'd feel it deep inside."

Surely she would know it. Wouldn't she? Annie knew she was getting close to the end of her rope. She hadn't had a single good night's sleep since Daniel had vanished. The initial shock had faded somewhat, but her secret fears sometimes escaped from the dark place where she managed to confine them most of the time. When they did, they nearly swamped her. Perhaps her beloved older brother really was dead.

She was exhausted. There had been too many decisions to make in the past few weeks, too many questions to answer, too much pressure from the people who had invested in her brother's company. And now that Joanna had told her about the baby, there was a whole new set of concerns to be faced.

"I'm not the only one who would know if Daniel were dead," Annie continued quietly. "Joanna feels as strongly about this as I do. We're both certain he's still alive."

"No one can survive in that water off the coast of Alaska for more than thirty or forty minutes," Oliver reminded her gently. "You know that."

"The thing that everyone seems to forget is that my brother was a certified genius. Furthermore, when he flew, he took precautions other people wouldn't bother to take. He carried a survival suit, for example. And a raft. And all kinds of equipment."

"Even a survival suit won't protect a person against hypothermia indefinitely."

"There are dozens of islands scattered between here and Alaska. Hundreds. Most are just little dots of land. He could have made it to any one of them. He would be able to survive on one until help arrived."

"The search-and-rescue operation was very thorough," Oliver said. "I made certain of it."

Annie widened her eyes. "You did?"

"Of course. I told you, Daniel was more than a trusted employee when he worked for me. He was a friend."

"I'm glad to hear that," Annie said grimly. "Because I've come to ask you for help. I'm hoping that your friendship with Daniel was strong enough that you'll agree to my plan."

Oliver studied her with an expression of subdued satisfaction. He had clearly been expecting this. "You want me to give you a buyout offer for the company."

"No." Annie shot to her feet and stalked to the floor-to-ceiling windows. She looked out at the slate-colored sky and gray waters of Elliott Bay. "No, that's the last thing I want. I told you, I won't sell Lyncroft Unlimited. Not if I can help it."

"I would be willing to agree to sell it back to your brother if he does reappear."

Annie glanced back over her shoulder. "That's generous of you, but I don't think it's such a good idea."

17

"Why not?"

She set her back teeth. "Because I have it on very good authority that you are a dangerous man, Oliver Rain."

He did not seem disconcerted by the news. "Is that right? Who told you that?"

"Daniel."

"Your brother always was rather intelligent."

"Right. A genius. Look, we both know that if I were to sell the company to you, I would lose control of it entirely. You could do anything you want with it. You might even refuse to sell it back to Daniel or if you did, you might put such a high price tag on it that he wouldn't be able to afford it."

"We could arrange the terms of the deal before you sign anything."

"I just don't like letting go of the company. Not even to you. The risk is too great. No offense, but frankly, I don't see anyone in his right mind surrendering rights to the kind of technology Daniel has created."

"I applaud your loyalty and determination. But in the meantime, you're under a lot of pressure from your brother's creditors. They can force you to sell or merge, Annie."

"I know." Annie closed her eyes briefly and then swung around to face him. "They've started to call every day. After that meeting two days ago I knew we were in real trouble."

"It was only a matter of time. They're running scared, Annie. Surely you see their position. Lyncroft Unlimited is a one-man company in all the ways that count and that one man has vanished."

"I have to buy some time. All I need is a little time."

"How much time?"

"That's just it, I have no idea. A few days or maybe weeks. Who knows how long it will take to find Daniel?"

Oliver took a slow, thoughtful sip of tea and set the cup down on its saucer. Annie followed the movement with her eyes. The delicate china looked very fragile in his powerful hands. But it also looked quite safe.

"Even if I give you all the time you wish, you can't hope to stave off the rest of the firm's creditors for long," Oliver said.

"Not by myself, no. I realize that. But they would be pacified if they thought the company was in good hands again. Everyone realizes that I don't know beans about electronics and neither does Joanna. Nor do we know anything about managing a company the size of Lyncroft."

"No," Rain agreed. "You don't."

Annie took an eager step forward. "But if an executive who had a brilliant reputation in the business world were to take the helm, I think we could hold off the investors indefinitely."

Oliver did not move, but there was an air of cool readiness about him now. "You're thinking of hiring someone to manage the company for you?"

"Sort of."

"I suppose it's a possibility. Have you approached anyone yet?"

"I had Barry Cork make a couple of discreet inquiries," Annie admitted. "He says the problem is that the people he approached all said they wouldn't do it unless they were guaranteed a permanent chunk of the company as part of their payment."

"That's a reasonable demand in such a situation. But you don't want to give away even a piece of Lyncroft Unlimited, do you?"

"No, I don't dare. Daniel probably wouldn't be able to get it back when he returns. Lyncroft Unlimited is going to be one of the hottest electronics firms in the country in five years. Everyone in the industry is aware of its potential."

"If you take on a partner now, Daniel will be stuck with him later, is that what you're afraid of?"

"Exactly. Partners can be major problems. Daniel told me once he never wanted one."

"You must understand that you have only two options at the moment. You can sell or merge Daniel's firm or you can take on a partner who can run it for you."

"I just can't take the chance," Annie said. "Daniel might never get back full control of his company."

Oliver reached for the teapot. "I'm sure I can be of some assistance, Annie."

Relief soared through her. "That was exactly what I was hoping you would say."

Oliver slanted her a speculative glance. "Were you?"

"Yes. The way I see it, you've got a lot at stake here, too. After all, it's in your best interests for my brother's company to survive and get its products into production, right?"

Oliver gazed at her over the rim of the cup. "It's true that I stand to make a considerable profit when the new technology starts hitting the market."

"Well, I've come up with an option that will give both of us what we want."

"Have you?" He sounded skeptical, but he was clearly intrigued.

20

"Yes, I have. It will protect Daniel's company and it will also protect your investment." Annie hurried back to her chair and sat down. Now that the moment had arrived to explain her idea, she was no longer so nervous. She leaned forward intently and folded her arms on the polished surface of the ebony desk.

"I'm listening, Annie."

"This is a little difficult to explain," she said. "But if you'll just hear me out, I think you'll agree that it could work. Keep in mind the plan won't have to be in effect very long because I'm sure we'll find Daniel any day."

Oliver paused in the act of pouring more tea. "This grows more interesting by the moment. Let's hear your plan."

"Okay, as you know, Lyncroft Unlimited is a family-held corporation. My brother and I control all of the stock. When Joanna marries Daniel, she'll receive shares in the company, too, but not before that time."

"I understand. But since she hasn't yet married your brother and Daniel is presumed dead, you now control all of the stock. You're the only member of the Lyncroft family around at the moment."

"That's right." Annie gathered herself for the plunge. "But if I were to marry, my husband would become a member of the family. I could give him an interest in the company."

Tea splashed on the surface of the ebony desk. Oliver abruptly set down the teapot. For an instant he stared at the small puddle of spilled tea as if amazed that his powerful hands had failed him. When he looked up again, his eyes were filled with frozen ice. "I didn't know you were planning to marry anyone."

Annie waved that aside. "I'm not. Not exactly, that is. Mr. Rain, I mean, Oliver, have you ever heard of a marriage of convenience?"

2

A stunned silence descended. Oliver's eyes narrowed, effectively masking his reaction. "Marriage of convenience?"

Annie leaned farther forward, intent on making him understand the brilliance of her plan. "By definition it's a marriage designed to benefit both parties in some manner but one that has nothing to do with love and affection. A marriage of convenience is essentially a business relationship."

"A business relationship." Oliver folded his big hands on the desk and regarded her with his chilling gaze. "You're contemplating such a marriage?"

"Yes."

"You intend to marry someone who is capable of managing Lyncroft Unlimited for you? Someone who will placate the investors and reassure Daniel's creditors?"

Annie was pleased that he was getting the picture so quickly. "You've got it. It would be strictly a business relationship, as I said. My husband will become a controlling partner in Lyncroft Unlimited on the day of our marriage. He'll take charge immediately. The man I have in mind has a legendary reputation in the business world so the other investors will be bound to accept him. They'll stop panicking."

"I see." Oliver's eyes did not waver.

"Do you understand how it would work?" she asked a little anxiously.

"I understand how you think it will work." Oliver fell silent for a moment. "What happens if Daniel does return?"

"Simple." Annie smiled triumphantly. "I file for divorce. Once it's final, my ex-husband will no longer own any part of Lyncroft Unlimited. The way Daniel set up his corporation, all shares in the company revert to the family in the event of a divorce."

"And if your husband takes you to court?"

"That's not likely, but I'll cover that possibility with a prenuptial agreement."

"You seem to have given this a great deal of thought."

"I have. I've discussed it with Joanna, and we both agree that it's the safest way to try to hold onto Daniel's company." She hadn't exactly discussed it with Joanna, Annie admitted to herself. She had more or less badgered her future sister-in-law into going along with the idea.

"It's a novel approach to the problem, I'll grant you that."

Annie felt a small flare of pride. "Thanks. I thought it was a pretty good idea myself."

"What's in this for your, ah, husband?"

Annie cleared her throat. "Well, obviously, the opportunity to protect his investment and his future profits in Lyncroft Unlimited."

"The man you have in mind is one of Daniel's creditors?"

"Yes. He's also someone who claims to be a friend of Daniel's. Someone who has offered to help me. Mr. Rain..."

"Oliver."

"Oliver, this is suddenly turning out to be a lot more awkward than I thought it would be." Annie's fingers tightened around each other. She realized her palms had grown damp. "It seemed like such a good idea at the time."

"Annie, are you by any chance proposing to me?" Oliver asked very softly.

She flushed, leaned back in her chair, and shoved her hands into the pockets of her emerald jumpsuit. "Yes."

"Ah."

Annie was tense enough as it was. She didn't need another dose of Oliver Rain's notorious inscrutability. "What does that mean?"

"It means I accept."

Annie stared at him. "You do? Just like that?"

Oliver's expression was as unchanging as ever, but there was an intensity in his gaze that had not been there earlier. "It would appear to be the only way I can protect my investment and my future profits as well as the only way of fulfilling my obligations as Daniel's friend."

"Don't you need time to think it over?"

"I have thought it over. It's not a difficult problem. The options are clear-cut. You'll hang onto the firm until it goes into bankruptcy if I don't marry you. Everyone will lose if I allow you to follow that path."

Annie went limp with relief. "I don't know how to thank you. Don't worry, I'm sure we won't have to stay married for long."

"You're quite certain Daniel will turn up, aren't you?"

Annie nibbled nervously on her lower lip. "I have

to believe he will. But even if he doesn't, I've still got to try to hold onto Lyncroft."

"Because of the future potential of the company?"

"No. Because Joanna's pregnant with Daniel's baby."

Oliver grasped the implications immediately. "In other words, if Daniel doesn't come back, you're going to try to save the company for his child."

Annie raised her hand in a small gesture. "What else can I do?"

"Nothing. I understand completely. I once found myself in a somewhat similar situation. One does what one must."

"I had a feeling you'd understand." Annie smiled. "Not everyone would go along with an idea like this. But there's something about you that's different. You're not the usual sort of business executive. And I know Daniel trusted you. He told me so."

Oliver ignored that. "Once more, I have to ask an obvious question. What happens to our little business arrangement if your brother doesn't return?"

Annie sighed, not willing to deal with that issue. "Naturally you want to know how long you're going to be stuck with a fake marriage."

"The marriage will be very real, won't it, Annie? Your scheme won't work if it's not legal."

"Oh, sure, it'll be real in the legal sense." She hesitated. "I suppose we could put a time limit on it if you'd like, but I really don't think there will be problems. The thing is, I believe Daniel will return any day."

"But if he doesn't?" Oliver persisted.

"Even if everyone's right and Daniel's gone forever, I think I could eventually learn to run Lyncroft on my own. But I'm certainly not qualified to take the reins now. The only business I've ever operated is Wildest Dreams, and I've only been running it for a year. I'd need time to learn the ins and outs of a high-tech firm like Lyncroft. It would also take time for the investors to learn to trust me."

"Yes, it would. Given your lack of background in the field, it would probably take a lot of time. Perhaps a couple of years. And that's assuming you're a fast learner."

Annie eyed him speculatively. "I couldn't ask you to stay tied up in a fake marriage for two years. Good grief, I don't want to be trapped in one that long myself."

"No, I don't imagine you do."

Annie came to a decision. "All right, let's set an outside time limit. Say six months. We'll reassess the situation at that point. If Daniel isn't back and if you want out of the arrangement, I won't try to convince you to stay."

"That sounds reasonable."

"I'm sure it won't come to that," Annie said more cheerfully. "Daniel will be found. You'll see."

"I hope you're right."

Annie smiled again in gratitude and relief. She felt better already. Things were under control. Oliver Rain could handle Lyncroft Unlimited. "You're really being very decent about this. I don't know how to thank you. I realize my plan must sound a little off the wall, but I really think it will work."

"It might at that."

"I just had a thought." Annie studied him closely. "Excuse me for prying, but are you, uh, romantically involved with anyone at the moment?"

"No."

Annie relaxed again. "Well, that makes everything much easier, doesn't it? I mean, it might have been a little difficult to explain our arrangement to another woman. Not that I would have even asked you to do it in the first place if you were involved with anyone else. After all, there are limits to the claims of friendship as well as business."

"What about you?" Oliver asked slowly. "Are you involved with anyone?"

"Nope. Starting up a small business takes up a lot of time, you know."

"I know." Oliver looked at her. "So there's no one else concerned here. Just you and me."

"Right. But if this thing drags on for a while, I want you to know I don't expect you to give up your private life entirely. You should feel quite free to date or whatever." It was hard to imagine Oliver on a date. "After all, it's not like this will be a real marriage."

"If word gets out that the marriage is a sham, your brother's creditors will panic. They might not believe we'll stay married long enough for me to save the company unless they believe we're in love."

Annie groaned and slouched deeper into her chair. "I suppose you're right. I hadn't really thought about that part. I guess we're going to have to make this thing look real, aren't we?"

"If you want it to serve the purpose you intend, yes."

"There will be questions, I suppose. People will be surprised at how quickly we decided to marry."

Oliver looked thoughtful. "We'll tell them we've been seeing each other for quite a while but preferred to keep the relationship private until such time as an

28

announcement seemed appropriate. Now, with Daniel gone and the company in need of leadership, we decided to go ahead and formalize our relationship."

"Hmm. Sounds okay. You already have a reputation for being something of a mystery. Still, there are going to be lot of little problems, aren't there?" Annie glanced uneasily around the study, wondering if she would actually have to move into Oliver's austere penthouse.

"Yes, you will," Oliver said politely as if he had read her mind. "No one will believe we're seriously married if you don't live with me."

Annie felt a brief stirring of genuine panic. "This is going to get complicated, isn't it?"

"Don't worry about it, Annie. I'll take care of everything. That's why you're marrying me, remember?"

29

3

It took the patience of a saint or the devil himself to propagate ferns from spores. Oliver had that kind of patience. He took quiet satisfaction in the process, even though it could take anywhere from six months to two years to see the results of his efforts.

Rain beat down on the huge rooftop greenhouse as he carefully misted a tray of tiny hybrids. Around him cascaded ferns of every size and description. Ferns were his passion, and the greenhouse was devoted entirely to them. Here on the roof above his penthouse he had created his own private rain forest.

There were many species represented in the greenhouse, although Oliver favored maidenhairs and staghorns. Adder's-tongues, tree ferns, glade ferns, and shield ferns occupied several rows of metal mesh benches. More plants hung suspended from the ceiling, forming a canopy of green. A few examples of some aquatic species floated on the surface of a small grotto pool at the far end of the structure.

The lacy young maidenhair ferns Oliver was misting were only an inch tall, but he was hopeful that he had created a new and interesting variety with this latest attempt. He would not know for certain, however, until the mature fronds appeared, which might not be for another year and a half. He was content to wait.

Oliver had learned a long time ago that patience was a virtue that nearly everyone else in the world lacked. Not that he minded that lack in others. It gave him a distinct advantage.

But in the matter of Annie Lyncroft, he had not had to exercise his singular talent for waiting at all. Two days ago she had announced she was prepared to hurl herself into his arms. Or at least into marriage with him.

Oliver allowed himself a faint smile as he contemplated the image of Annie Lyncroft in his arms. When he had first seen her at Daniel's engagement party, it had been rather like discovering an entirely new species of fern. She was unlike any other woman he had ever met. He had promised himself that he would find a way to collect her.

Oliver had decided that the time had come to find himself a wife. He thought Annie would suit him very well.

She was unquestionably unique. That did not altogether surprise him. After all, she was Daniel's sister and Daniel was an unusual man. Oliver had trusted Daniel Lyncroft during the years Lyncroft had worked for him. There were not many people Oliver trusted.

Annie's determination to save Daniel's company did not come as a surprise, either. A capacity for loyalty was obviously a family trait. It was also a trait Oliver required in his wife.

There was a strong, undeniable physical attraction between himself and Annie, which he could no doubt use to secure the bonds.

He had felt something deep inside himself respond to Annie almost on sight. It was not that she was spectacularly beautiful, rather the opposite. She had a subtle, haunting allure about her that fascinated him in a way more obvious beauty would not have done. He had always preferred ferns to roses.

He acknowledged to himself that he wanted Annie. Oliver rarely confided in others, but he made it a practice to be bluntly honest with himself. He reacted to everything about Annie, from the explosion of golden-brown curls that framed her huge hazel green eyes to the delicate sensuality of her soft, gently rounded breasts and thighs.

She was an intriguing creature. He knew from a remark Daniel had made that she was twenty-nine. The intelligence in her gaze was unmistakable. So was the clear, unwavering honesty. Oliver found that particular attribute extremely appealing. Perhaps it was because he himself was so skilled at concealing his own thoughts and plans from others.

She spoke blithely of a marriage of convenience, but Oliver was satisfied that with a little patience he could make her his in every sense of the word. He had, after all, been fully aware of the sensual aware-ness that had bloomed in Annie's gaze when she had looked at him the night of Daniel's engagement party.

Oliver had known then that, given time and strategy, he could have her. He had gone home that night and plotted a patient course of action that would eventually win him his goal.

But events had intervened before he could begin his campaign to seduce Annie. Daniel had disap-peared and Annie had found herself besieged by her brother's creditors.

To Oliver's surprise, Annie had taken matters into her own hands. He found the results interesting if somewhat disconcerting. He wondered if it was a sign of things to come. If so, his serene, well-ordered life was in jeopardy. But he would cope, Oliver assured himself. Annie was obviously the impulsive type, but she could be managed.

Oliver prowled through his rooftop jungle, sprayer in hand, and wondered how Annie expected the marriage of convenience to work. He gathered she anticipated a sort of roommate relationship.

Oliver paused amid a cluster of huge, billowing maidenhair ferns. He plunged his fingers into the rich soil to check the moisture level. The black earth was warm and damp and it felt very good.

The technology in the vast greenhouse was state-of-the-art. Everything from the heating to the irrigation system was monitored by the newest in electronic control systems. The instrument panel that governed temperature, rain, and humidity in this miniature world was housed just outside the glass-walled structure. The technology was sophisticated enough to allow Oliver to create microclimates in different sections of the glass-walled jungle.

Oliver used instruments to test the acidity of his potting soil, and he carefully calibrated moisture levels. He mixed fertilizers according to precise formulas and gaged light intensity with highly sensitive meters. But in the end he still relied on his senses and his instincts when it came to making most of his decisions.

There was no point trying to force ferns to accommodate themselves entirely to modern technology. The primitive green plants came from another time and place, remnants of an era that had long since passed.

Ferns were ancient survivors of a world that had

had no flowering plants, a world that had not yet seen the first dinosaurs, let alone the bothersome little creatures that would one day evolve into humans.

When Oliver walked through the time warp that was his greenhouse, he was filled with a sense of how the earth must have looked and felt hundreds of millions of years in the past. The journey gave him a link with his own past, back to the time when he had still been free to take another path. It was a path that would have led him down an entirely different road than the one he now traveled.

The door at the far end of the greenhouse opened. Bolt stuck his head inside. "Mrs. Rain is here, sir. Shall I tell her you're out?"

"There's not much point. She'll only return again later. Show her up here."

"She hates the greenhouse, sir," Bolt reminded him without inflection.

"I know."

"I'll send her up." Bolt vanished, closing the door behind him.

Oliver surveyed the young red fronds of a hacksaw fern. The fronds would turn green as they matured, but for now they lent an unexpected note of color to the surroundings. It occurred to him that Annie was going to have the same effect on his household. She would definitely add color.

The door of the greenhouse opened again a few minutes later. Sybil Rain, dressed in a stylish cream wool suit and cream suede pumps, walked into the humid warmth. Her discreetly tinted blond hair was cut in a sleek, sophisticated curve that ended at her chin. The pale hair was a perfect foil for her brown eyes and classic features.

Sybil had been a stunning beauty when she had married Oliver's father eighteen years ago. She was forty-six now, nine years older than Oliver, but she looked better than ever. Her face had actually developed some character over the years, much to Oliver's surprise. He had assumed she would remain a blond bimbo forever.

"Oliver."

"Sybil."

She frowned in annoyance as she walked down the aisle between two long fern-laden benches. Oliver wasn't concerned about her expression. Sybil frequently looked annoyed when she was in his presence. He understood her feelings perfectly. He experienced exactly the same reaction toward her.

The old animosity between them had existed so long it had become a habit for both. Each was capable of concealing it when others were around, but when they were alone, neither bothered.

"My God, it's like an oven in here. How can you stand it?" Sybil pushed the trailing fronds of a shoestring fern out of the way. The gold and diamond wedding ring Oliver's father had given her gleamed on her left hand.

"I like it this way." Oliver examined a row of covered glass dishes in which he was germinating some maidenhair spores. "More to the point, the ferns prefer it this way."

"The least you could have done was come downstairs for a few minutes so we could talk in comfort."

"I'm comfortable."

"And your comfort is all that matters, isn't it?" Sybil came to a halt on the walk. Her eyes were filled with an old bitterness.

35

"Was there something you wanted, Sybil? There usually is."

Sybil's mouth tightened. "Nathan and Richard tell me you're getting married."

"Yes."

"Yes? Just *yes*? Is that all you have to say about it?"

Oliver folded his arms and leaned against one of the plant benches. "Yes, I'm getting married. Tomorrow afternoon, in fact. A civil ceremony at the courthouse. You're welcome to attend if you like. Heather, Valerie, and the twins will be there."

"Damn it, Oliver, must you be so disgustingly arrogant? You can't just drop a bombshell like this on the rest of the family and not expect a few questions. Who are you marrying?"

"Her name is Annie Lyncroft."

Sybil furrowed her elegant brow. "Lyncroft. Never heard of her."

"No, I don't suppose you have. She doesn't move in your world."

"Don't try to tell me she moves in your social milieu, Oliver. You haven't got one. Your idea of a significant social engagement is a trip up the Amazon. Where did you meet this woman, anyway?"

"At her brother's engagement party."

Sybil tapped one well-shod toe. "You never go to parties."

"I went to this one."

"Why would you do that? You hate crowds. Wait a minute. Lyncroft." Her eyes narrowed. "Any connection to Lyncroft Unlimited, that electronics firm that you backed a couple of years ago?"

"Yes."

36

"The owner of the firm has been missing, hasn't he? A plane crash. I read about it in the papers."

"That's right. Annie is his sister."

"And now, one month after the crash, you're suddenly marrying her." Sybil stared at him with a look of dawning understanding. "Let me take a wild guess here. I'll bet this Annie Lyncroft has just inherited what could soon be the hottest electronics firm on the West Coast, hasn't she? A firm in which you've got a sizable stake."

"She owns the firm now, yes."

"Oliver, if you want the company, why don't you just buy her out?"

"Maybe it's not the company I want."

"You're saying this is a hot romance? Don't give me that," Sybil snapped. "I don't believe it for a minute."

"Even if I wanted to buy the company, Annie wouldn't sell. She thinks her brother is still alive. She wants to hold on to Lyncroft Unlimited for him. She's the steadfast, loyal type, you see."

"Lyncroft is dead. All the papers said he was." Sybil eyed him closely. "A small, growing company like Lyncroft would be in real financial trouble if it lost its owner. And you've got a considerable investment to protect."

"You always were very sharp when it came to business matters, weren't you?"

"What's going on here, Oliver? Don't tell me marrying Annie Lyncroft is the only way you can come up with to get your hands on Lyncroft Unlimited? That's a little outrageous, even for you."

"Don't you think it's just barely conceivable that

I've finally found the woman I want to make my wife?"

"No," Sybil said flatly, "I don't. I have a hard time envisioning you with a wife."

"I'm a man like any other."

"Bullshit." Under stress, Sybil tended to lapse back into the speech patterns of her youth. "You're not at all like most other men. You're weird and everyone knows it."

"I'm not that weird. Not when it comes to some things."

"Yes, you are. As far as I can tell, the only romantic liaisons you've ever gotten involved in are with the occasional botany instructor or fern collector during a field trip into some rain forest. Once you returned from the trip, all you cared about was the ferns you'd collected."

"I'm thirty-seven years old. It's time I started a family of my own."

"That's nonsense. You've got plenty of family."

That statement was unarguable, Oliver admitted to himself. The one thing he was not short of was family. He'd been responsible for his two sisters, two half brothers, and Sybil for fifteen years.

The responsibility had been thrust upon him that hellish day he'd learned his father had gotten on a plane at SeaTac Airport and vanished along with most of the Rain assets and a fortune in other people's money.

Oliver had known in that first shocking moment of shame and anguish that his whole world had changed. A rapid inventory of his father's business affairs had disclosed the fact that there was virtually nothing left.

Edward Rain's friends and colleagues were the first

ones in line to demand repayment on the loans they had made to him.

Faced with the prospect of five people depending on him, Oliver had done what had to be done. He'd given up his dreams of a career in botany and tackled the nearly overwhelming task of keeping the family together while he rebuilt his father's business empire.

He was content that he'd accomplished what he'd set out to do. He'd paid off every single one of his father's investors. The empire Oliver had then set about constructing had been larger and far more stable than the one Edward had inherited and destroyed.

Two years ago, Oliver had begun to liquidate his holdings. One by one he had sold off the various companies he had acquired. The sizable fortune he had received from the sales of his assets was now earning its keep in a variety of secure places. While he occasionally invested some venture capital in interesting start-up operations such as Lyncroft Unlimited, most of Oliver's money was in safe, dull investments that involved little or no risk.

Although large chunks of money could never be completely ignored, Oliver had succeeded in freeing himself up from the intense day-to-day supervision that had been required during the years in which he had built his empire.

Oliver took satisfaction in knowing that his brothers and sisters were well launched on their various paths in life. Heather had completed medical school. Valerie had graduated from college and was working as a curator at the private, very prestigious Eckert Museum.

The twins, Nathan and Richard, had just started their freshman year at the University of Washington.

They both claimed they were going for their MBAs. Oliver privately hoped they would change their minds by the time they reached their senior year. He himself had always disliked the world of business. The fact that he had been successful in that world did not alter his opinion of it.

As for Sybil, she was occupied with her endless round of charity benefits and social engagements. Thanks to Oliver, she was part of the world to which she had always aspired to belong.

He had done his duty by his family, Oliver concluded. And he would continue to do so. The family came first. But it was time to pursue a few personal goals of his own. It was time to marry.

"Believe me, Sybil, I'm well aware of the fact that I've got family," Oliver said. "It's not quite the same thing as having a wife and children of my own, however."

"Come off it. Don't try to convince me that you've suddenly developed an overpowering urge to become a devoted husband and father."

"Relax." Oliver reached out to stroke the long fronds of a nearby sword fern. "There's plenty of money to go around. Nathan and Richard won't be shortchanged if I decide to have children of my own. You know I'll always take care of them and my sisters. Just like I'll always take care of you. We made a bargain, you and I. Remember?"

The barb went deep. Sybil turned an unbecoming shade of red. "Damn you, Oliver Rain."

Oliver met her eyes and was satisfied that Sybil was recalling the day they had made their unholy pact. "I know exactly what you think of me, Sybil. It's not important. But I'd better make it very clear that you

40

are to behave yourself around Annie. I don't want her upset."

"Upset?" Sybil gazed at him in disbelief. "Doesn't she know you're only marrying her to get your hands on her brother's company? If she doesn't, she must be incredibly naive."

"You understand nothing about the situation. You will therefore keep your opinions to yourself."

A slow, malicious smile curved Sybil's mouth. "Well, well, well. What goes around comes around. Sixteen years ago you accused me of marrying your father for his money. And now here you are marrying a woman in order to control the business she's inherited. Isn't this fascinating? How long before she finds out she's been had in more ways than one?"

"As usual, you've managed to overstay your welcome." Oliver picked up a small trowel and went back to work.

"Don't worry, I'm on my way." Sybil started toward the door of the greenhouse. She paused at the far end and glanced over her shoulder. "Just one more thing, Oliver. Did you know Valerie has a new boyfriend?"

"No." He didn't care for the purr of anticipation in Sybil's voice.

"I think it might be serious this time. She shows all the signs of a woman in love."

"She'll bring him by to meet me if it's serious."

Sybil's smile was catlike. "Don't hold your breath waiting for her to get your approval on this one. She already knows you won't like him."

"Another unemployed artist?" Oliver asked without much concern.

"No. He's from the academic world. Teaches art history at the university." Sybil paused just long enough to get his full attention. "His name is Carson Shore."

Oliver went still.

"That's right, Oliver. Your sister is dating Paul Shore's son. Rather touching, isn't it? Reminds me of the Romeo and Juliet story. Very romantic. Do you suppose Valerie and Carson will succeed in uniting the two warring houses of Shore and Rain after all these years?"

Sybil went out the door and closed it loudly behind her.

Oliver stood quietly amid his ferns and recalled the day when he and Sybil had opened hostilities.

So long ago, he thought. Sixteen years. Sometimes it seemed like forever. At other moments it seemed like only yesterday.

He had been twenty-one at the time and enrolled in the botany department at the University of Washington. He had been looking forward to graduate work and eventually a Ph.D. in his chosen field. His imagination had been captured by the anticipation of unlocking the myriad mysteries of the plant world.

He'd had dreams of exploring the handful of exotic rain forests and jungles still left on the planet. He'd planned to spend his life searching old-growth forests for just a few of the millions of secrets still held fast in them. He knew the secrets were out there. Every botanist knew it.

Hidden deep in the ancient green worlds shrouded in endless twilight were the cures for terrifying diseases, clues to ways to feed an evergrowing population, answers to questions about the fundamental nature of life. Long ago Oliver had determined to be

42

a part of the adventure that awaited scientists who were committed to uncovering those secrets.

Oliver had lived on campus at the university since his sophomore year. He had moved out of the big house on Mercer Island not only because he wanted to be close to the school's libraries, labs, and greenhouses, but because that was the year his father, Edward, had chosen to marry a woman half his age.

Oliver had disliked Sybil on sight. She had been twenty-eight and at the peak of her beauty. He had taken one look at her and been certain she had married his fifty-seven-year-old father because of the Rain family fortune.

But Oliver had also realized with the intuition that was to serve him well in the business world that there was no point trying to convince his father that he'd been married for his money.

Edward had always been a distant, remote figure at best. He had been far more dedicated to making money than he had been to his wife and children. Oliver and his much younger sisters, Heather and Valerie, had learned their lessons in family love and unity from their mother. Mary Rain's death in a car accident two years before Oliver had graduated from high school had devastated all three of her children.

In his more optimistic moments, Oliver had told himself the alliance between Sybil and his father just might work. If Sybil was willing to play the role of a loving mother to Heather and Valerie in exchange for the social and financial status she had achieved by marrying Edward, Oliver was willing to keep his opinions to himself.

Heather and Valerie, at the tender ages of ten and twelve, had accepted Sybil with surprising ease. A year later when the twins, Nathan and Richard, were born, Heather and Valerie had good-naturedly accepted their baby brothers, too. No one could replace Mary Rain, but the household appeared to be functioning smoothly.

On that fateful afternoon Oliver had driven on impulse to the big house on Mercer Island to pay a surprise visit to his sisters and baby brothers. He had parked the car in the long drive and let himself into a side door with his key.

He had known something was wrong as soon as he stepped into the too-silent house. There was no sign of the housekeeper, his sisters, or anyone else, but he had sensed that the house was not empty.

Oliver's first thought was that there was a burglar in the mansion. He raced silently up the stairs to check the bedrooms. After finding the twins safely asleep in their own room, he went on down the hall.

He discovered Sybil in the luxurious master bedroom. She was in bed and she was not alone. The naked man who lay entwined with her in the pale blue satin sheets was as startled to see Oliver as Oliver was to see him.

"Shit." The man rolled out of bed and grabbed his clothes. "What the hell is this? Hey, I'm out of here, man. She never said anything about you. Told me her old man was a geriatric case, I swear it."

Sybil clutched the sheet. "Oh, God. Oliver."

Without a word Oliver turned and walked out of the door and down the stairs. He went into the living room and stood at the window. He spent a long time staring out at Lake Washington. By the time Sybil came warily into the room, he had made his decision.

"Look, Oliver," Sybil began nervously, "your father and I have an understanding."

"Some understanding."

"The relationship between Edward and myself is none of your business."

"You don't think so?" Oliver challenged softly. "What about the kids?"

"Don't you think I care about the children? I gave Edward two sons, didn't I?"

"Did you?"

Her eyes widened in horror. "For God's sake, don't you dare imply Nathan and Richard aren't Edward's children. I swear they are."

"Lucky for you they have his eyes and his hair, just as I do, isn't it? Otherwise we'd be talking about blood tests right now."

"You bastard," she breathed. Tears formed in her beautiful eyes. "You don't understand. Greg is the man I love. If things had been different, I would have married him."

"What was different?" Oliver asked coldly. "Wasn't he rich enough for you?"

"He's married, damn you." She took a step forward. "Oliver, please, listen to me. You're too young to know what this is all about."

"You're wrong. I know exactly what this is about. You've betrayed my father and this family. And now it's time for you to understand exactly how things are going to work from now on."

"What are you talking about?"

"I don't want Heather and Valerie subjected to any more emotional disruption. They've adjusted to you and they'd be confused and hurt if you were to leave. Little girls need mothers."

"I'm not leaving," Sybil shrieked.

"Nathan and Richard have a right to know their father. God knows he isn't around a lot, but they'd see even less of him if you were to take them away." Oliver set his teeth. "Boys need their fathers."

"Damn you, Oliver, I'm not taking them away."

"Children also need to believe that their mothers are angels." Oliver ignored the desperate look in Sybil's eyes. "So for the sake of my brothers and sisters, I won't tell my father what I saw this afternoon unless you force me to do so."

Hope and fear flared in Sybil's expression. "What do you want from me?"

"Your agreement on a bargain. Give my father what he's bought and paid for, a loyal wife and a mother for his children, and you'll get the money and the position you wanted out of this marriage. Screw up just once from here on in, Sybil, and I swear I'll make certain Dad knows exactly what kind of slut he married."

"I'm not a slut!" Sybil screamed. "You don't understand how it is between me and Greg."

"I don't give a damn about how it is between you two. All I care about is this family. We both know Dad would drop you in a minute if he learned you were sleeping around. So have we got a deal?"

"Edward would never believe you if you try to tell him about this afternoon," Sybil said with false bravado.

"Want to put it to the test? I'm his son. I know him better than you ever will. He'll listen to me." Oliver was not sure of that, but he discovered that day that he had a previously unsuspected talent for bluffing.

"Edward trusts me."

"Well, I won't make the same mistake," Oliver said. "I'm going to watch you like a hawk for as long as you're a member of this family. Step out of line just one time and you can kiss your share of the Rain money good-bye."

"You cold-blooded son of a bitch." Sybil was shaking. She dashed away the tears with the back of her hand. "What right do you have to interfere in my life? Who do you think you are?"

"I'm the man who can wreck this cushy setup you've made for yourself any time I feel like it. Remember that, Sybil. Because if I ever find out you haven't kept your end of our bargain, I'll pull the rug out from under you so fast you won't know what hit you."

She believed him. Oliver saw it in her eyes. Satisfied, he walked out of the house, got into his car, and left.

A year later Edward Rain disappeared, taking the fabled Rain fortune and a lot of money belonging to other people with him.

When Oliver closed the door on his own hopes and dreams for the future and turned to the task of picking up the pieces his father had left behind, he'd expected Sybil to head for greener pastures.

But she hadn't. She had realized within the first six months when all of Edward Rain's old friends and business acquaintances had politely turned their backs on the Rain family that Oliver was her best bet.

Sybil was a shrewd woman. She needed security not only for herself but for her two small sons. Oliver soon showed signs of being able to eventually give her back everything she had lost.

For his part, Oliver needed someone to look after

his sisters and brothers while he sweated blood day and night to rebuild the family fortune. He and Sybil had struck another bargain. The arrangement had worked. Sybil had stuck it out and been well rewarded.

Oliver always made good on his promises.

And he never forgot his enemies.

Which brought him to the matter of Valerie's new boyfriend. If Sybil was telling the truth, and there was no reason to doubt it in this instance, Oliver knew he would have to take action. He had no intention of allowing his youngest sister to get seriously involved with Paul Shore's son.

Oliver made a mental note to speak to Valerie. He would make it clear that Carson Shore was off-limits. He had never liked the Romeo and Juliet story.

4

Annie, I've got to tell you that I'm having a lot of second thoughts about this plan of yours. I wasn't overly enthusiastic about your marriage of convenience idea to start with. But now that you're actually going to move in with him, I'm getting downright scared."

"Calm down, Joanna. Everything's going to work out beautifully. You'll see. Oliver and I understand each other perfectly. We settled all the details on Monday. He's very good at details." Annie slashed open one side of the lid of a shipping carton with her knife. She turned the big box around and took aim at the next side.

She and Joanna were alone in the back room of Wildest Dreams. Annie's assistant, Ella Presswood, was out front handling two interior designers who had stopped in to shop for their clients.

There was less than an hour to go until Annie had to be at the courthouse for the wedding. Oliver had called that morning to say that he would send a car for her. When she had objected on the grounds that she could walk the few blocks from her boutique in Pioneer Square to the courthouse, he had politely overridden her protests. The car would arrive at three, she was told. Annie had been too busy with a customer at the time to argue the point.

"I don't know." Joanna twisted her hands. "I just don't know. I feel very uneasy about you moving into his penthouse. Rain has a reputation for being dangerous."

"I've gotten to know him very well during the past few weeks, Joanna. He's not dangerous in the least."

"Are you out of your mind?" Joanna stared at her. "Annie, you're not accustomed to dealing with this kind of man. For heaven's sake, he's not another Arthur Quigley or Melvin Finch. Rain is not a wounded bird in need of rescue."

"I know that. I'm not trying to rescue Oliver. He's going to rescue me."

"I seriously doubt that Oliver Rain has ever rescued anything except the Rain fortune in his entire life," Joanna muttered.

Annie slashed open another side of the shipping carton and glanced back over her shoulder. Joanna looked as worried as she sounded. There was tension in her pretty face and her gentle eyes were filled with uncertainty.

Annie had liked Joanna, who was a manager in a successful downtown property management firm, the moment her brother had introduced the two women. Annie had sensed immediately that Joanna was capable of the kind of love and unwavering devotion Daniel deserved. Joanna was as alone in the world as Daniel and Annie were; she longed to be part of a family.

Pale gold hair and fey blue eyes gave Joanna a deceptively ethereal look. But Annie knew there was rock-solid strength beneath the surface. That inner fortitude had emerged in the days following the news of Daniel's disappearance. Joanna was as convinced as Annie that Daniel was alive.

"Stop worrying," Annie said gently. "Oliver and I both understand that the marriage is a business relationship. He's not going to assault me in order to claim his marital rights, or whatever they call them these days."

"How do you know that?" Joanna demanded.

"Wait until you meet him. You'll understand." Annie slashed open the last side of the lid and peered into the carton. A large object shrouded in bubble wrap loomed inside. An emerald eye winked at her through the plastic. "Great. It's the leopard. I wasn't sure what I'd get when I ordered it. The guy who does these cloisonné animals is a little unpredictable. I'm still trying to move the elephant."

"Annie, stop fussing with the new merchandise," Joanna said, exasperated. "This is your wedding day and I have a ghastly feeling we're all headed for disaster."

"Don't be silly." Annie reached into the box, took a grip on the bubble-wrapped leopard, and started to haul him out. "You're letting your imagination run away with you, Joanna. It's the stress, I suppose."

"It's not the stress," Joanna wailed, "it's my common sense finally kicking in. This marriage of convenience idea is totally crazy. I should never have let you go through with it. I don't know what got into me. I must have been out of my mind to let you talk me into it."

"It's a brilliant idea and it's going to work just fine." Annie heaved the leopard halfway out of the box. "It's already working. I've had phone calls all morning from Daniel's investors and creditors asking if it's true that Oliver Rain will own half of Lyncroft Unlimited by tomorrow morning. When I told them it was true and that he was taking control of the entire operation, they all sounded incredibly relieved."

"It's you I'm worried about, Annie, not the company. Listen, it's not too late to call this whole thing off. Tell Rain you changed your mind."

"But I haven't changed my mind. We had blood tests and everything. You'll be glad to know we're both extremely healthy, by the way."

"I wasn't worried about your health."

"Well, there isn't anything else to worry about." Annie adjusted her grip on the bubble wrap and hauled the leopard a few more inches out of the carton. "Oliver and I are going to be roommates for a while. That's all."

"Annie, he's one of the most powerful men in the Northwest, and no one seems to know much about him. He might be, well, you know, strange or something."

"He is."

"Strange?"

"Uh-huh."

"Oh, my God."

"But in an interesting way, if you know what I mean." Annie had the plastic-bound leopard almost out of the box.

"No, I do not know what you mean," Joanna snapped. "This sounds worse by the minute. You've got to call off the wedding."

"I'm not going to call it off. This marriage is our best chance to hold things together until Daniel returns and you know it."

"At least wait until Barry Cork gets back from his trip to California."

"This isn't Barry's decision. I'm in charge of the company and I have to take the responsibility for deciding how to save it."

"Please," Joanna said desperately. "I know you're doing this at least partially for me and the baby. But I don't want you to take that kind of risk for us."

"I'm doing it for Daniel, too."

"Daniel wouldn't want you to do anything this drastic, either."

"It's not drastic. Not really. It's a simple, sensible way to deal with the situation. For the last time, Joanna, stop worrying. Oliver Rain is not going to be a problem."

"You keep saying that, but how do you know it? What makes you think you'll be safe in his penthouse? What if he turns out to be a sex maniac?"

"A sex maniac? Oliver Rain?" Annie started to grin. She couldn't help herself. She stood there clutching the bulky package containing the leopard and let herself get swept away with a vision of Oliver Rain as a sex maniac. Her grin turned into a laugh. It was the first time she had laughed since her brother had disappeared. "Not a chance."

"What makes you so certain of that?" Joanna challenged.

"He's just not the type." Annie made an effort to control her giggles. "Oliver reminds me of a medieval monk."

"A *monk*."

"You know, one of those very controlled, very stern types who wouldn't dream of being swayed by ordinary juicy passions like lust and vengeance and greed."

Annie had the leopard out of the box at last. She set it down on the floor and carefully stripped away the bubble wrap.

"From all accounts, Oliver Rain is no saint." Joanna warned.

"For the last time, stop worrying. Good heavens, look at him, Joanna. Isn't he beautiful?" Annie examined the large cloisonné leopard in delight.

The statue stood nearly as high as her waist. The exotic, intricate cloisonné design was worked in gold and green and turquoise over black. The spectacular beast had brilliant green eyes and sported a jeweled collar.

"Annie, please, listen to me."

"He's wonderful," Annie declared. "You know something, I can just see him in Oliver's study. Maybe I'll give it to him as a wedding gift."

"Maybe I'll accept," Oliver said quietly from the doorway.

Joanna gasped in dismay.

"*Oliver.*" Annie looked up quickly and saw her future husband looming behind Joanna.

He was dressed in a dark suit and a pale gray shirt with a gray tie. His heavy mane of midnight hair was tied back with a black ribbon. There was a trace of humor in his gray eyes. Annie had the uncomfortable feeling that he might have overheard her remark about his resemblance to a medieval monk. Blushing furiously, she hurried to fill the small, awkward silence.

"I didn't hear you come in, Oliver," she said quickly. "You remember my brother's fiancée, don't you? You met her at the engagement party."

"Of course." Oliver inclined his head. "I was extremely sorry to hear of Daniel's disappearance."

54

"He'll be back," Joanna said stiffly.

"I hope so, Ms. McKenna." Oliver gazed at her in an assessing manner. "Are you coming with us to the courthouse?"

"Only if I can't talk Annie out of this marriage."

The corner of Oliver's mouth curved slightly. He glanced at Annie. "Somehow I feel that might be rather difficult to do. I have the impression that Annie has made up her mind."

"I certainly have. And we'd better get going or we'll all be late." Annie picked up the cloisonné leopard in both arms and thrust it impulsively toward Oliver. "Here. He's yours if you really want him."

"Thank you." Oliver examined the beast as he cradled him. "I'm sure I'll find a place for him." He tucked the leopard under one arm and nodded to indicate that Annie and Joanna should precede him through the door.

Annie went into the front of the shop, pausing briefly to introduce Oliver to Ella and the two unabashedly curious designers. Then she led the way through her little shop crowded with the unusual, the outrageous, and the bizarre.

Walking through Wildest Dreams was akin to strolling through the attic of an eccentric collector.

Annie loved every piece in the crowded room. Each had been painstakingly selected or commissioned by her. Each was handmade, each chosen for its own indefinable appeal. In one corner was an etched-glass tabletop suspended on the wings of three large brass griffins. A collection of intricately designed lacquer boxes and trunks was stacked in another corner.

The gilded carousel with its assortment of mythological animals that she had tried to sell to Oliver glittered on a nearby shelf. Next to it was the cloison-né elephant. A huge fan decorated in an abstract design hung on the wall. Not far away was a magnificent folding screen with a surrealistic jungle scene painted on its three panels.

Annie glanced back once when she reached the front door. Oliver Rain was studying the contents of Wildest Dreams with cool interest. He still had the leopard under his arm.

It occurred to Annie that Oliver looked right at home here in this room full of strange and wondrous things.

Out on the sidewalk an expressionless Bolt politely opened the door of the black limousine. He was dressed as usual in his formal blue suit. Today he was wearing gold-mirrored sunglasses that hid his eyes and made him look more like an android than usual. Annie smiled tentatively at him as she scrambled into the back of the big car. Bolt did not return the smile.

Oliver handed the leopard to Bolt as Joanna got reluctantly in beside Annie. "Take care of this until we get home."

"Yes, Mr. Rain."

Bolt stuffed the leopard into the trunk, closed the lid, and then walked around the car and got behind the wheel. A moment later the big car pulled soundlessly away from the curb.

"Nice," Annie said as Bolt worked his way smoothly through the downtown traffic. "Very nice. But I still say it would have been easier to walk. Where will Bolt park? There won't be any space on the street at this time of day."

"I pay Bolt to solve problems like that," Oliver said.

There was a short silence.

"I really feel we should all talk this over before we go through with the wedding," Joanna announced.

"I appreciate your concern," Oliver said. "But I'm afraid there isn't any time left. I've been fielding calls from Daniel's major suppliers since the news of the marriage broke yesterday. They all told me they'll continue shipping only if they know for certain I'll be in charge."

"Face it," Annie said to Joanna. "Daniel's suppliers and investors are all a bunch of male chauvinist pigs who don't think two women can keep the business going on their own."

"It's not the fact that you're both female that worries them," Oliver said. "It's the fact that neither one of you has any experience or background in the electronics industry or in running a highly competitive business such as Lyncroft."

"All the same," Annie muttered as Bolt drew the limousine to a halt in front of the courthouse, "I think they would have reacted differently if Joanna and I had been male. Good lord, who are all those people waiting for us?"

Oliver glanced out the heavily tinted windows. "Family."

"Yours?" Annie shot him a quick, searching glance. She realized that even though Daniel had mentioned the Rain family in passing, she had not really imagined Oliver having real relatives.

"Mine." Oliver studied the small group. "The two young men on the left are my half brothers, Nathan and Richard. The two women on the right are my sisters, Valerie and Heather. Nathan and Richard are in college. Valerie is an assistant curator at the Eckert Museum and Heather is a doctor."

Annie noted the undercurrent of pride in his voice. "I'm impressed. And the woman in the peach suit?"

"That's Sybil, my father's second wife." Oliver's tone turned cool. "She's Nathan and Richard's mother."

Annie glanced at him but could read nothing in his eyes. She turned back to study the Rain tribe more closely as Bolt parked the limousine in a no-parking zone.

Oliver's half brothers were twins. Both were good-looking with the lean, graceful build and dark hair that seemed to be characteristic of the men in the Rain family. Heather and Valerie were equally attractive, although they both had light golden brown hair and softer, less angular features.

Heather looked every inch the professional woman with her short, stylish haircut and serious eyes. Her expensive, well-tailored tweed suit had a narrow skirt that ended just below her knees.

Valerie was equally stylish and equally businesslike. Her hair fell to her shoulders.

As Bolt opened the door, Annie realized that Sybil Rain was considerably younger than one would have expected. She was probably not more than a few years older than Oliver. She was also a strikingly attractive woman.

Annie decided that none of the rest of the Rain clan had Oliver's talent for keeping their expressions cool and unreadable. They all watched Annie and Joanna with unconcealed curiosity.

Annie surveyed her future in-laws-in-name-only and was glad she had taken the time to put on her hunter-green dress. The long sleeves and full sweep of the calf-length skirt gave her a more polished look than

58

she would have had in the slacks and sweater she had originally intended to wear.

"I suppose we'd better make a few introductions before we go inside," Oliver said. He took Annie's arm and steered her toward the rest of the Rains. Joanna trailed after them, looking extremely unhappy.

Oliver's proprietary grasp on Annie's arm drew the full attention of his family. As one, their eyes swung from Joanna and settled on Annie. Sybil's gaze narrowed.

"Trust Oliver to spring a surprise bride on us like this," Heather said as she shook Annie's hand. "He never gives out any clues about what he's going to do or when he's going to do it."

"Surprise is right," Valerie murmured. She shot her brother a speculative glance. "The rest of us are expected to get any potential spouses approved by him. But Oliver apparently didn't feel he had to get our approval for his own marriage. Hardly fair, big brother."

"Not much point in being the head of the family if you don't get to approve your own bride, right, Oliver?" Richard grinned at his brother as he shook Annie's hand.

"Yeah, old Oliver deserves a few perks as head of the clan. We'll let him get away with selecting his own bride," Nathan added cheerfully. "Looks to me like he's done a good job of it."

Sybil smiled without much warmth as she stepped forward. "It's not as though we have much choice, is it? Welcome to the family, Ms. Lyncroft. I certainly hope you know what you're doing by marrying Oliver."

"Annie knows exactly what she's doing," Oliver said coolly. "Don't you, Annie?"

"Definitely," Annie agreed. She was acutely aware of Oliver's big hand wrapped around her arm. He was holding onto her as if he thought she might try to flee.

Nathan looked at Oliver. "I'd better warn you that you're not going to be allowed to sneak away after the wedding. We've planned a little surprise of our own."

"That's right," Heather said. She smiled at Oliver. "Don't worry. Just a small reception. Family only. We know you wanted to keep this low-key, but you can't expect us to ignore your wedding altogether."

"After all," Sybil drawled, "your marriage is a major event in the family, Oliver."

Oliver accepted the news with apparent equanimity. "I don't mind if Annie doesn't."

"Well," Annie said cautiously, "I hadn't really planned on making a big deal out of this. It's just a little wedding, after all."

Everyone, including Oliver, looked at her.

"Just a little wedding?" Sybil repeated dryly. "Come now, Annie. It's a bit more than that, isn't it? You're marrying one of the wealthiest men in the state. Some might say this kind of alliance is more of a business move than a romantic one."

Annie flushed.

"I think we're ready." Oliver started forward with Annie in tow.

"Yes, let's get this over with," Annie muttered.

The formalities were completed in a blur as far as she was concerned. She realized that Joanna was on one side casting worried glances at her during the short ceremony, and she was very conscious of the assembled Rains hovering nearby. But mostly she was aware of Oliver. He seemed very large and substantial standing there next to her.

And then it was over. Annie breathed a sigh of relief as they all trooped back outside onto the sidewalk. She was telling herself that she had done the right thing and that this marriage was the only viable means she had of holding onto Daniel's company when a camera was suddenly thrust into her face.

"How does it feel to be Mrs. Oliver Rain?" A hard-eyed woman held up a microphone. "Does this marriage have anything to do with the fact that your brother has disappeared?"

Annie realized abruptly that she and Oliver were surrounded by a handful of reporters. Microphones and minicams were everywhere.

"Mr. Rain, how long have you two known each other?"

"Is it true you're going to take immediate control of Lyncroft, Mr. Rain?"

"Is it true you now own half of Lyncroft Unlimited?"

Oliver looked at the man who had asked the last question. "Yes."

"You're a partner in the firm, then?"

"The controlling partner?" another reporter demanded. "What does this mean for the company?"

"It means," Oliver said calmly as he and Bolt forged a path through the throng, "that Lyncroft Unlimited is safe and stable. We will proceed on schedule with Daniel Lyncroft's plans to bring the company's new technology to market."

"That's going to be good news for Lyncroft's investors," a woman said quickly. "Can you tell us if there will be any delays because of the loss of Daniel Lyncroft?"

"There will be no delays," Oliver said. "And now you'll have to excuse us. If you have any further questions, you can contact Lyncroft public relations tomorrow."

"But, Mr. Rain..."

"Wait a second, sir, this is major Northwest financial news. There were rumors Lyncroft was under pressure to sell or merge."

"Not any longer," Annie said swiftly.

"No," Oliver agreed. "Not any longer."

Richard caught Oliver's eye. "You two take the limousine. We'll bring Joanna with us. See you at the penthouse."

"All right," Oliver agreed.

Bolt finished carving a path through the swirling reporters for Oliver and Annie. They were within six feet of the waiting limousine when a shout came from the corner of the block.

"*Annie*! Annie, what the hell is going on here?"

Annie turned her head at the sound of the familiar voice. Barry Cork was charging down the sidewalk. His short brown hair was tousled as if he had been running frantic fingers through it. His handsome face were set in harried lines. His tie flapped back over his shoulder and his briefcase was bumping against his thigh as he rushed toward her.

"Barry. What are you doing here?" Annie smiled as he drew near. "I thought you were going to be in California for another few days. Have you met Oliver Rain?"

Barry came to a halt, breathing heavily, just as Oliver and Annie reached the limousine. "No, but I know about him." He glanced fleetingly at Oliver and then turned urgently back to Annie. "What's happening here? Is it true you just married him?"

"Yes, and everything's going to be fine, Barry." Annie was aware of Joanna and the Rains moving forward to surround them and in the process hold the curious reporters at bay. Oliver's hand tightened on her arm.

"What the hell do you think you're doing?" Barry hissed in a low voice. He shot another hard look at Oliver. "Have you gone crazy? You've given him half your company, haven't you?"

"Barry, listen, I can explain..."

"That's why he's married you. To get his hands on Lyncroft Unlimited."

"You've got it backward," Annie said. "I'll explain it to you later."

Bolt had the limousine door open. Oliver started to bundle Annie inside.

Barry grabbed her arm. His eyes were wild. "Are you nuts? Don't you know what's happening here? Oliver Rain has just taken over your company."

"Stop it, Barry," Annie said, pitching her voice low to avoid having the reporters and the rest of the Rains overhear. "You're getting hysterical. Lyncroft is perfectly safe. For now Oliver is my partner. That's all there is to it."

"You think so?" Barry demanded fiercely. "You think it's that simple?"

Oliver reached out and ripped Barry's clutching fingers off Annie's arm. "Take your hands off my wife."

Barry jerked his hand back as if it had been burned. But his desperate eyes never left Annie's face. "Ask him what happened to a guy named Walker Gresham. Go ahead, Annie. *Ask him.*"

"Let's go, Annie." Oliver prodded her gently but firmly into the limousine. Bolt stood close. His mirrored sunglasses reflected Barry's distraught face.

"Barry, I don't understand why you're so upset. Everything is going to be fine." Annie broke off as Oliver got her inside the car and slid in beside her.

Barry bent down to lean into the back of the car as Bolt started to close the door. "Annie, for God's sake, listen to me. Five years ago a man named Walker Gresham was a partner in a company Rain took over. Gresham died within months after the takeover. There were rumors, Annie. Do you hear me? There were rumors that Gresham's death was no accident..."

The car door slammed shut. Bolt got behind the wheel in the blink of an eye and a few seconds later the limousine pulled away from the curb.

Annie turned her head to glance out the back window. Barry stood on the sidewalk looking as if he had arrived late to a funeral rather than a wedding.

5

"I think the leopard works well in here." Oliver leaned back in his chair, steepled his fingers, and gazed at the jeweled statue with satisfaction.

As it happened, the exotic beast looked very much at home in his study. But he would have lodged it in here even if it had looked as ridiculous as the elephant and the carousel. The cloisonné leopard was, after all, a gift from his bride.

His bride.

He savored the deep sense of satisfaction he had been feeling since he had walked out of the courthouse with Annie at his side.

"You're sure?" Annie studied the leopard with a dubious expression.

"Yes." Oliver smiled slightly. "He suits the room very nicely."

His gaze went past the leopard to the rain-streaked darkness beyond the window. It was nearly eight o'clock, and he and Annie were finally alone. He thought that he had concealed his impatience well for the past few hours while his family produced the surprise reception. He admitted to himself that he had been oddly touched by their efforts, but he had been relieved to see everyone, including Bolt, leave a few minutes ago. This was, after all, his wedding night.

"Well, that takes care of the formalities." Annie blew

a small sigh and sank back into her seat. "No offense, but I thought your family would never leave."

"I was beginning to think I would have to ask Bolt to toss them out the door," Oliver said.

"Can't blame them for wanting to celebrate, I suppose. They think this marriage is for real. By the way, where did Bolt go? Into a closet somewhere?"

"Bolt has an apartment of his own down on the sixth floor of this building." Oliver masked the flare of irritation Annie's offhand comment about their marriage roused in him. He wondered how long it would take before she realized he had every intention of making this marriage very, very real.

"Oh." Annie glanced down at her hand and gave a small start. "Good heavens, I almost forgot. You can have your ring back now. The ceremony is over." She started to remove the simple gold band.

"Don't you think you'd better keep it on? It's customary, you know." And he was old-fashioned enough to want his wife to wear the symbol of her commitment to him in plain view.

"I hadn't thought about having to wear a ring all the time. Do you really think it's necessary?"

"Yes. We don't want any speculation at this juncture. The marriage must appear solid and secure."

Annie eyed the ring dubiously. "I suppose it won't hurt."

"It will shore up the image." He reached across the desk and took her hand in one of his. Her fingers were light, graceful, utterly feminine. He felt a small tremor go through her at his touch. Raw possessiveness flashed through him. He had not been wrong about her. She did want him.

She was his, Oliver thought triumphantly. Almost.

66

Oliver slid the gold band firmly back into place on her finger. When it was in position, she instantly started to tug her hand free of his grip. He searched for an excuse to hold onto her.

"Come with me." Oliver stood up, still grasping her hand firmly in his and walked around the edge of the desk.

"Where are we going?" She looked up at him with a mixture of sensual awareness and uncertainty in her huge eyes. She was still trying to pretend this was a business arrangement.

Oliver realized that for all her charming impulsiveness and her bold schemes to save her brother's company, Annie was not completely sure of herself tonight. The knowledge amused him and made him feel curiously indulgent. He would be patient with her, he promised himself.

"I want to show you something on the roof," Oliver said gently.

He tugged her to her feet and started for the door. He was ruefully aware of his semiaroused body. He was getting hard in spite of his best efforts at self-control. He would simply have to suffer the torments of the unsatisfied tonight, he told himself. It was too soon, much too soon, to seduce Annie.

"Are we going to look at the city lights?" Annie asked a little too brightly as he led her up the steps to the roof door.

"No."

He kept her hand tightly clasped in his, curious to see how she would react to the greenhouse. Something told him she would like it. He had never wanted to show off his private jungle to anyone else before, but now he wanted to see how Annie would look standing amid his ferns.

"Oliver, I don't want you to feel that just because we're sort of married you have to entertain me," Annie said earnestly as she hurried along beside him. "I really don't want to interfere with your normal evening routine."

He ignored her comment as he opened the door onto the roof. The huge greenhouse loomed in the shadows, its glass walls reflecting the rain-swept lights of the city.

"What's this?" Annie asked. Curiosity abruptly replaced the incipient nervousness in her voice.

"My private world." Oliver paused at the control panel to turn on the lights. Then he opened the door of the greenhouse. The primal scents of moist earth and growing plants enveloped them.

"Wow!" Annie took a deep breath as she stepped into the humid atmosphere and surveyed the lush, vibrant green foliage that surrounded her. "This is fantastic, Oliver. I've never seen such spectacular ferns. It looks like a slice of a rain forest."

"I thought you'd like it." He released her and stood back to watch as she walked slowly down the nearest fern-choked aisle.

He had been right. She looked perfect here among the lush, primitive greenery of his private world. Annie was as natural and real as the ferns were.

"Beautiful." Annie paused to admire a magnificent maidenhair. "Absolutely beautiful." She moved on to examine a tray of young plants.

"Do you like ferns?"

"Yes, indeed," Annie said. "I've killed dozens of them in my time. I don't have what you'd call a green

68

thumb, but I keep trying. How long have you been interested in them?"

"Since my college days." Oliver hesitated. "There was a time when I planned to make a career in botany."

Annie looked at him from between the fronds of a pretty little holly fern, her eyes sharp with perception. "Not business?"

"No. Not business. The last thing I ever wanted to be was a businessman."

Her eyes widened. "What made you change your mind and pursue your business interests as a full-time career?"

"I'm sure Daniel has told you about my father."

"I know he walked out on you and your family."

Oliver was not certain he liked the soft sympathy in her voice. He was not accustomed to sympathy. He wasn't certain how to deal with it. "He left a mountain of debts and I had four brothers and sisters to look after."

"You felt you had to pay off the debts and restore your family's financial security?"

He shrugged slightly and looked out through the glass wall of the greenhouse. "Yes."

"That was an enormous undertaking." Annie searched his face. "The interesting thing is that you seem to be every bit as good at business as you are at growing ferns."

"They're not unrelated. Both require patience. And self-control."

"And you have plenty of both, don't you?" Annie jerked her fascinated gaze away from his face and looked at the nearest fern, another maidenhair.

"Yes." He took cold satisfaction in that simple affirmation of what was, after all, the truth. Idly Oliver traced the delicate outline of the tightly curled crosier of a lady fern. He wondered if Annie's nipples would feel like the new frond, firm and full of passionate promise.

"Do you ever worry about being overcontrolled?" Annie asked. Her eyes were fixed on his finger as it traced the coiled crosier.

Oliver smiled at the naive question. "There is no such thing as having too much self-control."

"I suppose it's that attitude that's gotten you where you are today."

"Yes."

"You've paid a price, though, haven't you?"

Oliver met her eyes. "There's a price on everything."

"Uh-huh." She sounded unconvinced.

Oliver decided to change the subject. "About Barry Cork."

She jumped. "What about him?"

"I think it would be best if you did not tell him that our marriage is one of convenience."

Annie went very still. "Why not?"

"Let's just say I think he would have a difficult time keeping the information to himself." Oliver paused, thinking. "He seemed shaken enough as it was this afternoon. There's no telling how he would react if he thought our marriage was a sham. He might let it slip to the very people we're trying to convince."

Annie turned to study a row of glass-topped trays. Oliver saw the tension in her shoulders as she stood with her back to him. "I think Barry deserves some explanations. He was extremely upset this afternoon."

Oliver leaned against one of the benches and shoved his hands into the pockets of his charcoal gray slacks. "Go ahead, Annie. Ask me what that was all about."

She shot him a quick, searching look over her shoulder. "All right, what was Barry talking about? What did he mean when he said some people thought you had, uh, done in an executive of one of your acquisitions? What was his name?"

"Walker Gresham." Oliver concentrated on the night outside the glass walls. He fell silent, wondering how much of the story to tell her.

"Well?" Annie prompted after a few seconds of silence.

Oliver glanced at her, mildly surprised by the hint of asperity in her voice. "About five years ago I took over a medium-sized manufacturing firm that had found an active niche in the Pacific Rim market. I kept one of the former partners, Walker Gresham, on as a high-level manager. He was the one who had carved out the foreign markets for the company and he seemed to know what he was doing."

"What happened?"

"Your brother had just been put in charge of security. He walked into my office one morning and said he had reason to suspect Gresham was shipping something other than machine tools to some of his foreign customers. We set up a discreet investigation."

Annie watched him, intrigued. "And?"

Oliver shrugged. "And we found out Gresham was using my new machine tool exporting business as a cover for his real occupation."

"Which was?"

"He was an arms dealer. The bastard shipped black-market weapons to every two-bit terrorist and revolutionary around the Pacific who could pay for them."

Annie's eyes widened in astonishment. "That's awful. What on earth did you do? Report him to the FBI?"

"We never got the chance," Oliver said. "Daniel and I didn't know what we were onto at first. We thought it was just another white-collar business scam. We followed a computer trail that took us to a warehouse on a small South Pacific island where Gresham's stuff was being transshipped."

"What happened?"

"We went into the warehouse late one night looking for evidence and stumbled across Gresham and one of his clients instead." Oliver paused. "There was some trouble."

"Trouble?" Annie frowned. "I remember Daniel going out to the South Pacific on a business trip a few years ago. He never told me there was any danger involved. He just said everything had been straightened out."

Oliver chose his words carefully. "Everything did get straightened out. But in the process Walker Gresham was killed."

"*Killed.*" Annie gave him a horrified look. "Who killed him?"

Oliver saw nothing to be gained by telling her that he had fired the shot that had killed Gresham or that Gresham had been about to shoot Daniel at the time. Some things were better left unexplained, especially to someone like Annie.

Telling even a sanitized version of the story brought back unpleasant memories, however. Oliver suspected that the image of Gresham's blood-stained body lying on the concrete floor of the warehouse would haunt him off and on for the rest of his life. Perhaps it was only right, he thought. A man should not be able to kill, even in self-defense or to save someone else, and then be able to erase the memory of the killing.

"Your brother and I had gone into the warehouse armed just in case," Oliver said, choosing his words carefully. "We weren't sure what to expect. All hell broke loose. There was a flurry of shots and when it was over, Gresham was dead. It all happened a long ways from the States. The incident was not deliberately kept secret, but the island authorities handled everything very discreetly. It never made the Seattle papers."

"There was shooting? Someone was killed? My God. Daniel never said a word," Annie raged. "He could have been hurt. I'll strangle him. Why didn't he tell me what happened?"

"Probably because he knew you'd overreact." Oliver looked at her. "The way you're overreacting now."

"I am not overreacting. I'm furious."

"Annie, it happened five years ago."

"All the same, I should have been told. I'm his sister. Daniel had no right to keep me in the dark like that."

"He was obviously only trying to protect you. He didn't want you worrying about him."

"I don't need that kind of protection." Annie scowled. "I certainly hope you don't intend to try to keep things from me for my own good."

"Take it easy, Annie."

"I mean it, Oliver. I will not be treated as anything less than a full partner in this arrangement you and I have made. Is that clear? This whole thing was my idea right from the start and we'll do things my way. I don't want to be shielded or protected."

He pondered that for a long moment. "I'll keep your wishes in mind, naturally. But I doubt that you need to be kept fully informed of all the day-to-day details of running Daniel's business. It would be a cumbersome arrangement. And you have your own business to look after."

Annie nearly choked on her outrage. She took three steps forward and grasped the ends of Oliver's unknotted tie. "Now you listen to me, Oliver Rain, we're in this together. I thought you understood that. We're going to function as a team or not at all. Got that?"

He looked down into her fierce eyes. "I don't do business quite that way."

"You do now."

He smiled faintly. "Annie, you married me to gain my expertise. Let me do my job."

"But I want to be kept fully informed. I want to be involved in the decision-making process. I'm supposed to be learning the ropes, just in case, remember?"

"That will be impractical, Annie. Especially at this stage. Daniel's creditors and investors are expecting to see only me at the helm. And to be frank, I won't have time to run Lyncroft Unlimited and teach you how to manage it at the same time. At least not now."

"But, Oliver..."

He touched her cheek. Her skin was as soft as velvet. "Trust me, Annie. I told you I'd take care of everything for you, didn't I?"

"Well, yes." She frowned. "But I thought we'd be a team."

"I've never been a team player."

"This is a fine time to tell me," she muttered.

"Can't you bring yourself to put your trust in me?" he asked softly.

She released the ends of his tie and stepped back. "I'm overreacting, aren't I?"

"A little," he agreed.

"I'm tense."

"Understandable."

She bit her lip. "I'm scared, Oliver."

"I know." He put out a hand to catch hold of her before he could stop himself.

But Annie had already turned away and didn't see the move. He let his hand back fall to his side without touching her. Just as well, he thought. It was much too soon.

Annie folded her arms beneath her breasts and gazed into the sea of green that surrounded her. "I've tried to tell myself that this plan of mine will work. Most of the time I'm convinced that everything will come out all right. Daniel will return safe and sound and his company will be in good shape, waiting for him. But sometimes, like tonight, I wonder if I'm just fooling myself."

Oliver didn't know what to say in response to that. He was virtually certain Daniel Lyncroft was dead, but he didn't have the heart to keep insisting on it. He settled for the one promise he knew he could guarantee. "You don't have to worry about Daniel's company. I'll take care of it for you."

She shot him a quick, searching look over her shoulder. "You understand, don't you? You know why I'm doing this."

"Yes."

Her eyes narrowed speculatively. "Because you went through a similar experience after your father vanished, didn't you? You had to find a way to hold things together for your family."

75

"Yes."

"And pay off the debts he left behind."

Oliver nodded once, not saying anything.

Annie turned completely around to face him. "Your family appreciates what you did. It was clear tonight that your brothers and sisters admire you tremendously."

"I'm not sure admiration is quite what they feel for me."

Annie smiled. "They respect you. But you don't get along very well with Sybil, do you?"

"Sybil and I understand each other."

Annie tipped her head to one side. "Why don't you two like each other?"

"It's an old story," Oliver said gently. "And it doesn't concern you."

"Ouch." Annie grinned ruefully. "Okay, I know when I've been put in my place. No more questions about Sybil."

"I wasn't trying to put you in your place," Oliver said.

"Yes, you were. Don't apologize. Your relationship with your stepmother is your business and you don't owe me any explanations. Heavens, it's not like I'm really one of the family just because I married you."

"Why don't we change the subject?"

Annie flushed. "Right. Good idea. Let's change the subject. So, what about dinner? I don't know about you, but I'm starving."

"Bolt had instructions to leave dinner in the oven for us." Oliver glanced at the black and gold watch on his wrist. "It will be waiting when we go downstairs."

Annie's brows climbed. "Bolt cooks?"

"Bolt does anything I tell him to do."

"No offense, but he makes me think of a robot."

"Bolt is extremely useful." Oliver straightened. He took Annie's arm and started along the gravel path toward the door.

"I'm sorry I gave you the impression I don't trust you earlier," Annie said in a soft rush. "I didn't mean to imply that I don't have complete faith in you."

"Thank you."

Annie smiled. "You know something? You really are a very nice man. I think your basic problem is that you have difficulty communicating with others."

She came to a halt and went up on tiptoe to give him a quick, impulsive little kiss on the side of his face.

Desire roared through Oliver like an inferno. He stood like a rock, fighting for his self-control. It was as if Annie's small, meaningless caress had flipped a switch somewhere inside him. He had an almost overpowering urge to crush her into the nearest bank of ferns, lift up her skirt, and sink himself into her.

Even as he watched her watching him he saw the dawning awareness in her eyes. She took an involuntary step back. Wariness replaced the warmth in her gaze.

Oliver took a deep, steadying breath. "A lot of people don't think I'm very nice at all, Annie. And there's something you ought to know."

"What's that?" She whispered.

"I'm not a monk."

Her cheeks turned a vivid pink. "I was afraid you had overhead that stupid remark. I didn't mean it the way it sounded."

"Forget it," he advised brusquely.

"I never meant to imply that you were asexual or anything."

"It's all right, Annie."

"No, it's not all right." She was clearly flustered. "I wouldn't want you to get the wrong impression. I mean, I want you to know that I definitely think of you as a man."

"Thank you," he said dryly. It was all right now. He could feel his willpower taking hold again. He was back under control.

Annie's blush intensified. "Good lord, this is getting worse by the minute. I'm only trying to explain that I think you're quite normal."

"Normal, but strange?"

"In a very interesting way," she said, clearly desperate.

He smiled faintly. "Annie, I told you, it's all right."

"Yes, but I wouldn't want you to think that I..."

He stopped the frantic apology by the simple expedient of putting his hand over her lips. "That's enough. Let's stop right there with interesting. I like interesting."

"You do?" she mumbled into his palm.

"Yes. It so happens I find you very interesting, too."

"Really?" Her eyes widened above the edge of his hand.

"Yes. Really." It was too soon, Oliver thought, but he was going to kiss her anyway. He couldn't seem to stop himself. He leaned back against the bench, widened his stance, and pulled Annie slowly and inexorably between his thighs.

She resisted only briefly. The next thing Oliver knew Annie was leaning into him with a joyful abandon. Her hands splayed across his shoulders. Her eyes glittered with feminine anticipation. When he took his palm off her mouth he saw that her lips were slightly parted with sensual excitement.

"You remind me of one of my ferns," Oliver said.

"I do?" She appeared delighted by that information.

"Yes."

He bent his head. Slowly and deliberately he covered her mouth with his own. He felt the sexual electricity race through her, felt it add fuel to his already aroused senses.

She tasted exactly as he had known she would—fresh and vibrant and full of promise, the most exotic fern in his garden.

Annie's fingers tightened abruptly on the fabric of his shirt. She clung to him, greeting him with a deep, hungry curiosity that was sending small shivers through her.

And through him, Oliver acknowledged with a small shock. His hands were trembling a little with the force of his need. Annie's immediate, completely undisguised response filled him with a thundering satisfaction.

For a long moment he stood there, cradling her between his thighs, savoring the excitement and the anticipation. He could feel the softness of her breasts crushed against his chest. The curve of her hips pressed against his erection, making his blood run hot. She was just what he wanted, just what he needed. He had been right about her that night at Daniel's engagement party.

Oliver forced himself to let his mouth move slowly across Annie's, testing the extent of her desire for him. She mumbled something that sounded urgent against lips.

"What was that?" he muttered, not really caring. He took her earlobe between his teeth and bit carefully. Another shiver went through her. Once again he had a scalding vision of taking her right there in the greenhouse.

"I said this kind of thing could really complicate matters," Annie got out in a breathless little voice.

"No, it will simplify them." He was convinced of that. He knew for certain now that he could make her respond. Once he took her to bed, she would be his.

Annie held herself slightly away from him so that she could look up into his face. "How can you say that?"

"Annie, I want you. You want me. We're married. What could be less complicated than that?"

He knew as soon as the words were out of his mouth that he'd made a serious mistake. The expression in Annie's eyes altered swiftly. She pushed against his shoulders and stepped back out of his arms.

"Hold it right there." She eyed him warily "Just how did you think our little business arrangement was going to work?"

"Any way you want it to work," he said gently.

Some of the fizzy outrage went out of her. She wrinkled her nose. "I suppose I did sort of encourage you."

"Why don't we just say there seems to be a mutual attraction between us?"

She slanted him an uncertain glance. "Do you mean that?"

He smiled. "I don't think there's any doubt."

"Oh, God, I thought it was just me."

"And you thought I was a monk."

80

She glared at him. "Don't tease me about that. I've already apologized. Oliver, this is very awkward. What are we going to do?"

"What do you want to do?" he countered softly.

"I don't know." Distraught, she ran a hand through her sherry-brown curls. "I never thought about what would happen if we got involved. Physically, that is. In addition to a business involvement, if you see what I mean. This changes everything."

A distant alarm went off somewhere inside Oliver. He knew he had to block that line of thought immediately or she might file for divorce in the morning. "It changes nothing in regard to your brother's company. A deal is a deal, Annie. I intend to uphold my end of the bargain regardless of what happens between us."

"You do?" She gazed up at him intently.

Oliver forced himself to appear cool and unconcerned. "Of course. After all, I've got a lot at stake in Lyncroft Unlimited."

"Yes, you do, don't you? And I need you." The blush rose again in her cheeks. "To hold Daniel's company together, that is."

"The way I see it, we're looking at two separate issues." Oliver deliberately leached all nuance of emotion out of his voice. "Our relationship is one thing. Saving Daniel's company is another. There's no reason we can't handle each one independently of the other."

"Independently?"

"We'll divide up the responsibilities. I'll take care of the business problems. You make the decisions regarding the personal side of things."

"Me?" She looked amazed.

"Why not? Don't you think you can decide whether or not you want us to be roommates or lovers?"

"Of course I can make a decision like that," she sputtered. "That's not the point."

"What is the point?"

"The point is, I already know it's a very bad idea for us to be anything more than roommates."

"I don't think it's a bad idea at all. But the choice is yours. Just let me know whatever you decide. I'll go along with your decisions in that arena just as you've agreed to go along with mine when it comes to Lyncroft Unlimited."

Annie gazed at him, her mouth open. "I don't believe it."

"What don't you believe?"

"That you're prepared to be so cool and calm and rational about something like...like..."

"Sex?"

Her chin came up with a touch of defiance, even though her cheeks were still very pink. "Yes. Sex."

Oliver shrugged. "You obviously haven't had a lot of experience with monks." He took her arm and started toward the door again. "What do you say we go eat dinner? I've worked up an appetite."

6

I just can't believe you're married to him, Annie." Barry stabbed his fingers through his sandy hair and glumly eyed his cup of French-roasted coffee. "I can't believe I didn't know you and Rain were even seeing each other, let alone planning to get married. Dan never said a word."

"Oliver is a very private man. He wanted everything kept quiet." Annie wondered where and when she had acquired this marvelous ability to tell a social lie. It was certainly a useful skill. Nevertheless, she felt a jolt of guilt. Barry had, after all, been her brother's right-hand man. He deserved better than this.

She glanced covertly around to see if any of the handful of people at the nearby cafe tables could overhear her. There was no reason for alarm. The crowd was composed chiefly of tourists who had come to shop the galleries, bookstores, and craft shops of the Pioneer Square area. She didn't know any of them and they all seemed occupied with their own concerns.

"Private? That's putting it mildly," Barry complained. "Rain is a damned mystery. Ask anyone. They'll tell you he's strange."

Annie immediately felt compelled to defend Oliver. She wondered uneasily if the urge was a sign of budding wifely instinct. "He's not all that strange. He just likes his privacy. He didn't want a lot of speculation and gossip going around until we were ready to make an announcement. Then, after Daniel disappeared, he decided we had better move our wedding date forward in order to pacify the Lyncroft creditors and investors."

"Annie, I don't know what to say. This is all so damn sudden."

"Until Daniel disappeared, there was no real rush and Oliver does like to do things on his own schedule."

"You can say that again." Barry's mouth tightened ominously. "People who get themselves tangled up in Oliver Rain's schedule usually end up chewed into little pieces."

Annie waved that aside with a breezy movement of her hand. "The man's reputation has been blown out of all proportion." She frowned as a thought struck her. "It probably got that way because he doesn't feel any need to explain himself to others. His communication skills are a little weak."

"No shit."

"But he really is very nice and he's going to take good care of Daniel's company."

"Very nice?" Barry looked as if he were about to gag on his coffee. "That would be a joke if it weren't for the fact that the situation is so damned serious. Annie, Rain is as dangerous as they come. Don't you understand?"

Annie smiled reassuringly. "He's not dangerous. Not to us, Barry. He's going to protect Lyncroft Unlimited. Look at it this way. We've got the gunslinger with the toughest reputation in this part of the West standing guard over Daniel's firm."

"How can you be so naive?" Barry slumped despondently in his chair. "I don't like it, Annie. I'm scared for both you and Lyncroft."

"If you're uneasy because of that old rumor about Walker Gresham, forget it. I know the whole story."

"You do?" he asked sharply.

"Certainly. He told me everything. Gresham was running guns using one of Oliver's companies as a cover. Oliver and Daniel tracked him down and surprised him one night during a deal. There was some gunfire. Gresham was killed."

"That's Rain's story. Too bad Dan isn't here to back it up."

"How did you hear about it anyway?" Annie asked.

Barry shrugged. "Somebody mentioned it when word got around that Rain was Lyncroft's largest investor. Everyone was wondering what he would do. I guess we found out, didn't we? He married you. Shit."

Annie drew herself up. "I resent that, Barry.

"I'm sorry, but the man makes me nervous. Daniel's not here to protect you."

"I don't need to be protected from Oliver."

Barry's eyes narrowed. "Tell me something. What will you do if you find out that there really is a genuine reason to fear Rain?"

Annie sipped her coffee. It was obvious Barry was very worried on her behalf. It was touching. She sought for a way to ease his concerns. "You know Daniel set Lyncroft up so that only family members can own shares."

"I know." Barry's jaw tightened. "And you've just made Rain a member of the family. Given him an interest in the business."

"Well, if I ever had reason to get truly nervous

about Oliver's intentions," Annie confided, "I could divorce him. I have a prenuptial agreement that would effectively end his control over the company."

Barry's eyes never left her face. He slowly set his cup down on the table. "I hadn't thought of that."

Annie made a face. "Believe me, Oliver is well aware of it. He knows perfectly well that marrying me is not a surefire way to take over Lyncroft Unlimited."

"But he could use his power as a partner to maneuver Lyncroft into an untenable position."

"Lyncroft was already in an untenable position." Annie was getting exasperated. "If Oliver had wanted to force a sale or merger of the firm, he would have joined the other investors and suppliers who were putting pressure on us. He didn't have to marry me."

"I'm not so sure about that." Barry rubbed the back of his neck. "The man is devious. He knew you'd resist selling or merging the firm as long as possible. If you held out long enough, the company could have been ruined before he got his hands on it. And he had no way of being certain he would be the buyer. Hell, you might have found a white knight."

"And done a friendly merger with one of Rain's rivals?" Annie shook her head. "Not likely. And Daniel would have hated it. Look, Barry, you're going to have to trust me on this. I know what I'm doing. Besides, this will all become moot when Daniel returns."

Barry touched her hand lightly, his eyes troubled. "And if he doesn't return, Annie?"

"He will," Annie said.

Annie swept into the penthouse's designer kitchen at five-thirty that evening. She plopped two large bags of groceries onto the black tile counter and smiled brightly at Bolt.

"Didn't you get my note?" she asked.

"Yes, Mrs. Rain."

Annie eyed him uncertainly. "It said you wouldn't have to bother with dinner tonight. I'm going to cook it."

"Mr. Rain instructed me to cook dinner for both of you tonight. I take my orders from him." Bolt peeled a potato with machine-like precision. He looked awesomely efficient dressed in a spotless white apron over his white shirt and tie.

Annie refused to allow herself to be intimidated by the skillful manner in which Bolt wielded the paring knife. The man was good, she admitted it. Apparently he was good at everything. But she intended to cook dinner. She had been looking forward to it all day.

"I understand, Bolt," she said patiently, "but I'm telling you that I'll be cooking dinner. You can go home."

"As I said, Mrs. Rain, I take my instructions from Mr. Rain."

"You don't like me very much do you?"

Bolt picked up another potato. "My personal feelings have nothing to do with the matter. I work for Mr. Rain."

"Well, where is Mr. Rain?" Annie glowered at Bolt's impervious back. "I'll have him tell you that you can go home."

"Mr. Rain is busy in his study. He doesn't want to be disturbed."

Annie whirled around and started for the hall. "He won't mind me bopping in for a minute to tell him to send you home."

"He's with his sister," Bolt said crushingly. "I believe it's a private matter."

That brought Annie to a halt as Bolt had no doubt known it would. "All right, I'll wait until they're finished. Then I'll talk to Oliver. In the meantime, don't peel any more potatoes. I'm going to make tacos."

"We'll be having broiled salmon, Duchess potatoes, and artichokes," Bolt said. "It's one of Mr. Rain's favorite meals."

"I'll bet he likes tacos, too."

"Not particularly."

Annie gave Bolt a narrow-eyed glance. "He hasn't had my tacos."

She turned and stalked down the hall toward the elegant guest suite that had been assigned to her.

Bolt was going to be a problem, she decided. She had sensed from the start that he didn't like her. She had to admit it was an odd experience. She was accustomed to being liked. But if Bolt was going to draw battle lines, then she would stand her ground. After all this was her home for the foreseeable future. She was not going to be ordered about by a robot.

The sound of a tearful female voice rising in anger and frustration broke into Annie's thoughts. She glanced toward the closed door of Oliver's study. It had to be Valerie, she realized with a sympathetic pang. Somehow Annie could not envision the polished, self-confident Heather bursting into tears in the middle of an argument with her brother.

"Damn you, Oliver, I'm not going to let you run my life any longer." Valerie's distraught voice reverberated through the door. "I love Carson and if he asks me to marry him, I'm going to do it."

Annie could not overhear Oliver's response, but

that didn't surprise her. She doubted that Oliver would ever raise his voice in anger, regardless of the provocation. He had far too much self-control.

"I don't want to hear about what happened after Dad left. I've heard that story too many times already." Valerie flung open the door of the study and rushed out into the hall.

"It's ancient history," she shouted over her shoulder, her voice throbbing with emotion. "Sybil's right. You can't let go of the past."

"That's enough, Valerie," Oliver said quietly from the dark depths of the study. His voice was not harsh, but it was as unyielding as stone.

"I pity your new wife," Valerie declared with passionate contempt. She was shaking with the force of her anger. "Does she know yet that she's married a man who shapes his whole life around something that happened fifteen years ago?"

Valerie did not wait for an answer. She spun around, dashing the tears from her eyes.

She collided with Annie who was trying to get out of her way.

"Annie. My God."

"Excuse me." Annie steadied Valerie gently. "Are you all right?"

"Yes. No. I just want to get out of here." Valerie pushed past her. "I hope you know what you've done by marrying my brother, Annie. I think you're going to be very, very sorry."

Valerie rushed off down the hall. Annie gazed after her. A moment later the front door opened and immediately slammed shut. Annie turned around and glanced into the study.

Oliver sat unmoving behind his black lacquer desk.

The halogen light splashed across his folded hands and threw the rest of him into deep shadow.

Annie took a step forward and came to a halt in the doorway. In the corner of the room near the rock garden, the jeweled leopard crouched, watching her with the same unblinking gaze Oliver used to such effect.

"Your sister seemed a little upset," Annie ventured.

"She'll get over it."

"Is there anything I can do?"

"No." Oliver paused and then added very politely, "Thank you."

Annie hesitated, aware that she was being warned away just as she had been warned off the subject of Sybil last night. But she felt she had to at least try to get Oliver to communicate. "Would you like to talk about it? Sometimes it helps to discuss this kind of thing."

"I hope," Oliver said with a faint trace of amusement, "that you're not going to offer to help me get in touch with my feelings."

Annie glowered at him. "Forget it. If you don't want to talk about it, that's your problem. In the meantime we have another little matter that needs settling."

"What's that?"

"Bolt is fixing dinner."

"That's one of his duties here. He's an excellent chef."

"I'm sure he is." Annie crossed her arms and leaned one shoulder against the door jamb. "The man's a machine. He can do anything so long as he's plugged in. But we don't need a cordon bleu chef tonight. I'm cooking dinner."

"Are you?"

"Yes. We're going to have tacos. I picked up all the ingredients at Pike Place Market including a dozen of the best corn tortillas you've ever tasted. But first you have to kick Bolt out of my kitchen."

"Your kitchen?"

"You want me to duel with him for kitchen rights?" Oliver got to his feet. "No, I think we've had enough dramatics around here already this evening. If you're sure you want to do the cooking, I'll send Bolt home."

Annie smiled with satisfaction. It was a small battle, woman against machine, but she had won it. "Mind if I come along to watch?"

Oliver's brow rose as he started down the hall toward the kitchen. "Hoping to see a little blood spilled?"

"Certainly not. I just want to see Bolt's face when you let him know that I can give a few orders around here."

Oliver looked thoughtful. "It looks like I'm about to become an expert in the problems of domestic management. Do all new husbands go through this?"

"There is a period of adjustment in any marriage," Annie said loftily.

"I'll keep that in mind."

Bolt looked up from paring potatoes as Oliver and Annie walked into the kitchen.

"Sir?"

"We won't be needing your services tonight, Bolt. Take the evening off," Oliver said.

Bolt glanced at Annie. His face showed no hint of emotion, but it was obvious he knew he'd lost the skirmish. "Yes, sir."

Annie immediately felt guilty. Poor Bolt. He had a

91

right to feel as if he'd been usurped. She was the newcomer around here. "Here, let me help you." She hurried over to the sink and began cleaning up the potato peelings. "Why don't you take the potatoes home with you, Bolt? You can use them for your own dinner."

"No, thank you, Mrs. Rain." Bolt took off his apron and hung it on the inside of the pantry door.

"Would you like to join us for tacos?" she asked, feeling desperate.

"I don't care for tacos." Bolt walked out of the kitchen.

Annie felt as if she'd spent the afternoon pulling wings off flies. She turned to Oliver with a stricken expression. "Do you think he's really upset?"

"Who? Bolt?" Oliver opened a small door that concealed a wine rack. He perused the bottles consideringly. "Why should he be upset?"

"Well, I did sort of get him kicked out of here. I hope I didn't hurt his feelings too badly."

"He's not out of a job," Oliver said dryly. "He's just got himself an evening off."

"Yes, but I'm not certain he sees it that way."

"Annie, you got what you wanted. Bolt is out of your kitchen." Oliver applied the corkscrew to the top of the wine bottle. "There's not much point in being the winner if you start feeling sorry for the loser."

"An interesting philosophy of life." Annie pulled a package of aged cheddar cheese, lettuce, and some fresh plump tomatoes out of the grocery sacks. "Did you come up with it all by yourself?"

"I'm sure I'm not the first man who ever thought of it." Oliver poured red wine into two glasses.

"Probably not." Annie rummaged around in a drawer. "Where's the grater?"

"I have no idea."

"Figures." She opened another drawer and peered inside. "You leave all the grating to Bolt, right?"

"Right."

"Ah-hah. Here it is." She pulled out the flat stainless-steel grater and went to work on the cheddar cheese. "Where did you get him, anyway? From a factory?"

"Bolt? He came to work for me about three years ago."

"Where did he work before you hired him?" Annie asked as she grated the cheese.

"For a company that specialized in international security for large corporate clients."

Annie frowned. "What did he do?"

"I believe his specialty was antiterrorism security arrangements. His expertise was in electronics."

"Like Daniel?"

Oliver's brows rose. "Not quite. Your brother was, I beg your pardon, I mean your brother *is* a genius with electronics, but he was never much good when it came to the basics of security."

"I resent that," Annie said heatedly. "My brother is brilliant."

"Yes, I know. But not when it comes to security matters. He didn't really have an aptitude for it."

"He tracked down that gunrunner for you."

"Finding Gresham was an accident. Daniel stumbled across the evidence. He didn't go looking for it. Daniel was always too trusting for security work. He had a strong tendency to assume the best about people unless someone showed him evidence to the contrary."

"Okay, so my brother is not suspicious or paranoid by nature. Is that a crime?"

"It's not a crime, but it can lead to some very serious mistakes in judgment," Oliver said mildly. "Personally, I try to avoid those kinds of mistakes."

"No wonder you don't have a lot of friends," Annie muttered under her breath.

"What was that?"

"Nothing. Tell me more about Bolt. Why did he quit his job with the international security firm?"

"There was an incident," Oliver said softly. "Innocent people were killed. It was not Bolt's fault, but he took the responsibility for it. He suffered what used to be politely called a nervous breakdown." Oliver sipped his wine as he watched her grate the cheese. "By the time he recovered, he had lost his wife and his career."

"How awful," Annie breathed. "Now I feel absolutely terrible for kicking him out of here. That poor man. He's been through so much, and I come along and treat him like a robot."

"You're too soft in some ways, Annie. Bolt will survive being kicked out of his kitchen."

Annie scowled at him. "You know something, Oliver? I've been thinking."

"About what?"

"About your basic problem in life."

"I wasn't aware I had one."

"Well, you do." Annie bore down on the cheddar cheese. "Your problem is that you can't be bothered with explaining yourself. Also you're a trifle insensitive. And you lack interpersonal communication skills. The end result is that you've acquired a reputation for being devious and mysterious and rather arrogant."

"Is that a problem?"

"Yes, it is. Especially when you apply that approach to family matters." Annie did not look at him as she set aside the cheese and picked up a tomato. "Take that little scene with Valerie, for example."

"Are you going to throw the tomato at me?"

Annie glared. "She was in tears, Oliver."

"She'll recover."

"Will she?" Annie put the tomato down on the cutting board. "Look, I know this is none of my business."

"True, it's not."

"But I think you handled Valerie very badly."

"Is that right?" Oliver lounged against the refrigerator. He appeared fascinated.

"Yes, that's right." Annie started to slice the tomato. "I take it you don't like her new boyfriend?"

"I've never met him."

Annie put down the knife in surprise. "You're kidding me? You came down on her like a ton of bricks for dating a man and you don't even know him?"

Oliver studied the wine in his glass. "I know who he is, that's enough."

"Well? What is he? An ex-con? A sociopath? Some kind of creep?"

"He's Paul Shore's son."

Annie considered that as she picked up her own glass of wine. "I don't know the Shores. I've never moved in those circles. But I've certainly heard of them. Paul Shore has a major real estate development company headquartered here in Seattle. Does big high rises and malls. That kind of thing."

"Among other things."

"A designer friend of mine is doing the Shore home

for the annual arts benefit he and his wife give every year. The Shores are very active on the local art scene. They run a foundation or something."

"Yes."

"So what's wrong with Paul Shore? Why don't you think his son is good enough for Valerie?"

Oliver took a swallow of the wine and savored it thoughtfully. "I suppose that since you're part of this family, you have a right to know a little history."

Annie smiled encouragingly and went back to work on the tomato. What Oliver had just said wasn't strictly true, at least as far as she was concerned, but at least he was finally starting to open up. It boded well. "I'm listening."

"It's not a long story. Shortly after my father walked out, I discovered that he was deeply in debt to a handful of his old friends. Paul Shore was among them."

"What happened?"

"I went to Shore and asked him if, for the sake of his past friendship with my family, he would give me an extension on the loan."

Annie went still. "He said no?"

"He said no. He wouldn't give me any maneuvering room at all. He said he wanted the money paid back immediately, even though it would mean selling off the only asset I had left, the house. Even that would only cover a portion of the debt."

"That was a terrible thing for Mr. Shore to do," Annie said quickly. "He must have realized that your family was already under terrible stress. If he was an old friend, he should have helped you."

"I won't bore you with the unpleasant details of how I survived those first two years and got back on my feet financially. Let's just say I did it and Paul Shore gave me no quarter, let alone any assistance."

"I see. You've never forgiven him for turning his back on your family after your father's disappearance."

"It's not the kind of thing you forgive, Annie."

"Whew." She tossed the tomato slices into a bowl. "I can see why you're not real fond of Paul Shore."

Oliver acknowledged that remark with a small inclination of his head. Quiet satisfaction pooled in his eyes. "I thought you would understand."

"And I can also see why it makes things a little complicated."

Oliver's gaze turned cautious. "How?"

"Well, naturally, you're not predisposed to like Paul Shore's son."

"No."

"I imagine you wish Valerie had found another boyfriend."

"She will find another boyfriend," Oliver said evenly.

"Maybe. Maybe not." Annie held up the knife and fixed him with a pointed look. "In the meantime, you will have to do the generous, intelligent thing."

Oliver blinked slowly like a hunting cat that has decided it's time to stop indulging the prey. "Which is?"

"Accept the fact that your sister is dating a man who had absolutely nothing to do with what happened between you and Paul Shore all those years ago. Give Carson Shore a chance. For Valerie's sake."

Oliver did not move. He continued to prop one shoulder against the refrigerator and gazed at her as if she were a somewhat odd species of fern. "I'll set the table," he said at last.

He straightened away from the refrigerator and started hunting through cupboards and drawers.

Annie bit back a dismayed oath. "He might be a very nice man, Oliver. Valerie obviously thinks so."

"Shall we eat in here at the kitchen table?" Oliver asked gently. "No sense using the dining room. We don't have Bolt here to clean up afterward."

Annie dashed around the edge of the kitchen island and planted herself directly in his path. "You're ignoring the issue here, Oliver."

"There is no issue." He stepped around her and with great precision began to position the place mats, silverware, and napkins on the black metal and glass table. "But there may be a small misunderstanding."

"I knew it." Triumph shot through Annie. "That's the whole problem. A misunderstanding. I knew you weren't an unreasonable man."

"Thank you."

"You can simply explain to Valerie that initially you had some problems with the idea of her dating Carson Shore based on ancient history. But now that you've had a chance to think it over, you realize you can't go around visiting the sins of the fathers onto the sons, or whatever the old adage is."

"What I will tell Valerie," Oliver said calmly, "is that if she marries Carson Shore, it will be an act of betrayal against her family. She will not be welcome among us again. Furthermore, she will go to him without a dime to her name. I will cut her off entirely from the family money."

"What?" Annie stared at him, aghast. "You can't do that, Oliver."

"Of course I can do it."

"What if she goes ahead and marries him, anyway?"

"Don't worry. It will never happen."

"How can you be so certain of that?" Annie demanded.

"That's my business," Oliver said. "It doesn't concern you."

Annie searched his face, seeking some sign of softness. She found nothing to give her any hope, but she still could not bring herself to believe that Oliver was as unyielding as he was making himself out to be.

"This is ludicrous. I can't believe you're being so hard-hearted about this."

"I suppose that while we're on the subject of the Shores, we should cover another matter."

"I don't think I want to hear this," Annie muttered.

"I realize that as far as you're concerned, this marriage of ours is not quite real. But in the eyes of the world, you're my wife. Agreed?"

"Agreed." Annie was learning to be wary when Oliver spoke in that especially even tone.

"Everyone knows there are certain things my wife would not do."

"How would everyone know that when you've never before had a wife?" Annie was rather pleased with that comeback.

"Let's just say that my reputation precedes me," Oliver said calmly. "In any event, the point I am trying to make here is that one of the things my wife would definitely not do is get involved in any way with a member of Paul Shore's family."

"I'm not involved with anyone in his family. I don't even know any members of the Shore family."

"Keep it that way, Annie. For however long this marriage lasts, you're Mrs. Oliver Rain. I'll expect you to act the part."

She stared at him. "What exactly does that mean?"

"It means," he said very softly, "that your first loyalty is to me."

"I don't believe this." Annie banged one of Bolt's professional-weight frying pans down onto the stove. "That's the most outrageous thing I've ever heard. No wonder Valerie was upset. You probably talked to her the way you're talking to me. Well, if you expect me to take orders like that, you've got a real surprise coming, Oliver Rain."

"Any time you want out of this marriage," Oliver said neutrally, "you're free to end it."

Annie stood frozen in shock at the threat. Then she collected herself and whirled around to confront him. "You earned your reputation the old-fashioned way, didn't you? You worked hard at it."

He finished setting the last plate on the table and glanced at her. "Annie, I would rather eat tacos than argue with you."

Annie smiled grimly. "That's because you don't know how to argue properly. You just issue orders and back them up with threats. It seems to me that you've got a few things to learn about being a husband, Oliver Rain. You need to learn to communicate."

"Is that right?" He went back to the counter and picked up his glass of wine. "Who's going to teach me?"

"Me," Annie said rashly.

"That should prove interesting," Oliver said.

7

Annie's bravado had faded somewhat by the time she went to work the following morning. It had been a long night. She had spent it lying awake for hours in her elegant gold and gray bedroom, stewing over her situation.

She had told Oliver that he had a problem, but the truth was, she had an even bigger one. She was making plans to commit the cardinal error of trying to change him.

Big mistake, she told herself as she opened the front door of Wildest Dreams. Conventional wisdom held that any woman who married a man thinking she could change him was a fool. Common sense told her that since the marriage was in name only and not expected to last very long, it was even more foolish to think about remolding Oliver Rain.

She had married him strictly to save Lyncroft. It wasn't her problem if he chose to run his life and his family with an iron fist sheathed in a velvet glove.

She winced at the image as she turned on the lights. Last night's scene with Valerie made the description a little too apt. Oliver had definitely taken off the glove.

Daniel had told her that Oliver Rain was dangerous, Annie reminded herself. And Daniel, as Oliver had remarked, tended to look for the best in people.

Ella Presswood breezed into the shop shortly after ten looking disheveled and disorganized. That was not an unusual state of affairs. Ella had perfected an image of artistic chaos. She reinvented herself daily with new hair color, new clothing combinations, and tons of heavy, jangling jewelry. Today her hair was tinted a vivid shade of fuchsia and slicked down with something wet and sticky. She was wearing a mustard-colored T-shirt under a business jacket that had been designed for a large man. There were rows of clunky fake gems around her throat.

"'Morning, Annie. Sorry, I'm late. I was on the bus from hell. Very high freak factor among the passengers. Hey, didn't expect to see you here today."

Annie waved a feather duster over the cloisonné elephant. "I thought I explained to you that Oliver and I are postponing our honeymoon until after Daniel returns."

"Yeah, I know. But you've only been married a couple of days." Ella eyed her curiously. "Most people would take some time off."

"No point. I'd have spent it alone. Oliver went straight into my brother's office this morning. He says it's important to let everyone see him there."

"Makes sense. I know how much you've been worrying about your brother's business lately." Ella busied herself behind the counter. "You know, I still can't believe I never had a clue about you and Oliver Rain. You're not usually so secretive, Annie."

"I know. But Oliver wanted things kept quiet."

"Too bad you had to rush the wedding for business reasons. You didn't get to do it up big. No gown, no china, no nothing."

No nothing was right, Annie conceded ruefully to

herself. Not even a few old-fashioned marital rights. But that was her choice, according to Oliver. If she wanted to go to bed with him, he was willing.

"Oliver wouldn't have wanted a big production, anyway," Annie said. "He's a very private person."

"Private, huh?" Ella surveyed her slicked-down hair in the trompe l'oeil mirror that hung on the wall. The mirror had been painted to show a reflection of a room. "No offense, but he seems a little weird."

"Coming from you, that's rather humorous. At least Oliver doesn't color his hair pink."

"True, but you've got to admit we don't see many men of his type wearing it long the way he does," Ella mused. "But I wasn't talking about his hair. He seems sort of dark and mysterious, if you know what I mean. I would never have guessed you'd fall for a guy like him."

Annie frowned. "What type did you think I'd go for?"

Ella shrugged. "Someone like Quigley next door. Or that cello player you were seeing for a while. That reminds me." She turned away from the mirror. "You got a package from him yesterday. Guess he heard the news about your wedding."

Annie brightened. "A package from Melvin Finch? Where is it?"

"Behind the counter."

Annie hurried around the corner of the long counter and discovered the small package. She tore into the wrappings and found a note.

To Annie from Melvin. Congratulations on your
marriage. Hope you found a guy who's straight
out of your wildest dreams. You deserve the best.

"How sweet," Annie said, touched. "It's a compact
disc featuring music performed by that Midwest
symphony orchestra he joined."

Ella grimaced. "Figures."

"Now, Ella, Melvin is a very nice person."

"Another of your wounded birds, as Joanna calls
them. You found him, patched him up, and, when
he was ready, released him to fly away."

"Melvin had to follow his dreams," Annie said
wistfully. "He and I were never really in love. We
were just good friends."

"You mean you felt sorry for him," Ella said. "And
Melvin enjoyed having you feel sorry for him."

The door of Wildest Dreams crashed open with
nerve-jarring force just as Annie finished stowing
Melvin's gift in a drawer.

A raven-haired woman dressed from head to toe in
fire-engine red swept into the room. She pursed her
crimson lips and waited until she had Annie and Ella's
full attention.

"Darlings," she announced grandly, "I'm back for
another look at some of your odd little pieces."

Annie laughed. "You mean you're going to give us
another chance, Raphaela? I thought you said
everything in Wildest Dreams was too tacky for your
project."

Raphaela, born Martha Lou Stotts, had opted to
use her singular pseudonym when she set herself up
in business as an interior designer two years ago. In

addition to eschewing a last name, she was always careful to wear only red in public. It was her trademark color she had once explained to Annie.

Two months ago Raphaela had descended upon Wildest Dreams to announce that she had been selected to "do" the interiors of the Paul Shore residence for the annual arts benefit. She had been ecstatic. It had been a great professional coup for her.

Annie had been very hopeful at first that Raphaela would use something from Wildest Dreams in her design. It would have been great publicity for the boutique. But Raphaela had hedged.

"You're in luck, Annie." Raphaela dropped her red leather briefcase onto the floor and smiled beatifically upon Annie, Ella, and Wildest Dreams. "I find that I have come to a point in my project where I do, indeed, need something that will jar the senses and amuse the eye."

"That's great," Annie said enthusiastically. "How about the elephant?"

Raphaela rolled her eyes. "Don't be ridiculous. The elephant would never do. I'm going with an exotic fantasy look that will be combined with a touch of neo-deco."

"How about the carousel?" Ella suggested.

Raphaela eyed the glittering carousel. "A possibility. But I think the jungle print folding screen would be a better bet."

"Use whatever you like," Annie said quickly. "I really appreciate this, Raphaela. It's going to be great advertising for us."

"Think nothing of it." Raphaela gave her a fond look. "What are friends for?"

Annie's response was interrupted by the ringing of the neon telephone on the counter.

Ella picked up the glowing receiver. "Wildest Dreams." She listened a minute. "Sure, I'll get her. May I tell her who's calling? Right." She covered the phone with her palm. "Sybil Rain," she mouthed.

Surprised, Annie took the phone. "This is Annie."

"I was wondering if we might do lunch today." Sybil's voice was brisk. She was clearly not expecting to have her offer turned down. "We haven't had a chance to really get acquainted."

Annie's first instinct was to find an excuse. She had a feeling that she and Sybil were not cut out to become close friends. Still, the woman was technically her new mother-in-law. Make that stepmother-in-law, Annie corrected herself. "That will be fine, Sybil. Where shall I meet you?"

Sybil named the elegant dining room of one of the downtown hotels and hung up the phone.

"Trouble?" Ella asked.

"Not really. Sybil Rain wants to have lunch with me."

Raphaela's eyes widened in astonishment. "Sybil Rain? Why on earth would she want to have lunch with you?"

Ella chuckled. "Because Annie married Oliver Rain the day before yesterday."

"*Married*. Annie and Oliver Rain? Oh, my *God*." Raphaela's eyes swung back and forth between Ella and Annie. "This is a joke, right? You're teasing poor Raphaela."

"No joke." Ella assured her. "Big surprise, but no joke."

"*Oliver Rain*? That weird guy who used to own half of Seattle before he sold his holdings?"

"He's not weird," Annie said, annoyed.

"I'm surprised you haven't heard about the wedding, Raphaela," Ella said. "It was in the business section of the papers this morning."

"Why on earth was it in the business section?" Raphaela demanded.

"Because Rain is going to take over the management of Lyncroft Unlimited," Ella explained with a sidelong glance at Annie.

"Just until Daniel returns," Annie said firmly.

Ella and Raphaela looked at her with pitying eyes, but they did not argue.

"Sure," Ella said kindly. "Just until Daniel returns."

"This is incredible," Raphaela breathed. "You're married to Oliver Rain. I can't believe it." Her eyes narrowed speculatively. "Tell me, what do the interiors of his new penthouse look like? Is it true the whole thing was done in black? I've been hearing rumors."

"There's a lot of black and gold," Annie said. "And gray. It's very striking."

"Black and gold, hmm? Sounds too dark for a Seattle residence. And not your style at all." Raphaela smiled encouragingly. "As his new wife, you might want to lighten things up a bit. Keep me in mind if you decide to make some changes."

"Something tells me Oliver wouldn't tolerate too many changes," Annie admitted.

"Nonsense," Raphaela said. "Making changes in a man's life is what a wife is for. Just ask any of my ex-husbands."

Three hours later Sybil dipped a spoon into a bowl

of lobster bisque and looked at Annie who was seated on the other side of the table. "We were all quite stunned by the suddenness of this marriage."

"I understand." Annie picked at her shrimp cocktail. She was not very hungry. The minute she had sat down, Sybil had begun grilling her. Annie was beginning to feel like one of the entrées on the restaurant's overpriced menu.

"Of course Oliver has always been secretive," Sybil said smoothly. "One never really knows what his real plans are until he chooses to reveal them."

"I realize he's a very private man." The phrase was rapidly becoming a litany, Annie thought.

Sybil smiled, but the smile did not reach her eyes. "Some people feel he's a very dangerous man."

"I'm sure his reputation is exaggerated."

Sybil's mouth tightened. "Take it from me, Annie, it's not. I can personally testify to that." She put down her spoon. "Look, there's no point in beating about the bush. I asked you to have lunch with me today because I think there are some things you need to know."

"About Oliver?"

"Yes." Sybil paused for effect. "I think you should be aware that there is every reason to believe that Oliver married you in order to get control of your brother's company."

Annie looked up from her shrimp. "That's not true."

"Annie, believe me, I know him infinitely better than you do. I know what he's capable of doing to achieve his own ends. And I know that love would be Oliver's last reason for getting married. He doesn't even understand the word."

"I'm not so certain about that," Annie said gently.

"It seems to me he's been very good to his family. He's taken care of all of you, hasn't he?"

An old bitterness flashed briefly in Sybil's gaze. "For a price. That's what I advise you to remember when you deal with Oliver. There is always a price tag attached."

Annie stirred uneasily in her chair. "There's no reason to worry about me. I knew what I was doing when I married Oliver."

"Did you?" Sybil studied her closely. "I hope you're smart enough to know that if you married him for his money, you wasted your time. You'll never get your hands on it. Oliver is much too clever to allow any woman to fleece him."

Annie was incensed. "I didn't marry him for his money."

"If you married him for love, you're going to be even more disappointed."

Annie gave up on the shrimp. "I don't think there's much point in continuing with this friendly little get-acquainted lunch. If you'll excuse me, I have to get back to my shop."

"Annie, wait." There was sudden desperation in Sybil's expression. "Please don't leave. I've got to talk to you."

"I don't want to talk to you about Oliver or my marriage."

"You don't understand. There's more involved here than just your marriage. I know you're concerned about your brother's business. We need to talk."

"If you're going to issue another warning about what Oliver has planned for Lyncroft, forget it. I'm not in the mood to listen." Annie started to rise from the chair.

"Just a minute." Sybil broke off and looked up quickly as a tall man came to a halt beside the table. Anxiety tempered with relief appeared in her eyes. "Jonathan. What are you doing here?"

"Hello, Sybil." The man turned a charmingly rueful smile on Annie. Behind the lenses of his glasses his eyes reflected a measure of understanding. "Sorry about this. Allow me to introduce myself. I'm Jonathan Grace. A friend of Sybil's."

"How do you do." Annie examined him curiously. Her first thought was that Jonathan Grace did not live up to his name. Instead of being built on lean and graceful lines, he was solid and sturdy looking. One could imagine him as having played football in high school or college. Some of the muscle had turned to middle-aged spread. Annie guessed he was in his late forties or early fifties. He had broad, somewhat heavy, but generally pleasant features.

"You shouldn't be here," Sybil said quickly.

"I think Annie will understand and keep our little secret, won't you, Annie?" Jonathan sat down at the table. He signaled to a waiter.

"What secret?" Annie asked warily as the waiter poured coffee in Jonathan's cup.

"Sybil and I are planning to be married," Jonathan said easily.

Sybil sucked in her breath. There was a haunted look in her eyes. "We agreed it was much too soon to say anything about our plans, Jonathan."

"It's all right, darling." Jonathan patted Sybil's hand and turned his amused brown eyes on Annie. "I'm afraid my lovely Sybil has been living in fear of her stepson for so many years she can't get used to the idea of being open about our relationship."

"He'll cut me off the instant he hears I'm thinking of remarrying," Sybil said nervously. "He's been looking for an excuse to get rid of me for the past sixteen years and this will be it."

Jonathan squeezed her hand. "You know you won't have to worry about your financial security, honey. I can take care of you."

"It's the principle of the thing," Sybil said tightly. "I've told you that. Damn it, I'm entitled to my share of the Rain fortune. Oliver has no right to deprive me of it. It's all so unfair. He owes me for what I did for him. He *owes* me."

Jonathan smiled tenderly. "And I'm sure in his eyes he's repaid you. You've admitted that Rain has been quite generous ever since he started making money on his own. Your sons have had everything they needed, including a father figure."

"I'll admit he's been good to them. They never knew their real father. Oliver stepped into the role. He was always available for them and the girls, even during the times when he was working eighteen hours a day. But he only tolerated me because of them."

"I'm sure that's not true, Sybil," Annie said.

"It's quite true." Sybil looked down at her beauti-fully manicured hands. Her mouth tightened. "He hates me."

Annie was appalled. "I don't believe that."

"You don't know him."

"Why should he hate you?"

Sybil sighed and glanced away for a moment. "He always resented the fact that his father married me after his mother died. Oliver never accepted me."

Annie tilted her head to one side. "You think Oliver still resents you, even after all these years?"

"I know he does. He'll never forgive me for trying to take his mother's place." Sybil met her eyes. "Oliver never forgives or forgets. Everyone knows that. Just ask Valerie. She's in love with Carson Shore, the son of one of Oliver's old enemies. I talked to her this morning. She was in tears because Oliver has ordered her to sever the relationship."

Annie swallowed. She knew that much was true. There was no reason to doubt that Sybil's story was equally true. All things considered, Oliver did seem to be the type who carried a mean grudge. But once again she felt an inexplicable need to leap to his defense.

"Oliver has been very good to me." Annie folded her hands in her lap. "And he's taking care of my brother's company until Daniel returns."

Jonathan frowned in concern. "Sybil mentioned that your brother died in a plane crash."

"They never found his body," Annie said stoutly. "I believe he's still alive."

"I can understand your not wanting to give up hope," Jonathan said quietly. "I lost my own brother several years ago. It was...difficult."

Annie smiled gratefully. "Daniel is all the family I have."

"You may be holding onto your hopes, Annie, but everyone else has given up," Sybil said. Surprisingly, although the words were brusque, her voice was not totally lacking in sympathy. "Including the business community. And that is why Oliver has been so good to you, as you put it. He's merely looking after his investment in Lyncroft Unlimited."

Jonathan slowly stirred his coffee, his eyes troubled. "I'm afraid Sybil's right about one thing, Annie. I've been in Seattle long enough to have heard some of the gossip about Oliver Rain. They say he always has his own reasons for the things he does. The rest of the world rarely discovers what those reasons are until it's too late."

Annie carefully folded her napkin and put it down on the table. "Please excuse me. I must get back to work."

Sybil's head jerked up in alarm. "I hope you won't feel compelled to tell Oliver about this conversation, Annie. He'll accuse me of interfering in his private affairs. It will give him one more reason to despise me. God knows he hates me enough as it is."

Annie hesitated, not wanting to be sucked into even such a small conspiracy. Then she saw the earnest plea for understanding in Jonathan's eyes.

"For Sybil's sake, Annie," he murmured, "maybe it would be best if you didn't mention what was said here today."

"Is this how everyone handles Oliver?" Annie demanded. "They deliberately keep him in the dark?"

"The less Oliver knows, the better for all of us," Sybil said. "He uses every scrap of information for his own ends. You would do well to remember that, Annie."

Annie could find no adequate response to that. She got up and walked out of the restaurant without a backward glance.

Three nights later Annie sat alone in the penthouse living room. Dressed in a pair of well-washed jeans and a green sweater, she was curled deep in a leather sofa. She gazed moodily out into the rainy night where a ferry glided across Elliott Bay. The lights of the vessel glittered like so many pearls strewn across the black velvet of the cold water.

Annie was enjoying the view alone. For the past several days, ever since she had come to live here, Oliver had vanished into his study every night after dinner.

She knew he was working. Oliver spent hours going over her brother's files and the reports submitted by Lyncroft's managers. If he followed his usual pattern tonight, he would be up long after she went to bed.

Until tonight Annie had busied herself during the evenings just as she had when she had lived alone in her apartment. The monthly bookkeeping chores required of a small business such as Wildest Dreams were neverending. Tonight she had paid her taxes and the rent, gone over invoices, and written paychecks for herself and Ella. But she was deeply aware of Oliver's presence in the penthouse. She knew she would sleep restlessly again tonight until she heard him go down the hall to the master bedroom suite.

Last night she had heard his footsteps pause briefly outside her bedroom door. She had held her breath, wondering what she would do or say if he opened it. But he had not. Her chief reaction had been an unnerving sense of disappointment.

She wanted him, she thought with a shattering jolt of realization. She had never experienced such an intense physical and emotional desire. This was what had been missing in her relationships with men like Arthur Quigley and Melvin Finch.

Annie knew now there was no way she could continue to ignore her reaction to Oliver. The elemental excitement he ignited within her had been there from the first time she had seen him. Proximity was doing nothing to squelch it. She had never been so deeply aware of a man in her life. Of course, she reminded herself, she had never lived in a man's home before, either.

A marriage of convenience was proving to be a very strange and unsettling sort of relationship, not at all the casual, businesslike association she had anticipated. Try as she would, she could not bring herself to feel like Oliver's roommate.

The complex, enigmatic man down the hall was beginning to haunt her. Her emotions were in a constant state of turmoil these days. Part of her longed to reach out to Oliver, to lure him from his dark lair into the light. Another part of her warned that any move to rescue Oliver could lead to disaster for herself.

Unable to concentrate on the stack of invoices she had been studying, Annie pushed the papers aside and got to her feet. She crossed the gray slate floor and went down the hall to the kitchen. Maybe a cup of tea would snap her out of her strange mood.

She flipped on the light and smiled wryly at the gleaming surfaces. Bolt had cooked tonight, so naturally things were immaculate. Annie wondered what he did when he went downstairs to his own apartment in the evenings. Now that she knew something about his past she could no longer think of him as an android.

Annie filled the stainless-steel kettle and set it on the stove. While she waited for the water to boil, she rummaged around in the cupboards for tea and a pot. A moment later a faint whistle from the kettle announced the water was ready. Annie reached for it.

It wasn't until she realized that she had made

enough tea for two that she knew what she was going to do. She put two cups and saucers on the tray before she could change her mind. Then she picked up the tray, went back down the hall to the study, and knocked once.

"Come in." Oliver's voice was a dark rumble behind the door.

Annie took a deep breath, pushed open the door, and walked into the room.

Oliver was seated behind the ebony desk. His black hair was tied back in a ponytail as usual. The collar of his gray shirt was unbuttoned and the sleeves were rolled up on his forearms. When he looked up, the bright halogen light from his desk lamp gleamed on the lenses of his reading glasses.

Annie liked the glasses. Oliver looked more approachable when he was wearing them.

"What is it, Annie?"

"I thought you might like some tea."

He removed his glasses with a deliberate gesture and glanced at the tray in her hands. There was cool pleasure in his gaze when he raised his eyes to meet hers. "Thank you."

She set the tray down on the desk and poured two cups. She was chagrined to realize that her fingers were trembling. "How are things going?"

"Fairly well. I've finished going through the financial data. I'm looking at the research and development reports now." Oliver took the cup from her hand. "Your brother was a true genius. Not many men have a talent for both invention and management."

"You mean he *is* a genius," Annie corrected. She lounged on the edge of the desk and swung one leg as she sipped her tea. "He'll be back, Oliver."

"I hope for your sake that he will return."

Annie swung her leg a couple more times. "You know, I've been wondering if I should be in here in the evenings, going over the same reports you're going over. It probably wouldn't hurt for me to familiarize myself with the inner workings of Lyncroft."

"We've discussed this before, Annie. I thought we agreed that you would trust me to handle Lyncroft for you until Daniel returns."

"Of course I trust you," she said quickly. "It's just that it's my brother's firm and I do have an obligation to keep an eye on things."

"You're busy with a business of your own. If you get too involved with Lyncroft, Wildest Dreams will suffer. A small business needs the full attention of its owner."

"I know." She chewed on that one for a minute. "All the same, I feel I should know more about what's going on at Lyncroft."

"I see." Oliver put down his cup and got to his feet. He walked over to the Zen rock garden and stood studying the pattern in the sand for a long moment. "Your renewed insistence on taking a more active interest in Lyncroft wouldn't have anything to do with whatever it was you and Sybil talked about at lunch a few days ago, would it?"

Annie abruptly stopped swinging her leg. "You knew I had lunch with her?"

"Yes."

"How did you know about that, Oliver?"

"Does it matter?"

Annie bit her lip. "Yes, I think it does. I didn't mention it to you."

"Why didn't you mention it, Annie?"

117

The very softness of the question made her go quite still. "Sybil said you might be annoyed if you knew she'd taken me to lunch. She asked me to keep quiet about it."

"And you did as she asked."

"Well, yes. I felt a little sorry for her if you must know the truth. I think you frighten her."

"Do I frighten you?"

"Of course not."

"I see." He continued to brood over the sand. "If I asked you to do something for me, would you agree as readily as you agreed to go along with Sybil's request?"

"Depends what you ask of me," Annie whispered.

She could feel the stalking tension in him now. It pulsed silently across the room, reaching her, sinking into her, wrapping itself around her insides. She realized with a start that she could no more have walked out of the study at that moment than she could have flown.

"I would like you to promise me that you will never lie to me, Annie. Not even to protect someone else."

The odd, melancholy tone in his voice nearly broke Annie's heart. She suddenly understood that Oliver knew only too well that the members of his own family, the family he had struggled so hard to protect, frequently kept things from him out of fear of his reaction. He knew it and hated it. But he was helpless to figure out how to make the people he cared about trust him with their secrets. He had isolated himself emotionally and he had no clue how to break through the self-imposed barriers that kept him from communicating properly with his family.

"Oh, *Oliver*." Annie put down her cup and leaped to her feet.

She dashed across the room to where he stood with his back turned toward her. Wrapping her arms around his waist from behind, she hugged him with fierce tenderness. It was like hugging a live leopard. He was all sleek sinews and warm muscle. The masculine scent of him inundated her senses.

"I swear I will never lie to you, Oliver," she said into his shirt.

He turned around abruptly, taking her by surprise, and framed her face in his strong, calloused hands. Annie shivered beneath the heat and the sheer intensity in his eyes. She could feel the strength in him, but far from alarming her, it sent a thrill of knee-weakening desire through her.

"Thank you, Annie," Oliver said. "In return, I swear I will never lie to you. Do we have a deal?"

"Yes." She knew he was going to kiss her. She wanted his kiss more than anything else in the whole world.

That was when Annie finally admitted to herself that she was in love with Oliver Rain.

And then she could not think clearly at all because his mouth was on hers, blotting out everything else around her except the knowledge that he wanted her and she wanted him.

8

Annie knew she was going to let him make love to her the instant he took her into his arms. No, she thought, she had known what would happen even earlier when she carried the tea into his study. She had made her choice.

It wasn't just because she wanted him in a way she had never wanted any other man. It was because she knew somehow that he needed her as much as she needed him.

Even as his mouth moved slowly, powerfully on hers, she knew better than to hope he would put his feelings into words. It was too soon for that. Such an admission would be far too threatening to his all-important sense of self-control.

Annie had a hunch that deep inside Oliver had probably decided that as long as the words were unspoken, they could be safely ignored. If he were ever forced to acknowledge his need aloud, Oliver would have to confront that need. He would probably see it as a weakness.

It was better this way, Annie told herself as she twined her arms around his neck. For now she would do the surrendering for both of them.

For her there was no sense of weakness, simply a great joy in being able to bestow the gift of herself on a man who deserved some happiness.

"Annie?" Oliver kissed the corner of her mouth and then her ear. His hands glided down her spine to her waist.

Annie shivered. The urgency in him was an enthralling drug that was setting fire to her blood. She stroked her fingertips along his sleek hair and then touched his hard face. "Yes. Oh, yes, please, Oliver."

Satisfaction flared in his gaze. Oliver scooped her up in his arms without another word. The strength in him was greater than she had realized. He cradled her effortlessly against his chest as he carried her across the room to the long window seat. Images of Persephone being carried off into the Underworld danced in Annie's head.

He set her down amid the black and gold cushions and then straightened to rake her with a gaze that burned straight through her clothing. Pale moonlight illuminated the stark hunger in his face.

"You're sure?" he asked.

"Yes." She could hardly speak. "What about you?"

He smiled faintly. "I've been sure since the beginning. But you must be absolutely certain, Annie. After tonight there will be no going back to being roommates."

"I know," she whispered. Once Oliver had become her lover, she would never be able to pretend he was just a friend. For an instant a tremor of primitive female fear drove out some of the excitement she was feeling.

She would never be the same after tonight. She knew that with a certainty that first chilled and then warmed her.

"I'm glad you came to me tonight," Oliver said. "It hasn't been easy waiting for you."

Annie went hot beneath Oliver's unrelenting gaze. She could feel her insides turning to liquid. A deep, heavy ache seized her lower body. She reached out to catch hold of his rough hand. "Have you really been waiting for me?"

He sank slowly down onto the cushions beside her. His warm palm settled on her breast in a gesture that was both reverent and possessive. "For longer than you know."

She smiled tremulously. "I wanted you to want me since that first night at Daniel's engagement party."

"I wanted you then." He leaned over her, caging her between his arms. "I want you even more now." He bent his head and slowly kissed the soft, vulnerable curve of her throat.

Annie arched convulsively in reaction, twisting to get closer to him. Oliver moved his hand to the curve of her hip. He squeezed gently.

Annie sucked in her breath when she felt his long, sensitive fingers slide between her legs. They seemed to scorch through the fabric of her jeans.

"Oliver?"

"I'm right here." He pushed the hem of her sweater up a few inches and lowered his head to drop random kisses across her midsection. "I'm not going anywhere."

Annie fumbled urgently with his shirt, needing to feel his bare skin beneath her palms. He did not resist but he did nothing to aid her, either. When his shirt finally parted, she saw the mat of crisp, black hair that covered his chest. Eagerly she splayed her fingers through it and found herself entranced by the hard, muscled contours of his body.

He felt so good. Perfect. Everything she had ever dreamed a man could be.

Annie was astounded by the whirlwind of desire that tore through her. She had never experienced anything resembling this in her life. She was literally on fire. It was an incredible sensation. This was what the poets called passion, she thought with glorious certainty. She wanted to shout her elation to the world.

"Hurry, Oliver." She clutched at him. "Please hurry."

His answering smile held satisfaction and masculine promise. His palm was warm between her legs. "You're already wet."

"Oh, God, Oliver." She lifted her hips against his questing hand, aware that her jeans were rapidly turning damp. "I've never felt like this."

"I'm glad." He leaned over her again, kissing her with a deep thoroughness that left her breathless. All the while his hand stayed pressed between her thighs, moving gently against her.

Annie thought she would go mad. She closed her knees, trapping his fingers, begging him silently to touch her even more intimately.

Oliver laughed softly in the shadows. Annie's eyes flew open in astonishment. She realized she had never heard Oliver laugh. The sound was unique, somewhere between a low growl and a gruff purr. It delighted her. She looked up at him and saw moonlight reflected in his eyes.

"It's all right, Annie," he said against her mouth. "I'll take care of everything."

She wanted to ask him what he meant by that, but she could not find the right words. Even as he captured her mouth in another kiss, she heard the rasp of metal on metal and knew he had unfastened her jeans.

And then his hand was inside her panties, searching out the damp, hot, aching place between her legs. Annie fought for breath. When she felt his finger slide slowly inside her, she stopped breathing altogether for a few seconds. Then she inhaled sharply.

"*Oliver*. Now. Please. I can't wait. *I can't wait*."

"You don't have to wait." His voice was husky. He stroked his tongue into her mouth at the same instant that he gently pushed a second finger into her feminine channel.

Annie moaned as he stretched her slowly, opening her completely to his touch. A strange, pulsing tension was building within her. She wrapped her arms around Oliver, clinging to him, trying to bring him closer. His fingers moved on her, finding just the right place.

"*Oliver*. My God, please."

"Let me see you fly, Annie. You're safe. I'm here to catch you."

Something exploded inside her. The tension that had gripped her so tightly a moment earlier suddenly found its release in an exquisite explosion of sensation. Her body convulsed around his probing fingers. And then the ripples of pleasure began.

She heard herself whispering Oliver's name over and over again in a breathless voice she hardly recognized as her own.

A moment later she went limp in his arms. Oliver held her as she coiled languorously against him. His hand traced the length of her spine in a soothing, gentling movement.

"Beautiful." Oliver kissed her shoulder. "Spectacular.

But, then, I knew from the start that you would be one of a kind."

She looked up at him through heavy, drooping lashes. "That was amazing. Absolutely amazing."

His smile was one of satisfaction, as if he had found his own release. "I'm glad."

"I have never felt anything like that before in my life. Nothing has ever been like that."

"Good."

Maybe it had been so special because she knew she was in love, Annie thought in dreamy wonder. That realization brought another in its wake.

Annie looked up at Oliver in consternation. "You haven't even gotten undressed."

"There's plenty of time." He kissed her damp forehead. "All night, in fact."

"Yes, I know." Her voice trailed off.

Something was wrong. She could feel it. She searched Oliver's face in the shadows. His eyes still burned with the desire she had seen in him earlier. She could feel the sexual rigidity of his body. He was fully aroused. She could also feel the iron-willed control he was exerting over himself.

It was then she realized just what was bothering her. From the moment she had told Oliver that she wanted to go to bed with him, he had taken charge. Everything that had just happened had been carefully orchestrated by him. He had controlled the passionate interlude just as he controlled everything and everyone in his life.

"Don't you want me?" Annie whispered.

"More than you can possibly guess. And I'm going to have you when the time is right."

"I thought the time was right," she muttered.

"Soon." Oliver got to his feet, reached down, and scooped her up into his arms.

Annie clung to him, still boneless from the aftereffects of her climax. A small chill went through her, washing away some of the lingering warmth. It was clear that as much as Oliver seemed to desire her, he had no intention of allowing himself to be at the mercy of his own passion.

Or hers.

It occurred to Annie that Oliver was determined to prove to himself and to her that he was in complete control. Apparently he would not allow himself to surrender to anything, not even pleasure.

A glint of green near the rock garden caught Annie's attention as Oliver strode toward the door with her in his arms. She glanced down and saw the emerald-eyed leopard watching her as she was carried off into the night.

A long while later, after the pale gray sheets of Oliver's bed were damp and twisted from the mind-shattering lovemaking that he had visited upon her, Oliver finally claimed his exhausted bride.

He loomed over her, his shoulders and the sleek contours of his back glistening in the moonlight. His control had cost him something, Annie realized when she saw the sheen of sweat on him. At least it hadn't been easy for him.

The bottom line, however, was that after three hours of passion, Oliver was still in complete command of himself. It was profoundly depressing to know that she did not have the same effect on his senses that he had on hers. He wanted her, but he wanted her on his terms, his way, and in his own good time.

"Look at me." Oliver brushed his lips across her forehead. "I want to see your eyes when I make you mine."

Annie obeyed, too tired now to argue. Her gaze met his and she nearly dissolved completely beneath the searing heat she saw in his eyes. He thrust himself into her with a slow, tender, very calculated movement of his body. She realized that even in this final act of consummation he had to prove he was still in control.

Annie almost swore in frustration even though she had never been so physically satisfied in her entire life. But at that moment he sheathed himself completely within her, filling her to the core. Annie was flooded with sensation once more. Incredibly, her weary body could still respond.

"So tight," Oliver whispered. His forehead rested on hers as he waited for her body to accommodate itself to him. "You fit me like a glove, Annie."

He pulled out slightly and then pushed slowly back into her. Annie shuddered. Her body clenched around his.

"That feels so good." Oliver's voice was tight and thick.

Annie dug her nails into his shoulders. Then she lifted herself cautiously, testing the length and breadth of him. He seemed huge inside her. The weight of him was crushing her into the sheets.

Oliver gritted his teeth. "*Yes*. Just like that. God, yes." He reached down between their bodies and found the sensitive place in the nest of curls above her legs. Annie shrieked softly.

127

He waited until she had almost finished convulsing around him. Then and only then, did he finally allow himself to savor his own release.

Annie was so exhausted she fell asleep before he eased himself out of her body. Her last thought was that this situation would not do at all. Oliver needed to learn there was such a thing as too much self-control. She did not know how many nights of this she could take.

Annie awoke later to a moonlit room. For a moment she was disoriented. A feeling of unreality held her in thrall causing her to wonder briefly if she was caught up in a dream. Then she became aware of the weight of Oliver's arm across her breasts. The fiery memories came back in a rush.

She turned her head on the pillow and saw that Oliver was asleep beside her. The pale light from the window illuminated the planes and angles of his harsh features. Somewhere along the line his midnight dark hair had come free of the band that he used to tie it back. It spilled across the elegant pillow giving him a primitive, untamed look. She had gone to bed with a pagan.

Annie lay very still, recalling her first sight of his nude body during the night. The power in him was physical as well as mental. He was a strong, lean, well-built man who had not allowed himself to soften. The coordinated masculine grace she had always admired in him was infinitely more impressive when he had his clothes off.

Annie sat up slowly amid the gray sheets and looked around the room. She had peeked into the master bedroom suite once when she had moved into the penthouse, but she had never actually been inside it. An invisible gate had barred the way until now. She suspected few women would have had the nerve to walk into this most private and personal of rooms without an invitation.

The bedroom was filled with deep shadows. A black lacquer chest of drawers stood against one wall. Next to it was a severely styled gray metal chair. The soft light from the moon picked out the gold threads in the austere, abstract design embroidered on the black quilt.

Restlessly Annie slipped out from beneath the weight of Oliver's arm, pushed aside the tangled sheets, and got out of bed. She felt vulnerable as well as cold so she picked up the first article of clothing she came across. It was the shirt Oliver had worn earlier. She put it on and went to the window.

The neon lights of the Seattle waterfront glittered far below. When she looked out over Elliott Bay, however, she could see nothing but an endless sea of night.

"What are you doing, Annie?"

She jumped at the sound of Oliver's low voice. She glanced quickly back over her shoulder. He was watching her from the shadows of the bed, his eyes reflecting the cold moonlight. He sprawled across the rumpled pillows with the natural arrogance of a jungle cat. His dark, tangled mane drifted across his sleek, muscled shoulders.

"I thought you were asleep," she whispered.

"I felt you leave the bed. Is anything wrong?" There was genuine concern in his voice.

"No. There's nothing wrong." He was a good man,

she thought. But he definitely had some problems. "I just got out of bed to look at the view."

"The view is very nice from here," Oliver said, his tone darkening with lazy sensuality.

Annie could feel his eyes on her. She pulled his shirt a little more snugly around herself. "Oliver?"

"Yes?"

Annie couldn't think of what to say next. She had no idea of how to go about complaining about his incredible lovemaking. How did a woman tell a man he was too good in bed, she wondered wryly. "Nothing. I was just thinking about us."

"I'm glad to hear it. That's exactly what you should be thinking about tonight."

Annie heard him get out of bed. He crossed the gray carpet without making a sound. The next thing she knew his hands were on her shoulders. He pulled her gently back against his hard, solid body and wrapped his arms around her, pillowing her breasts on his forearms. She felt his warm breath in her ear.

"I will never forget tonight as long as I live," Oliver said as he kissed the curve of her shoulder.

"I won't either." She melted instantly beneath the warm sensuality of his words. The scent of him reassured her on some primitive level. So did the strength in his arms. Some of her uneasiness faded.

She leaned back and slowly relaxed into his warmth. She told herself she was getting upset over nothing. So Oliver had as much control over his sexual passions as he did over everything else in his life. Why should that bother her? What else had she expected?

"You're cold." Oliver dropped another small, tantalizing kiss on the nape of her neck.

"Not really." Not now that he was holding her like this, warming her with his powerful body. It was going to be all right, she thought.

If she was honest with herself, she had to admit that she knew why she had overreacted to this latest demonstration of Oliver's amazing self-control. It was because deep in her heart she wanted to be the one person on the face of the earth who could make him lose it.

"Annie?"

"Hmm?" She nestled against him. The hair on his chest was crisp and a little rough on the skin of her back.

Oliver nibbled gently on her earlobe. One of his hands found its way inside the edge of the shirt and drifted down over her belly. "What did you and Sybil talk about at lunch?"

Shock hit Annie like a shaft of lightning. She froze. An instant later outrage washed over her in an icy wave. "You son of a bitch. You bastard. How *dare* you?" She clawed at his arms, trying to free herself.

Oliver released her immediately. "Annie? What the hell is the matter with you?"

"What's the matter with me? *Me*?" She whirled around and took two quick steps back so that she was just beyond his reach. "Who do you think you are? What kind of a sneaky, low-down, underhanded trick was that?"

Oliver's eyes narrowed. "Calm down."

"No, I will not calm down." Annie swung around and began striding furiously back and forth in front of the window. She clutched the unbuttoned edges of his shirt, holding them tightly closed across her breasts. "That was despicable. Unconscionable."

131

"I asked you a simple question."

"Oh, sure. A simple question, my foot. That was not a simple question. You were trying to trick me into answering it. You were trying to seduce me into telling you about my conversation with Sybil. You should be ashamed of yourself."

"I thought we had an agreement," Oliver said very softly. "You promised not to lie to me."

She shot him a scathing glance. He was standing with his feet braced slightly apart, his hands on his hips. He seemed completely unconcerned that he was stark naked. Of course, with a body like his, why should he be concerned, Annie thought resentfully.

"I gave you my word," she said proudly. "I won't ever lie to you."

He smiled slightly. "Then tell me what happened between you and Sybil this afternoon."

"What happened between me and Sybil," Annie said grimly, "is none of your damned business."

"Whatever happens in this family is my business, Annie."

"Not necessarily. In any event, I certainly do not intend to discuss this particular issue with you. Not now."

"What about your promise to me?"

"I am not lying to you," she raged. "I am simply refusing to tell you about a private conversation I had with someone else."

"It's the same thing."

"No, it's not," she retorted. "In any event, I more or less let Sybil think I would not discuss the matter with you. She's trusting me to respect her privacy. I would do the same thing for you. I don't intend to tell her about any confidential conversations you and I might have."

"If you ever do, there will be hell to pay."

Annie glared at him in frustration. "Tell me something, Oliver. Why are you so hostile toward Sybil? After all these years how can you still resent the fact that she took your mother's place?"

Oliver's brows rose. "That's not why I dislike her."

"So maybe she was a little young for your father." Annie waved a hand in dismissal. "That wasn't any of your concern."

"Is this the explanation she gave you?" Oliver asked.

She slanted him a quick, uneasy glance. Her mouth went dry as a thought occurred to her. "Oliver, you weren't by any chance in love with her yourself at the time, were you?"

"No." He sounded disgusted. "Annie, will you stop trying to analyze my relationship with Sybil? It's got nothing to do with what we're dealing with here."

"I think it does." Relief that he hadn't had a young man's crush on Sybil drained off some of Annie's outrage. "I think it has a lot to do with what we're talking about. Tell me why you hate her."

Oliver's face was unreadable. "I don't hate her. But I sure as hell don't trust her."

"Why not?"

"Because I walked into my father's house one day and found Sybil in bed with one of her old boyfriends," Oliver said through his teeth. "I don't trust her because I know for a fact that she's capable of betrayal. Does that answer your question?"

Annie blinked, taken aback by the passionate anger that seethed just below the surface in him. She must never forget that Oliver's cold self-control concealed some very deep, very turbulent waters.

"I see," she said weakly. "I suppose that would be fairly traumatizing for a young man. Finding your stepmother in bed with a stranger couldn't have been easy for you."

Oliver bit off a muttered exclamation. He obviously had his temper back under full control. "I was not traumatized. It was an educational experience. I learned everything I needed to know about Sybil that day."

"Is that right?" Annie studied him curiously. "Did you tell your father?"

"No."

"Why not, if you're so big on trustworthiness?"

"It was simple. The kids needed her," Oliver said coldly. "Believe it or not, she was fairly good with Valerie and Heather. And I knew that if I got her kicked out, Richard and Nathan would never know their father. I knew Dad well enough to know that he wouldn't have gone out of his way to maintain the relationship at a distance."

"I see. So you let her stay for the sake of the family."

"To be blunt, yes."

Annie eyed him curiously. "What did you say to Sybil that day?"

Oliver shrugged. "I told her that if she wanted to enjoy any part of the Rain fortune, she had better walk the straight and narrow."

"And you've been terrorizing her ever since, haven't you?"

Oliver frowned. "I haven't terrorized her."

"Yes, you have. She thinks you hate her."

"Well, I'm not exactly fond of her," Oliver admitted.

"That unfortunate incident must have happened years ago."

"Sixteen years ago to be exact. Why?"

"For heaven's sake, Oliver, people change. If you want to improve your relationship with Sybil, you're going to have to let go of the past."

Oliver gave her an amazed look. "Why would I want to improve my relationship with Sybil? The one she and I have now works just fine as far as I'm concerned."

"Good grief. Everyone thinks you're incredibly shrewd, but personally I think you're as dumb as dirt when it comes to some things." Annie stopped pacing and turned to face him. "For the record, Oliver, you do not have a good relationship with your stepmother."

"For the record, Annie, I don't give a damn. Now, what did the two of you talk about at lunch?"

Annie drew herself up with determination. "I," she said clearly and distinctly, "have absolutely no intention of telling you a thing about what transpired during my lunch with Sybil. So there."

Oliver nodded agreeably, as if accepting her response. "What did you think of Jonathan Grace? Any chance he might actually marry her?"

Annie's mouth dropped open in astonishment. "How did you know Jonathan Grace was with us?"

"Bolt keeps track of that kind of thing for me," Oliver said easily.

"*Bolt*?" Annie heard her voice rise to a squeak of outrage. "You had Bolt spying on me?"

"He wasn't spying on you, Annie." Oliver paused. "I told him to keep an eye on you, because I suspected that sooner or later Sybil would try to get you alone.

I wanted to know if she started feeding you poison about me."

"I don't believe this." Dazed, Annie staggered over to the chair and dropped down into it. "You had me watched."

Oliver looked concerned. "Are you okay, Annie? You look a little ill."

"I might throw up at any minute."

He started toward her. "Here, let me help you get to the bathroom."

She held up a stern hand. "Do not, I repeat, *do not* touch me."

He stopped a pace away from the chair. "Annie, if you're ill, we should get you to an emergency room."

"I am not ill. Not in the way you mean. Don't worry, I won't throw up on your rug." Annie drummed her fingers on the arm of the chair. She narrowed her eyes at Oliver. The look of concern on his face was genuine, she realized. "You'll have to forgive me, Oliver. I'm a little confused at the moment. You don't happen to have a twin, do you?"

"A twin?"

"Are there two of you?" she asked patiently. "A nice Oliver and a nasty Oliver? Is this one of those stories in which there's a good twin and a bad twin?"

"No." He smiled slightly.

"I was afraid of that. Which means we have to work with what we've got." Annie shot to her feet, still clutching his shirt around herself. "I think I'm beginning to get a hint of the true nature of the monumental problem we have here, Oliver."

"I'm glad one of us is."

Annie resumed her pacing, her mind working furiously. "It's obvious you've gotten away with murder over the years."

"Not quite."

She sent him a quelling glance. "In a manner of speaking. The truth is, you manage your family the way you manage your financial empire. You're an old-fashioned feudal lord at heart. And now you think you can manage a wife the same way."

"Annie, you're getting a little carried away here."

She spun around and stabbed an imperious finger at him. "Your problem is even more complicated than I first thought."

"I believe you said something about me not being a great communicator."

"This goes beyond your inability to communicate."

"We've already been over this, haven't we?" Oliver asked politely.

Annie lifted her chin. "I've done some more detailed analysis."

"I see."

"Now, then, you have a strong, natural tendency to dominate everything and everyone in your world. Probably a result of all the responsibilities you were forced to assume at an early age. Then, again, maybe you were born that way. You, Oliver, are what they call a controlling personality."

"I'll keep that in mind." Oliver took a step toward her. He halted as she shook her finger at him. "There's more?"

"Much more. You've been allowed to become a tyrant. No one stands up to you. Your family respects you and admires you, but they're all far too much in awe of you. You get away with your dictatorial tendencies because no one confronts you head on and

137

draws a line. I, however, am not afraid of you, Oliver."

"I'm glad." He took another step toward her, stalking her slowly, with infinite patience.

Annie retreated a step and then stood her ground. "There are going to be some changes made around here."

"Are there?"

"Yes, there are. For starters, I do not want Bolt spying on me. It gives me the creeps. Think how you would feel if someone were lurking about watching you."

Oliver weighed that. "All right."

She eyed him warily. "I mean it. I won't have him skulking about in the bushes wherever I go."

"I said all right."

"Really?" Annie was disconcerted by the ease of her first victory. "You promise you won't have him spy on me?"

"He wasn't spying on you. He was keeping an eye on you for your own good. But, yes, I promise I won't have him do it any more. I don't think it's necessary, now that we've had this discussion. I can understand your point of view."

Elation swept through Annie. She smiled at Oliver with approval. "That's wonderful. I knew you weren't truly insensitive, just a little thickheaded."

"Thank you."

"From now on, we're going to talk about things as they come up," Annie said earnestly.

"I'll try. But I'm a little rusty at this kind of thing. Will you be patient with me?"

"Of course I will," she assured him.

Inside she was ecstatic. Oliver cared enough for her

138

to try to change himself. A woman could hardly ask more of a man than that. He might even be falling in love with her, Annie thought happily.

"I'm glad we had this little talk," Oliver said.

"So am I. The thing is, Oliver, you can't go through life manipulating and bullying people, even if you think it's for their own good."

"I see."

"You have to learn to trust others if you want them to trust you. Trust builds trust. Suspicion just creates more suspicion."

"I appreciate your thinking on the matter." Oliver opened his arms. "Can we go back to bed now?"

Annie went to him at once. "Yes," she said against his bare chest.

He picked her up in his arms and carried her back to the shadowed bed.

139

9

Oliver centered himself and then slowly, deliberately lowered his body from the yoga shoulder stand into the plough position. Without a break in the flowing rhythm, he turned onto his belly and arched his body smoothly into the cobra. His muscles coiled and uncoiled easily, obeying every command he gave them. Energy pumped through his veins.

He could not recall when he had last felt as good as he did today. He took his excellent health for granted most of the time, but this morning he was keenly aware of the vibrant sense of well-being that filled him. The yoga routine he ritually went through every day was astonishingly easy to complete today. He moved from one difficult posture to the next without any effort.

Annie was his, he thought with deep satisfaction as he stretched his body out into the full locust. Last night she had become his wife in every sense of the word. She had responded to him as if she had been made to order for him.

His self-control had been tested to the limit during the long hours in bed with Annie. He had wanted her more than he had ever wanted any woman. But he knew only too well that at this stage his hold on her was tenuous at best. As far as she was concerned, their marriage was still a temporary affair.

His goal was to slowly and surely bind her to him as completely as possible. The strong bond of physical attraction was an invaluable tool.

With such a crucial objective in mind, Oliver had been able to deny his own needs. He had worked hard to ensure that Annie's first experience with him would make her forget any other relationships she might have had in the past. Not that there had been many for her, he thought, pleased. He had known from the way she reacted to her first orgasm that her experience had been extremely limited.

He was not surprised, he thought as he sat up slowly and put his left foot over his right knee. When Annie gave herself, she surrendered completely. That was one of the first things he had learned about her last night. He sensed she would not take such a risk lightly. The fact that she had taken it with him was proof of her growing commitment to him. He twisted himself into the new position, feeling the stretch of muscle from his shoulders through his thighs.

He was satisfied that he had accomplished his goal last night. Over and over again he had brought Annie to the point of release and then sent her flying over the edge. She was a beautiful instrument, and he had played her to perfection. She had told him of her pleasure in a hundred tiny cries and murmurs. He had been certain that he had satisfied her.

He drew himself up out of the twisting stretch and into one of the balance postures. He frowned, aware that he was not paying full attention to the movements. He had practiced them for so many years that he could run through them on automatic pilot. But that was not the point of the exercise. The point was to focus and concentrate, mind and body together in a disciplined routine that strengthened his sense of control.

Oliver was ruefully aware of the nature of his concentration problem this morning. His body was going through the motions, but his mind was still full of heated images from last night. The result was that he was going to end this morning's yoga with the same fully aroused body that had brought him awake a short while ago.

He glanced back toward the rumpled bed. Annie was sound asleep in an exhausted sprawl. Her face was turned away from him but he could see the sweet, enticing curves of her shoulder and hip beneath the black and gold comforter. In the predawn light her hair was a billowing halo on the pillows.

She would definitely remember last night, Oliver told himself. And so would he.

Desire surged through him, as hot and fresh and demanding as it had been during the night. He wanted nothing more than to go back to the bed and pull Annie's warm, soft body against his own. The urge to feel her melt for him once more was almost overpowering.

But the sheer strength of the compulsion was reason enough to resist. He was not a man who was at the mercy of his passions. Oliver deliberately overrode the urge to go back to bed, coiling himself instead into another complex posture.

"Doesn't that hurt?"

Surprised at the sound of Annie's voice, Oliver glanced over his shoulder. She had turned her head on the pillow and was watching him intently. Her face was soft and flushed from sleep. There were shadows beneath her eyes.

"No," he said. "It doesn't hurt."

"It looks painful." Her eyes widened as she took in the size of his erection pressing against the fabric of his briefs. "I'm not sure you should be doing something like that in your, uh, condition." She blushed furiously. "I mean, you could hurt yourself."

"I haven't had any serious accidents so far." Oliver slid into another stretch, determined to exercise his thundering hormones into submission.

"What time is it, anyway?"

"Six o'clock."

"It seems earlier," she muttered.

"You don't have to get up with me. After I finish this I'm going to spend some time in the greenhouse."

"That's all right. I usually get up by six." Annie pushed back the covers and slid her bare legs over the side of the bed.

Oliver saw that she was still wearing his shirt. She clutched it tightly closed as she stood. She appeared to be embarrassed.

"I think I'll take a shower," she finally said. "I'll use the bathroom in my bedroom."

"All right," he said gently, throttling back the new wave of desire that swept through him. She was his wife. "I'll join you for breakfast in about an hour."

In spite of his determination to control his passion, his gaze lingered on the curve of her thigh. He remembered how soft the insides of Annie's legs were. He quickly forced himself into the next stretch as she hurried from the room. He held the rigorous posture until every muscle in his body was straining with the effort.

Then he straightened slowly and at last allowed himself to walk over to the bed. The scent of last night's lovemaking still hung in the air. For a moment he stood there, recalling the heat and the passion and the shimmering satisfaction.

Then he turned and forced himself to walk into the bathroom where he quickly turned on the shower.

Half an hour later, dressed in a pair of jeans and a fresh shirt, he bounded up the stairs to the roof. A sense of exhilaration still gripped him. He checked the array of dials and gages on the environmental control panel and then opened the door of the greenhouse.

His private rain forest was waiting for him. Oliver picked up a sprayer and a trowel and went to work.

He was examining a tray of tiny new staghorn hybrids when the greenhouse door opened. He looked up as Annie entered. She was carrying two steaming mugs.

"I thought you might like some tea." She offered him one of the mugs.

Oliver smiled, pleased by the wifely gesture. "Thank you." He walked down the fern-choked aisle to where Annie stood and took the mug from her hand. He studied her over the rim, enjoying the sight of her freshly scrubbed face and shining hair.

Annie examined him just as intently. "Oliver, are you upset?"

He frowned in surprise. "Upset?"

"As in annoyed. Or angry. Or hurt?"

"Of course not. Why do you ask?"

"Well, you've been acting a little weird this morning."

"More weird than usual, would you say?" he asked blandly.

A rush of warm color suffused her cheeks. "I didn't

144

mean to imply you were acting really strange or anything."

"That's a relief."

She scowled. "This is not funny. I'll admit I haven't ever been married before, but to the best of my knowledge, most new husbands don't bounce straight out of bed in your condition and start doing yoga."

"My condition?"

Her blush deepened. "You know what I mean. You were obviously somewhat, well, somewhat aroused. But you didn't seem interested in sex. And then you charge up here and go to work on your ferns. I just wondered if you were annoyed or something."

He smiled and sipped his tea. She looked sexy as hell in the mornings, he thought. "Why should I be annoyed?"

She watched him closely. "Because of the argument we had last night. I thought you might have been hurt or angry because I told you that things were going to be a little different around here. That I wouldn't tolerate being spied upon. That you needed someone to stand up to you."

Oliver resisted the urge to laugh. Something told him Annie would not appreciate humor at the moment. Instead, he set down his mug. Without a word he removed hers from her hand and set it beside his own. Then he drew her into his arms and kissed her thoroughly. He did not raise his head until she was clinging to him, her mouth open beneath his.

"Would it relieve your mind to know that I had completely forgotten all those things you said last night?" he asked at last.

She drew back, looking uncertain. "Not exactly. I just didn't want you to be too offended, that's all."

Her earnest expression charmed him. Oliver wondered if all husbands felt this indulgent in the mornings. "Don't worry, Annie. I am not in the least offended."

"I'm glad to hear that." She searched his face anxiously. "But you don't really mean you've forgotten everything we talked about, do you?"

"No. I just mean our conversation doesn't bother me. Don't worry, I have never forgotten a single word you have ever said to me." Oliver brushed his lips across the tip of her nose. "By the way, who is Melvin Finch?"

"Melvin?" She looked blank. "Oh, *Melvin.*"

"Bolt said you received a wedding gift from him."

Annie wrinkled her nose. "How did Bolt know about Melvin's gift?"

"Apparently you left it lying on the table in the hall last night. There was a card attached to the package."

"That's right. I was going to tell you about it, but it slipped my mind," Annie said easily. "Melvin is an old friend. He left Seattle a couple of years ago to join a symphony orchestra in the Midwest. He's a wonderful cello player."

"How did he learn about our marriage?"

"Someone must have mentioned it to him on the phone. It's not exactly a secret. Melvin and I have a lot of mutual friends here in Seattle."

"How close were you and Finch?"

"I told you, we were friends. Melvin was an accountant here in Seattle when I knew him. He played his cello on the side. I knew as soon as I met him that he hated accounting. What he really wanted to do was make a career out of the cello."

"So why didn't he?"

146

"His father didn't approve," Annie explained sadly. "Mr. Finch insisted Melvin stay in what he called a real job instead of trying his luck in the music world. I told Melvin he should give music a try. If it didn't work out, he could always go back to accounting."

Oliver frowned as the picture began to emerge. "So you convinced him to defy his father and follow his star?"

"Not exactly. The problem was that Melvin and his father didn't communicate very well. Every time Mr. Finch laid down the law, Melvin reacted as he had when he was a child. I encouraged him to deal with his father as an adult. It worked. Mr. Finch eventually accepted Melvin's decision and wished him well."

"So you helped Melvin develop some backbone and the first thing he did was split for the Midwest, is that it?"

"His first offer was with a symphony in the Midwest," Annie clarified carefully.

"Why didn't he take you with him?"

She shrugged. "As you said, he was following his star."

"Do you miss him?" Oliver asked more harshly than he had intended.

"Not really." Annie smiled reminiscently. "I'll probably always be rather fond of Melvin, though. He's very sweet. And his cello playing is nothing short of brilliant. Wasn't it nice of him to send us that compact disc?"

"Very thoughtful." Oliver reined in the jealousy that had begun to gnaw at his insides. There was obviously no reason to concern himself any further with Melvin Finch. Annie showed no signs of pining over her cello player.

"This greenhouse is absolutely amazing," Annie said cheerfully. She glanced around with interest. "I didn't get a chance to see all of it the other evening when you brought me up here. Why don't you give me a complete tour this morning?"

Oliver's thoughts shifted direction instantly. "Are you really that interested in it?"

"It's fascinating." Annie ambled over to the tray of glass-covered dishes. "Ferns are different from flowering plants, aren't they?"

"Very different." Oliver walked over to stand beside her. "Flowering plants grow from seed. But ferns have a much more complicated life cycle."

"How do you propagate them?"

She really was interested, Oliver realized. He felt ridiculously pleased. "When they're ready, I collect the spores from under the mature leaves. I sow them by tapping them from a sheet of paper onto a growing medium in the glass jars."

Annie peered more closely into the jars. "You just dump the spores in there?"

"No. It's a little more complicated than that. The whole process has to be done under relatively sterile conditions, for one thing. I don't allow anyone else in the greenhouse when I'm sowing spores." Not that anyone else was all that interested, he reflected.

"What do they look like?"

"The spores? They're very small. I'll show you." He unsealed a small paper packet containing what looked like fine rust-brown dust and tapped the contents out onto a sheet of paper. "These are from *Woodwardia fimbriata*, better known as a giant chain fern."

148

"What happens after you sow them in the glass jars?" Annie asked.

"When the spores germinate, they form what is called the prothallia."

"A baby fern?"

"Not quite." Oliver picked up one of the glass jars and showed her the tiny green organisms inside. "Those are prothallia, and they have to be kept moist so that the sperm can fertilize the egg cells. The result of that process eventually produces young ferns."

He moved to another bench to show her the tray of hybrids he was growing. Annie followed with a string of questions.

Neither thought of breakfast for nearly an hour.

At eleven o'clock the following morning Oliver removed his reading glasses and set them down on Daniel's desk alongside the report he had been studying. He reached over and punched the intercom.

"Ask Barry Cork to come in here, please, Mrs. Jameson."

"Yes, sir."

Oliver got to his feet and walked to the window, idly rubbing the back of his neck. It looked like he was going to have to pay a personal call on one of Daniel's main suppliers. That meant a trip out of town. Oliver was not looking forward to it. It would mean being away from Annie overnight. Not a pleasant thought.

He gazed at the view beyond the window. The headquarters of Lyncroft Unlimited occupied a sprawling jumble of two-story industrial buildings in the south part of Seattle. The company had grown so fast that Daniel had had a hard time finding sufficient space.

Oliver could see the curve of the Kingdome from the window. Beyond it was the Pioneer Square neighborhood where Annie was no doubt hard at work. His soft, sweet, exquisitely passionate Annie. Oliver smiled to himself.

A knock on the door broke into his thoughts.

Oliver turned his head. "Come in."

Barry Cork stepped into the room, a wary, slightly anxious expression on his face. Oliver was accustomed to that look. Most of the people who worked for him had it.

"You sent for me, Mr. Rain?" Barry assumed a respectful stance.

Oliver shifted his gaze back to the window. "What's the problem with Featly and Moss?"

Barry cleared his throat. "As I explained in my report, they're unwilling to keep Lyncroft as a priority client now that Dan is out of the picture. I've tried talking to them. That's where I was, in fact, when you and Annie got married. But they're under a lot of pressure from other clients."

"And they think Lyncroft might not make it, so why keep us at the top of the hot list, is that it?"

"Well, yes. I guess that's about it." Barry hesitated. "No offense, Mr. Rain, but Featly and Moss are in California."

"So?"

"So they're, uh, not quite as aware of your reputation down there as the Northwest suppliers are."

Oliver nodded. "In other words, they have no reason yet to think Lyncroft is going to survive Daniel's absence."

"I'm afraid that's about it in a nutshell."

"We need their shipments and we need them on a reliable basis. It looks like I'll have to go down there and talk to them myself." Oliver turned around, deliberately erasing all expression from his face. "Get me everything you have on William Featly and Harvey Moss."

Barry frowned in confusion. "You mean on the company?"

"No, Cork," Oliver said with a patience he did not feel. "On the two men who own it."

"You mean personal stuff?"

"Exactly. I want to know where they went to school, who they've worked for in the past, whether they drink or gamble. The usual."

"I see." Barry adjusted his tie and cleared his throat again. "The thing is, I don't think we have too much information on the guys who own it. I've met both of them. They seem okay."

Oliver eyed him coldly. "Didn't Daniel maintain files on the people he dealt with?"

"Not *personal* files." Barry looked aghast. "Why would he? We've got a fair amount of financial information, naturally, but not what you'd call personal stuff. I think maybe Featly's married, if that helps."

"Not much." Oliver was irritated. Daniel had worked for him long enough to know the value of gathering background information on the people with whom one did business.

"I don't know what else I can offer you." Barry pushed his glasses higher on his nose. "I guess I could try making some phone calls."

"Never mind. I'll take care of it." Oliver walked back to his desk and sat down. "Contact Featly and Moss.

151

Tell them I'm flying down to see them this week. Let's make it Thursday. Have Mrs. Jameson make the travel arrangements."

"Right." Barry backed toward the door. "Anything else, Mr. Rain?"

"No." Oliver picked up the report he had been reading. He waited until the door closed before he put the report back down and reached for the phone. He dialed the private number of his penthouse.

"Rain residence," Bolt said in his machinelike voice.

"Bolt, I want you to track down whatever you can on a couple of Lyncroft suppliers named Featly and Moss. I'll fax what I've already got on them to you in a minute. It's not much, just some financial and accounting data. For some reason Daniel Lyncroft doesn't keep any useful files of personal information on people like this."

"Yes, sir."

"There isn't much time. I'm going down to California to see Featly and Moss the day after tomorrow. Just get me whatever you can between now and when I leave. You can fill me in when you drive me to the airport."

"Yes, sir."

"I only expect to be gone overnight." Oliver paused. "Try not to get into any major skirmishes with Mrs. Rain while I'm away."

"Understood, sir." If Bolt saw any humor in the remark, he managed to conceal the fact admirably.

Oliver hung up the phone and sat quietly for a moment, contemplating the notion of having Annie waiting for him when he came back from a business trip.

It was a pleasant thought. Something to look forward to in fact. For the past few years, ever since he had achieved his financial objectives, he had not really had a lot of events in his life that he could anticipate with a sense of genuine pleasure. Since he had met Annie, he found himself looking forward to something besides watching ferns grow.

Annie studied the museum poster hanging behind Valerie's desk. It showed a photograph of a savage-looking feline deity carved in sheet gold. The title of the Eckert Museum's upcoming exhibition was printed boldly across the top of the poster, The Golden Jaguar: A Survey of Pre-Columbian Gold.

"Very impressive," Annie said, admiring the poster. "I wouldn't mind having him in my shop."

"I doubt if very many of your customers could afford him," Valerie said dryly. "The piece is practically priceless."

"The workmanship is certainly sophisticated looking. How old is it?"

"The jaguar is Chavin," Valerie said impatiently. "It dates from around 800 B.C. And you're right, the workmanship is very sophisticated. Better than anything that was being done in Europe at that time. Pre-Columbian craftsmen were absolute masters."

"I hadn't realized they had worked with gold."

"They certainly did," Valerie said. "In fact the Aztecs called gold the excrement of the gods."

"No shit," Annie murmured.

Valerie gave her a sharp glance.

"The Golden Jaguar is going to be an impressive exhibit," Annie continued politely. She glanced around the room at the jumble of books and photographs that were spread out on every available surface.

The pictures showed exquisitely carved golden ornaments, headbands, vessels, and figurines. All combined the elements of savagery and sophistication that had been captured so perfectly in the golden jaguar in the poster.

"Pre-Columbian art is my area of expertise." Valerie toyed with a pencil in her hand. Her eyes were troubled. "The exhibit opens in less than two weeks. Right now I'm preparing for the preview."

"Who gets to go to the preview?" Annie asked quickly.

"Anyone who has given over ten thousand dollars to the Eckert Museum during the past year."

"Oh." Annie sat back in her chair. "I guess that lets me out."

"Oliver is invited," Valerie said grudgingly. "He made a sizable contribution this year. As his wife, you're also welcome. But don't hold your breath. Oliver almost never attends that kind of thing."

"We'll see," Annie said, feeling optimistic. Oliver was proving cooperative lately. "What did you want to talk to me about, Valerie? I told my assistant I'd only be gone for an hour."

Valerie continued to hold Annie's eyes for a moment and then she broke the contact. "I'm sorry you had to witness that scene between Oliver and me the other evening."

"These things happen in families," Annie said sympathetically. "I've got an older brother, too."

Valerie shot her a quick, curious glance. "Oliver says you think your brother is still alive even though everyone else believes he's dead."

"Not quite everyone else believes that. His fiancée, Joanna, thinks he's still alive, too."

154

Valerie's expression held a degree of understanding. "This must be a hard time for you. I know how I'd feel if Oliver disappeared. As arrogant and overbearing as he can be, I still can't quite imagine the world without him."

"Brothers are like that, I guess. You get used to having them around."

"All of us are definitely used to having Oliver around. He was always there for the rest of us," Valerie said quietly. "Even before Dad left, Oliver was the one we turned to after Mom died. Oliver was the one who took care of things. Do you know what I mean?"

"Yes, I know what you mean."

"After Dad was gone, Oliver was all we had left. We depended on him. Oliver is very, very dependable." Valerie suddenly slammed the pencil down onto the desk. "I love him, but I swear to God, he can be a real bastard at times."

"I know." Annie smiled slightly.

Valerie gave her a sharp glance. "How long, exactly, have you known him?"

"Long enough to know he's got a domineering streak a mile wide. But I feel he's trainable. He's basically a good man. I think, given a little time, that I can work with the raw material available."

"Is that right?" Valerie flashed her an annoyed look as she got to her feet. "What do you intend to do with Oliver? Mold him into a sensitive, sweet, lovable teddy bear?"

Annie grinned. "I didn't say I could accomplish miracles. Oliver reminds me of the golden jaguar in that poster, an interesting blend of savagery and sophistication. But I'll see what I can do with him."

155

"Lots of luck."

"Thanks."

"He's so damned stubborn," Valerie sighed.

"He's very concerned with being in control," Annie explained. "It's easy to see how he got that way. Sheer willpower and incredible self-control are what made it possible for him to hold your family together and recreate the Rain fortune."

"I suppose so, but they also create a lot of problems."

"I'm aware of that." Annie glanced surreptitiously at her watch.

"I know you're in a hurry." Valerie went back to her desk and sat down. "Look, I'll try to make this short and coherent. I asked you here today because I wanted to know if Oliver said anything to you about that argument I had with him."

"Why do you want to know?"

Valerie closed her hands into fists. "I need to know what he's thinking. I need to know if there's any way I can reach him, make him listen to reason. Did he say anything at all?"

Annie picked her words carefully. "Not much. Just something about not liking the man you're currently dating."

"He doesn't even know Carson," Valerie said tightly. "He's never met him. Oliver hates Carson's father because of things that happened years ago. It's a feud that has nothing to do with Carson and me. But Oliver can't separate Carson from his father."

"I understand."

Valerie eyed her. "I've usually done what Oliver wanted me to do. We all have. To be perfectly honest,

156

most of the time he's right about things. But he's wrong about Carson."

"How did you meet Carson?"

"He teaches art history at the university. I consulted with him on a couple of exhibitions. We got to know each other. His family has a tradition of supporting the arts." Valerie tapped one mauve nail on the desk. "In fact, Mr. and Mrs. Shore are hosting their annual benefit for the arts on Friday evening."

Annie nodded, not quite sure what was expected of her. "I know."

"I'm going." Valerie raised her chin. "Carson has invited me to attend as his guest."

Annie winced. "Oh."

Valerie nodded grimly. "You're right, Oliver is going to be furious when he finds out."

"Maybe not," Annie said, trying to look on the bright side. "I mean, attending events that raise money for the museum is practically part of your job description, isn't it?"

"That's one way of looking at it. But Oliver will never look at it that way." Valerie's eyes glistened with tears. "Why does he have to be so damned stubborn? Why can't he give Carson a chance?"

Annie sighed. "I suppose you want me to talk to Oliver for you?"

Valerie gave her a desperate look. "Would you?"

"I can try. But we both know it might not do any good. As you said, your brother is remarkably stubborn."

"I have a feeling he'll listen to you. I think he feels, well, sort of indulgent toward you."

"What makes you think that?" Annie asked, flattered and pleased.

Valerie gave her a wry smile. "He's got that ridiculous cloisonné leopard you gave him on display in his study, doesn't he?"

* * *

"Why are you going down to California?" Annie asked Oliver that night when she took the tea tray into his study.

"To see one of Daniel's chief suppliers, Featly and Moss. They haven't restored Lyncroft to a priority status since I took over." Oliver set some papers aside and removed his reading glasses. "I've got to convince them to return to their original shipment schedule or we'll be in trouble within three months."

"They must still think Lyncroft is doomed in spite of the fact that you're in charge now." Annie sat down across from him and poured the tea.

"Cork says the problem is that they don't know much about me so they have no reason to think Lyncroft is in safe hands." Oliver accepted the teacup.

Annie grinned. "You mean the folks down in California haven't heard about your amazing reputation? How embarrassing."

Oliver's brows rose slightly. "I'll try to give them a clearer picture of what I intend to do with Lyncroft. By the way, do you happen to know if Daniel kept any files away from the office?"

Annie looked at him in surprise. "Not that I know of. Why do you ask? Is something missing?"

"There are no personal files on Featly and Moss or anyone else for that matter."

"Personal files? You mean personnel files? I'm sure there must be a lot of them. Lyncroft employs dozens of people. There have to be personnel files."

"Not personnel files." Oliver sipped his tea with a

considering air. "I'm talking about files of personal background information on the people with whom Daniel does business. Details on their personalities, problems, habits, that kind of thing."

"What on earth are you talking about?" Annie put her teacup down with a clatter. "Daniel runs a corporation, not the Central Intelligence Agency."

"I assumed that while he worked for me he at least learned the value of maintaining personal data on major suppliers and investors."

"Obviously, Daniel doesn't agree that it's necessary to spy on people in order to maintain sound business relationships." Annie scowled at him. "Are you telling me that your penchant for poking around in other people's affairs extends outside the family?"

"I don't poke around in their affairs." Oliver swallowed more tea. "I keep myself informed."

"That's euphemism if I ever heard one." Annie shook her head in disgust. "Oliver, you have got to learn that you will never make any friends by spying on people."

"I don't need friends. They're unreliable at best. But I do need information."

Annie tapped her foot. "That's ridiculous."

"No, it's not." Oliver's eyes hardened almost imperceptibly. "I learned that lesson when I picked up the pieces my father left behind."

Annie groaned. "Must you take such a hard line on everything?"

"You married me so that I could save Lyncroft," Oliver said softly. "Let me do my job."

Annie flushed. She didn't want to argue with him tonight, least of all about why she had married him. Nor was this a good time to talk to him about Valerie and Carson. Perhaps this was one of those moments when a wise wife changed the subject.

"How long will you be gone?" she asked quietly.

"With any luck, just overnight. I should be back on Friday."

"Okay."

He studied her in silence for a moment. "Will you miss me, Annie?"

"Yes," she admitted.

"Good," he said. "I'm glad."

But he didn't look really glad about it, Annie thought. Oliver's eyes gleamed with an expression that could more properly be described as arrogant satisfaction.

"That's about it as far as Featly and Moss are concerned." Bolt eased the limousine through the heavy airport traffic with the precision of a professional sniper taking aim. "Nothing unusual in their backgrounds, at least not that I could turn up in forty-eight hours. Just a couple of good businessmen making a substantial living supplying parts for companies like Lyncroft."

"Some other firm must have convinced them that Lyncroft was no longer a major player and that Featly and Moss should shift their priorities," Oliver observed. He flipped through the short printout Bolt had given him to read. "If that's the case, maybe I can convince them to change their minds."

"Yes, sir." Bolt slid the limousine into an incredibly minute slot near the curb. "One more thing, sir."

"Yes?"

Bolt turned and rested one arm on the back of the

seat. His gold-mirrored sunglasses reflected the scene on the sidewalk outside the car.

"I didn't turn up anything useful on Featly and Moss," Bolt said, "but there was something strange about that last trip Barry Cork made down to California to see them."

Oliver stuffed the printout into his attaché case. "Go on."

"Cork supposedly went down there specifically to talk to Featly and Moss. Right?"

"Right."

"As far as I can tell, he only spent an hour with them."

Oliver looked up as he snapped the case shut. "He was gone for several days. Where was he the rest of the time?"

"I couldn't trace his movements for the entire period, but I could place him at private meetings with at least two of Lyncroft's biggest competitors."

"I'll be damned." Oliver felt something click into place.

"Furthermore, those meetings were not held at the offices of the firms involved," Bolt concluded. "They were held in a hotel room."

"Thank you, Bolt. You never fail to earn your salary."

"I do my best, sir. Will you want me to keep an eye on Mrs. Rain while you're out of town?"

Oliver hesitated. "No," he said finally. "That won't be necessary."

10

Arthur? Where are you? Are you in here?" Annie surveyed the musty interior of Quigley's Bookshop, searching for Arthur among the ceiling-high aisles crammed with old volumes.

"Up here, Annie. I'll be right down."

Annie glanced up and saw Arthur at the top of a ladder. He was wedging an old leather-bound book carefully into place on a shelf full of other ancient tomes.

"I need a book," Annie said. "At least, I think I need one."

"Sure. What book?" Arthur started down the ladder. He was a small, wiry man with a receding hairline and kind brown eyes. He wore a pair of horn-rim glasses perched on his nose. He was dressed in a pair of brown corduroy trousers, a rumpled sweater, and loafers.

"I don't know exactly what book I want," Annie explained as Arthur reached the bottom of the ladder. "I just know the subject."

"And that is?"

"Sex."

Arthur blinked at her from behind his horn-rims. "You want a book on sex?"

"A manual or something." Annie blushed. She lowered her voice. "It's for my husband."

162

"Ah." Arthur blushed, too. "Your new husband. That would be Oliver Rain."

"Right." Annie glanced curiously down one aisle labeled Health. This was turning out to be a bit more awkward than she had expected. But Arthur was a good friend. He would understand.

"I see." Arthur cleared his throat. "Would that be a basic manual? Intermediate? Advanced?"

Annie considered the question with a small frown. "Advanced. He knows the basics. He knows the intermediate stuff, too." She felt herself turning even pinker. "In fact, he knows a lot about sex. A great deal more than I do. The problem isn't technique."

Arthur looked sympathetic. "Would it be a problem of premature ejaculation, then?"

"Lord, no," Annie muttered. "Sometimes I wish it were. Actually, it's more of a communication problem."

"Ah," Arthur said again, nodding wisely this time. "A communication problem. What, exactly, does Rain have trouble communicating?"

Annie tried to think of a delicate way of explaining the situation. "My husband is a very assertive, take-charge sort of man. Very much in control. Of everything, if you see what I mean."

"I think so," Arthur said slowly.

Annie smiled, grateful for his understanding. "I want to be the one to take charge. I want to show him what it's like to be the one who's not in control."

"I think I have just what you're looking for," Arthur said. He led the way down an aisle labeled Exotica.

He stopped in front of a row of ancient volumes and plucked out one.

Annie studied the title engraved on the old leather

binding: *Three Nights Among the Amazons*. "Don't you have anything newer than this?"

"Yes, but nothing better for your purposes."

"Okay, I'll give it a try." Annie looked up. "How much do I owe you?"

Arthur smiled. "Consider it a wedding gift."

"How nice of you."

"Don't be ridiculous, Annie. I owe you more than I can ever repay. If it hadn't been for you, I would never have married Elizabeth."

The warm gratitude in Arthur's gaze embarrassed Annie. "How's the baby?" she asked quickly to change the subject.

Arthur grinned proudly. "Getting bigger every day. You won't recognize him when you see him."

"Have Elizabeth bring him by for a visit."

"I'll do that."

Annie smiled. "I've got an elephant I think might interest him."

"I don't know why I thought it would help if I came out here to the beach cottage for a while," Joanna said.

"It's all right. I understand." Annie kept her eyes on the winding road. A light winter rain obscured the view of the beach. The turnoff to Aunt Madeline's old cottage was only a short distance ahead.

"When I phoned to tell you I was going to drive out here, I didn't mean to make you feel you had to come with me," Joanna said.

"I don't mind. An overnight stay on the beach will do us both good." Actually, Annie had not particularly wanted to drive out to the coast on the spur of the moment this afternoon. It was a two-hour trip, and she had a lot to do at Wildest Dreams.

But Joanna had sounded so depressed and anxious when she had called, Annie had known she couldn't allow her to make the trip alone.

"It's the stress," Joanna confided. "It's getting to me, Annie." She dabbed at her eyes with the tissue she had been using for the past hour. "Sometimes I get so frightened. I seem to be crying more and more often lately."

"I know what you mean." Annie saw the turnoff ahead and slowed her candy-red compact. "If I let myself think about Daniel too much, I get scared to death, too. So I try to focus on other things."

"It was nice of you to offer to come with me."

"No big deal. Oliver's out of town tonight. Ella can take care of Wildest Dreams for the rest of the afternoon. We'll spend the night and drive back in the morning. I'll be at the shop shortly after it opens tommorrow. No problem."

"I haven't been out here with Daniel for months." Joanna surveyed the weathered cottage as it came into view. "He came out here alone a couple of times just before our engagement party, but I didn't come with him. He was in what I call his full work mode."

"Daniel has always had a habit of coming out here to stay by himself whenever he's working on a particularly difficult problem."

Annie parked the car in the drive and sat looking at the little house through the soft rain. For a moment she was still, her mind flooded with memories. "After our parents were killed in the car crash, Aunt Madeline brought us here to live. Daniel and I both love this place."

"I know. Daniel told me how much it means to both of you. I know how much you two cared about your aunt."

Annie smiled wistfully. "Aunt Madeline was a little eccentric, but she loved us. She never made us feel like a burden."

"How was she eccentric?"

"She was an artist," Annie explained. "A fairly good one. Her stuff sold quite well. But her art was her first passion, and she spent a lot of time working at it. Daniel and I learned to entertain ourselves, which was probably not a bad lesson."

Tears streamed down Joanna's cheeks. "God, Annie, what are we going to do?"

"What we've been doing all along. We wait." Annie knew it would not take much for her to break down and cry, too. She steadied herself and opened the car door.

An hour later Annie sat with Joanna in front of a cheerful fire and realized she was feeling much better. Joanna's mood had lightened, too. At least she was no longer teary-eyed.

"I feel closer to him here for some reason." Joanna gazed around at the rustic cottage, taking in its faded drapes, old braided rug, and heavy wooden furniture. "I'm glad we drove out here."

"So am I." Annie propped her feet on the scarred wooden coffee table. She closed her eyes and let the atmosphere of the cottage sink into her bones.

Images of Daniel drifted through her mind: Daniel teaching her to play poker. Daniel teaching her how to drive when she was fifteen. Daniel comforting her when her first date ditched her at the last minute for another girl. Annie smiled at that last memory. She'd found out later that Daniel had challenged the boy to a fistfight because the kid had made Annie cry.

"He's not dead," Joanna said, touching her stomach.

"No." And Annie was somehow more certain of that than she had been for several weeks. She would know if her big brother was gone forever.

Joanna tucked one leg under herself and leaned back into the corner of the faded sofa. "Tell me the truth, Annie."

Annie opened her eyes, surprised at the odd demand. "About what?"

"You and Rain. Your marriage of convenience isn't working out the way you thought it would, is it?"

Annie made a face. "You're very perceptive. No, it's not."

"You're in love with him, aren't you?" Joanna asked softly.

"Yes."

"I was afraid of that. I knew there was something between the two of you right from the start. I saw the way Rain looked at you the night he met you. It was like watching a big cat stalk a butterfly."

"Good lord." Annie stared at her in astonishment. "What a thing to say."

Joanna shrugged. "It's true. And you were aware of him the whole time he was in the room, weren't you?"

"Guilty as charged."

"Well, I guess now we know what put that insane notion of a marriage of convenience into your head. Basic lust."

"I resent that," Annie grumbled. "It was an incredibly astute business decision that had nothing to do with the fact that I had the hots for him."

Joanna chuckled. "If you say so. I've got to admit, I have a hard time imagining the two of you together. You're so different from each other."

"Don't you dare ask me what he's like in bed," Annie warned.

"Wouldn't dream of it." Joanna slanted her a laughing glance. "Just tell me one thing."

"What's that?"

"Is there anything kinky involved? Velvet whips maybe? Feathers? Little golden balls?"

"*Joanna.*"

Joanna grinned. "You can't blame me for being curious. The man's got a reputation for being strange. Just how weird is he?"

Annie hesitated. "No whips, no feathers, no little golden balls."

"Gee, that's a disappointment. I was sure there would be something interesting and exotic to report."

"Ferns," Annie said softly, recalling the passionate enthusiasm in Oliver the morning he had explained fern reproduction to her. "The man is very good with ferns."

The ringing of the telephone on the end table interrupted whatever Joanna was going to say in response. Annie jumped.

"No one knows we're here," Joanna said, staring at the phone.

"Bolt knows. I left him a note." Annie scooped up the receiver. "Hello?"

"Good evening, Annie." Oliver's voice was a perfect monotone. "I didn't know you had plans to go out of town while I was gone."

"Hi, Oliver." Annie flopped back against the sofa cushions. "I assume you got this number from Bolt."

168

"He said you left a note on the kitchen table." There was an almost indiscernible pause. "A very brief note."

"No point writing a long letter to Bolt. He and I don't communicate all that well, anyway." Annie was amazed at how good it felt to hear from Oliver. He was acting like a real husband, phoning while out of town on business. It made her feel warm and cozy inside to know he cared enough to call.

"Bolt tells me you're at a cottage on the coast?"

"That's right," Annie said. "Aunt Madeline's old place. Daniel and I inherited it."

There was another infinitesimal pause. "And you're there with Joanna?"

"Uh-huh." Annie glanced at Joanna. "She and I drove out here this afternoon."

"The decision to go out there was a spur-of-the-moment one, then?"

"Well, yes." Annie frowned slightly, wondering why the conversation was focusing so intently on the fact that she was here with Joanna. "Joanna was feeling kind of blue and wanted to come out here. I decided to join her. We'll be driving back in the morning."

"I see."

"Is anything wrong, Oliver?"

"No."

But something in his voice alerted her. "Are you sure?" Then a thought struck her. Outrage poured through her, washing away the sense of marital warmth in a split second. "Good grief, don't tell me, let me guess. You're not absolutely certain it's Joanna I'm with, are you? This is probably Bolt's fault. What did he do? Did he imply I was out here having a wild orgy?"

"Annie..."

169

"That does it," Annie announced. "I'm going to have a long talk with Bolt when I get back. And I'd better warn you, Oliver, if he doesn't shape up, I may fire him."

"Fire Bolt? That should be interesting."

"I mean it. I won't have him giving you biased accounts of my activities."

"I didn't receive a biased account," Oliver said. "I got a very factual account. That's the only kind of account Bolt knows how to give."

"Hah. Never trust a robot. Inside they all secretly long to be human."

"Annie, calm down."

"No, I will not calm down. I'm annoyed, Oliver. Pissed off, if you want to know the truth. You're calling here to check up on me, aren't you?"

"I called to talk to you," he said calmly. "Is that so strange?"

"I don't know. With you, it's sometimes hard to tell what's normal and what's not." Annie's fingers clenched around the phone. "Do you want to talk to Joanna? That will at least prove I'm not here with some man."

Oliver hesitated briefly. "No, I don't want to talk to Joanna."

But his slight pause before answering was more than enough to further infuriate Annie. "You had to think about it before you answered, didn't you? Admit it! You'd really like some concrete proof that she's the one who's here with me."

"Annie, will you please calm down?"

"No." Annie thrust the phone toward Joanna. "Say something to Oliver, Joanna."

Joanna rolled her eyes as she took the phone.

"Hello, Oliver," she said ruefully. "Hope you're having a nice trip. Ours is turning out to be a little strange."

Annie snatched the phone back. "There. Did you hear her?"

"Yes, Annie, I heard her."

"Of course, that doesn't prove much, does it?" Annie continued vengefully. "We could have brought along a whole car full of hot young studs to entertain us."

"I don't doubt that you and Joanna are there alone, Annie," Oliver said.

"Wonderful," she snapped, still feeling disgruntled. "I do believe we're making progress. Now, then, how is your trip going?"

"I thought you'd never ask."

"Did you make any progress with Featly and Moss?"

"I think so." Oliver was silent for a moment. "They seemed surprised to learn that Lyncroft was going ahead with Daniel's plans for the development of the new product line."

"Why did that surprise them?"

"Apparently the rumor down here in Silicon Valley is that one of Lyncroft's rivals has made a sudden leap forward in basic developmental technology. It's expected to beat Lyncroft to market with its own line of wireless products."

"That's impossible," Annie declared. "Lyncroft was way ahead of everyone. Daniel told me that himself."

"Not any longer. Lyncroft is still ahead, but the competition is catching up. And that competition was willing to cut a very good deal with Featly and Moss."

"So they're now getting priority on the parts that we need? Why those bastards. Oliver, you've got to stop them."

"I think I have," Oliver said with a cool certainty that implied he knew he had. "For the next six months, at least, Lyncroft is guaranteed to receive the parts it needs on time. But that still leaves us with another problem, Annie."

"What's that?"

Oliver allowed another long, exceedingly thoughtful silence to elapse. "There is some question about just how Lyncroft's rival managed to close the developmental lead that Daniel held."

"Maybe they made a technological breakthrough on their own," Annie suggested.

"Maybe they had help," Oliver said softly.

Annie's feet hit the floor as she sat up abruptly. "What are you saying? Are you talking about a leak?"

"They call it industrial espionage."

"Oh, my God," Annie wailed. "What are we going to do?"

"Put a stop to it," Oliver said. "We'll discuss it when I get back."

"You'll be home tomorrow?"

"Yes. But probably not until late tomorrow night. I need to talk to some more people down here. I assume you're planning to be back from the beach by the time I get home?"

"Don't be sarcastic, Oliver. It doesn't suit you. Of course I'll be back from the beach."

"All right." Oliver paused. "Give my best to Joanna."

"What about the hot young studs?"

"Tell them to get lost."

Annie smiled. "I'll do that." She saw Joanna watching her with an amused expression. "Take care of yourself, Oliver."

"I will."

"I miss you."

"Do you?" Oliver sounded deeply satisfied.

Annie wrinkled her nose in exasperation. "Yes. Now you're supposed to say you miss me, too."

"I miss you, too. Goodnight, Annie. Drive safely on the way home tomorrow."

"I will."

Annie kept the phone close to her ear until she heard a faint click on the other end. Then she sighed and hung up.

Joanna studied her curiously. "Was Oliver actually afraid you were here with some man?"

"I don't know." Annie leaned her head back against the sofa cushions. "The thing about Oliver is that it never occurs to him to simply trust people."

"Not even a wife?"

Annie's mouth tightened. "No. And especially not a wife whom he thinks married him for business reasons."

"I see the problem. You did marry him for business reasons."

"Yeah, but I didn't start sleeping with him for business reasons. I hope he understands that."

"A fine distinction," Joanna murmured.

"No, it's not." Annie was annoyed. "It's a major distinction."

"It seems to me," Joanna observed slowly, "that you have just as big a problem as Oliver does."

"What do you mean?

"I mean, you have to ask yourself why he was so willing to alter the arrangements of your marriage of convenience, don't you? The real question here, Annie, is not why you're sleeping with him. I know the answer to that. You've fallen for him, hook, line, and sinker."

"So what's the real question?"

"Why is he sleeping with you?" Joanna asked quietly.

Two hours later Annie was still lying awake contemplating Joanna's question. There was a very simple and obvious answer, she told herself. It was the answer Oliver had given her himself. He was sleeping with her because he was attracted to her. Real basic stuff.

But of all the men Annie had ever met, Oliver was the one least likely to act simply to assuage a physical desire. He had far too much self-discipline to allow himself to be swayed by something as elemental as his hormones.

Annie sighed. She had firsthand evidence that there was passion in him, but he was definitely the master of that side of his nature, just as he was the master of everything else in his world.

So why was he sleeping with her, Annie wondered uneasily. She knew he wanted her, but she had to face the fact that he would not have made love to her simply because of that.

The one thing everyone said about Oliver was that he always had a hidden agenda.

Unable to sleep with such thoughts mushing about in her brain, Annie pushed aside the covers and got out of bed. She yawned as she padded barefoot down the cold hall to the kitchen to get a glass of water.

When she passed through the small shadowed living room, she noticed the dark shape of the desk near the window. She glanced at it wistfully. Daniel had liked to sit at that desk when, as a teenager, he had sketched strange, clever machines that looked like objects from outer space. Years later he still sat there when he was doing some of his most creative thinking.

Annie walked over to the desk. She touched the marred wooden surface with her fingertips. She was in an odd mood tonight, she realized. The old memories of Daniel were combining with her concerns about Oliver to produce a curious uneasiness that she did not know how to combat.

"Annie?" Joanna appeared in the doorway. She was wrapped in a terry cloth robe. "What are you doing?"

"Thinking." Annie smiled wryly. "I don't know if it's a particularly good idea."

"What were you thinking about?"

"About how much time Daniel used to spend here when he was a teenager. He always used this desk when he worked on his drawings."

"He never mentioned that," Joanna said softly.

"His drawings were wonderful. I'd love to show you some. Wait…maybe there are still a few left in one of the drawers." Annie started opening the desk drawers. She saw a small, flat object in the second one. "Here's something."

"A drawing?" Joanna came closer.

"No." Annie frowned as she removed the object from the drawer. "It's a diskette. There's a label on it."

"What does it say?" Joanna came closer, a curious expression in her eyes.

Annie stared down at the label. She couldn't believe what she was reading. "'Annie or Joanna, if you find this, take it to Oliver Rain. He'll know what to do with it.'"

"My God," Joanna whispered. "What on earth do you suppose is on that diskette?"

"I don't know." Annie sat down abruptly in the nearest chair. Her pulse was suddenly pounding. She frowned intently as she reread the simple message. "But I think we had better do exactly what it says. I'll give this to Oliver as soon as he gets home tomorrow night."

Joanna slid her hands inside the sleeves of her robe. "I don't know about you, but I just felt a strange chill go down my spine."

"I know what you mean." Annie looked up. "Joanna, you don't suppose there's any connection between this and Daniel's disappearance, do you?"

"How could there be?" But the uncertainty in Joanna's eyes told its own story. "His plane went down at sea. How could there be any connection between the accident and that note on the diskette?"

"I don't know. I guess my imagination is running wild. I wonder if we could find a way to read this before Oliver gets back."

"I doubt it," Joanna said. "Knowing Daniel, if he meant for only Oliver to read it, he would have taken precautions. Whatever is on that diskette is probably protected with a password or a code of some kind."

"You're right," Annie agreed. After all, Daniel had been an electronic security expert. He'd know about things like codes and passwords. And so would Oliver. "I hope Oliver doesn't get delayed for another day down in California."

Annie had the diskette in her shoulder bag when she strode into Wildest Dreams at ten-fifteen the next morning.

Ella popped up from behind the counter. She was sporting green hair today. "You don't look rested and refreshed, boss."

"What did you expect? I just had a two-hour drive. I need coffee." Annie tossed her purse into a drawer under the counter. "Anything exciting happen yesterday afternoon?"

"Not unless you count another visitation from Raphaela. She's in a panic over last-minute preparations for her big night at the Shore residence."

"That's right. Tonight is the evening of the benefit, isn't it?"

"Uh-huh. She bopped in here three times yesterday trying to make up her mind about what to use from our shop. She's torn between the folding screen with the jungle scene on it and the carousel. I expect she'll be in at any minute to make the final decision."

The front door of the shop crashed open. Annie turned her head. "Speak of the devil."

Raphaela swept into the room, a vision in a red swing dress and a red heels. "Darlings, I'm back."

"Make a decision, Raphaela?" Annie asked.

"You'll be glad to know I've made up my mind. It's got to be the carousel. No question about it. It will be the perfect counterpoint for the neo-deco theme I'm using in the solarium."

Annie glanced around the room at all the bright, whimsical objects on display. "You're sure you don't want to go with the paneled screen?"

"No, darling. The carousel will be perfect." Raphaela surveyed her choice with evident satisfaction. "I'll have someone drop by and pick it up this afternoon."

"How did the design work turn out?" Annie inquired.

"It will be my finest hour, if I may say so. The Shore residence will look positively fabulous tonight. I do wish you could see it."

Ella grinned. "Fat chance. To get on the Shore's guest list, you'd have to give at least five or ten grand a year to that arts foundation of theirs."

"Personally, I give to the food bank and the homeless shelters," Annie remarked. "I figure patronizing the arts is for the very wealthy."

Raphaella arched her finely penciled brows. "I've got news for you, *Mrs. Oliver Rain*. You are now counted among Seattle's richest citizens."

Annie felt a stab of chagrin. There was no way to explain that she didn't consider her position as Mrs. Oliver Rain as a permanent post yet. "I guess I haven't gotten used to the notion of being married to Oliver." she murmured.

"What an odd thing to say." Raphaela headed for the door. "I do believe I could adjust quite quickly to marrying a fortune the size of Rain's. On the other hand, that probably wouldn't get me an invitation to the Shore's benefit, would it? Everyone knows that Paul Shore and Oliver Rain aren't on speaking terms."

The door slammed shut behind Raphaela. Annie watched her disappear down the street and wondered what everyone was going to say tonight when Carson Shore and Valerie Rain were seen together at the benefit.

Oliver was going to be furious. He would no doubt view Valerie's actions as a betrayal of the family.

Two hours later Ella got ready to go to lunch. "See you in half an hour, Annie."

"All right." Annie waited until the door had closed before she took her purse out of the drawer.

She had been thinking about the diskette all morning. Her imagination was still working overtime, concocting elaborate and chilling reasons to explain why her brother had left the diskette in the desk drawer.

She took the small square object out of her purse and reread the message on the label.... *take it to Oliver Rain. He'll know what to do with it.*

Annie had an urge to hide the diskette somewhere other than her purse. Purses got snatched all the time in downtown Seattle. She'd had a short, brisk wrestling match with a would-be purse snatcher herself a few months ago. She'd managed to hang onto her bag, but it had been a near thing.

She glanced around the shop. Her eyes fell on the cloisonné elephant. She remembered the hidden drawer in the base. It was the perfect spot. The diskette would be safe there for the rest of the day. Tonight when she closed up Wildest Dreams, she would retrieve the diskette and take it home to Oliver.

Annie hurried across the room and pushed on one of the elephant's scarlet toenails. The secret drawer sprang open. The diskette fit securely inside. Annie carefully closed the drawer, feeling much better. The diskette was safe.

At four-thirty that afternoon Annie got a call from a designer who was working on a Pioneer Square loft residence.

"Can you come up and take a look, Annie? I think it needs a finishing touch from your shop. The address is just three blocks from your shop. I'll meet you at the lobby door and let you in."

Annie glanced at her watch. "Okay, I'll be there in ten minutes." When she hung up the phone, she looked at Ella. "I should be back by five-thirty. If I'm not, go ahead and close up."

"Right, boss."

But Annie got seriously delayed with the designer when the client showed up and took an active role in the decision-making process. It was nearly six by the time she got back to Wildest Dreams.

The minute she let herself into the darkened boutique she knew something was terribly wrong.

In a glance she saw the cloisonné elephant with the diskette inside was missing.

Annie forced herself to take several deep breaths in order to keep from dissolving into hysterics. When she could control her fingers, she frantically dialed Ella's home number.

There was no answer. Annie slammed down the receiver and tried to think of the names of some of Ella's spacy friends. In desperation, she just kept dialing her home number again and again. After fifteen minutes, Ella finally answered. Annie didn't even say hello. "Where's the elephant?" Annie yelled into the phone when her assistant came on the line.

"The elephant? What elephant? Annie, is something wrong?"

"I can't find my elephant. The one with the scarlet toenails. Where is it?"

"Oh, that elephant. I guess I forgot to leave a note. Raphaela has him. She made a last-minute decision. She's not using the paneled screen or the carousel."

"She's using my elephant?" Annie yelped.

"Yeah. Anything wrong with that?"

180

"Oh, my God." Annie dropped the phone back into its cradle.

One thing was clear. She had to get her elephant back tonight. And that meant going to the Shore's party this evening.

Annie glanced at her watch. The benefit would be starting soon, if it hadn't already. She could hardly show up at the door dressed in slacks and a sweater.

She tried to think. She would have to rush home to the penthouse, slip into a decent-looking dress, and then rush off to the Shore's residence on Lake Washington. Fortunately she had the address because Raphaela had given it to her.

Annie rushed out of Wildest Dreams, hoping Oliver would not get home until very late tonight. She did not relish the prospect of having to explain to him that his wife had crossed the threshold of his long-time enemy.

11

What do you mean Annie isn't at home?" Oliver asked from the back seat of the limousine.

"Just what I said, sir." Bolt found an opening in the airport traffic and slid the limousine into it. "She left a note on the kitchen table."

"Another note on the kitchen table?" Oliver glanced at his black and gold watch. It was after eight o'clock. He had been looking forward to a drink and dinner with Annie.

"Yes, sir." Bolt's gaze never wavered from the car ahead of the limousine.

"This is getting to be a habit." Oliver refused to acknowledge his disappointment and concentrated instead on his irritation. "What did the note say?"

"I assumed you'd want to read it so I brought it along with me." Without taking his eyes off the traffic, Bolt opened a small compartment in the dash. He reached inside and removed a tiny piece of paper. He offered no comment as he handed it to Oliver.

Oliver frowned as he studied Annie's almost illegible scrawl.

Welcome home, Oliver. I'll be back soon.
Something unexpected came up at work. Tell you

182

all about it when I get back. Hope you had a good trip. Love, Annie.

Oliver reread the last two words. "Love, Annie." She probably signed all her notes and letters "Love, Annie," he decided. Then he refocused on the message.

"What does she mean, something unexpected came up?" he asked Bolt.

"No idea, sir."

Oliver picked up the car phone and dialed the number of Annie's shop. After seven rings he realized there probably wasn't going to be an answer. He hung up and tried to recall the name of Annie's assistant. Ella Something. Ella Presswood.

When he got through to Ella's apartment, he got her roommate.

"She's still at the Outer Limits," the woman said cheerfully.

"What's that?"

"It's a coffeehouse in the Belltown area. This is double-latté night. Two for the price of one."

"I see." Oliver grimly hung onto his patience. "Can you give me the number?"

"Sure. Hang on a sec."

A few minutes later he got through to the Outer Limits. A helpful soul on the other end offered to fetch Ella. Oliver looked down and saw that he was drumming his fingers on the armrest while he waited. He forced himself to stop.

A moment later Ella's voice came on the line. "Yeah? Who wants me?"

"This is Oliver Rain."

"No kidding? *Oliver Rain*?"

"I'm looking for Annie. I have a note from her saying that something came up regarding her business. But she doesn't say in the note what that something was. I wondered if you knew, Ms. Presswood."

"Oh, yeah. I think she went after the elephant."

Oliver clamped down on a sudden urge to grind his teeth. "What elephant would that be?" he asked very politely.

"The ugly one with the scarlet toenails. You know, the one she once tried to palm off on you. She was real upset because she found out Raphaela had changed her mind at the last minute and taken it instead of the carousel."

This required more patience than propagating ferns, Oliver thought. "Who is Raphaela and where did she take the elephant?"

"Raphaela's a designer. She took the elephant to finish off her project at the Shore residence."

Oliver went cold. "Paul Shore?"

"Yeah, she did their home for the arts benefit tonight. It was a very big deal for her careerwise. And Wildest Dreams is going to get a nice bit of publicity out of it because Raphaela is using an item from the shop. Now do you understand?"

"Are you telling me that damned elephant is at the Shore home?"

"Uh-huh. I got the feeling Annie was headed there. Said she had to find the elephant. I don't know what she thinks she's going to do even if she gets into the benefit. She can hardly walk back out the door with the elephant under her arm. People would think she's stealing it. Raphaela would go bonkers."

"Thank you, Ms. Presswood," Oliver said evenly. "You've been extremely helpful."

"Hey, I live to be helpful. Like, I think it's going to be my full-time career, you know? Bye."

"Good night." Oliver replaced the phone very carefully. "Bolt?"

"Yes, sir?"

"I've changed my mind. We're not going home yet. I want to stop at an address on Lake Washington first."

"What's the address, sir?"

Oliver gave him Paul Shore's address. It was indelibly engraved on his memory, even though it had been years since he had last been there.

He had gone to see Shore twice following his father's disappearance.

On the first of those two unforgettable occasions, he had asked Shore for an extension on the loan that had been made to his father. Shore had refused. The fires of the humiliation of that moment would burn forever within Oliver.

The last time Oliver had gone to the mansion on Lake Washington he had paid off the loan. The repayment became possible after Oliver had sold the Rain home on Mercer Island and plunged every dime of the proceeds into some very high-risk investments in the commodities market. The memories of that period in his life still sent an icy trickle of dread through him.

He had staked the family's entire future on his knowledge of botany in order to make some educated guesses regarding some crucial harvests. Those guesses had paid off. The harvests had been far better than insiders had predicted. Oliver made his first fortune virtually overnight.

But he had been well aware of the enormous risks he had taken and he had not liked the feeling. Oliver had never again played the volatile commodities market. He did not like dealing with the random factor of luck. He preferred investments that allowed him a greater degree of control.

He gazed out the tinted window and recalled the evening he had taken the check to Paul Shore's home.

Shore's surprise had eaten at Oliver like acid. When Shore had clapped him on the back and told him he might turn out to be twice the businessman his father had been, Oliver had been almost blinded by a red haze of fury. But even then the icy veneer that was to serve him so well was already firmly in place. Oliver had controlled his rage.

He had simply turned around without a word and walked out the door. He had not spoken to Paul Shore since that fateful evening.

Anger and a deep, painful sense of betrayal clawed at Oliver's insides as Bolt guided the limo into the elegant residential section that fronted Lake Washington.

Annie had gone to Paul Shore's home. Oliver's hand tightened into a fist on his thigh. His wife was in the home of his enemy.

Getting inside was the hard part. Annie, dressed in the first thing she had found in her closet, a slim black sheath, almost didn't make it past the young blond man in the tux who guarded the front door.

"No, I don't have an invitation," she explained for the third time. "But I assure you, I have a very good reason for going inside. If you would please just ask someone in authority to come out here, I can explain."

The young man, who had the look of an unemployed model, wrinkled his fine brow. "I'm sorry, ma'am, but I'm afraid Mrs. Shore is busy at the moment."

Annie decided she had nothing left to lose. "Kindly tell her that Mrs. Oliver Rain is at the front door."

"Who?"

"Mrs. Oliver Rain."

The young man consulted a piece of paper. "I'm afraid your name doesn't appear on the guest list."

"I know that. I'm trying to tell you…"

"*Annie*. What are you doing here?"

Annie glanced past the moonlighting male model and saw Valerie, stunning in an off-the-shoulder silver evening gown, in the doorway. A good-looking man with dark hair and serious eyes stood beside her. He was dressed in formal black and white.

"Am I glad to see you, Val." Annie darted around the blond in the tux. "Look, can I talk to you for a minute? I need to get inside. There's this elephant, you see."

"Elephant?" Valerie frowned in surprise. "Never mind. First, I want you to meet Carson." She smiled tremulously up at the serious-eyed man standing beside her. "Carson, this is my brother's new wife, Annie."

"How do you do, Annie?" Carson took Annie's hand in a firm grasp. "Come on inside. I'll tell my parents you're here. I'm sure they'll be delighted."

"Thanks." Annie hurried on up the steps. "Actually, there's no need to say anything to your folks. I just want to find my elephant."

Valerie stared at her. "What's all this about an elephant? What's going on? Does Oliver know you're here?"

"It's a little hard to explain," Annie said. "But somewhere in this house, there's an elephant with scarlet toenails. He's from my shop. The designer who did your parents' home for the evening took him without telling me. I had something important stuffed into his hidden drawer. And no, Oliver doesn't know I'm here."

"Scarlet toenails, hmm?" Carson smiled. "I think I saw him in the solarium."

"That's a relief." Annie threw him a grateful look. "Can you lead me to him?"

"Sure, right this way." Carson turned and started to forge a path through the glittering throng of guests. "But don't think you're leaving tonight without meeting my parents. My mother will throttle me if I don't introduce you."

Valerie turned anxious eyes on Annie. "What about Oliver?"

"What about him? As far as I know, he's not even back from California yet. He got delayed." Annie surveyed the crowded room curiously. "Nice place."

That was an understatement, she acknowledged to herself. The shore home was a mansion by any definition of the word. The rooms were elegantly proportioned with high ceilings and endless, polished wooden floors. A long row of formal French doors revealed a breathtaking view of Lake Washington.

"The house has been in Carson's family for four generations." Valerie explained in an undertone. "It was built by his great-grandfather."

"He and Valerie's great-grandfather were partners

in a shipping operation," Carson said over his shoulder.

Annie glanced at Valerie in surprise. "I didn't realize the connection between your family and the Shores went back so far."

"The Shores and the Rains did a lot of business together over the years," Carson explained. "The feud is a new twist." He smiled warmly at Valerie. "Val and I hope to end it."

Valerie's mouth tightened. "It won't be as easy as Carson thinks. He doesn't know my brother."

"We'll see," Carson said.

A moment later he led the trio into a long, white room that was studded with glass. Annie saw immediately that Raphaela had gone ahead with her plans to create a fantasy land.

Colorful awnings and huge, overstuffed pillows had been used to create a lush, exotic backdrop. Brass palm trees towered over a bubbling champagne fountain in the center of the long room.

And there, standing placidly near the fountain, was the elephant.

"There he is," Annie announced, vastly relieved. She rushed forward and came to a halt beside the cloisonné beast. Valerie and Carson followed.

"So what is it about this elephant that's so important?" Valerie asked.

Annie reached down and pushed on one scarlet toenail. "It's not the elephant. It's what I left inside."

The hidden drawer sprang open. Annie saw the diskette and relaxed. She picked it up and stuffed it into her purse.

"Looks like a computer diskette," Carson observed.

"It is." Annie turned to smile at him. "You're welcome to keep the elephant for the rest of the evening. I've got what I wanted." She broke off, suddenly, aware that her words sounded far too loud in what had been a rather noisy room.

Belatedly she realized that a muted hush had fallen over the crowd.

A horrible sense of premonition gripped her. Along with everyone else in the solarium, Annie glanced toward the entrance. Oliver stood there, a dark, avenging god wearing a suit and tie.

His eyes found Annie in that instant of silence. He started forward, striding through the crowd with cool disdain for everything and everyone around him. The murmur of voices rose again toward a more normal level, but this time there was an undertone of collective curiosity and anticipation in the muted conversations.

"If he makes a scene, I will just die." Valerie's face was frozen. Her lips were drawn into a thin line and her eyes were filled with anxiety. "I swear to God, I will just die."

"Calm down," Annie said soothingly. "Oliver's not going to make a scene. He's probably here because he figured out that I was here. I'll explain everything to him and that will be the end of it."

"You're out of your mind," Valerie said. "We'll all pay for this." She straightened her spine. "But I don't care. This is my life and I'm going to live it my way."

'Atta girl. Stand up to him. That's my advice." Annie patted her reassuringly on the shoulder.

Carson watched Oliver's approach with a thoughtful expression. "This, I take it, is my ferocious future brother-in-law? Remind me not to get between him and a chunk of raw meat."

"He's not that bad. His growl is much worse than his bite," Annie said quickly.

"If you say so." Carson looked unconvinced.

"Annie doesn't know him very well yet," Valerie muttered.

Annie decided it was time to take charge of the situation. She was aware of the expectancy in the crowd around her and she reminded herself that Oliver could be difficult when he chose. Smiling determinedly, she went forward to intercept him.

"There you are, Oliver." Annie planted herself squarely in his path. "I'm so glad you could make it. I was afraid you wouldn't get back to town in time."

He came to a halt. "What are you doing here, Annie?"

She put one hand on his shoulder and stood on tiptoe to brush her lips across his cheek in what she hoped was a typical wifely greeting. "Behave yourself," she muttered for his ears only. "I promise I'll explain everything later."

For a tense moment Oliver looked as though he were going to ignore her demand. A cold rage burned behind the even colder mist of his rain-colored eyes.

"You will definitely explain this later," he said very softly.

His hand closed around her arm in what probably looked like a polite gesture of affection to those standing nearby. Annie, however, felt as if she had been caught in a steel trap. He was not hurting her, but she knew she could no more have pried herself free of his grasp than she could have flown. She kept her smile plastered on her face as Oliver guided her toward where Valerie and Carson stood.

Realizing that Oliver was going to speak to Valerie,

191

Annie rallied for another attempt to defuse the explosive situation.

"Oliver, I don't believe you've met Valerie's friend, Carson Shore, have you?" she said brightly. "Carson, this is Oliver Rain, Valerie's brother."

Carson smiled politely, but his eyes were cautions. "My pleasure." He held out his hand. Beside him Valerie looked brave but despairing, as if she were facing a firing squad.

When Oliver did not immediately respond to Carson's proffered hand, Annie threw caution to the winds. She brought the heel of her black pump sharply down on the toe of one of Oliver's Italian leather shoes.

A slight, but unmistakable, flinch went through Oliver. He slanted an unreadable glance at Annie and then, to her enormous relief, he held out his hand to Carson.

"I know your father," Oliver said enigmatically as he gripped Carson's hand in what had to be one of the briefest handshakes on record.

"So I've been told." Carson retrieved his hand and put it around Valerie's shoulder in a proprietary gesture. "I hope you won't make the mistake of assuming my father and I are clones."

Valerie swayed slightly against Carson, her eyes bleak.

Annie turned up the wattage in her smile. "Oliver always keeps an open mind. He never makes snap judgments, do you, Oliver?"

Oliver's eyes skimmed over Annie's brilliant smile. "No. I gather as much information as possible before I make any decision. But once in a while I discover

I've made a mistake. When that happens I correct it immediately."

Annie decided to read that statement in the most positive light. "Yes, I know, dear. That's why you've been so wonderfully successful. By the way, I've been talking to Valerie about the new exhibit of Pre-Columbian art that she's curating at the Eckert Museum. We'll want to attend the preview, won't we?"

"Will we?"

"Naturally. No point being related to the curator if you can't get into a few private showings. Now, then, say good-bye to Carson and your sister. I know you've had a busy trip and you must be exhausted. We'll go straight home and have a nice, relaxing dinner. I have so much to tell you."

"I have a few things to say to you, too," Oliver said. He looked at Valerie. "Good night, Val."

"Good night, Oliver," Valerie said stiffly. There was a flicker of relief in her gaze, however, as if she had just realized that the firing squad wasn't going to fire. At least not tonight. She cast a quick, anxious look at Annie. "I'll see you later."

"Right." Annie looked at Carson. "Thanks again for helping me find the elephant."

"Any time." Carson was still watching Oliver.

"Let's go home." Oliver tightened his grip on Annie's arm and turned her toward the entrance to the solarium.

A distinguished, well-dressed couple walked into the solarium at that precise moment. The man appeared to be in his late sixties. He carried himself with a stiff military posture that made him appear taller than he was. He was almost bald. A fringe of gray hair was cut close to his skull. He had a beak of a nose and there were deep indentations beneath his cheekbones.

The woman, who was probably in her late fifties, was fashionably slender and fit looking. The skin around her eyes and mouth was strikingly free of the wrinkles one would have expected in a woman of her age. She wore her silver hair in a smooth, short curving wave.

Annie knew from the way the distinguished couple moved through the crowd, nodding at the guests and murmuring politely, that she was looking at none other than Mr. and Mrs. Paul Shore.

"Before you try that trick with the heel of your shoe a second time," Oliver said softly to Annie, "I'd better warn you that I'm not going to shake hands with the bastard."

"Now, Oliver, there's no need to be hasty here."

"Take some advice. Don't push your luck any farther than you already have tonight. You're on thin ice as it is." Oliver urged her toward the solarium entrance.

The crowd parted, leaving Annie and Oliver on a collision course with the Shores. Oliver did not slow or hesitate. He simply kept moving forward like a shark through water. Annie was appalled. It was obvious the four of them would all collide in a tangled heap if someone didn't change direction or get out of the way.

Paul shore glanced up and saw Oliver and Annie bearing down on the doorway. A startled expression crossed his face.

Mrs. Shore turned with a gracious smile. It was clear she did not immediately recognize Oliver. Then her eyes widened. Her smile turned uneasy. She shot

Annie a quick, worried glance as if she wondered if there would be any help forthcoming from that direction.

"Hello, Rain," Paul Shore said stiffly as Oliver moved toward him. "Didn't know you'd be here tonight."

Oliver said nothing. He just kept moving toward the entrance as if the other man did not exist. Annie was keenly aware of the fascinated gazes of those watching the small scene.

Mrs. Shore made a noble effort. "We enjoyed meeting your sister earlier this evening. Such a lovely young woman. I understand you're newly married?"

Oliver still did not respond. He was headed toward the entrance with the single-minded concentration of a predator intent on prey.

Annie had had enough. Aunt Madeline had always claimed that good manners were all that stood between civilization and savagery.

Annie dug in her heels, more or less dragging Oliver to a halt. A shudder of fresh anticipation went through those who stood nearby.

"Good evening, Mrs. Shore. I'm Annie Rain. Nice to meet you. Lovely party. I'm so sorry we can't stay. Something's come up."

"Yes, of course, I understand." Mrs. Shore looked almost pathetically grateful for the short burst of social patter. She glanced quickly at Oliver. "So kind of you to drop by."

"Been a long time, Rain," Paul Shore said gruffly.

"Not long enough." Oliver spoke so softly that only the four of them could hear.

Shore's face flushed a dull red. "It would appear

that your sister and my son have become rather close lately. Perhaps we should talk. For their sake."

Oliver studied him without any evidence of emotion. "Maybe you're right. Give my secretary a call. We'll set up an appointment."

Shore's eyes narrowed at the curt manner in which he had been told to deal with a secretary. But he made no comment on the not-so-subtle insult. "All right. I'll do that."

Oliver inclined his head with chilling grace. Then he tightened his grip on Annie's arm and swept her out of the room.

Bolt was waiting near the limousine in the long, curving drive. Oliver stopped briefly to speak to him.

"Take the car back to the garage," Oliver said. "I'll drive Annie home. We won't be needing you for the rest of the evening."

"Yes, sir." Bolt gave Annie a brief, unreadable glance. Then he turned away to get behind the wheel of the limo.

Oliver drew Annie toward her little red compact, which was parked on the street. "Let me have the keys."

Annie fished inside her purse for her key ring. "Want me to drive?"

"No."

"I didn't know you drove," she said, skipping a step to keep up with him. When Oliver slanted her a strange glance she added quickly, "I mean, I thought Bolt did all your driving for you."

"I can drive. Why do you think I keep two cars in the garage?"

Annie remembered the Mercedes that was always

parked in the slot next to the limousine. "But you never drive it."

"You haven't lived with me long enough to know when and if I drive it, have you?"

"I guess not. Say, Oliver, I want to thank you for behaving yourself somewhat decently back there. I know how hard it must have been for you."

"Do you?"

"Yes, and I hope you realize that Valerie was especially grateful that you didn't punch out Paul Shore or tear the place apart. I told her you wouldn't make a scene."

"I don't give a damn whether or not Valerie was grateful. I'll deal with her later. What I want to know is, why were you there, Annie?"

"It's a long story."

"Shorten it."

Annie blinked as he came to a halt beside her car and opened the front door. "Are you really angry?"

His brows rose as he held the door for her. "You have to ask?"

"Sometimes with you it's hard to tell just what you're thinking or feeling." Annie slipped into the front seat.

Oliver's gaze followed the long length of leg revealed by her short black dress. "I see you dressed for the occasion," he said as he slammed the door.

Annie buckled her seatbelt and reached into her purse as Oliver went around the front of the car. When he got in beside her, she waved the diskette in front of him. "You want a short explanation of my presence here tonight? This is it."

He frowned at the diskette. "What's on that?"

197

"I don't know. I found it at the cottage after you called last night. See the note on it?"

Oliver glanced at the label. "Daniel left this for me?"

"Yes. Very strange, don't you think?"

"Very." Oliver turned the key in the ignition and eased the car away from the curb. "What has that got to do with your being at the Shores' this evening?"

Annie sighed impatiently. "I hid the diskette in the elephant. Remember the little drawer in the base?"

"I remember."

"While I was gone this afternoon, a designer friend of mine took the elephant to use as an ornament at the Shore's benefit. I discovered it was missing about an hour ago. I was frantic. Thank heaven Valerie and Carson were there."

"Why?"

"I don't think I could have talked my way into that fancy shindig without them. The guy at the door kept saying I wasn't on his list."

Oliver slanted her a sidelong glance. "Did you try telling him you were Mrs. Oliver Rain?"

"I've got news for you, Oliver. Not everyone in town turns to jelly at the mention of your name. I don't think the guy at the Shores' front door had even heard of you."

"He has now," Oliver said.

Annie blinked. "How did you get in?"

"I walked in."

"I mean, how did you talk your way past the guy at the door?"

"I didn't try to talk my way past him," Oliver said. "I walked up the steps and he got out of my way."

"Oh." Annie wrinkled her nose. "I can see where that technique would work better for you than it would for me. I lack a sufficiently intimidating presence or something. I guess I don't look like a Mrs. Oliver Rain."

"You look exactly like Mrs. Oliver Rain," Oliver growled.

"If you say so. At any rate, that's my story. Are you going to buy it or do I have to walk across hot coals to prove I'm telling the truth?"

"I believe you." Oliver looked oddly resigned to the inevitable. "Your story is too bizarre to be anything but the truth."

Annie smiled complacently. "That's one of the things I like about you, Oliver. Deep down, you're really very nice. Reasonable, even. Hard to understand why everyone, even your own family, has gotten such a bad impression of you over the years."

"Maybe I'm just the victim of a long series of unfortunate misunderstandings," Oliver suggested grimly.

12

Oliver felt slightly light-headed. The sense of relief he was experiencing was so great it almost amounted to euphoria.

Naturally Annie had had a perfectly reasonable excuse for being in the home of his enemy, he thought ruefully. He should have expected as much.

Oliver sank his teeth into a slice of the mushroom and olive pizza Annie had ordered for dinner. The pizza had arrived a few minutes earlier, still piping hot even after the elevator ride to the twenty-sixth floor. Annie had served it in the study in front of the portable notebook computer he kept on his desk.

In an artless act of graciousness that Oliver thought highly suspect under the circumstances, she had invited Bolt to join in the impromptu feast. Oliver didn't know whether to be amused or annoyed that Annie had arranged not to be alone with him.

Holding the slice of pizza in one hand, Oliver leaned forward and typed in *ice*, another of the handful of passwords he recalled from the days when Daniel had worked for him. The screen flickered.

"Ah-hah." Annie peered intently at the screen. "That's it, Oliver. Look, something's happening."

By rights he should have been simmering with fury, Oliver thought as he watched letters form on the screen. He was still vaguely astounded that he was not having to exert every ounce of self-discipline he possessed to control his rage.

But somehow there was no room for the anger he ought to have been feeling under the circumstances. Whatever else she'd had in mind when she went to Paul Shore's home, she certainly had not deliberately betrayed his trust.

She had been frantic because of the missing diskette. He knew Annie's list of priorities these days was very short, and there was no question but that anything regarding Daniel was at the top.

Oliver wondered if he would eventually get used to the feeling of being second on Annie's list.

He forced himself to put aside the knowledge that her primary allegiance was still toward her missing brother. Oliver reminded himself that he had known where he ranked in the general scheme of things before he had accepted Annie's offer of marriage.

"Interesting," Bolt said, watching the screen with unwavering concentration. "Looks like a series of memos regarding Barry Cork. Dates, times, and observations."

"Bolt's right. This stuff is about Barry." Annie stared at the screen. "Why would he leave you a bunch of information on him, Oliver?"

Oliver glanced impassively at the names and dates that filled the screen. "It looks like Daniel had figured out that Cork was selling Lyncroft proprietary information to the competition."

"What? I don't believe it."

"It's true, all right." Oliver punched a button to page through the data Daniel had compiled on Barry Cork. "Apparently Daniel got suspicious a few weeks before he disappeared."

"But why would Barry sell off Lyncroft's secrets?" Annie asked, looking genuinely bewildered.

"The usual reason." Oliver glanced at her. "Money."

"But Barry worked for Daniel. My brother trusted him." Annie shook her head in disbelief. "Barry was his *friend*."

Oliver resisted the urge to remind Annie of her naîveté. He studied her as she sat curled in the black leather chair beside him. She had changed clothes while waiting for the pizza to arrive. The little black dress that had revealed such an enticing length of leg was gone. In its place was a pair of jeans and a ribbed knit pullover that hugged her small waist and fitted snugly over her high breasts and the sleek curves of her thighs. There was a fresh, glowing sexiness about her that made him think of his ferns.

Oliver turned his attention back to the screen. "I'm surprised Daniel didn't fire Cork as soon as he realized what was happening."

Annie frowned. "Maybe he wasn't absolutely certain Barry was guilty. Maybe he was looking for evidence."

"He didn't need any more evidence than this list of names and dates," Oliver said absently. "It's obvious Daniel already had most of the facts."

Annie studied him. "You don't seem very surprised by all this bad news on Barry."

"I'm not." Oliver punched up another page of Daniel's notes. "A lot of it correlates with what Bolt and I turned up during the past few days."

"You and Bolt knew about this? And you didn't tell me?"

"I was going to tell you as soon as I walked in the door tonight," Oliver said. "I had planned to give you the whole story over a glass of wine. But you weren't

202

here waiting for me. If you will recall, I had to track you down first."

"Oh, no you don't," Annie retorted. "Don't you dare try to excuse your secretiveness by using that pathetic excuse. You must have had a strong hunch about what was going on before you even left for California."

"I found out on the way to the airport. Bolt filled me in."

"You had Bolt investigate Barry Cork?" Annie cast a fulminating glance at Bolt who did not take his eyes off the computer screen. "Without checking with me first?"

"I had Bolt investigate Featly and Moss," Oliver said patiently. "In the process he turned up some un-expected information on Cork's last trip to California. Cork recently held some very interesting meetings in motel rooms with important people who represent Lyncroft's competition."

"I should have been kept informed," Annie declared, clearly outraged.

"You're being informed right now," Oliver pointed out.

She narrowed her eyes at him. "Oliver, this is anoth-er example of your incredibly poor communication skills. What's more, I think it was deliberate this time."

"Annie, be reasonable. I just found out about Cork myself."

"You must have known something when you called me last night," she shot back.

"I didn't want to talk about it over the phone."

She pursed her lips disapprovingly. "I've told you

I want to be kept informed of any major developments that affect Daniel's company."

"Yes, I know. His precious company comes first at all times, doesn't it? I know what my role in all this is. I'm supposed to save Lyncroft for you. Believe me, I'm doing my best."

"Oliver, I didn't mean you weren't doing your best, just that you are sometimes very uncommunicative."

Oliver glanced at her. "I told you in the beginning that you were going to have to trust me, Annie."

Annie slid an embarrassed glance toward Bolt who was stoically ignoring the quarrel. "We'll talk about this some other time," she muttered.

"Agreed. We'll table it for the meeting we're going to have later. There are a couple of other items on that particular meeting's agenda."

"Don't you dare try to intimidate me, Oliver Rain. It won't work."

"If you say so." Oliver frowned thoughtfully at the screen. "This looks like the last of your brother's notes."

Annie leaned closer to the screen to read over Oliver's shoulder. "Those are dated only a week before Daniel disappeared."

There's been a change in the pattern. I suspect Cork has a new contact in Seattle. Not related to the California crowd as far as I can tell. This is a fresh development and I don't like the feel of it. There's something more involved here than a little routine corporate espionage. Cork's more nervous than he was a few weeks ago. And there's a lot of money involved. Too much money. I checked Cork's bank accounts. I pay the man well, but not that well. I could fire the son of a bitch now and be done with it. But I'd rather find out more about this new arrangement before I give him the ax.

Rain, if you're reading this, it's because Annie has found this diskette and asked you for help. It means that for one reason or another, I'm not in the picture. I don't know what to tell you, because I haven't got anything more to go on than Cork's actions, evidence of the money he's salting away, and a solid hunch that this is more serious than I thought at first. You and I both know things can get tricky when there's a lot of cash involved.

If Annie comes to you, my friend, I'm going to hold you to that promise you made to me five years ago. Take care of Annie and Joanna for me and we'll call it even. Deal? By the way, my advice is to keep Annie out of this. If I know her, she'll be on a one-woman crusade for truth and justice. You'll want to handle this with your own methods, and she probably won't approve of the way you do things.

Annie spun around in the chair to confront Oliver. "What on earth does Daniel mean by that last bit? And what's that part about you making him a promise five years ago? What exactly did you promise him and why?"

Oliver blanked the screen. The sharp, bright light from the halogen desk lamp provided a circle of illumination over the desk and threw the rest of the room into deep shadow.

He picked up another slice of pizza and deliberated over his answer. "I told you about the incident five years ago."

"That business with the gunrunner? Gretchen or Grissolm or something?"

"Gresham." Oliver took a bite out of the pizza, letting the memories of what had happened in the island warehouse flicker through his head. "I told your brother that night that I owed him for uncovering the operation and for helping me put a stop to it. I also told him if I could ever repay the favor, he was to let me know."

Annie gazed at him for several thoughtful seconds. "I see." She sank deeper into her chair. "Since Daniel seems to think you should be in charge around here," she said very carefully, "what are you proposing that we do now?"

Oliver did not like the expression in her eyes. "Annie, your brother didn't mean to imply that he didn't trust you."

"Don't you think I know that? But he sure as heck doesn't believe I'm capable of handling this thing on my own, either."

"Why would he think you could?" Oliver asked calmly. "You haven't had any more experience in dealing with industrial espionage than you've had with running a corporation the size of Lyncroft. You did the right thing when you turned everything over to me."

She chewed on her lower lip. "Did I? Somehow it all seems to be getting extremely complicated."

"I know you're upset, but this isn't the time to start having a lot of second thoughts."

"I know." Annie watched him from behind lowered lashes. "We're in this together, aren't we?"

"Yes." He wondered what she was thinking now. Perhaps she was beginning to regret the hasty marriage.

"So what are we going to do about Barry Cork?" she asked bluntly. "Fire him?"

"I don't think so. Not just yet." Oliver glanced at Bolt. "It's always better to know your enemy before you make decisions. We'll do what your brother intended to do. We'll give Cork enough rope to hang himself and in the process maybe we'll find out who his new client is here in Seattle. That information might be useful in the future."

Annie ran a hand through her hair, creating further havoc among the golden brown curls. "It's hard to think of Barry Cork as the enemy."

"You haven't had much experience identifying enemies."

Annie gave him an odd look. "You know something, Oliver? There are times when I can see why you make people nervous."

"But I don't make you nervous, do I, Annie?"

"No." There was a touch of defiance in the single word.

Oliver glanced at Bolt and silently indicated the door. Bolt got up without a word and left the room. Oliver allowed the silence to fall as the door closed behind Bolt.

Annie started to get restless after less than a minute. She shifted position, sliding one ankle onto her knee. The nails of her right hand tapped out a meaningless rhythm on the arm of the chair. Then, with a small exclamation, she shot to her feet and stalked across the room to the rock garden.

"I suppose you'll assign the robot to watch Barry?" Annie asked, her back to Oliver.

"Bolt is good at surveillance work."

"He certainly gets to keep his skills sharp working for you, doesn't he?" Annie's voice turned brittle. "Lots of work within the family to occupy him in addition to keeping an eye on your business competition."

Oliver abruptly realized the leaps her agile, unpredictable mind was making. "I didn't assign Bolt to watch you while I was out of town."

"You obviously knew right where to find me."

"Not because Bolt had followed you around while I was gone. I found you by calling Ella, your shop clerk. She guessed you'd gone after the elephant."

Annie glanced at him quickly, her eyes searching his in the shadows. "Is that the truth?"

"I may not be as communicative as you would like on occasion, but I have never lied to you and I never will."

She stared at him for another minute and then something within her seemed to relax. "I believe you." She turned back to study the darkened rock garden.

"What's wrong, Annie?"

"Everything. I've been worried enough about Daniel as it is. But I thought I was handling it. I thought I was doing what needed to be done to hold things together until he got back."

Oliver contemplated the blank computer screen. "You mean you thought that by marrying me you assumed you had taken the necessary steps to protect Daniel's company and his child."

"Exactly. And now this stuff about Barry comes up." She waved a hand vaguely in the direction of the notebook computer. "Something more is going on than we first thought, isn't it?"

"Maybe."

"What do you mean, maybe?" Annie dug the toe of her shoe in the fine pearl gray sand, marring one of the carefully raked lines. "Those notes Daniel left for us put a whole new perspective on his disappearance, don't they?"

"Not necessarily. We don't know if there's any connection between Barry Cork's little espionage sideline and your brother's disappearance. In fact, I think it's highly unlikely that there is."

"Why?" she demanded, obviously seeking reassurance.

Oliver shrugged. "For one thing, corporate espionage is a white-collar crime. It rarely involves murder. And that's what frightens you now, isn't it? The possibility that Daniel might have been murdered?"

Annie shuddered visibly. "It's a possibility I hadn't even considered until I saw what was on that diskette."

"The Barry Corks of this world are usually not murderers."

"What makes you so sure of that?"

Oliver got to his feet and went to stand behind her. "Trust me on this, Annie. Cork is a liar and a thief, but he's probably not a killer."

"Oh, God, I hope you're right." She turned around to meet his eyes. Tears glittered on her lashes. "But Daniel was uneasy enough about him to leave that diskette for us."

"Yes."

"He must have thought there was some danger. He specifically asked you to take care of me and Joanna if something happened to him."

"Yes."

Annie dashed the back of her hand across her eyes. "And that's precisely what you're doing, isn't it?"

"I'm doing my best, Annie."

"You're a good friend, Oliver," Annie whispered. "Daniel said you would be. He said you were dangerous, but that he trusted you."

Oliver caught her chin gently on the edge of his hand. "You and I are more than friends now, Annie. We're lovers, who happen to be married."

"I guess so," she said forlornly.

"I know so." Oliver bent his head and brushed his mouth lightly, persuasively across hers, searching for the response he knew now that he could draw so beautifully from her.

"What are we going to do?" Annie threw her arms around his neck and hugged him fiercely.

Oliver could feel her tears dampening his shirt. Tears for Daniel, he thought. He wondered if Annie would ever cry for the man she had married. The man who happened to be her lover.

"It's going to be all right," Oliver said into her tousled hair. "I'll take care of everything."

"Just as you always do?" She gave a choked little laugh and burrowed her face against his chest. "Try not to make me too nervous in the process, will you?"

He smiled. "The last thing I want to do is make you nervous, Annie." He lifted her into his arms and carried her to the door.

Annie snuggled against him, her eyes closed as he

strode into the darkened bedroom. She did not protest until he put her down on the bed.

She opened her eyes then, blinked owlishly, and abruptly sat up. She held up a hand as if to ward him off. "Oh, no you don't, Oliver. Stop right there."

Oliver felt a chill go through him. This was the first time in the short history of their marriage that she had not melted instantly at his touch. "Is something wrong, Annie?"

"Yes, I think there is." She studied him with a speculative gaze. "Sort of."

He smiled. "That time of the month? Annie, that's not a problem."

"No. It's not that. It's something else."

"Tell me," he ordered gently. He sat down on the edge of the bed.

She promptly scuttled off the far side and stood, facing him. "Have you ever noticed, Oliver, that you're always the one in charge in the bedroom as well as everywhere else?"

"I wasn't aware that you had any complaints." He rose to his feet again, watching her carefully.

"I think it's time we tried what international diplomats like to call a 'shift in the balance of power.'"

He stared at her in blank incomprehension. "Annie, are you trying to tell me something?"

Annie gave him a daring little smile that held a hint of uncertainty. "Tell me something. Would you be afraid to let me run things around here for a while?"

Oliver felt something tight inside him begin to untwist in silent relief. She wasn't trying to push him away. "I'm not afraid of you, Annie."

"Prove it."

"How?" He had never particularly cared for the

element of unpredictability, but in Annie it was occasionally amusing.

"To begin with, stay right where you are." She circled the bed to stand directly in front of him. "Don't move."

"If that's what you want." Curiosity consumed him as he looked down at her. "What are you going to do?"

"We're going to play a game. First, I'm going to undress you." Annie went to work on the buttons of his shirt. Her fingers were unsteady, but it was clear that she was determined.

"All right." Oliver reached for the hem of her ribbed pullover.

"Oh, no you don't." Annie stepped back and lightly slapped his hand aside. "You can't touch me. It's one of the rules."

"We're playing this game by a set of rules?"

"Yes." She moved in close and went back to work on his shirt buttons.

He smiled, prepared to be indulgent. But when her fingertips skated down his chest, he sucked in his breath. "Annie..."

"You're not supposed to move, remember?" She looked up at him from beneath her lashes as she pushed his shirt off his shoulders. "I've been telling you all along, Oliver, that you've got a very strong, controlling personality. You need to learn to lie back and let someone else take charge once in a while."

"But I like being in charge." He nuzzled her throat as his shirt fell to the floor at his feet. "Especially of you."

"I know you do. Stop that. You're not allowed to kiss me yet."

"Why not?"

"Because I said so. This is my game, remember?" Annie stepped back and surveyed his bare chest. Her eyes warmed with feminine appreciation. She reached out to stroke the curve of his shoulder.

The look in her eyes sent desire pulsing through him. No doubt about it, she definitely wanted him, just as she had from the beginning. Oliver felt himself suddenly turn very hard, very fast. It occurred to him that it was getting increasingly difficult to control himself around Annie.

Instinctively he took a step toward her, but he stopped obediently when she shook her head and gave him a mysterious smile.

"Aren't you going to take your clothes off?" he asked as she fumbled with his belt.

"Eventually."

"That sounds like a long time from now." He drew in his stomach when he heard the metallic slide of the zipper. Damn it, he was already fully aroused and Annie hadn't even got her own clothes off yet.

She kissed him full on the mouth, but before he could get his tongue between her lips, she was moving, sliding sinuously down the length of him. Her lips brushed his chest, his right nipple, and then his navel.

Then she was on her knees in front of him. Oliver groaned as Annie's hands slipped inside the waistband of his trousers and pushed them down over his thighs. His briefs went to the floor along with his pants.

He shuddered, acutely aware of his heavy erection. He could feel Annie's breath on him. When her fingers circled him with a featherlight touch, he wondered in shock if he was going to explode right then and there. What in hell was happening to him, he wondered.

"You're beautiful," Annie whispered.

"Annie, this has gone far enough." He buried his fingers in her hair. "Let's get into bed."

"All right." She rose smoothly. Her eyes were shimmering as she reached down to toss back the black and gold comforter. "Go ahead, lie down."

He tried to wrap his hand around the nape of her neck and pull her close. He wanted to put his tongue into her mouth and sink his throbbing manhood into her sweet heat. This was insane. One night away from her and he was wild.

"Oh, no you don't. Not yet. On the bed." She planted her hands against his chest and urged him backward.

Oliver allowed himself to be pushed down onto the gray sheets. He reached up for Annie, but she side-stepped his groping hand.

"What about you?" he asked, frowning.

"I'm going to get undressed."

"About time," he growled. "I'll help."

"No, you'll watch." She crossed her arms beneath her breasts, grasped the hem of her pullover, and eased it off over her head.

Oliver felt the fever within him rise several more degrees at the sight of her breasts cupped in a lacy little black bra. It occurred to him that he had never seen Annie wear black lingerie. He watched, fascinated, as she reached behind herself to unfasten the clasp of the bra. An instant later her breasts were free.

Oliver's mouth went dry. Her breasts enthralled him. They were perfect, elegantly shaped, and crowned with full, rosy nipples. He remembered the taste of them and suddenly he was starving. Once more he reached for her. Once more she stepped back.

"You're taking your time about this, aren't you?" he asked roughly.

Annie's fingers paused on the fastening of her jeans. She gave him an uncertain, disappointed look. "Don't you like it?"

He stared at her breasts, his body wracked with an aching need that was rapidly driving him to the brink of sanity. "I like it very much."

"I'm glad." She wriggled out of her jeans, leaving behind only a triangle of black satin. She took a tentative step toward the bed.

Oliver caught the faint, tantalizing scent of her arousal. His whole body clenched in response. He dragged his eyes from the black satin panties to her face.

"Come here," he ordered, his voice husky with desire.

She shook her head and put one knee on the bed. She wrapped her palm around the rigid muscle of his upper thigh and squeezed. "Not just yet. We have a long way to go, Oliver. A very long way."

"The hell we do." He reached for her.

Annie scooted quickly out of the way. "This is my game, remember? I'm the one in charge."

He swore under his breath and sprawled reluctantly back against the pillows. "Annie, I can't take much more of this little game of yours."

"Really? I'm surprised at you, Oliver." She got up off the bed and walked over to the black-lacquered chest of drawers. "You're the one who taught me this game."

He scowled at the pale, rounded curve of her shoulder and buttocks. "What are you talking about?"

She turned toward him, holding up two silk ties that she had taken from the drawer. "You've been giving me lessons in this game since the first night you made love to me, although I'll admit you never actually tied me to the bedposts."

"Hell." It finally dawned on him just what she intended to do. He eyed the neckties warily. "You're not serious about this, are you? I thought I was the one with the reputation for being weird."

"Don't worry, the neckties are merely symbolic," she said quickly. "We both know they couldn't hold you. Not if you really wanted to be free."

"Look, Annie, I'm willing to play bedroom games, but I think this is taking things a little too far."

She walked to the side of the bed and looped one of the ties around his left wrist. "You're not afraid of me, are you, Oliver?"

His eyes met hers. Surely she didn't think he was actually going to submit to being tied to the bed. Anger flowed through his aroused body. He'd had enough of this crazy game. He was going to rip his hand free of the stupid strip of silk and then he was going to drag Annie down onto the bed. He was going to make love to her until she couldn't even think, let alone dream up bondage games.

"Oliver?" Annie looked down into his face and hesitated again.

He saw the new awareness in her eyes. She knew the idiotic game had gone too far. She sensed that he was going to take control once more.

He was always in control. He had to be in control because he could not trust anyone else.

216

But even as Oliver started to twist his hand free, something stopped him. In a disconcerting flash of insight, he realized that this was no game to Annie. She was trying to make him understand something that was very important to her.

For a few seconds neither of them moved. Then Oliver slowly relaxed against the pillows. "If you want to play games, Annie, go ahead."

Her smile was brilliant. "That's another thing I like about you, Oliver, you're willing to play fair."

Annie wasted no time. With a few deft movements, she anchored his left wrist to the bedpost. Then she scrambled over the top of him and quickly went to work on his right hand. Oliver closed his eyes and gritted his teeth when he felt the touch of her satin panties against his throbbing erection. It was going to be a long night.

13

It was a thousand times worse than Oliver had expected. Annie was far from being a skilled courtesan, just the opposite, but her effect on him was devastating. Her somewhat naive but nevertheless passionate assault upon his body constituted a scene straight out of an erotic dream.

Make that nightmare, he thought ruefully at one point.

She was all over him, warm and silky and exquisitely female. Her fingers traced the contours of his chest, sending ripples of intense pleasure through him. Then they dipped lower, clenching lightly in the dark, curling hair below his abdomen. When her head bent to follow her questing hand, Oliver experienced an ecstasy that was just short of agony. He held his breath.

"Annie," he managed, his voice tight and harsh, "I don't think this is going to work."

"How can you say that?" Her breath was tantalizingly warm on his stiff, rigid flesh. "It's working beautifully. Just the way the book said it would." Her teeth nipped gently.

Oliver clenched his jaw. "What book?"

"The one I read to get ready for tonight. It's called *Three Nights Among the Amazons*."

Oliver realized he was rapidly losing the thread of the conversation. "You've been studying for this?"

"Of course. I wanted to get it right." Annie touched him intimately with the tip of her tongue.

Oliver thought he would shatter. It was all he could do not to tear his hands free of the strips of silk that bound him. "Why did you feel you had to study for this?"

"I wanted you to understand what it's like, Oliver."

"What the hell are you talking about?"

She kissed the inside of his thigh. "I wanted you to know what it feels like to be the one who isn't in control."

Oliver tried to concentrate on what she was saying and failed. Her teasing mouth had moved down to his knee. He wanted her lips back where they had been a moment ago, covering him like a liquid glove. "Later," he bit out. "We'll talk about this later."

"All right."

Her soft voice was a hot flame on his tortured skin. Oliver was stunned to discover that the insides of his legs were so sensitive.

"That's enough, Annie," he said persuasively. "Let's finish this the way it was meant to be finished."

"There's no rush. We've got all night. Isn't that what you tell me whenever I start to beg?"

Oliver slitted his eyes. He could see her tousled curls moving between his legs. The sight drove him closer to the edge. "I'm not begging," he said very deliberately. "I'm telling you that if you don't finish what you've started, I'll finish it for you."

Annie lifted her head, her eyes filled with silent, sensual laughter. "If that's what you want to do, I can't stop you."

"I'm glad you realize it."

"You're a lot bigger than I am." She smiled with blatant satisfaction as she stroked his aroused body. "Big enough and strong enough to free yourself. But that would ruin my game."

"Annie, for God's sake, sweetheart, enough is enough. I can't last any longer."

"Now you know how I feel." She cupped him gently in her hand. "Let yourself go, Oliver. I'm the one in control tonight."

"You think you're in control here?" he asked in disbelief.

"Yes." Annie glided up along his body, crushing him softly beneath her. Breasts pillowed against his chest, she kissed his throat. "And I'm going to try to prove it."

"How?"

"You'll see." She nibbled on his ear and squirmed lightly on top of his aroused manhood.

Oliver thought he was going to lose his mind. His fingers clenched around his silken bonds. No woman had ever made him feel this close to the edge. "Annie, you don't know what you're doing."

"Yes, I do. I read the whole book first. My goal is to make you lose control tonight, Oliver. I want to make you go wild."

He stared at her, utterly baffled. "Why would you want to do that?"

"Because it's what you do to me." She nipped his shoulder. "I'm going to show you what it's like to be helpless. I'm going to give you a taste of your own medicine, Oliver. I'm going to take you to the edge if I can and I'm going to push you over."

"What about you?" he said through his teeth.

"Me?" Annie raised her head and smiled again. "I'm going to watch you."

"*Watch me*?"

"That's right. The way you watch me when you make love to me."

"You like the way I make love to you," Oliver whispered. "I know you do. You can't hide it."

"No, I can't hide it, can I? But I don't like being the only one who loses control when we make love. I don't like feeling that I'm a puppet and you're the puppet master. I don't like knowing that I don't have the same effect on you that you have on me."

"This is crazy."

She ground her hips against his, clamping him firmly between her thighs. He could feel her black satin panties gliding along his engorged shaft. It was almost too much. Oliver nearly exploded then and there. He fought and won the battle for his self-control one more time, but he knew he probably would not win the next skirmish.

"You know what, Oliver?" Annie shifted enticingly. "After you've surrendered, I just might make you do it again. And again. And again. Until you can't stand it any more. And then, when I'm ready, maybe I'll let you come inside me."

Outrage pulsed through Oliver, mingling with the hot lava of desire that was already pouring through his veins. "This has gone far enough."

"We haven't even begun."

"The hell we haven't." Oliver tore his hands free of the silk ties that had bound him to the bed. He reached for Annie.

She did not attempt to draw back as his hands closed around her arms. There was no fear in her, only an unmistakable gleam of triumph in her eyes. Oliver ignored it as he rolled her onto her back and covered her body with his own. Nothing else mattered now except sheathing himself inside her.

"Sweet witch." Oliver reached down between their bodies and yanked at the scrap of black satin that barred his way. "What have you done to me?" Her panties were damp, he realized. She was ready for him.

The panties tore in his hands. Startled by the sound of rending silk, Oliver stopped fumbling with the scrap of fabric. He grabbed Annie's knees, lifting them, pressing her thighs open. His fingers brushed against her inviting warmth, parting her.

"God, yes." He plunged into her, driving himself to the hilt in one long, heavy stroke.

Annie gasped at the invasion. Oliver was shocked back into full awareness. He knew at once that although she was moist, she wasn't anywhere near the point of release. He was way ahead of her, almost to the edge.

Dismay collided with passion as Oliver realized he could not muster enough control to last long enough for a second stroke.

It was all over in an instant. His scorching climax swept through him like a firestorm, hot and ungovernable.

He was out of control.

* * *

Oliver roused himself a long time later. He pushed himself up on his elbows and looked down at Annie. She smiled tentatively. In the cold light of his returning sanity and self-control, Oliver saw the wariness in her eyes.

Oliver touched her cheek. "Is that what it's like for you?"

"I don't know." She searched his eyes. "How did it feel?"

"Intense." He thought about it. "Good, but not good enough."

"Why not?"

"You weren't with me."

"That's how it feels when you make love to me, Oliver. It's an incredibly erotic experience, but I feel like I'm going through it by myself. It's as if you're always holding back, watching me."

"Pulling the strings?"

"Yes."

"Hell." Oliver eased himself from Annie's body and rolled onto his back beside her. He was grimly aware that she had not found her satisfaction. "If you'd let me stay in charge, we both would be in the same condition now."

"No, we wouldn't. You'd still be exercising that amazing self-discipline of yours. You'd make me come two or three more times before you'd allow yourself to finish."

Oliver slanted her a sidelong glance. "I *make* you come?"

"Well, yes. That's what it feels like." Annie turned onto her side, folded her arms on top of his chest, and gazed soberly down at him. "Over and over again. As often as you want. I've never felt so helpless in my life as I am when you make love to me."

"And you don't like feeling helpless in my arms, is that it?"

"You don't understand. Sometimes it feels great to

be helpless. But not all the time. I need to know that I have as much power over you as you do over me."

"This is about power?"

"In a way. I want us to be equals in this, Oliver. After all, we're lovers, right?"

"Damn right."

"Well, then, sex should be something we share, not a contest of wills."

"I didn't realize you saw it as a contest of wills."

Annie smiled. "I know. You just wanted to please me. I appreciate it, Oliver. Honest, I do. But I want to know that I can please you, too. Don't you understand?"

He studied her intently. "I think I'm beginning to figure out what's going on here."

Disappointment welled up in her eyes. "And you don't like it, do you?"

"I didn't say that." He threaded his fingers through her wild curls. "It's just that the basic concepts are new to me. You've got to give me time to make adjustments."

Annie brightened. "Don't worry, I will. All the time you want, Oliver. I promise."

"Thank you. I'll do my best to get it right." He slid his hand down over her hip and buried his fingers in the triangle of honey-colored curls that shielded her softness.

"Oliver?"

"If we're going to try for a more egalitarian approach to lovemaking, we both have to start off on an equal footing. Don't you agree?"

"I suppose so." Annie shivered delightfully as his fingers found her.

"We want to be sure we start even." He wrapped

his hand around the back of her head and brought her face down to his. "That means you have to catch up with me."

"Maybe we should talk about this a bit more. I'm not sure you've really got a handle on the concept I'm trying to get across here."

"This time we'll make it happen together, Annie. I swear it."

"You're sure?"

"I'm sure."

She sighed happily and ducked her head to kiss him. "I knew you'd get the point. You're not nearly as arrogant and thick-headed as everyone seems to think you are."

"I appreciate your confidence in me. A man needs to know his wife believes in him."

A long while later Annie curled contentedly against the hard length of Oliver's warm body. There were definitely some positive aspects to her husband's formidable self-mastery. He had promised her they would reach the peak together, and he had delivered on that promise. He had been with her all the way.

They had gone over the edge together, and it had been a stunning experience.

Annie was feeling quite optimistic about the future tonight. She stirred against Oliver. When his arm tightened around her, she knew he was still awake.

"Oliver, I've been thinking."

"I hope this isn't about another book you've been reading."

"I'm not joking," she said.

"Who's joking?" His mouth curved faintly. "All right, what were you thinking about?"

"The way you handled Paul Shore tonight." She smiled. "I was very proud of you."

Oliver did not move. "I barely spoke to him."

"Yes, I know, but you agreed to talk to him when he suggested it. You invited him to meet with you. It was a wonderful first step."

"Is that how you saw it?"

She turned her head on the pillow and studied his expressionless profile. "I know it must have been difficult for you after all these years and after all that happened between the two of you."

"It was not exactly a pleasure," Oliver said without any inflection.

"I realize that. But you did the right thing. You took the olive branch that Paul Shore extended. Valerie and Carson must be feeling enormously relieved tonight.

"Do you think so?"

"I'm sure of it." Annie put her arm behind her head and gazed up at the shadowed ceiling. "Something tells me that the meeting between you and Shore will go very well."

"Forget Shore." Oliver turned and gathered her into his arms. "There's something I've been meaning to ask you."

"What's that?"

"Where did you get the book you used to study for this evening's performance?"

"*Three Nights Among the Amazons*?" Annie chuckled. "Arthur Quigley, the man who owns the bookshop next to Wildest Dreams, recommended it to me. All in all, I think it was a good choice."

"You asked the owner of that bookshop for a recommendation?"

Annie sensed that Oliver was not pleased. "There's no need to be embarrassed," she assured him. "Arthur is a very good friend of mine. He understood."

"What exactly," Oliver asked, "did this good friend of yours understand?"

"Don't worry, I was very subtle about the whole thing."

"Tell me, how do you make a subtle request for a book like *Three Nights Among the Amazons*?"

Annie cleared her throat discreetly. "I merely explained that I wanted a book that would give us some inspiration."

"Inspiration?"

"Arthur was very nice about it. After all, we're newlyweds, remember. People realize that newlyweds fumble around a lot at first."

"Fumble around?" Oliver repeated ominously.

"It's nothing to be ashamed of," Annie said quickly. "No one expects you to be a perfect lover right from the start."

"I don't believe this."

Annie bit her lip. "Are you angry?"

"Me? Angry? Whatever gave you that idea? Just how good a friend is this Quigley?"

"I told you, very good. Arthur used to have a terrible problem with shyness. He would bury himself in his bookshop and virtually ignore his customers. It was sad. He didn't sell many books and he never dated. A very lonely man."

"Until you came along?" Oliver asked coolly.

Annie smiled and shrugged. "Arthur and I became friends a few months before I opened up my shop. We went out together for a while. But I wouldn't say we dated. Mostly we talked business. I always knew

Arthur and I would never be more than friends and I think Arthur knew it, too."

"Is that right? What did you two do when you got together?"

"We talked a lot. And after a time he began to get over his shyness."

"Amazing."

"It was really. And rather gratifying," Annie admitted proudly. "He even began to date. In fact, I introduced him to the woman he eventually married. She was a little shy, too. Arthur helped her get over it. They had a lot in common."

"Quigley sounds like another Melvin Finch."

"Melvin?" Annie considered that. "Oh, no, Arthur and Melvin are really quite different. Melvin had a problem relating to his father if you'll recall. He wasn't shy like Arthur."

"How many Arthurs and Melvins do you know?"

Annie frowned. "I don't understand."

"Never mind." Oliver sat up amid the rumpled sheets. "Where are my neckties?"

"They're probably crushed by now. Don't worry, I'll iron them for you." Annie scrabbled about behind the pillow until her fingers closed around a strip of silk. She held it aloft triumphantly. "Got one. I'm sure the other is around here somewhere."

"That's all right." Oliver took the necktie from her. He grasped it firmly in both hands and pulled it taut, testing the strength of the silk. "One will do nicely."

"What are you going to do?"

"Fumble around a little." He reached out and caught her gently by the wrist.

"*Oliver.* You wouldn't."

But she saw the new sexy laughter in his eyes and

228

something within her responded joyously. She started to giggle. It was going to be all right, she thought. Oliver was finally learning how to play in bed.

At eleven o'clock the next morning Annie sat behind her desk at Wildest Dreams. She was gazing at the pile of paperwork spread out on her desk, but her thoughts were on the events of the preceding evening.

Oliver was making terrific progress.

True, he would probably have occasional lapses, she thought. It was only to be expected. A leopard did not change its spots overnight. She had to remember that he was not accustomed to the notion of sharing power in anything, let alone in a relationship. He was accustomed to being the one in command. But he was learning. That was the important thing.

Deep down, Oliver was a fundamentally decent man, an honorable man. His problem was that he'd been forced to be strong for so long that it was second nature to him now. He instinctively exercised power in everything, including his interpersonal relationships.

But last night he had proven he was capable of modifying his behavior. He was trying to change. For her sake.

Annie hugged the knowledge to her and began to hum a cheery off-key tune as she pored over a small catalog.

She was preparing an order when a slight sound in the doorway made her look up. She smiled when she saw who stood there. "Hi, Valerie, come on in."

"I'm sorry to bother you." Valerie's eyes were shadowed. "I like your shop. You have an interesting collection."

229

"Thanks. No priceless Pre-Columbian gold, but we're getting by. Sit down." Annie waved her to a seat on the other side of the desk. "How did things go at the Shores' benefit after Oliver and I left?"

"Fine. No one made any acutely embarrassing comments about Oliver to my face if that's what you mean."

"Not exactly."

Valerie hesitated. "Annie, I want to talk to you about last night."

Annie closed the catalog. "What about it?"

"I heard Oliver ask Paul Shore to schedule a meeting."

"Yes, I know." Annie grinned smugly. "A good first step, don't you think?"

Valerie searched her face anxiously. "That's what I wanted to ask you. Do you really think Oliver intends to make his peace with Mr. Shore?"

"Yes, I do." Annie leaned back in her chair, feeling very wise and very sure of her analysis of Oliver. "Your brother is a bit stubborn."

"You can say that again."

"And he's a trifle arrogant."

Valerie grimaced. "Tyrannical would be a better word."

"But," Annie said as she held up a hand, "he's also very smart."

"Okay, I'll give you that."

Annie chuckled. "Smart enough to know when he's fighting a losing battle. I think he realizes that the relationship between you and Carson is not something he can control. So he's decided to mend some fences with Paul Shore in an effort to create harmony between the families."

Valerie twisted her hands in her lap. "I wish I could believe that. I want to believe it."

"Believe it." Annie smiled. "And give your brother some credit. He's doing this for you, Valerie. Family always comes first with Oliver."

Valerie gave her an odd look. "But he made terrible threats."

"That's all they were, empty threats. He would never tear the family apart," Annie said gently.

"The other night when I talked to him he made it clear he would do anything in his power to prevent me from marrying Carson."

Annie shrugged. "Oliver probably just needed a little time to think things over. To accept the fact that he was powerless to stop you. It wasn't easy for him. Oliver hates being powerless, you know."

"I realize that." Valerie sighed. "And I know that the family is all-important to him. Everything he's done since Dad died was for us. He was more like a father than a brother. A real, old-fashioned patriarch."

"I understand." Annie smiled. "The problem with patriarchs is that they have the defects of their virtues. The qualities that make them strong enough to hold a family together during hard times are the same qualities that can get in their way when it comes to dealing with people in a sensitive, understanding manner."

"My brother doesn't know the meaning of the words *sensitive* and *understanding*. As far as he's concerned, things get done his way or they don't get done at all."

Annie stopped smiling. "Don't you think you're being a little hard on Oliver? He's not nearly as tough and uncompromising as you seem to think he is."

"You don't know him as well as the rest of us do."

Valerie eyed her with sudden, hopeful speculation. "But maybe you're right. Maybe you're having a positive effect on him. Maybe marriage is mellowing him."

Annie laughed, aware of a bubbling sense of optimism welling up within her. "Count on it."

The phone rang again on Monday. Annie was busy rearranging a display featuring a giraffe-shaped coat rack. She let Ella take the call.

"Wildest Dreams." Ella listened and then beckoned Annie toward the counter. "She's right here. Hold on a minute." She clamped a palm over the receiver. "It's for you. The other Mrs. Rain."

Annie stifled a groan as she walked back to the counter and picked up the phone. "Hello, Sybil."

"I just talked to Valerie," Sybil said without preamble. Her voice was laced with urgency. "She told me what happened Friday night."

"You're referring to Oliver and Paul Shore running into each other at the arts benefit, I assume?"

"What's going on? Did Oliver really tell Shore he would meet with him?"

"Yes, that's exactly what happened," Annie confirmed proudly. "Oliver and Mr. Shore are going to mend the breach for Valerie and Carson's sake."

"Damn."

"I know. Valerie was equally stunned. You know something, it seems to me that none of you give Oliver enough credit for being a basically reasonable human being."

"Reasonable." Sybil sounded dazed. "You're right. That's not a word that crops up a lot in conversations about Oliver. Annie, this is so sad. Poor Valerie. And poor Carson. He's really a nice young man. But I knew Oliver would never allow the two of them to get together."

Annie glared at the receiver. "What are you talking about? I just told you that Oliver is going to meet with Shore."

"If you think that Oliver is going to talk peace at that meeting, you're even more naive than I originally believed. Listen to me, Annie, if Oliver has agreed to meet with Paul Shore, it's because he's got ammunition to use against him."

"That's not true." Annie was outraged. No one, apparently, had any faith in Oliver's underlying integrity.

Sybil ignored the outburst. Her tone turned thoughtful. "My bet is that Oliver's got something on Shore, something he's held in reserve all these years, just in case he ever needed it. And now the time has come."

"That's ridiculous."

"He'll probably use whatever he's dug up to blackmail Shore into forcing poor Carson to break off the engagement."

"You're making my husband sound like Machiavelli," Annie stormed.

"Oliver could have given Machiavelli lessons."

"Damn it, Sybil, I refuse to believe Oliver is scheming to blackmail Paul Shore."

"Then you're a fool. I've known Oliver Rain a lot longer than you have. I know what he's capable of doing. I also know how much he hates Paul Shore. Oliver would never tolerate a marriage between Valerie and Carson. Even if they managed to elope, Oliver would find a way to destroy their happiness. He'd break up the marriage if it was the last thing he did. But knowing Oliver, he'll stop it before it even takes place."

"You're wrong."

"Think so? Wait and see. You've got a lot to learn about the man you married. Good-bye, Annie." Sybil hung up the phone.

Annie stood listening to the dial tone for half a minute.

"Problem?" Ella asked.

"No." Annie tapped her toe. "At least I don't think so. But maybe I'd better not take any chances."

She dialed the number of Daniel's office, knowing his secretary would answer.

"Lyncroft Unlimited." Mrs. Jameson's voice was warm and businesslike, as usual.

"It's me, Annie."

"Hello, Annie. Good to hear from you. I suppose you want to talk to Mr. Rain? Unfortunately, he just left."

"No," Annie said quickly, "I don't want to talk to him." She thought quickly. "I just need to know his schedule. I'm supposed to coordinate something around it. I understand Oliver and Paul Shore might be meeting in the near future?"

"Oh, yes. Mr. Shore's secretary called first thing this morning. Mr. Rain and Mr. Shore are doing lunch today."

Annie was floored. "They are?"

"As a matter of fact, Mr. Rain is on his way to Mr. Shore's club even as we speak."

Annie was overwhelmed by a horrible sense of foreboding. Realistically speaking, she had to admit there was a very faint possibility that Sybil might just be right. Annie didn't want to believe that Oliver was scheming to ruin Valerie's happiness, but she suddenly didn't want to take any chances, either. Oliver had only just begun to change his ways, after all.

Better to be safe than sorry.

"They're meeting today, you say?" Annie clutched the receiver tightly and glanced at her watch. "Do you know which club, by any chance?"

"Certainly. Mr. Shore's secretary gave me the information." Mrs. Jameson rattled off the name of the exclusive club. "It's right downtown."

"Thanks." Annie hung up the phone.

"Everything okay?" Ella asked.

"Yes," Annie said. "I'm sure it is. But I'd better make certain. I'll be back after lunch."

She grabbed her purse and tore out of the shop at a run. Paul Shore's club was only a few blocks away.

It was unfortunate that it was raining.

14

Oliver was unpleasantly aware of the uneasy, almost eerie feeling he experienced when he walked into the dining room of Paul Shore's club.

His father had once belonged to this club. It was the first time Oliver had been inside it since Edward Rain's disappearance. Oliver did not belong to any private clubs. He was too much of a loner by nature. Even if he had chosen to join one, he reflected, it would most definitely not be this one. Paul Shore was, after all, a member.

Little had changed in the club in the years since he had last been here, Oliver noted. With one obvious exception. Today there was a handful of women wearing expensive business suits sitting at a few of the tables. Apparently the old boy network had been invaded to some degree.

But other than that, it was all much the same as it had been the day his father had brought him here to buy him a drink. The occasion had been Oliver's twenty-first birthday. He remembered it well. It was one of the very few times when he and his father had simply sat and talked to each other. The conversation had not been particularly memorable. Edward had asked Oliver how his studies were going. Oliver had waxed enthusiastic about his plans for graduate

236

school. Nothing earthshaking. They had just talked for a while, father and son.

Everything looked the same as it had on that day. The walls were still paneled in rich, dark oak. There was a muted sound of fine silver and china clinking in the background. An air of hushed importance hovered over the tables where the movers and shakers of Seattle met to talk about politics and the economy of the Pacific Rim.

Memories of his twenty-first birthday made Oliver's stomach tighten when he walked past the table where he and his father had sat. He wondered fleetingly what he would have said to his father all those years ago if he could have foreseen the future. The words rose, hot and furious in his mind.

You son of a bitch, you can't do this to us. You can't just walk off and leave us, you bastard. It's not right. What about the girls? They'll be devastated. Now that Mom's gone, you're all they've got left. And you've got two young sons who need you. Nathan and Richard are just babies. They need their father. Hell, I need you. Don't we matter to you? Don't you care about your family, goddamn it?

Oliver clamped down on the raging anger and pain. If he could go back in time to that day when he had sat here talking with his father, he would not have pleaded with him. Oliver clenched one hand into a fist at his side. He would not have begged, he promised himself. He would not have sacrificed his pride in an effort to persuade Edward to do his duty by his family.

But deep inside Oliver knew that was exactly what he would have done. If there had been even a ghost of a chance of convincing his father to stay, Oliver knew he would have gone down on his knees.

Now, sixteen years later as he walked into the club, he faced the truth that had been with him all along. He had never begged for anything in his life. But if he could go back to the day of his twenty-first birthday knowing then what he knew now, he would have shredded his pride to ribbons in an effort to keep his father from walking out.

I've done the best I could but there were so many times when it wasn't enough. So many times when I wasn't sure what to do. They needed you, Dad. You were their father. You were my father. And you left us behind as if we didn't matter at all.

Oliver confronted the evidence of the weakness that still resided within himself. He tried to will it out of existence but he knew it would never disappear. He would fight it for the rest of his life.

"Mr. Rain?" The maitre d' loomed in Oliver's path.

"Yes."

"Mr. Shore is expecting you. Please follow me, sir."

Paul Shore was sitting at a table near the window. Like an aging gunslinger hardened from too many years of dealing with young guns, he sat facing the room, his back to the wall. There was a half-finished martini on the table in front of him. He nodded brusquely in greeting as Oliver sat down, but he did not offer his hand.

"Can I get you something from the bar, Mr. Rain?" the waiter asked.

Oliver glanced at Shore's martini. "No."

Something flickered in Shore's gaze as the waiter handed over the menus and withdrew. "Well, Rain, it's been a long time."

"Has it?" Oliver did not touch the menu.

"This isn't going to be easy, is it?" Shore took a sip of his martini, as if fortifying himself.

Oliver studied his nemesis, assessing again in the light of day the impression he'd gotten Friday night. There was no doubt about it, Shore looked a lot older than he had on the occasion when Oliver had gone to pay off the Rain debt. It was not simply a matter of the years that had passed. There was a deep weariness etched in Shore's face. There was also caution. But underlying it all, Oliver thought he detected a silent plea for a truce.

That hint of an unvoiced appeal was all Oliver needed. It signaled a weakness he knew he could use to his own advantage.

"There's no point wasting our time in a rehash of the past," Oliver said.

"Isn't there? When you get to be my age, Rain, you'll find that you spend a great deal of time rehashing the past. You look back and wonder what you might have done differently if you had the chance to do it over again."

"Don't tell me you have any regrets."

"We all have regrets. You'll know what I mean thirty years from now."

Oliver looked at him. "I'll keep that in mind."

"You do that." Shore took another swallow from his martini and then pushed the glass to one side. "Why did you agree to meet with me today?"

"You know the answer to that."

"Carson and Valerie."

"Yes."

"I realize that finding out about their intention to marry must have come as a shock to you," Shore said.

"It certainly did to me." His gaze sharpened. "But there's something I want you to know."

"What's that?"

"Carson is a fine young man. I'm proud of my son." Shore rubbed the bridge of his nose. "I used to think he was weak."

"Did you?"

"I was furious when he chose the academic world instead of my world. It was hard for me to accept the fact that he wasn't cut out for business. But he's not weak. In fact, lately I've begun to believe that he's stronger than I ever was."

"An interesting assessment," Oliver said.

Shore narrowed his eyes. "What I'm trying to make you understand is that Carson is not like me. Or you, for that matter."

"What's that supposed to mean?"

"It means I don't want your judgment of him to be biased because of your old hatred of me, damn it."

Oliver felt cold satisfaction. Shore was more vulnerable than he could have imagined. Desperate, even. The older man's control was close to snapping. There was no point drawing out the cat-and-mouse game any longer. It was time for the kill.

"I think we should talk about your son," Oliver said very softly.

Relief flared in Shore's eyes. "I'm hoping you'll give him a fair chance. He's going to be very successful in his field. And he cares very deeply about Valerie. She'll be good for him. Hell, my wife says they're made for each other. I want my son to be happy, Rain."

"Do you?"

Shore frowned. "I'm assuming you're here today

because you want the same for your sister. It's time for you and me to make peace."

"You misunderstood me, Shore," Oliver said. "When I said we should talk about your son, I was referring to your other son, Hammond."

"Hammond," Shore repeated in disbelief.

"You remember him. He's the one you had to pack off for an extended vacation abroad two years ago after you found out he'd defrauded investors in that development firm you bought for him."

Shore's face sagged. "Jesus, man, how did you find out about that?"

Oliver shrugged. "A little research. Tell me, Shore, how much did it cost you to buy your oldest son out of that mess? You did a neat job of it, I'll grant you that. There wasn't a hint of it in the media. And no charges were filed. Very smoothly handled."

"My God, that's why you agreed to meet me today." Shore's eyes widened. "You're going to blackmail me, aren't you? You're going to threaten to leak the whole story to the press if I don't find a way to force Carson to end his engagement to your sister."

Oliver said nothing. He was content to let the full impact of the revelation take its toll before he went on to the next stage of his carefully orchestrated battle plan.

He was weighing the effects of his first missile, choosing the next target site, when a small flurry of commotion across the room caught his attention.

Annie's voice sang out, clear as a bell above the muted hum of serious conversation. "Kindly take your hands off me. I told you, I'm Mrs. Oliver Rain and I'm here to join my husband. He's right over there."

Startled, Oliver turned his head just in time to see

241

Annie, her curls a wild, frizzy halo around her head, break free of the grasp of the maitre d'. She dashed across the room, sailing toward the table where he and Shore were seated.

"I'm sorry, madam, but I cannot allow you in without an invitation from one of the members," the maitre d' said urgently as he trotted after her. "If you will please wait in the lobby, I'm sure we can settle this matter."

"There's nothing to worry about," Annie called back over her shoulder. "I told you my husband was here."

She skidded to a halt beside the table Oliver was sharing with Shore. "Hi, Oliver." She bent her head and gave him a quick wifely peck on the cheek. "Had a little trouble getting in here. I told you I don't look like a Mrs. Oliver Rain."

She was breathless, Oliver realized. And damp from the rain. She must have run all the way from Wildest Dreams.

"What are you doing here, Annie?" he asked as he got slowly to his feet. "Is something wrong?"

"Not a thing." She patted him reassuringly on the shoulder and turned her radiant smile on Shore. "Good afternoon, Mr. Shore. Lovely party. Hope you made lots and lots of money for the arts."

Shore gazed at her in obvious confusion. "Mrs. Rain."

"You remembered my name," Annie said in delight as she seated herself. "Wasn't Raphaela's work terrific? Raphaela was the designer who did your place for the benefit. I don't know if you happened to notice the cloisonné elephant in the solarium. It came from my shop."

"Did it?" Shore looked even more confused.

"Yes, and I must say, it looked right at home in your solarium." Annie leaned forward and added in a confidential tone, "It's for sale, you know."

"I see."

The maitre d' apparently realized he would not have to throw Annie out. He backed off hurriedly and signaled to a waiter.

Shore stared at Annie. "I wasn't aware you were joining us today."

"Neither was I," Oliver said coldly.

Annie's smile did the impossible and brightened another few watts. "I managed to get free for lunch after all. Thanks for waiting for me." She picked up a menu. "I'm starving. This is your club, Mr. Shore. What do you recommend?"

"The halibut," Shore said automatically. "They do it very nicely here." He couldn't seem to take his eyes off Annie.

"Sounds great." Annie looked up at the waiter. "I'll have the halibut. No salad. And coffee, please."

"Yes, ma'am."

"Now, then." Annie folded the menu with a snap. "What is everyone else having?"

Shore glanced from Annie to Oliver and then turned to the waiter. "Halibut."

Annie gave Oliver an expectant look. "What are you having, Oliver?"

"I wasn't planning on having anything," Oliver said pointedly.

"Nonsense. You don't have to diet. You get plenty of exercise." Annie gave the waiter a sunny smile. "He'll have the halibut, too."

"Yes, ma'am." The waiter nodded quickly, apparently having decided that Annie was in charge. He turned away before Oliver could cancel the order.

Oliver gazed thoughtfully at Annie and wondered how she'd look being carted out of the club over his shoulder. "How did you know where to find me?"

"When I phoned your office, Mrs. Jameson told me you were meeting Mr. Shore for lunch."

"I must remember to fire Mrs. Jameson when I return to the office."

"Don't even joke about doing any such thing. You'd be lost without her." Annie turned back to Shore. "I didn't mean to interrupt the conversation."

"The hell you didn't," Oliver muttered. He was almost certain he knew what was going on. Annie had gotten wind of this meeting and had surmised it was not going to proceed along the lines she thought it should. He wondered who had tipped her off. He had confided in no one, which probably meant Sybil had talked to her. Sybil knew him all too well.

"Please continue with whatever it was you were discussing when I arrived," Annie urged Shore.

Shore looked at Oliver. "We were talking about my son," he said quietly.

"Carson?" Annie nodded. "He seems awfully nice. I understand he teaches art history. You must be very proud of him."

"I am," Shore said, his eyes still on Oliver.

"We weren't talking about Carson." Oliver frowned. It dawned on him that Annie's presence was going to make things awkward, just as she must have known it would.

Annie looked inquiringly at Shore. "You have another son?"

"Yes, I do," Shore said evenly. "His name is Hammond."

"Does he live here in Seattle?" Annie asked.

"Not at the moment." Shore hesitated. "He's living out of the country. A company in which I have an interest has recently expanded overseas. Hammond is working at one of their foreign offices."

"How interesting," Annie said.

"Your husband certainly seems to think so." Shore signaled for another martini. "He's going to try to blackmail me because of it."

Annie's relentlessly cheerful smile vanished in the blink of an eye. "Don't be ridiculous. Oliver would never blackmail anyone. Would you, Oliver?"

"Of course not," Oliver said very softly.

"I think," Annie said firmly, "that someone should tell me what is going on here."

Shore's eyes were bleak as he met Oliver's across the table. "Your husband has somehow learned that my son Hammond got himself into serious financial trouble two years ago. There were questions of fraud. I took care of the matter. I reimbursed those who had been hurt by my son's actions. And then I sent Hammond out of the country for a while."

"How terrible for you," Annie said with gentle sympathy.

Oliver ground his back teeth. He had a sudden vision of his plan falling apart before his very eyes. Anger simmered in his veins. This time Annie had gone too far. Tying him to the bed was one thing; involving herself in family matters was another.

"Your husband knows I do not want this information to become public," Shore continued. "He knows how much it would hurt my wife. What it would do to all of us."

"I understand completely." Annie shook her head dolefully. "As Aunt Madeline used to say, there's one in every family."

"One what?" Shore asked.

"A black sheep." Annie gave him a commiserating smile. "The scoundrel who can't resist blotting the old escutcheon. The one who embarrasses everyone else in the family. In my family it was Great-Uncle Charlie."

Oliver swore silently, aware that the situation had slipped irretrievably beyond his control.

"Great-Uncle Charlie?" Shore stared at Annie, bemused.

"Yep. Great-Uncle Charlie liked to rob banks."

"Banks." Shore was clearly dumbfounded.

"Uh-huh. Aunt Madeline says his father was so humiliated, he wouldn't allow Charlie's name to be spoken in the house." Annie made a tut-tut sound. "It would have been one thing if Charlie had been forced into robbing banks in order to feed his family or some such noble goal. But that wasn't the case at all."

Shore gazed at her in unwilling fascination. "Why did he rob banks?"

Annie glanced quickly from side to side and then lowered her voice. "For the thrill of it, as far as we can tell. Great-Uncle Charlie *liked* to rob banks. That's why there was no stopping him. He did time for bank robbery, but when he got out, he went right back to his little hobby."

"How interesting." Shore did not seem to know what to say next.

"I met him once," Annie went on in a chatty tone.

"When I was a little girl. He was very nice. Took Daniel and me to the zoo. Told Daniel not to start smoking or robbing banks because once you started either one it was hard to quit. Daniel promised him he wouldn't. And he never did."

"What happened to your great-uncle?" Shore asked as the plates of grilled halibut arrived.

"Oh, he got shot robbing a bank. He was seventy-eight at the time. Went out in a blaze of glory. Aunt Madeline took us to the funeral and warned us to beware of a life of crime." Annie picked up her fork. "She also warned us about something else."

"What was that?" Shore asked.

"She told us that we shouldn't ever be ashamed of having Great-Uncle Charlie in the family. That's when she explained that every family had a black sheep and that no one else should feel responsible for that person's behavior. Ultimately we're each responsible only for ourselves."

"The actions of one member of the family can hurt and humiliate the whole family," Shore said slowly.

"Yes, I know." Annie forked up a bite of halibut. She glanced briefly at Oliver. "I think everyone at this table understands that only too well. You've suffered because of the actions of your son, Mr. Shore. I saw how my uncle hurt my relatives. And Oliver, as you know, went through all sorts of hell after his father took off."

Oliver's simmering anger flashed into raw fury. "That's enough, Annie."

"I'm sorry." She gave him a misty smile. "I didn't mean to dredge up old memories. But surely you can see that you and Mr. Shore have a lot in common."

"No, by God, we do not have a lot in common."

Oliver wanted to shake her, anything to make her shut up. Instead he was forced to sit there, throttling back his rage as he mentally envisioned a cage door swinging closed on him.

"Yes, you do, Oliver. You and Mr. Shore have both been through absolute misery because of the actions of a family member."

"I said that's enough, Annie. I meant it."

Shore looked at him. "I'm well aware that I contributed to the problems you faced when your father disappeared, Rain. I've never apologized. I'm doing so now."

Oliver turned on him. "I don't want your goddamned apologies."

"I realize that. You'd rather have revenge." Shore continued to hold his gaze. "I think this is as good a time as any to explain why I could not give you any slack fifteen years ago. I was in a precarious situation, financially speaking, when your father left town. I needed the money he owed me. I needed it badly."

"I don't want to discuss this," Oliver said.

"I know you don't," Shore said in a low voice. "But I want you to understand what it was like for me in those days. I was heavily into junk bonds and real estate. Like everyone else, including your father, I was leveraged to the limit. I wasn't sure if I could stay afloat. When he cut out, leaving me holding the bag for a group of investors, it was the last straw. I had two sons and my wife to think of."

This was all Annie's fault, Oliver thought savagely. Everything was falling apart because of her. "I said I don't want to talk about the past, Shore."

"I don't expect you to forgive me. I just want you to understand," Shore insisted. "I needed the money your father owed me more than I had ever needed money in my life. I also wanted revenge for what he had done to me. He was supposed to have been my friend, damn it. I trusted him."

"Let's drop this right now," Oliver rasped.

Shore ignored him. "I couldn't get my hands on him, so I lashed out at you. I thought I was ruined. I never expected you to come up with the cash within six months. How the hell did you do it, anyway? You never told me."

"It was none of your damned business," Oliver said through his teeth.

"I know. But you must understand. Deep down, I've always wondered how you got that money so quickly. I've wondered if I drove you to some desperate act."

Annie frowned. "Oliver didn't rob any banks to get that money, if that's what's worrying you, Mr. Shore."

"Then where did it come from?" Shore demanded.

Annie's eyes widened. "I don't know." She looked at Oliver inquiringly.

Somehow Oliver managed to get control of his rage. "I played the commodities market for six months."

"Jesus." Shore looked awed. "I didn't think anyone except the dealers made that kind of money in commodities."

"I got lucky," Oliver said roughly.

"I doubt if it was luck," Annie said in tones of boundless admiration. "More like sheer brilliance."

Oliver impaled her with a look he knew must have reflected a fair portion of the frustration and anger he was feeling.

Annie did not flinch. She turned back to Shore.

"Well, I'm glad that's all out in the open. The thing to remember, as Aunt Madeline said, is that neither of you is responsible for what your relatives did. No matter how much it hurt you or your families, you aren't to blame."

"Is that a fact?" Oliver asked grimly.

"Yes, and as for what happened afterward, you were both victims of circumstances beyond your control. But you both survived and flourished and that's the bottom line, isn't it?"

Oliver closed his eyes in disgust.

Shore spoke quietly. "That doesn't mean your husband can't do a great deal of damage to my family if he wishes to, Mrs. Rain."

"He won't," Annie said gently.

Oliver opened his eyes and stared at her.

Annie swallowed and looked away. "By the way, this halibut is really very good. You two had better eat it before it gets cold."

"What about my son?" Shore asked quietly.

Oliver switched his gaze back to Shore's anxious face and knew the bitter frustration of the predator deprived of its prey. Out of the corner of his eye he saw Annie smile encouragingly at him. He could feel her willing him to do what she thought was the right thing.

In that moment Oliver knew he had lost the battle. For some totally incomprehensible reason he could not bring himself to go through with his plans to crush Shore. At least not with Annie sitting there, glowing with such serene faith in his integrity.

It was one thing to avenge himself on Paul Shore. Oliver knew he could have gone through with that without a qualm. But disappointing Annie was another matter.

"Forget Hammond," Oliver muttered. "Forget the whole damn thing."

Shore's relief was painful to behold. "Thank you, Rain. If it's any consolation, I think I know what you're feeling right now. I owe you."

Shore was going to go free, and there was every possibility that the Rain family would soon be related by marriage to the Shore family. Oliver wondered if he had lost his mind when he had married Annie.

"Carson and Valerie are such a perfect couple," Annie said with a cheerfulness that grated on Oliver's raw nerve endings. "You know, this whole thing sort of reminds me of Romeo and Juliet."

251

15

Annie knew something was wrong the minute she opened the front door of Oliver's penthouse that evening. The silence was deafening, but the heavy brooding quality that permeated the atmosphere told her someone else was already home.

Home. It struck her that she was starting to think of Oliver's apartment as her home.

She shook the last drops of rain off of her umbrella, slowly removed her raincoat, and hung it in the closet. The uneasiness that had been growing in her all afternoon blossomed into a dark flower of dismay as she wandered across the marble foyer.

She had known there might be problems tonight after the scene with Paul Shore. She had sensed the churning emotion deep inside Oliver when he had walked her out of the club. On the surface, of course, he was as calm and controlled as always, but she had not been fooled. He had not said a single word until they were outside on the sidewalk.

"Bolt will bring the car around in a minute."

"That's all right," Annie had assured him. "I'd rather walk. It's only a few blocks to the shop."

"It's raining."

"I've got my umbrella."

"As you wish." His eyes locked with hers. "I'll see you at home this evening."

252

Annie touched his arm. "Oliver, do you want to talk?"

"No. Not now."

Before she could respond the black limo had arrived at the curb with the stealth of a shadow. Oliver had gotten inside and shut the door without looking back at her.

That was when Annie had known for certain that the luncheon with Shore had not gone nearly as smoothly as she had at first thought. She had walked slowly back to Wildest Dreams through the cold, driving rain. By the time she reached the shop, she was convinced she had screwed up royally.

But looking back she did not see how she could have handled things any differently.

Now Annie paused in the doorway of the kitchen. "Bolt?"

There was no sign of Oliver's household robot. The lights were off in the kitchen. Normally Bolt would have been midway through preparations for another gourmet meal. His absence was definitely a bad sign.

Annie trailed reluctantly down the hall into the living room. It was empty, too. The rain slanted steadily against the expanse of windows.

That left the study. Annie knew Oliver would be waiting for her there in his ebony and gold lair.

She had to force herself to make the long trek down the gray-carpeted hallway. When she finally arrived, the door was closed.

For some reason that annoyed Annie. She straightened her shoulders, opened the door without knocking, and stalked into the room. She came to a halt just inside, letting her eyes adjust to the subdued light.

Oliver was sitting at his desk, a leopard crouching in his cave. His face was in shadow. The halogen lamp created a ring of sharp, white light on the polished surface of his desk, revealing his folded hands. For some strange reason her eye was caught by the golden gleam of his wedding ring.

"Hello, Oliver." Annie stomped defiantly over to a chair and threw herself down into it.

"Good evening, Annie."

"Where's Bolt?"

"I told him to leave early today. We won't be needing him this evening."

She groaned. "You're angry, aren't you?"

"Let's just say I've been thinking about this relationship."

Annie winced. "You really are pissed."

"I have tolerated a great deal from you, Annie. But today you went too far."

Icy fingers traced the length of Annie's spine. "I didn't do anything." But she knew that wasn't true. And so did Oliver.

"You interfered in a situation that was no concern of yours."

"I didn't exactly interfere, Oliver. I just invited myself to lunch with you and Shore, that's all."

"Why?"

She blinked. "Why? Well, I suppose because I was a little worried."

"About what?" Oliver prompted very softly.

Annie struggled with that one. "I was afraid you might do something you'd wind up regretting."

"Regrets? Annie, I made it a policy a long time ago not to have regrets."

"The thing is," she said earnestly, "you've been

254

carrying a grudge against Paul Shore for so long, I didn't know if you would be able to think clearly when you were actually face-to-face with him. I thought that having someone else there at the table would help defuse the situation. And I was right, wasn't I? Admit it."

"You deliberately involved yourself in a matter that had nothing to do with you."

"Damn it, Oliver, I just sat there and chatted over lunch. I didn't involve myself in anything."

Oliver said nothing. An intimidating silence ensued.

"Stop that," Annie ordered.

"Stop what?"

"Stop trying to intimidate me." Annie shot out of her chair and went to stand at the window. "It won't work, Oliver. I won't allow you to use those tactics on me."

"And I will not permit you to involve yourself in matters that are the sole concern of myself and my family."

"Oliver, I am part of your family. I'm your wife."

"That status, according to your own words, is temporary."

Annie's stomach knotted in pain. "I know that."

"You're the one who wanted a marriage of convenience."

"Yes, I know, but..."

"I did not find our marriage very convenient today, Annie."

"Damn it, will you stop sounding as if you're conducting a court-marshal? I get the impression you're going to strip me of my rank and insignia and make me walk the plank or something."

"It's obvious we need to arrive at a clearer understanding of how this marriage is going to work," Oliver said. "I won't tolerate any more interference in my affairs."

"Is that so?" Annie's frustration made her reckless. "What are you going to do about it?"

There was another heartbeat of shattering silence. "Have you forgotten that you need my help to save Lyncroft?" Oliver finally asked very softly.

The shock of the blatant threat robbed Annie of her breath. It took a few seconds for her to recover. When she did, her anger drowned out any fear she might have felt. She swung around to confront him, her hands in fists at her sides.

"How dare you?" she shouted.

Oliver's eyes were colder than the rain on the window. "You came to me for help to save your brother's business. You proposed the marriage of convenience. You need me, remember?"

"Don't threaten me. Don't you dare threaten me."

"I'm not threatening you. I'm pointing out certain facts. You have a lot more at stake in this marriage than I do. I can survive very nicely without the profits I might ultimately see from Daniel's wireless technology."

"Is that so?"

"Yes. You, on the other hand, are up against the wall. You're desperate to hold Lyncroft together. And I'm the only one who can do it for you, Annie."

"What are you saying? That if I don't stay out of your family affairs, you'll abandon me and the company to our fates?"

Oliver's jaw tightened. "I don't think it will come to that, will it? You're impulsive, but you're smart. Smart enough to know when you've gone too far.

You crossed a line today, Annie. Don't ever cross it again."

Annie threw up her hands. "Why are you so mad at me? What did I do that was so wrong?"

"I told you what you did. You chose to involve yourself in a family matter, a matter that was none of your business. You should have stayed out of it, Annie."

"I just sat there and talked."

"You deliberately ruined everything," Oliver said evenly.

She glanced quickly at him. Oliver's grim face was as expressionless as ever, but something in his voice warned her that he did not have himself as firmly under control as he would have her believe.

"I ruined everything?" Annie echoed. "Come on now, Oliver. Are you telling me that I have that much power? Are you admitting that just by inviting myself to lunch I managed to trash all your carefully arranged plans?"

"Stop it, Annie."

She took a step toward him. "Are you saying that I, little Annie Lyncroft, purveyor of tacky art, had the power to force the mighty Oliver Rain to scrap his clever schemes for revenge?"

"Annie, I'm warning you."

She took another step toward him. "Good God, Oliver, it boggles the mind. To think that I could change the course of history so easily."

"I said, that's enough, Annie. I meant it. What does it take to stop you?"

"Why, Oliver, I'm not sure anything can stop me." She made a sweeping gesture with her right hand. "Heck, I'm a force to be reckoned with, according to you. I have the power to alter your whole life. Just by inviting myself along to lunch. Lord only knows what would happen if I ever invited myself to join you when you're having dinner with one of your enemies."

Oliver sat unmoving. His hands were still clasped on the top of the desk. Annie noticed that his knuckles had gone white.

"Do you or do you not want me to save Lyncroft for you?" Oliver asked.

"Forget the threats." Annie walked to the door. She turned, her hand on the knob. "You know damn well you aren't going to follow through on them."

"No?"

"No. And I'll tell you why. Because you know as well as I do that I didn't force you to give up your plan to use Shore's son as a weapon. You're the one who abandoned the scheme. You're the only one who had the power to give it up."

Oliver still did not move.

"You could have gone ahead and blackmailed Shore if that was what you really wanted to do. I couldn't have stopped you. No one could have stopped you." Annie opened the door.

"Come back here, Annie."

"I understand now why you're mad. You're furious with me because I made you stop and think today. Having me there at the table forced you to consider exactly what you were doing."

"Come back here, Annie."

Annie leveled a finger at him from the doorway. "You're the one who changed his plans today, Oliver. I didn't change them. We both know I don't have that kind of power over you. How could I? I'm just a business associate you happen to have been sleeping with lately. I'm not even a real wife."

Annie went out into the hall and slammed the door behind her as loudly as possible. The crashing thud jarred a black glass vase on a nearby table and made her feel much better. She stalked on down the corridor toward the foyer.

The study door opened behind her. "Where are you going?" Oliver asked in a voice that was approximately twenty degrees below absolute zero.

"Out." Annie picked up the keys lying on the black marble table near the front door. She did not turn around, but she was acutely aware of Oliver rapidly closing the distance between them. He reached the door just as she did.

"I asked you a question." Oliver held the front door shut as Annie tried to twist the knob. "Are you walking out on me?"

"No." Annie lifted her chin. "If I ever walk out on you, I'll tell you about it. As it happens, I'm going downstairs to visit Bolt."

"*Bolt.*"

"Yes, Bolt. And when you're ready to apologize, you can come and get me. Kindly remove your hand from the door or I shall scream bloody murder."

Oliver gave her an incredulous look. "Why in hell are you going down to Bolt's apartment?"

"Because I feel like it." Annie yanked at the door. To her surprise, Oliver slowly removed his hand.

Annie slipped out through the partially open door, took three strides across the corridor, and punched the elevator call button. She was aware of Oliver standing in the doorway, watching her as she waited for the elevator to arrive. She did not look back.

When the elevator doors slid open, Annie stepped inside and hit the button for the sixth floor. She held Oliver's eyes as the doors started to slide shut.

"You're not going to get away with blaming me for the fact that your conscience kicked in this afternoon," she declared.

It wasn't until she stepped out into the corridor on the sixth floor a moment later that she realized she had a problem. She knew the number of Bolt's floor, but she didn't know the number of his apartment.

There were six doors on the sixth floor. Annie prowled past each of them. There were name tags inserted over the doorbells of five of the apartments. The slot above the sixth was blank.

Annie leaned on the unidentified button.

The door opened almost instantly. Bolt looked down at her without any sign of surprise.

"Mr. Rain said you were on your way down here," Bolt said.

Annie grimaced. "Figures. I'll bet he'll call back in a minute to see if I arrived. Can I come in?"

"Yes." Bolt stepped aside. A chime sounded softly above a wall panel full of sophisticated electronics. Bolt pressed a button. "Yes, Mr. Rain?"

"Is she there?" Oliver asked over the intercom.

"Yes, Mr. Rain."

"See that she gets dinner. She hasn't eaten yet."

"Yes, Mr. Rain." Bolt released the intercom button.

"What did I tell you?" Annie walked on into the apartment, glancing around curiously. "I knew he wouldn't be able to resist checking up on me."

Annie surveyed Bolt's headquarters. It was no penthouse, but it was spacious and well appointed. The windows provided a different slant on the same view that Oliver enjoyed twenty floors above. The furnishings were Spartan, each piece arranged with military neatness. Books were filed in orderly ranks in a bookcase. Magazines were stacked fastidiously.

A computer screen glowed on a table in a corner of the living room. Annie wandered over to take a closer look.

"What would you like for dinner?" Bolt asked without any sign of emotion.

"Nothing, thanks. I'm not hungry."

"Mr. Rain said I was to feed you."

"Don't worry about it." Annie frowned as she bent down to read the lines of type on the computer screen. "What are you working on? Some sort of spy report for Oliver?"

"No." Bolt moved suddenly, reaching past her to push a button on the keyboard. "As it happens I'm working on a personal project at the moment." The screen went blank.

But Annie had seen enough to astonish her. She looked up at Bolt, her eyes widening in awe. "That was fiction, wasn't it? Bolt, are you a writer?"

"I haven't been published yet," he muttered.

Annie realized he was turning a dull red. "I've never known anyone who wrote. What kind of stuff is it?"

"Suspense."

"No kidding? This is exciting. No wonder you're kind of strange. This explains everything."

Bolt gazed at her impassively. "It does?"

"Of course. Everyone knows writers are strange. Have you finished a manuscript?"

"I'm working on the last few chapters of one." Bolt started for the kitchen again. "I'll fix you something to eat."

261

"Forget it. I'm really not hungry."

"Mr. Rain said you were to be fed."

"Okay, okay. Whatever Mr. Rain wants, Mr. Rain gets." Annie followed Bolt into the sleek kitchen. "I'll take a glass of wine if you've got it. I could use one. And maybe a pretzel or something."

"I don't have any wine. I have beer."

"Beer will do." Annie seated herself on a stool behind the counter and watched as Bolt took a can from the refrigerator, opened it, and poured the contents into a glass. "Bolt, can I read what you're written?"

He looked at her, startled. "You want to read it?"

"I'd love to."

"I don't know." It was the first time Bolt had ever looked indecisive. "No one has ever read anything I've written."

"Someone will have to read it eventually," Annie said persuasively. "I read a lot of suspense. I really enjoy that kind of stuff."

Bolt hesitated. Then he gave Annie a direct look. "Will you be honest with me about it?"

Annie mentally crossed her fingers behind her back. "Absolutely." One could always find something nice to say about an artist's creation, she reminded herself.

"All right then." Bolt put some pretzels on a plate. "But if you don't like it or if it bores you, I want you to put it down and tell me the truth. Agreed?"

"Sure." Annie took the glass of beer and the small tray full of pretzels and went back into the living room.

Bolt picked up a stack of neatly printed pages and handed them to her. "Why did you come down here?"

Annie made a face. "Can't you guess? Oliver and I quarreled."

"So why did you come here?"

"You know Oliver." Annie took a swallow of the beer. "He'd worry if he thought I had actually left the building. He'd probably send you after me to keep an eye on me. This way neither of us gets wet and I get to read a good book while I wait for him to come to his senses."

Bolt frowned. "Come to his senses and do what?"

"Apologize." Annie munched a pretzel.

Bolt looked blank. "Why would Mr. Rain apologize?"

"Because he's in the wrong and he knows it. Don't worry, I won't be here all night. He'll come down to fetch me eventually. Oliver plays fair."

"You don't know him very well yet, do you?" Bolt sat down in front of the computer screen. "Mr. Rain plays to win. No, I take that back. Mr. Rain does not play at all. He goes to war."

"He's changing. You'll see. Do you write all night?"

"Sometimes."

"You know, Bolt, I'm getting a whole new view of you."

"That makes us even."

"How come you don't like me, Bolt?"

Bolt's fingers froze above the computer keys. "What makes you think I don't like you?"

"Call it a strong hunch," Annie said dryly. "Is it because you think I'll take advantage of Oliver? You don't have to worry, you know. Oliver can take care of himself."

Bolt gave her an odd look. "I'm aware of that."

"I won't get my greedy little hands on all his money."

"No," Bolt agreed. "You won't. Not unless he wants you to get your hands on it."

"So how come you're worried about me hanging around?"

Bolt gazed into the depths of the computer. "He's grown somewhat fond of you," he said at last.

"I'd like to think that was true," Annie said. "But to be honest, he's not fond of me at all tonight."

"He's not accustomed to dealing with anyone quite like you, Mrs. Rain."

"So?"

"So, I'm afraid he may on occasion suspend his normally extremely sound judgment where you're concerned."

"Hah. You think I'm going to wrap him around my little finger?"

"I think you already have." Bolt went back to work as if she weren't in the room.

Annie propped one leg over the arm of the chair and settled in the corner. She swung her foot absently as she started to read Bolt's manuscript.

Everything was back under control. For the moment, at any rate.

Annie was downstairs with Bolt just as she had said she would be.

Oliver released the intercom switch. Christ, his hand was trembling. He glowered at the offending fingers as he deliberately flexed them. From somewhere he dredged up the will to crush the incipient panic that had threatened to twist his insides into jelly.

It was all right; Annie hadn't left him.

Of course she hadn't left him. She still needed him, he reminded himself.

Oliver walked to the window. He stood gazing unseeingly out into the darkness and wondered what the hell to do next. He could not recall the last time he had found himself at such a complete loss.

There was no need to rush into a decision, he told himself. Annie was safely at hand. There was time to think this through, time to figure out how to handle his wife.

"Damn it to hell."

The fact that his first instinct was to rush downstairs and retrieve Annie only went to show that he had been letting her influence him far too much lately. Her tendency toward rash, unpredictable behavior was starting to rub off on him.

The woman was invading every corner of his life. She was taking over, interfering in his most private affairs. She was causing him to do things he would never have done if she were not around.

He had never realized that marriage to Annie would turn out like this. Nothing was going the way it was supposed to.

Oliver turned and walked out of the study. He went down the hall to the steps that led to the rooftop greenhouse. He needed to think.

Outside on the roof he paused beside the control panel and switched on the lights inside the greenhouse. Then he opened the door and went inside.

At once he felt calmer, more in control. The warm, humid scents of his own private jungle soothed him as nothing else could have done.

Here in the greenhouse time felt different than it did outside. This was a different place, a different

265

world. Here he could recover his sense of direction, his patience, his control. Here he could refocus on his goals and lay plans for reaching them. Here among his precious ferns he could make clear-sighted, rational decisions.

Oliver walked through his green world, losing himself in the incredible lushness of it, letting himself absorb the ancient aura of living things that had defied time for over three hundred million years.

He stopped at the small grotto and stood looking down at the mat of green ferns that floated on the surface of the water. He wanted to think about the past and how it affected the future.

But all he could think about was Annie waiting for him downstairs in Bolt's apartment.

He could not believe that she actually expected him to apologize. After what she had done today, she should have been on her hands and knees trying to make amends. She should have been frantic at the possibility that he might abandon her brother's company to its creditors.

She needed him, damn it, and she knew it. She had come to him. She had practically pleaded with him to marry her and save Lyncroft Unlimited. He was the one holding the power in this situation.

He always held the power. It was the only safe position to occupy.

Oliver picked up a small trowel, realized that he wanted to hurl it against the greenhouse wall, and willed himself to put it carefully back down on the bench.

He moved on to a bank of staghorns and wondered at the coldness in the pit of his belly.

He had learned one thing today and that was that

Annie could not be easily bluffed. She hadn't believed for one minute that he would actually toss Lyncroft Unlimited to the wolves.

She had been right. He had been trying to intimidate her, but he'd never had any intention of destroying Lyncroft Unlimited. He had made a commitment and he would fulfill it. Daniel had been a good friend, one of the few Oliver had ever had.

He should have remembered his own rule, Oliver thought. Never make threats. Make promises.

His mouth twisted into a humorless smile. If he went downstairs and apologized, Annie would probably revel in the proof of her growing power over him.

Then again, maybe she wouldn't. Oliver frowned at that thought. Annie would not take an apology as a sign of victory for the simple reason that she did not use power with the same cold, conscious awareness that he himself used it. She did not take satisfaction in the development of strategy or in the manipulation of means to achieve ends. Annie would never know the icy pleasure of revenge.

Annie was not like him. Her motives were difficult, perhaps impossible for him to comprehend. The only thing he could be certain of was that they were different from his own.

Along with that realization came another. Oliver suddenly saw with terrifying clarity that the problem in dealing with Annie was that she was going to insist on holding him to her own standards.

She had assumed from the beginning that his actions were based on noble, honorable goals. She saw him as a misunderstood knight in tarnished armor.

God help him, Oliver thought, because it was becoming increasingly difficult to disappoint her.

Oliver was not certain what to expect when he went downstairs to fetch Annie home. He definitely did not like the sense of uncertainty that filled him when he leaned on Bolt's doorbell. But he knew that at least he had his expression under control a moment later when the door opened.

"Where is she?" he asked Bolt.

"In the living room." Bolt hesitated. "Reading."

Oliver crossed the small entryway and walked into the living room. Annie was sprawled in an armchair, a stack of printed pages on the floor beside her. She looked up. Her eyes were warm and welcoming.

"Hey, Oliver, did you know that Bolt is writing a book?" She set aside the handful of papers and jumped to her feet. "And it's fabulous. A little violent in some places and I told Bolt he needs to stick some romance in it, but the suspense is terrific. I can't wait to finish it."

Oliver glanced speculatively at Bolt. "I didn't know you were a writer."

Bolt's gaze did not quite meet Oliver's. "Unpublished."

"But not for long, I'll bet," Annie said. "I can't wait for you to write the last chapter, Bolt."

Oliver noticed that Bolt was turning a strange shade of red. The battle between Bolt and Annie was over, whether Bolt knew it or not. Chalk up another conquest for Annie. Bolt was going to be putty in her hands from now on.

Oliver looked at Annie. "Are you ready to go home?"

"Yes." Annie glanced at Bolt. "Can I take the rest of the manuscript with me? I can't quit now."

Bolt looked strangely disconcerted. "All right."

"Thanks." Annie smiled at Oliver as she gathered up the unfinished portion of Bolt's manuscript and tucked it under her arm. "Okay. I'm ready."

Oliver met Bolt's eyes and inclined his head once in a brusque acknowledgment of gratitude. Bolt nodded and said nothing as he opened the door.

"You know something? Bolt can really write," Annie confided as she stepped into the elevator. "I wouldn't have believed it if I hadn't seen it with my own eyes. Looks like I'm going to have to take back all those nasty cracks I made about him being an android." She waved the manuscript. "This is good. Terrific, in fact. I hope it sells."

Oliver looked down at her as the elevator doors closed. "Are you waiting for an apology?"

Annie smiled serenely. "You came and got me. I figure that's probably as close to an apology as I'll get. Don't worry, I know you're sorry or you would never have come downstairs to fetch me home."

"So now you've convinced yourself that I've apologized," Oliver mused. "Don't you ever worry that looking at the world through rose-colored glasses is a good way to trip and fall flat on your face?"

"I'm not quite as naive as you seem to think, Oliver."

"That's a matter of opinion." Oliver smiled wryly. "I, on the other hand, am not quite as inarticulate as you seem to think. I apologize for saying the things I did to you earlier. I was wrong to blame you for the fact that I didn't go through with my plans to pressure Shore into trying to stop the marriage."

Annie clutched Bolt's manuscript to her breast. Her smile was wistful. "Why did you change your mind?"

"Today at lunch I came face-to-face with something I haven't wanted to deal with."

"What was that?"

"After all these years, I finally understood that Paul Shore was never the real target of my revenge. He was just a stand-in."

"For your father?" Annie asked.

Oliver told himself he should not have been surprised at her perception. He had better get accustomed to it. "Yes."

"I understand. You never had a chance to confront your father over the fact that he abandoned you and your brothers and sisters. Naturally you turned your anger on the next available target. It was easy to blame Paul Shore for a lot of what had happened because he had been involved in the mess. Is that it?"

"Part of it," Oliver agreed.

Annie tilted her head to one side. "You had every reason to hate what your father did to your family."

Oliver watched the elevator doors slide open. "It's true, I hated him for what he did to the family. But there was more involved. I've hated him all these years for what he did to me."

"To you?"

"Don't you see, Annie?" Oliver got out his key as he walked off the elevator. "Because of Edward Rain, I became the one thing I swore I never would become. A man like my father."

270

16

Dumbfounded by Oliver's assessment of himself, Annie stood frozen in the elevator. She gazed after him, mouth open in shock, as he crossed the hall without a backward glance. The elevator doors started to close.

"Oliver, are you crazy?" Annie recovered the powers of speech and movement just in time to leap between the narrow opening left by the closing doors. "You're not anything like your father."

"How would you know? You never met him." Oliver shoved his key into the lock and pushed open the door of the penthouse.

"Just because I never met the man doesn't mean I don't know a heck of a lot about him."

"I'd rather not discuss this, if you don't mind," Oliver said.

"Well, we're going to discuss it. This is no time for you to go into your faulty communication mode."

"Forget it, Annie."

"Oh, no. We're not going to forget it." Clutching Bolt's manuscript, Annie rushed through the door behind Oliver. She dashed past him into the wide foyer, spun around, and came to a halt directly in front of him. "Stop right there. We're going to talk."

He looked down at her, eyes filled with a deep, brooding melancholy. "There's nothing to talk about."

"There most certainly is." Annie slammed Bolt's manuscript down on the black marble table. Then, hands on her hips, she confronted Oliver. "Your father was the kind of man who would abandon a wife, five children, and all of his responsibilities. You would never do such a thing."

Oliver rubbed the back of his neck with a weary gesture. "That's not the point."

"Oh, yes, it is." Annie reached up and grabbed two fistfuls of his shirt. She stood on tiptoe and put her face very close to his. "It's the most important point there is. Ask any woman. Or any kid whose father has walked out. Ask any creditor who got left holding the bag."

"Annie..."

"For crying out loud, Oliver, look at you. Look at what you are."

His mouth curved humorlessly. "I have looked at what I am. I don't like what I see."

"Then you're blind." She used her grip on his shirt to try to shake some sense into him. She exerted all of her strength, but Oliver stood like a rock. Frustration leaped within her. "You're a fine man. An admirable man. You've accomplished an incredible amount."

"I made some money. That's nothing. My father made money, too."

"The money isn't important. What's important is that you saved your family. Oliver, you held things together when they could easily have crumbled. Your brothers and sisters have all gotten off to a successful start in life because you became the head of the family."

"Annie, I've got work to do."

She gave him another shake that had no effect. "You gave everyone in your family what they needed most after your father walked out. You gave them security, a sense of strength. They knew they could count on you. Don't you know how important that is? Okay, so you've got some communication problems. So who doesn't? We can fix that."

"Excuse me." Oliver's hands closed around her waist. He lifted her up and set her to one side. Then he walked straight past her down the hall toward his study. He did not look back.

"Don't you dare walk out on me when I'm arguing with you," Annie yelled at his back.

"You walked out on me earlier, remember?"

"That was different. I told you, I didn't leave you, I just went to visit Bolt." Annie rushed down the hall. "Oliver, for the last time, you can be irritating, uncommunicative, insensitive, and downright difficult on occasion, *but you are not anything like your father*."

Oliver reached the door of his study. "You don't know what you're saying."

"Oh, yes I do." Annie had a sudden, horrible fear that their combined destinies were somehow riding on the outcome of this confrontation. Panic seized her. "Oliver, listen to me."

"You've already said enough, Annie."

"I know you are not like your father, do you hear me? I know enough about your father and enough about myself to know that I could never have loved a man like him."

Oliver went absolutely still, his hand motionless on the doorknob.

It seemed to Annie that everything in the entire

universe had ceased moving except her heart. It was pounding.

Oliver broke the spell, turning toward her very slowly. There was a fierce storm of emotion gathering in his eyes. "What are you saying, Annie?"

Annie's mouth was suddenly very dry. Her pulse was racing so fast she was dizzy. She wished she had time to think. But there was no time. "I'm saying that I love you."

"You love me." Oliver repeated the words carefully as if testing each one for flaws or weaknesses.

"Yes." Annie smiled tremulously. "For goodness sake, don't tell me you didn't know."

"How would I have known?" He searched her face. "You never told me."

"I thought it must have been obvious."

Oliver walked slowly back along the hall until he stood in front of her. "The only thing that was obvious was that I could make you want me. And that you needed me to save Lyncroft."

"Let me be perfectly blunt about this, Oliver. I would never have proposed a marriage of convenience to any of Daniel's other creditors or investors."

"No?"

"Absolutely not. I think I started falling in love with you that night at Daniel and Joanna's engagement party. In fact, to be honest, I think the only reason I came up with the idea of a marriage between us to save the company was because I was already in love with you."

"Annie." Oliver's voice was rough with some unidentified emotion. He framed her face carefully with his powerful hands. He bent his head slowly and took her lips.

The familiar excitement flowed through Annie when she felt Oliver's calloused palms against her skin. She twined her arms around his neck as his mouth moved urgently, demandingly on hers.

"Annie," he said again.

"Yes," she whispered.

There were no more words as Oliver picked her up in his arms and carried her into the darkened bedroom. But Annie told herself the words would come eventually. Oliver was in love with her. He had to be in love with her.

Surely he could not touch her like this, the way he touched his ferns, if he was not in love with her.

A long time later Annie stirred beside Oliver. "There's something I've been wondering about."

"What's that?"

"Did you ever find your father? I know you must have gone looking for him eventually. I can't see you not wanting to track him down."

"I found him." Oliver's voice was toneless. "Or rather I found his grave. He died in a sailing accident in the Caribbean about three months before I finally got a lead on him. He'd covered his tracks well."

"Did you ever find out why he left?"

Oliver's jaw tightened. "The people who knew him down there in the islands said he'd talked a lot about wanting to be free. Rich and free. I guess the responsibilities and the debts he'd accumulated got to be too much for him."

"But you never had a chance to confront him."

"No. Maybe it's just as well." Oliver's hand moved on her arm. "I'm not sure what I would have said or done."

"What did you tell your family?"

"The truth. There are times when you can't protect them."

Annie touched his face with gentle fingertips. "I think you've done a very fine job of protecting your family from all the perils that could have destroyed them, Oliver. You're the true head of the Rain family, not your father. You didn't buckle under the weight of the responsibilities you had to assume."

He pulled her close and held her to him for a long time before they both fell asleep.

The one thing I never wanted to be: a man like my father. Oliver's painful admission was still haunting Annie the following afternoon as she worked with a designer who had brought his client with him to Wildest Dreams.

"Something with an amusing, somewhat gaudy edge to it, Annie." Stanford J. Littlewood, owner and sole proprietor of Stanford J. Littlewood Designs, scanned the contents of Annie's shop with a coldly critical eye. He turned to his client with a condescending smile. "As you can see, Annie specializes in the whimsical look. Some of her pieces have a certain charm when used with discretion."

Annie set her back teeth. She was well aware that the phrase, "used with discretion" was a blatant warning to the uncertain client. The message was that she should not even contemplate selecting an item from the shop on her own. She must remember that she needed Stanford J. Littlewood's professional advice.

Annie smiled benignly at Littlewood's client. Charlotte Babcock was a pleasant woman in her early thirties who was obviously going through the trauma of dealing with an interior designer for the first time.

"Some of my pieces do require a certain boldness on the part of the client, Mrs. Babcock." Annie stroked the cloisonné elephant that Raphaela had returned after the Shore benefit. "Designers often decide to play it safe when it comes to choosing a finishing touch. But a single stroke of daring can do wonders for a room."

"Yes, I'm sure you're right." Charlotte glanced uneasily at Littlewood.

Littlewood smiled condescendingly again. "When one is dealing with a finishing touch, one must always ask the vital question that separates the good, the bad, and the ugly."

"What's that?" Charlotte asked anxiously.

Littlewood gave the cloisonné elephant a derisive, dismissing glance. "Is it art or is it just plain tacky?"

Annie resisted the urge to stick her tongue out at him. He was deliberately intimidating his client. But, then, Littlewood was very good at intimidating clients.

Today he was at his most impressive. His wavy silver hair had been moussed and blow-dried so that it swept straight back from his artificially tanned face. He was dressed in an off-white shirt, off-white tie, silver-gray suit, and off-white tassled loafers.

"Did you bring some sketches of the interiors with you, Stan?" Annie asked. Out of the corner of her eye she saw Ella hide a quick grin. Everyone knew that Littlewood hated to have his first name shortened to "Stan." "And can you give me some idea of the colors you're using?"

Littlewood peered down his nose. "Naturally." He

flipped open his off-white leather briefcase and fished out some drawings and color swatches.

The phone rang on the counter just as Annie started to study the sketches of Charlotte Babcock's residence.

"It's for you, Annie." Ella held the phone aloft.

"Please take a message, Ella."

"He says it's important."

Annie glanced up in concern. "Who is it?"

"He won't say. I'm not even sure it's a man." Ella's eyes were conveying a message of urgency. "I think you had better talk to him. Or her. Or whatever."

Annie smiled at Charlotte. "Excuse me."

"Certainly."

"I'll take it at my desk." Annie walked past the counter and into her small office.

She lifted the receiver of the desk phone. "This is Annie Lyncroft. What can I do for you?"

There was a scratchy sound on the other end of the line. A low, barely audible voice spoke in a sexless whisper. "If you want to know what happened to your brother, find the mechanic."

Annie went numb. For an instant she couldn't think. "What is this? What are you talking about?"

"Find the mechanic who worked on Lyncroft's plane the day he disappeared. He can tell you what really happened."

"Wait." Annie gripped the phone with a feeling of desperation. She sensed the caller was about to hang up. "Who are you?"

"Let's just say this is someone who wants to see justice done," the voice rasped. "One more thing. If you want to find the answers, don't ask Rain for help. In fact, if you value your life, don't tell him you're going to track down the mechanic."

"Are you crazy? Who is this?"

"Find the mechanic on your own, Ms. Lyncroft. And keep in mind that the only person who has benefited from your brother's disappearance is Oliver Rain." There was a slight pause. "Be careful, Ms. Lyncroft. Be very, very careful."

"Wait, please..."

But the caller had cut the connection. Annie realized she was holding the receiver so tightly her fingers hurt.

"Oh, my God." She put the receiver down very slowly, willing herself to think.

Find the mechanic.

"Annie?" Ella poked her head around the corner. Her brows drew together in a frown when she saw Annie's face. "Everything okay?"

"Yes. Everything's fine." Annie sat down in the chair behind her desk. "I'm not feeling well, that's all. Would you mind making my excuses to Stan and his client? Let them look around and get some ideas.I'll get back to them later."

"Sure. Maybe you should go home."

"I might just do that. But first I want to make a phone call." Annie pulled the telephone directory toward her. "Close the door, will you?"

"Are you sure you're going to be okay?"

"I'm fine, Ella. Just a little queasy."

Ella started to grin. "Hey, you don't suppose you're pregnant, do you?"

"Close the door, Ella," Annie said.

"Right." Still grinning, Ella shut the door.

Annie's hands trembled as she opened the phone book to the listings under aircraft service and maintenance. She ran a fingertip down the list of companies until she came to a familiar name. It was the firm Daniel always used when he rented or chartered a plane.

Annie had to punch in the number of the aviation service company twice. The first time her nervous fingers slipped. A woman answered after what must have been the tenth ring. She sounded as if she had been running. Annie could hear the roar of private aircraft propellers in the background as she identified herself.

"Sure, Ms. Lyncroft. I remember you. I talked to you the day your brother disappeared. I'm Sarah."

"Oh, yes. The flight instructor."

"Among other things," Sarah admitted dryly. "What can I do for you?"

Annie closed her eyes, trying to calm herself. Sarah had been very kind to her that awful day. "Sarah, I was wondering if I could speak to whoever serviced the plane my brother used."

There was a brief pause on the other end of the line. Sarah's voice was muffled as she apparently spoke to someone over her shoulder. "Tell him I'll be out in a minute." Her voice got clearer. "What? Right. The mechanic. That was Wally."

"Wally?"

"Yeah. Wally Thorpe. He's not with us anymore."

A strange feeling of disorientation swept through Annie. "Where did he go?"

"Don't know. He quit two days after Daniel disappeared. Just walked off the job and said he wasn't coming back. Haven't seen him since." Sarah's voice grew muffled again. "I said I'll be right out. Damn it, tell him I won't charge him for ground time, will you?"

"Sarah, please, I know you're busy," Annie said quickly. "But could you give me Wally Thorpe's phone number? Or his address? I'm very anxious to speak to him."

"Hang on, I should have both in my file." Drawers banged over the angry whine of a revving aircraft engine. "Got it. You ready? The address is on Bainbridge Island."

"I'm ready."

Annie hastily jotted down the number and address.

"Ms. Lyncroft?" Sarah sounded concerned now. "What's this about? The authorities talked to Wally the day after Daniel disappeared. The maintenance records were all in order. The plane was in excellent condition. And Daniel always did a thorough preflight check."

"I know. This is about something else. Thanks, Sarah."

Annie hung up the phone and sat staring at the number on the pad in front of her for a long time. Then, slowly, she punched out each digit with great care.

Annie let Wally Thorpe's phone ring for what seemed like forever. There was no answer.

"Well, well, well." Sybil surveyed Daniel Lyncroft's office with amused disparagement. She took in the metal file cabinets; plain, serviceable furnishings; and the sophisticated computer and shook her head. "Not quite your usual style, is it, Oliver? I know a designer who could do wonders with this place."

"I don't need a designer," Oliver said.

Sybil smiled coolly as she sat down. "No, I don't imagine you'll be running Lyncroft Unlimited personally for very long, will you? You rarely involve yourself in the day-to-day operations of any of your companies. When are you going to install a management team?"

"Not for another few months." Oliver hesitated. "It may not be necessary. Annie expects Daniel to return any day."

"I know. Poor Annie. I'll say one thing for her, she's born optimist." Sybil crossed her legs and adjusted the hem of her pale-blue wool skirt. "She's been living with you for, let's see, nearly two weeks now, isn't it?"

"Almost."

"Nearly two weeks of sharing your board and," Sybil smiled blandly, "I assume your bed?"

"Annie is my wife," Oliver said coldly.

"Ah, yes. Your bed. Two weeks of living quite intimately with you and she still isn't cured of her naïveté. Amazing."

Out of long habit Oliver forced himself to sink deeply into a bottomless ocean of patience. He kept his expression impassive. "I assume you have a reason for dropping by my office today?"

Sybil regarded him with open speculation. "I want to know what's going on, Oliver. I have some rights. So does Valerie."

"What does Valerie have to do with this?"

"Don't act like I'm an idiot." Sybil lifted her chin. "I know you're up to something. You're always up to something. You're devious and cunning and everyone knows it except, maybe, little Miss Pollyannie. But do you know something, Oliver? Somehow I never thought you'd sink so low that you'd use your own sister as a pawn."

"Do you want to explain exactly what you mean, Sybil, or are we going to play guessing games?"

"I'm talking about this matter of you and Paul Shore supposedly declaring a truce." Open accusation flared in Sybil's eyes. "Valerie is so happy, she's dancing on air."

"An interesting trick."

"Tell me, Oliver." Sybil leaned forward. "Are you going to feel any guilt at all when she comes crashing down?"

"Why should she crash?"

"Because all of her happiness is based on a stack of completely false hopes." Sybil paused. "Isn't it?"

Oliver glanced down at his folded hands and then raised his eyes to meet Sybil's. "I don't know if Valerie's relationship with Carson Shore is going to work or not. But if it fails, it won't be because of me."

Sybil's polished nails bit into the expensive leather of her purse. "Are you telling me the truth? You're not going to try to crush Valerie's relationship with Carson?"

"No." It occurred to Oliver that the members of his family held a remarkably jaundiced opinion of him.

"You really did seal a truce with Paul Shore at lunch yesterday?"

"In a manner of speaking." Oliver glanced at his watch. "Sybil, if you don't mind, I've got a lot of things to do this afternoon."

"I don't believe it."

"Fine." Oliver unfolded his hands and picked up a pen. "Believe whatever you want to believe. But as I said, I'm busy at the moment."

"Oliver, look at me." Sybil stood up and stepped to the edge of the desk. "Do you swear to me that you're telling the truth? You don't have any tricks up your sleeve? You aren't hatching any schemes to stop Valerie from marrying Carson?"

Oliver gazed thoughtfully at her. The last time he had seen that beseeching look in her eyes had been sixteen years ago when he had confronted her after finding her in bed with her lover. "Sybil, you're a very suspicious person."

"Everything I know about suspicion I've learned from you." Sybil narrowed her eyes. "I'm serious. I know you hate my guts, but I'm asking you to please level with me this one time."

Oliver put the pen down very slowly. "I don't."

"You don't what?" she demanded.

He practiced the deep breathing he used when he did his yoga exercises. "I don't hate you."

Sybil stared at him. "Of course you do. You've always hated me. You didn't like me the day your father married me, and you thought I was beneath contempt that day you found me in bed with Greg."

"Greg? Was that his name? I'd forgotten."

"Yes, that was his name." Sybil's voice was very tight. "Greg Taylor." She swallowed visibly. "I loved him, you know. Oh, I realized later that he didn't love me. He had never loved me. He just used me. But at the time, I loved him."

"Even though he was married to someone else? And so were you?"

"It's true, Greg and I were both married." Sybil looked down at her wedding ring. "There are a lot of reasons for marriage and they don't all include love. You should know that better than anyone."

"One more comment about my marriage and I'll throw you out of this office."

"I'm sorry." Her mouth tightened. "Believe it or not, I didn't come here to quarrel with you. But let's be honest, you're not exactly a model for loving, romantic, devoted husbands everywhere, are you?"

"Annie seems content," Oliver said evenly.

He wondered if Sybil had even the slightest hint of how hard he had to work to keep his tone cool and his words restrained. Inside he was practically shouting out the secret he had held close all day long.

Annie loved him. He wanted to tell Sybil. He longed to tell the whole world. He longed to say the words aloud so that they would seem more real, but he was half-afraid to give them voice. He was desperate to go home this afternoon just so he could hear Annie tell him again that she loved him. Maybe if she told him often enough, he would eventually allow himself to believe her.

"Annie seems content?" Sybil repeated incredulously. "What does that mean? Are you trying to tell me you've seduced her into thinking that you actually love her?"

"Sybil, I suggest we change the subject."

Sybil tilted her head slightly, reacting to the ice in his voice. She had known him long enough to know when she had pushed too far. "All right. Let's do that. There's one more thing I want to know before I leave."

"What's that?"

Sybil held his eyes for a moment longer. Then she broke the contact and walked over to the window. She stood with her back to him. "I want to know how far the mellowing of Oliver Rain has gone."

"Try being more specific."

"Is Valerie the only one who is going to benefit

from the magical effect Annie is apparently having on you?"

Oliver studied the rigid set of Sybil's shoulders. "I take it you want to know if it's safe to tell me about your affair with Jonathan Grace?"

"Christ. You really are a bastard, aren't you?" Sybil did not turn around. "How long have you known?"

"Does it matter?"

"I suppose not." She sighed wearily. "I don't know why I even bothered to try to keep my relationship with Jonathan under wraps."

Oliver thought about it. "Maybe you tried because you're genuinely serious about him."

"I haven't felt like this since Greg," she whispered. "I love him, Oliver. Are you going to ruin it for me?"

"Let's not get melodramatic. I can't and won't stop you from marrying anyone. I don't have that kind of power over you."

"You're wrong," Sybil said. "You do have that kind of power. And you know it as well as I do. All you have to do is threaten to cut me out of the Rain fortune and I'll drop any dreams I have for marrying Jonathan. Just like that." She snapped her fingers.

"The money is that important to you?"

"Yes, goddamn it." Sybil whirled around, her face a tight mask of fear and anger. "Yes, it's that important. You think you had it tough because your father walked out and left you holding the bag, but you don't know how tough life can be, Oliver Rain."

"But you're going to tell me, right?"

"You didn't grow up on welfare. You didn't have to live in a housing project. That neighborhood was so dangerous my mother wouldn't let me play outside for fear I might get raped. My father didn't walk out when I was twenty-two, Oliver. He left before I was even born. Yes, the money is that important to me."

"Doesn't Grace have money?"

"He has money, all right, but that's not the point. I want the money I earned. I need to know I have money of my own. And I did earn my share of the Rain fortune, Oliver. You know I did. We made a bargain and I help up my end of it. Admit it."

Oliver wondered what Annie would say if she were here. "The money is yours, Sybil. You're right, you earned it. You'll continue to get your share regardless of whether you decide to remarry."

Sybil's eyes widened with shock. Then hope glimmered in them. "Do you mean it?"

"Yes."

"You give me your word?"

"Yes." Oliver reached out and switched on the computer. "Now, if you don't mind, I'd like to get something done this afternoon. I'm trying to keep Lyncroft afloat."

Sybil moved slowly toward the door. She looked dazed. "My God, Annie really is having an impact on you, isn't she? I would never have believed it."

"Good-bye, Sybil." Oliver punched up the cost-analysis data he had been studying earlier.

Sybil paused, her hand on the doorknob. "Oliver?"

"Yes?"

"I know this is going to sound stupid, but I'm suddenly dying of curiosity. Is there the remote possibility that you've actually fallen in love?"

"Good-bye, Sybil."

"I knew it was a stupid question. Good-bye, Oliver. Oh, one more thing. Are you going to Valerie's preview tomorrow night?"

Oliver frowned, remembering that Annie had said something about attending. "I don't know yet."

"If you decide to come perhaps I'll introduce you to Jonathan. I think you'll like him if you'll give yourself a chance."

Oliver looked up. "One thing, Sybil."

"What's that?"

"You're a wealthy woman."

"Thanks to you," she murmured graciously.

"What do you know about Grace?"

Sybil's expression became immediately wary. "What are you implying? That Jonathan might want to marry me for my money now that I can be certain of keeping it?"

"It's something that needs to be considered."

"I've got news for you. Jonathan asked me to marry him weeks ago even though I told him there was a good chance you'd cut me off."

"I see. Sounds like the noble type. Would you feel a little more secure if I had Bolt look into his background?"

Sybil scowled. "I don't know whether to be furious or flattered. Are you, in your own nasty, suspicious way, trying to protect me?"

"You're part of the family," Oliver said quietly.

"I don't believe it." But Sybil was suddenly smiling. "You *are* trying to protect me."

"Maybe I'm just trying to protect your share of the Rain money."

"All right, I'll buy that. Still, coming from you, it's rather sweet." Sybil laughed. "You must be in love, Oliver. Why don't you admit it? I hope for your sake that Annie loves you. I don't want to be within a thousand miles of you if it turns out she's just using you to save Lyncroft."

17

Annie eased her foot off the gas pedal as she rounded another curve in the narrow, winding road. Although it was only four-thirty, it was already dark. The thick woods that loomed on either side of the pavement didn't help matters. She told herself she could have done very nicely without the light fog that drifted in the beam of her headlights.

There were no street lights on the old island road, and she had not passed a house nor seen another car for over a mile. The sense of being totally alone was unnerving.

Annie brought the car to a complete halt when she came to a small signpost. She peered through the windshield, struggling to read the faded lettering. Marston Lane.

According to the address Sarah had provided and the map Annie had brought with her, this was the right spot. She turned into the lane.

The pavement was rough and broken, forcing Annie to slow her pace to a crawl. She saw the bulk of an old cabin in a stand of trees ahead. There were no lights in the windows and no car in the drive.

Annie brought her little red compact to a halt, switched off the engine, and sat behind the wheel, studying Thorpe's cottage. The eerie silence made her nervous. She realized that having come this far, she was uncertain about what to do next.

Oliver would have known what to do, she thought. Oliver always knew what to do.

But Oliver wasn't here. He had been out of the office when she had called from the ferry dock. Something unexpected had come up, Mrs. Jameson had explained. He had left immediately after receiving a call from someone named Bolt. She had not known when he would be back.

Annie retrieved the flashlight Daniel always insisted she keep in the glove compartment. Then she opened the car door. The chunking sound was very loud in the foggy silence.

The biting cold attacked her the instant she stepped out of the warmth of the front seat. Annie fastened her coat and pulled on a pair of gloves. She wished very badly that Oliver was with her.

This was ridiculous. She did not even know what she was going to do other than knock on the door and perhaps peek in the windows. It occurred to her that if there was someone inside the house, he might mistake her for a prowler if she was not careful.

Annie forced herself to walk briskly to the front door of the cottage. She knocked loudly.

"Is anyone home?"

A faint sighing in the trees overhead was the only answer. But Annie felt an odd trickle of awareness go down her spine. She spun around, convinced for a terrifying instant that she was not alone.

"Hello," she called. "Is someone there?"

The silent fog ebbed and flowed in the flashlight beam. Annie whipped the light across the space in front of her but saw nothing.

"All right, calm down," she told herself aloud. "You came here for answers. Don't panic or you won't get any."

She walked to the nearest window and pointed the flashlight through the dirty glass. The narrow beam picked out the dark shapes of a sagging couch and an ancient armchair. Magazines were scattered across the coffee table.

Annie went to the next window and found herself looking into a kitchen. There were dishes piled on the drainboard. A box of cereal stood on the counter.

The evidence of recent habitation made Annie take a quick step back. She stumbled over a clump of bushes. The flashlight beam waved wildly about until she regained her footing.

"Take it easy," Annie instructed herself through gritted teeth. "So you're a little new at this. You've seen enough television to know how it's done. You'll get the hang of it."

She continued her trek around the small cabin, pointing the flashlight through each window. The bedroom was in disarray. Wally Thorpe apparently did not believe in making his bed or in emptying his trash. The closet doors stood open. Annie peered more closely and saw that there were no clothes hanging inside.

Curiosity began to overcome her nervousness. When she reached the back door and found that it was unlocked, Annie took a deep breath, steeled herself, and opened it.

The cabin had a musty odor, as if it had been closed up for a long time. But that wasn't the worst of it. The smell of decaying food in the kitchen was the clearest indication that no one had been living here in some time. The cottage reeked.

Annie walked slowly through the rooms, careful not to touch anything. She had been right about the clothes in the closet. There weren't any. Nor were there any clothes in the drawers. There were towels on the bathroom floor but no sign of shaving gear.

It finally struck Annie that there was a general air of a hurried departure about the cottage. It was as if Wally Thorpe had come home one day, thrown his clothes and personal belongings into a suitcase, and fled.

Annie walked back into the kitchen. The smell was worst in that room. She started to retreat, but her eye was caught by the sight of a calendar featuring nude models on the wall near the phone.

It wasn't the unreal size of the featured lady's bare breasts that fascinated Annie. It was the fact that the woman in the picture proudly bore the title of Miss October that riveted her attention.

This was late November. Wally Thorpe had not been around to change the calendar to the new month. He had been gone several weeks.

Holding her nose, Annie went closer. The calendar had a square for each day of the month. There were short, cryptic notes in some of the squares.

The seventh of October, the day her brother had disappeared, was circled in red.

Annie stared at the calendar in mounting horror. A coincidence, she told herself. Perhaps Wally Thorpe had decided that was the day he was going to quit his job. No, Sarah said he had left two days later.

Then Annie noticed the phone number that had been scrawled across the fifth of October. There was something familiar about it although she could not immediately identify it. Then it hit her. She had dialed that number herself on more than one occasion in the recent past.

There was a pen hanging on a string near the calendar. Annie reached for it with her gloved hand and used it to jot down the number Thorpe had written on the calendar.

She was stuffing the paper back into her purse when she heard a board squeak somewhere in the distance. For an instant Annie thought her heart was going to stop. A split second later adrenaline pumped through her like an icy wave of electricity. It shot across her nerve endings and stirred the hairs on the back of her neck.

She switched off the flashlight and was immediately shrouded in cold darkness.

She couldn't tell if the squeak had come from inside the house or from the steps outside the front door. She strained to listen and heard nothing. The sensation of being watched was stronger than it had been earlier.

Annie was afraid to move and at the same time compelled to run. She fought for control of her muscles and managed to take one step toward the back door.

With great concentration, she succeeded in taking another step. And then a third.

She reached the back door and twisted the knob slowly. The door made a soft groaning noise as she opened it.

Annie hesitated in the doorway, staring into the unfathomable darkness. Nothing moved outside, at least nothing that she could see. She gathered her courage and went cautiously down the steps.

She stopped in the blackest shadows cast by the side of the house and looked longingly at her car in the drive. She was going to have to make a dash for it.

Annie gripped her keys in her fist and ran for the car.

No one stopped her. No one called out. No one fired at her. A moment later she was safe inside the car. She locked the doors and jammed the keys into the ignition. The engine started with a roar of protest.

Annie snapped the car into reverse, glanced over her shoulder, and sent the compact rocketing back down the drive. She didn't breath until she reached the main road. Then she jammed the pedal to the floor. If she hurried, she could make the next ferry back to Seattle.

Annie didn't know what was going on, but she very much wished she had brought Oliver along for the ride.

"What the hell do you mean, you don't know where Annie is?" Oliver snarled softly into the receiver.

There was an instant of startled silence on the other end of the line. Oliver swore silently. Terrorizing innocents would not get him the answers he wanted.

"Sorry," Ella stammered. "Hey, look, she left around three and I haven't seen her since. I closed up the shop without her. She probably got hung up with a client."

"What is the name of this client?"

"I don't know. I mean, I'm not even sure she went out on business. She just left. Said she had some errands to run or something. Maybe she went shopping. It's only six-thirty. Is something wrong, Mr. Rain?"

"No. Nothing's wrong." Oliver forced himself to speak calmly. "Thank you, Ella."

"Sure. Sorry I couldn't help. She's probably on her way home right now."

"Yes."

Oliver hung up the phone and looked at Bolt. "Ella last saw her around three o'clock."

"Are you going to call Joanna McKenna?" Bolt asked.

"If I do, she'll undoubtedly panic. Ms. McKenna has had her doubts about me from the beginning. She is very likely to put an unpleasant construction on this current turn of events."

"It wouldn't surprise me." Bolt's mouth thinned. "May I remind you, Mr. Rain, that we would not find ourselves in this situation if I'd been keeping an eye on Annie for you."

"I don't need you to tell me that, Bolt." Oliver got to his feet, shoved his hands into his pockets, and began to prowl the study. "Are you certain she didn't leave a note?"

"I searched everywhere. And I listened to the calls taken by the answering machine twice."

Oliver curled his hand into a fist inside his pocket. He was getting edgier by the minute. Something was very wrong, and he was utterly helpless. "Goddamn it, Bolt. We don't even know where to start looking."

"It's only six-thirty."

"She's always home by a quarter to six."

"True," Bolt agreed. "Nevertheless, I must point out that you haven't lived with her long enough to know all her habits and idiosyncrasies. For all we know, she went out to one of the malls and got delayed in traffic."

"She should have called."

Bolt shook his head. "She doesn't have a car phone."

"Get her one. Better yet, make certain you drive her wherever she wants to go."

"Yes, sir."

"She's not single any more," Oliver muttered. "She's supposed to keep me informed. She ought to let me know when she's going to be late."

"Yes, sir."

"Damn it to hell." Oliver stared down at the carefully raked sand in the rock garden. The possibility that something had happened to Annie was turning his insides to ice. It was an unthinkable possibility that he had been pushing aside for the last forty minutes. Nothing had happened to her, he told himself. She was late getting home, that was all.

Bolt stirred. "You're worried that there may be a connection between what happened to Cork today and the fact that Annie's missing, aren't you?"

Oliver braced himself. "Yes."

"The odds are against it, I think," Bolt said in a considering tone. "Regardless of what Cork might have been up to, there's no reason Annie would be a target. If someone wanted to see Lyncroft Unlimited broken up by its creditors, it would make more sense to get rid of you."

Oliver realized Bolt was trying to reassure him. "We don't even know if Cork was a target or just the victim of bad luck and bad driving."

The message that Barry Cork had been pulled out of a single-car freeway accident and taken, unconscious, to Harborview Hospital had reached Bolt shortly after three. He had immediately called Oliver who had left the office to meet him at the hospital. There they had learned nothing except that Cork might not live.

A faint, discreet *bong* announced that the front door was being opened. Oliver spun around, galvanized by the soft, muted tone.

"Bolt?" Annie's voice came from the foyer. "Oliver? Where is everyone?"

Oliver started for the doorway. "I'm going to strangle her."

"*Sir.*"

Oliver paused briefly, surprised by the urgency in Bolt's normally emotionless voice. "What is it?"

Bolt looked at him. "I just wanted to remind you, sir, that Mrs. Rain has only been living here for a very short time."

"So?"

Bolt coughed discreetly. "So she may not yet be fully conversant with your, uh, requirements vis-à-vis a wife."

"Are you trying to tell me I shouldn't come down on her like an avalanche just because she's put me through hell for the last hour?"

"There is an old saying, sir. You can catch more flies with honey than you can with vinegar. And it *is* only six-thirty, sir."

"I'll be damned," Oliver muttered. "The woman reads your manuscript, tells you it's wonderful, and the next thing I know she's got you eating out of the palm of her hand. What the hell is going on around here?" He turned and stalked out the door without waiting for an answer.

Annie poked her head out of the kitchen. Her eyes looked huge and serious. "There you are. I was wondering where everyone was."

Oliver scowled at the sight of her. Annie looked disheveled and anxious. Her hair was even more wildly tangled than usual. There was dried mud on her shoes and her stockings were snagged. A terrible fear ripped through him.

"Annie, what happened?"

Annie stared at him, her lower lip trembling. Her eyes filled with tears. Then, with a small, indecipherable exclamation, she hurled herself straight into his arms.

"For God's sake, what's wrong?" Oliver crushed her to him. She felt small and soft and so very vulnerable. "Are you all right?"

"I'm okay." She sniffled loudly against his shirt as she wrapped her arms fiercely around his waist. "Honest. Just a little shaken, that's all."

"Where have you been? Why are you late?"

"I went to Bainbridge Island."

"To see a client?" Oliver held her gently away from him so that he could search her face.

"To see a man named Wally Thorpe."

Oliver's fingers tightened roughly on her shoulders. "Why in God's name would you want to see Thorpe?"

Annie blinked the last of the tears out of her eyes. "You know who he is?"

"He's the mechanic who serviced Daniel's plane the day he vanished."

Annie frowned. "How did you know that?"

"I told you, I made certain that the investigation of your brother's accident was very thorough."

"Yes, you did, didn't you?"

299

"I didn't talk to Thorpe myself but the authorities did," Oliver said. "The company that rented the plane to your brother cooperated in every way. There was no evidence that anyone had tampered with the plane or that anything had been overlooked in the servicing of the aircraft."

"Nothing at all?"

"No. Annie, why did you suddenly take it into your head to talk to Thorpe today?"

"I didn't talk to him. He wasn't there."

Getting the answers was not going to be easy. Annie was frazzled and nervous. Oliver summoned all of his self-control and patience.

He put his arm around Annie's shoulder and steered her down the hall to the study where Bolt waited. "What made you decide to look for Thorpe?"

Annie started to answer and then broke off when she saw Bolt. She smiled weakly. "Hi. Sorry I'm a little late. Hope dinner's okay."

"There is no problem with dinner, Mrs. Rain." Bolt's eyes skimmed over her, noting her unkempt appearance. "Are you all right?"

"Uh-huh." Annie dropped into the nearest chair. She stuck her feet out in front of her, leaned her head back, and rested her arms wearily on the arms of the chair.

Oliver sat down behind his desk. "Bolt, will you please bring us some tea?"

"Yes, sir." Bolt disappeared through the door.

Oliver felt his insides gradually unclench. She was all right. She was safe and sound, that was the important thing. He could breathe freely again. But something had happened, and he had to find out what it was. He deliberately gentled his voice.

"Tell me why you tried to find Thorpe, Annie."

She regarded him solemnly. "I got a phone call this afternoon. The caller didn't identify himself." Annie paused. "Or maybe it was a woman. I really couldn't tell. The voice on the other end of the line just said that if I wanted to find out what had happened to my brother, I should find the mechanic who had serviced his plane."

"*Shit.*"

Annie blinked. "Yes, well, at any rate I called the aviation service firm Daniel had used and got Thorpe's address. I took the ferry to Bainbridge, looked around, and came back here."

"Hold it right there." Oliver folded his hands on the desk and leaned forward into the light cast by the halogen lamp. "Are you telling me some bastard deliberately tried to make you think Daniel's plane had been sabotaged?"

"I suppose that was the implication, wasn't it?"

"And that Thorpe was the culprit?"

"That was kind of how it sounded."

"And that knowing these facts you went tearing off by yourself to investigate?"

Annie held his gaze. "Yes. That's what I'm telling you."

Oliver lost his temper, an event so rare that he almost didn't recognize what was happening. "*You little fool.* Don't you have an ounce of common sense? Do you have any idea of what I've been going through, wondering where the hell you were?"

Annie opened her mouth, clearly about to defend herself, but stopped as Bolt walked in with the tea tray. She smiled thankfully at him. "Thanks, I need that."

"You're welcome," Bolt said. He set about pouring three cups.

Oliver fixed Annie with a look. "I want an explanation."

"You're getting it." She accepted the cup and saucer from Bolt with another grateful smile. "I'll tell you the truth, Oliver, at several points, I rather wished you were with me. It was a little spooky. I've never done any housebreaking before."

Hot tea splashed on Oliver's fingers as he took the cup and saucer from Bolt. "You broke into Thorpe's house? Damn it, Annie, I don't believe this."

"I didn't find much," Annie admitted. She seemed to be getting herself back under control. "But it looked as though Thorpe packed and left in a hurry. All the clothes were gone from his closet. There was still food in the kitchen. Nobody had emptied the garbage in a long time."

Oliver put down his teacup very deliberately. He stood up, planted both hands on the desk, and leaned forward. "Why in hell didn't you call me and tell me what you were going to do?"

Annie stirred uneasily in her chair. Her gaze went to the cloisonné leopard and then returned to his face. "I did call. You were out of the office."

"So you went ahead on your own."

"Yes. Oliver, this is probably a good time to tell you something else the caller said. He or she made a point of telling me that if I wanted answers about Daniel's disappearance, I should not tell you I was going to look for Thorpe. I was told not to ask you for help because I might be putting myself in danger by doing so."

302

Oliver felt as if he'd been kicked in the stomach. "You were warned not to tell me about any of this?"

"That was how it sounded. Like a warning."

Oliver did not take his eyes off her. "Then why are you telling me now, Annie?"

"I had a long time to sit and think on the ferry ride back to Seattle. I put all the evidence together and came up with an interesting conclusion."

Out of the corner of his eye Oliver saw Bolt take a step closer to the desk. "What was that conclusion?" Oliver asked very carefully.

"It seemed to me," Annie said slowly, "that someone was deliberately trying to set you up. Someone wants me to believe you're behind Daniel's disappearance."

A screaming silence filled the study.

"A very logical conclusion," Oliver finally said grimly. He exchanged a silent glance with Bolt. Then he looked at Annie again. "Did the caller say anything else? What was this evidence you mentioned?"

"He didn't say much. At least not on the phone." Annie opened her purse and drew out a small slip of paper. "But while I was in Thorpe's house I found a calendar. The date Daniel disappeared was circled on it."

Bolt frowned. "Not surprising. Your brother's disappearance would have been a major event for Thorpe and everyone else at the aviation service firm where he worked. It's not every day a company like that loses an aircraft."

"That wasn't all I found on the calendar." Annie put the piece of paper on the desk in front of Oliver. "Someone had written this phone number down two days before my brother rented the plane."

Oliver glanced at the number and recognized it instantly. "Damn it to hell." He sank slowly back down into his chair.

"What is it?" Bolt stepped forward and peered at the phone number Annie had scribbled on the paper. "That's one of the lines you've got here in the penthouse, sir. It's your private number."

"Yes." Oliver said nothing more. He couldn't think of anything to say. He watched Annie intently as he fought to deal with this new twist in a situation that was threatening to escalate out of control. "Did you recognize it, Annie?"

"Yes, of course."

Bolt picked up the piece of paper. "Looks like we've got a problem with security, sir. Only members of the family have this number."

"I'm aware of that." Oliver couldn't tear his gaze away from Annie's face.

She was watching him just as intently, but although she still appeared worried, there was no fear or suspicion in her expressive eyes. She trusted him, he thought. In the face of all the damning evidence, she trusted him.

"So how did Wally Thorpe get your private phone number?" she asked finally, breaking the silence.

"An interesting question." Oliver sat down again and picked up his teacup. "And one for which I don't have an answer." He finally managed to wrench his gaze away from Annie. He looked at Bolt. "I believe we had better try to find Thorpe."

"Yes, sir." Bolt took a swallow of his tea. "I'll see what I can do."

Annie crossed her legs and idly swung her foot. Her gaze switched back and forth between Bolt and

Oliver. "I reached a couple of other conclusions while I was sitting on that ferry."

"Yes, Mrs. Rain?" Bolt asked politely.

"We agree that someone wants me to believe that Oliver is up to no good," Annie said slowly.

Bolt flicked a searching glance at Oliver and then nodded. "Apparently so."

Oliver couldn't think of anything to add to that. He was too busy trying to control the talons of rage that were digging into him. Someone had gone to a great deal of trouble to try to destroy Annie's trust in him.

"We have to ask ourselves why anyone would do that." Annie got to her feet and began to pace back and forth across the study. "There is only one obvious answer. Someone hopes I'll conclude that Oliver is behind my brother's disappearance. That same someone must want me to divorce Oliver so that he can no longer control Lyncroft Unlimited. But who would benefit from that?"

"No one," Oliver said grimly. "All the creditors and investors stand to gain if Lyncroft stays in one piece."

"There is a faint possibility that someone in the family might want vengeance against you, Mr. Rain," Bolt said quietly. "She might see the destruction of Lyncroft as a way to achieve that goal."

Annie scowled. "You're talking about Sybil, aren't you? Forget it. The last thing she would do is hurt Oliver financially. It wouldn't be logical. She likes the Rain money."

Oliver's mouth curved ruefully. "Good point."

"People are not always logical when it comes to vengeance." Bolt gazed impassively at Oliver. "There are other possibilities besides Sybil. An old business opponent such as Paul Shore might be looking for a way to avenge himself."

Oliver leaned back in his chair. "I've made my peace with Shore." He glanced at Annie. "At least I think I have. In any event, this kind of thing isn't his style."

Bolt shrugged. "There may be others, sir, who do not wish you well."

Oliver looked at him. "Thanks for the testimonial to my ability to win friends and influence people. I'll admit that not everyone I've dealt with over the past fifteen years sends me Christmas cards, but I can't think of anyone who would do something like this to get revenge."

"Why not?" Annie asked with blunt curiosity.

"Losing Lyncroft wouldn't hurt me very badly," Oliver said, deciding to be equally blunt. "Granted, I'll make a nice profit along with everyone else if it stays whole, but the bottom line is that if Lyncroft goes under, it would only cause a minor blip on my financial screen."

Annie studied him closely. "I see. I hadn't realized it was that unimportant."

"I didn't say it wasn't important," Oliver said quietly. "But the financial considerations are the minor ones. I told you in the beginning why I agreed to save Lyncroft."

She gave him a misty smile. "Because of Daniel."

"That was part of it." Oliver turned back to Bolt. "I think we can discount the idea of a competitor who is out to get even for an old grievance."

Bolt processed that information. "There's another angle to consider. Don't forget that whoever called Annie and warned her off you may be connected to Barry Cork and his schemes."

306

"I'm aware of that." Oliver looked at Annie. "Which brings me to the reason I nearly went out of my mind when you disappeared this afternoon."

"I didn't realize you were upset just because I was a bit late," she said in surprise.

"I was more than upset. But we'll let that go for now. Annie, Cork was in an accident this afternoon. A single-car freeway mess. He was taken to Harborview. At last report he's unconscious. He may not live."

"Oh, my God," she breathed. "Poor Barry."

"The police are investigating, but the assumption is that it was an accident. There doesn't appear to be any evidence to the contrary," Bolt added.

Annie's stunned eyes went to him. "I take it that means you're not so certain?"

"No," Bolt said simply. "We're not entirely certain."

Annie clasped her hands very tightly in front of her. She gazed straight at Oliver. "You told me that the kind of white-collar industrial espionage Cork was involved in doesn't usually end in murder."

"Not usually," Oliver said. "But given this afternoon's events, I think we're going to have to reconsider that assumption."

"Maybe we should go to the police," Annie said.

Bolt sat in stony silence.

Oliver studied the arrangement of the rocks in his garden. "That, of course, is one option."

Annie's eyes widened. "Good grief, we can't do that, can we? They'd probably jump to the conclusion that you're the prime suspect."

"Probably." Oliver kept his tone noncommittal.

Annie's teeth sank into her lower lip. "They might think that you're the only one who had any clear

307

motive to get rid of Daniel. You can sit there and say that gaining control of Lyncroft was no big deal financially for you, but others might not see it that way."

"True," Oliver admitted.

"And who knows what they would decide about your connection with Barry Cork? The cops might think you tried to kill him because he was selling your new company's secrets. No, we absolutely can't go to the police at this point."

A deep warmth flowed through Oliver. Annie really did trust him. More than that, she was trying to protect him. He could not recall the last time anyone had tried to protect him.

"I'll admit it might complicate things," he agreed. "But there are two other good reasons why it might be better to keep our speculations private for the moment."

"What reasons?" Annie demanded.

"The first involves lack of proof. We have no evidence that Daniel's disappearance or Cork's freeway crash are anything more than accidents. Also, that phone call you got today is not likely to impress the police. There's no proof it even took place or that anyone implicated me or Thorpe."

"What's the second reason why we should keep the information to ourselves?" Annie asked.

"Bolt and I want to ask a few questions of our own. It will be easier for us to do so if the authorities aren't involved."

Annie stared at him, dawning excitement in her eyes. "You're going to look for some answers yourself? Oliver, that's a great idea. I'll help."

"No," Oliver said, "you will definitely not help. You will stay out of this. Furthermore, you will not go anywhere outside this penthouse or outside your shop on your own. You will keep me informed of your whereabouts at all times. There will be no more impulsive trips to Bainbridge or anywhere else. Is that clearly understood?"

A storm began to brew in Annie's eyes. "Oliver, I told you at the start of our marriage that I would not allow you to keep me under surveillance. There's a possibility that this mess involves my brother. I have a right to be a part of the investigation. I won't let you keep me in the dark."

Oliver glanced at Bolt. "I think that will be all for now, Bolt. Don't worry about fixing dinner. We'll take care of ourselves tonight."

Bolt gave Annie an uncertain glance as he started for the door. "Yes, sir. I'll be downstairs if you need me." He let himself out of the study, closing the door softly behind himself.

Annie glowered at Oliver. "I mean it, Oliver. I realize you only want to protect me, but I'm not going to let you keep me under lock and key and I'm not going to let you shut me out of our investigation."

"Annie, it's for your own good."

"A reason that is one hundred percent guaranteed to make me fight you every inch of the way. How would you feel if someone said that to you?"

"I wouldn't tolerate it," Oliver admitted. "But that's beside the point. You came to me in the first place because you wanted help saving Lyncroft. We made a bargain, you and I. It's true that neither of us could foresee how complicated things would get, but our deal still stands. I handle matters involving Lyncroft."

"This marriage is more than a bargain," Annie argued.

Oliver didn't dispute that. Instead he tried a different tack. "Annie, we've got a difficult situation here. One with a lot of unknowns in it. I don't want you taking any more of the kind of risks you took this afternoon."

She flushed. "I didn't take a risk. I just followed up on a clue."

Oliver set his teeth against his rising temper. "You took a risk. We don't even know yet how dangerous that risk was. I don't want you finding out the hard way."

"You can't keep me out of this. I'm in the middle of it, whether you like it or not."

She was right. But Oliver knew he would do anything within his power to keep her as safe as possible. He had no scruples when it came to protecting Annie. "I don't intend to argue with you."

"Good." She gave him a warm, approving smile. "You know something, Oliver, you really are making progress. In the old days I'll bet you would have just laid down the law and the hell with my feelings on the subject. But now we're actually talking like equals."

"I'm glad you approve of the new Oliver Rain." Oliver got up and walked around the desk.

"I like him very much." Annie eyed him with a trace of wariness as he came toward her. "What are you doing?"

He stopped in front of her, put his hands on her shoulders, and kissed her full on the mouth. He deliberately deepened the kiss until she sagged warmly against him. Then he lifted his mouth from hers. "I'll give you one guess."

"What about dinner?"

"Dinner can wait twenty minutes. I can't." He eased her back against the desk and moved between her legs. He pushed her skirt up above her knees with one hand and lowered his zipper with the other.

"Only twenty minutes, Oliver?" Annie's eyes were full of loving laughter.

"Fifteen at the rate I'm going."

"Go for twenty," she advised in a husky whisper. "I don't want to have to borrow Arthur's book on the problem of premature ejaculation."

18

The following evening Annie stood with Valerie in the central gallery of the Eckert Museum. She surveyed the crowd that had turned out for the museum's preview. "You must be thrilled, Val. The exhibition is obviously a hit."

"Gold has a way of capturing the imagination," Valerie said modestly.

"You've done a fantastic job." Annie admired a collection of ancient gold jewelry in a nearby display case. The images of strange deities and animals had been rendered with astounding artistry on a variety of arm bands, necklaces, and earrings. "There's an exciting feel to the way you've arranged the pieces. People will love it."

Valerie glanced down at the case. Her eyes glowed with pride. "Thanks, but it would have been tough to ruin this collection. As you said the other day, there's a wonderfully savage sophistication about Pre-Columbian art."

Annie moved on to study a ferocious feline figure carved in gold. "Another jaguar?"

"Yes, it was a common motif. That particular piece is Diquis."

"It would look great in Oliver's study," Annie observed.

Carson appeared at Valerie's elbow. "I've never

seen his study, but I agree it would probably fit right in. There's a certain resemblance between Rain and that big cat."

They all glanced across the crowded gallery to where Oliver stood talking with a small group of people.

"You can say that again," Valerie murmured. "Annie, I can't believe the effect you're having on my brother. He's a changed man these days."

"Do you think so?" Annie asked wistfully.

"Are you kidding?" Valerie laughed. "Oliver is actually mingling tonight. I can hardly believe my eyes. In the past he almost never attended this kind of thing, let alone tried to socialize."

Annie watched Oliver covertly for a moment. All right, he was mingling, but it was still rather like watching a large leopard trying to appear innocent while standing amid a herd of antelope. There was no getting around the fact that he would never be one of the crowd.

Oliver was not actually doing much talking as far as she could see, but at least he was with a group. He wasn't holding himself entirely aloof from those around him the way he had that night at Daniel's engagement party.

But she was not certain just how changed Oliver really was. True, there were signs that he was making a serious effort to be more sensitive in his dealings with the members of his family. And he had declared a truce with Paul Shore. But as far as Annie was concerned, he was not making vast progress communicating with her except in bed.

He had not yet told her that he loved her.

She was determined to remain optimistic, however.

313

Sooner or later she knew she would hear the words from him. She was certain he was falling in love with her.

Richard and Nathan, looking like younger versions of Oliver in their formal attire, wandered over to join Annie, Valerie, and Carson.

"Great job, Val." Richard nodded toward the nearest display case. "Bet the museum shelled out a bundle for this stuff, huh?"

"Some of it's on loan from a couple of local private collections. But Eckert owns a fair amount. Many were acquired years ago before it was considered extremely valuable and before the various governments involved clamped down on exports."

Nathan swept the room with a single glance and frowned. "What's with Mom tonight? I thought she was planning to be here."

"Sybil said she was going to be a little late," Valerie explained. "I think she's planning a small surprise."

"What sort of surprise?" Nathan asked.

Richard raised his brows in a manner that was startlingly reminiscent of Oliver. "I'll bet she's going to bring Jonathan Grace with her."

Nathan glanced at him. "Yeah? She's going to stop trying to hide him from big brother?"

"I got that impression," Richard said. He grinned. "And I've got five bucks that says big brother probably already knows about him, anyway. No one in this family can keep a secret from Oliver."

"That," Nathan intoned in a sepulchral voice, "is because big brother sees all and knows all."

"As a matter of fact," Heather said as she joined the group, "I talked to Sybil this afternoon. She said she definitely planned to bring Grace tonight so that she

314

could introduce him to Oliver. She seemed very up-beat about the idea."

"Oliver must have given his approval in advance," Nathan remarked.

Valerie smiled. "Probably because of Annie."

Heather looked at Annie. "I think we've got a white witch in the family. You've cast some sort of spell on Oliver, Annie."

Annie shook her head quickly. "No one could change Oliver. Not unless he wanted to be changed. There's no spell on him. It's just that he's been practicing interpersonal communication skills, that's all."

"Oliver's been working on his interpersonal communication skills?" Richard laughed. "Hey, that's great. Like they say in Hollywood, what a concept."

Heather frowned thoughtfully. "He wasn't so bad about communicating some things. Remember how he used to make us all join him in his study after dinner every night?"

"Don't remind me." Richard grimaced good-naturedly. "He made us do our homework there with him while he went over business papers. We spent every evening in my brother's study while the rest of our friends were watching TV and playing video games."

"It didn't hurt us one bit," Heather said stoutly. "Taught us good study habits for one thing."

"And it gave you time with Oliver, for another," Annie observed softly.

"Yeah, I guess so. But I don't think you get the picture, Annie." Richard grinned. "The biggest lesson we learned there in Oliver's study was that if one of us screwed up in school, it was a reflection on the whole family. No one dared embarrass the family by getting a failing grade because no one wanted to explain the failure to Oliver."

"Oliver was better at intimidation than interpersonal communication," Nathan said. But he sounded remarkably cheerful about it.

Heather smiled her serious smile. "My brother does seem different lately. If I had to put my finger on what has changed about him, I would say that he seems happier. And that must be because of you, Annie. Nothing else has occurred that could account for the transformation."

"I appreciate the positive feedback," Annie said, "but let's not get carried away. There hasn't been a huge transformation, just some minor modifications."

"You're wrong," Heather said simply. "The changes are major."

"Heather's right." Richard looked at Annie. "Maybe this is a case of Beauty and the Beast."

Annie bristled. "Oliver was never a beast."

"That's what you think," Valerie said dryly. "Don't get me wrong, I love him dearly, but Oliver can be a real pain when it comes to getting what he wants. And he always knows what he wants."

"Yeah, not only for himself, but for everyone else," Richard added.

"He means well," Annie said quickly.

"We're not saying he doesn't," Nathan said wryly. "But with Oliver it's usually a case of do it his way or don't do it at all."

"He's not that bad," Annie said.

"No?" Nathan chuckled ruefully. "Last year I came up with the brilliant idea of postponing college for a year while I did some traveling in Europe. Oliver didn't agree. You will notice that I am at the university this year, not drinking coffee on the Via Veneto."

"Here comes Mom," Richard said. He nodded toward the doorway. "And she's got Grace with her. Looks like she really is going to introduce him to Oliver." He whistled soundlessly. "This is serious stuff."

"Do you like Jonathan Grace?" Annie asked curiously as she watched Sybil and Jonathan make their way through the room.

"He's okay," Nathan said noncommittally. "What matters is that Mom is happy."

"You mean Oliver has finally condescended to allow her to be happy," Valerie said bluntly. She glanced at Carson. "I know how Sybil's been feeling these past few months."

Carson shrugged. "Your brother doesn't seem so bad to me."

"You never knew him B.A.," Valerie said.

Carson slanted her a questioning look. "B.A.?"

"Before Annie," Heather murmured. "Sybil looks terrific tonight, doesn't she?"

Annie had to agree that Sybil looked radiant in a soft green sheath that highlighted her upswept hair. Beside her Jonathan Grace was distinguished looking in his expensively tailored formal clothes. He had Sybil's arm tucked protectively under his own, and there was an expression of intense satisfaction in his eyes. Annie realized he was watching Oliver, who had not yet noticed Sybil's arrival.

Annie glanced at Heather inquiringly. "I thought Sybil said Oliver and Jonathan had never met."

"They haven't," Valerie said. "Sybil's been afraid to introduce them. Cross your fingers and hope this

317

works. Otherwise, I'm afraid Sybil's going to be heartbroken. I think she's really in love with Grace."

"It'll be okay," Annie assured her.

Oliver chose that moment to abandon the small group of people with whom he had been standing. He searched the room with a single glance, found Annie, and started toward her.

In typical Oliver fashion, he looked neither to the right nor to the left as he cut a swath through the crowd. He didn't seem to notice people moving aside for him; he simply walked where he wanted to walk and a path miraculously appeared before him.

When he reached Annie and the others, he nodded at Carson and then looked at Valerie. "The exhibition is impressive, Val. Congratulations."

Valerie glowed. It was obvious Oliver's praise meant a great deal to her. "Thanks."

Carson smiled proudly. "She's one of the best on the West Coast when it comes to Pre-Columbian art. Eckert is lucky to have her."

Before Oliver could respond, Sybil glided up with Jonathan at her side.

"Good evening, everyone." Sybil's eyes were bright with pleasure. "Valerie, the exhibition is terrific. It's bound to attract a lot of attention."

"I hope so," Valerie said.

"It will. The reviews are going to be great." Sybil turned smoothly to Oliver. "I'd like you to meet Jonathan Grace, Oliver. Jonathan, this is Oliver. I believe I've mentioned him."

"Several times." Jonathan smiled, but his eyes were watchful. "It's a pleasure to meet you at last. I must admit, you're not quite what I had imagined."

"What were you expecting?" Oliver asked mildly.

"There was something said about fangs and claws, but I don't see them," Jonathan said. "I understand you're going to have me investigated."

"*Jonathan*," Sybil hissed in dismay.

"It's all right." Jonathan patted her hand affectionately. "I appreciate the fact that he wants to protect you, darling. You should appreciate it, too."

Sybil raised her eyes toward the ceiling, but there was a delicate blush on her cheeks.

"Feel free to check out whatever you like," Jonathan said seriously to Oliver. "I'll have my accountant forward some copies of my recent income tax forms if that will be of any help."

"Thank you," Oliver said. "That will be very useful."

Sybil glowered at him. "I'm warning you, Oliver. Don't you dare embarrass me."

"I wouldn't think of it, Sybil." Oliver turned to Annie. "Are you ready to go?"

Annie looked at him in surprise. "Are we leaving already?"

"Yes."

Annie started to argue, but something in Oliver's expression stopped her. She turned to Valerie. "Well, in that case, congratulations again, Valerie."

"Thank you," Valerie said softly. She stepped forward and gave Annie a brief, affectionate hug. "For everything."

Annie smiled, embarrassed, and said her farewells to the rest of the Rains. Oliver took her arm and started toward the door. As usual, a path magically appeared.

Bolt was waiting at the curb with the limo. He got out from behind the wheel to open the door.

"Why are we in a hurry?" Annie demanded as

Oliver stuffed her neatly into the back of the car. "I was enjoying myself."

"Sorry, we're on a schedule," he told her as he got in beside her.

"Whose schedule? What schedule?" Annie tried to read his face in the shadows as Bolt eased the limo away from the curb.

"I have a business appointment this evening." Oliver glanced at the glowing face of the limo's digital clock. "I'm going to take you home, and then Bolt will drive me to the meeting. I should be back within a couple of hours."

"You never said anything about an evening appointment. You never have evening meetings. What are you up to, Oliver?"

"It's nothing that concerns you, Annie."

"Which means it most definitely does concern me. I'm warning you, Oliver, if you don't tell me what's going on, I'll follow you to this so-called appointment of yours."

He looked startled by the threat. "No, Annie, you will not follow me."

"Tell me where you're going."

"I'd rather not."

"Wait a second, this has something to do with what's been happening, doesn't it?"

Oliver hesitated. "In a way. It involves Barry Cork."

"What about him?" she asked quickly. "He's still unconscious, isn't he?"

"As far as we know." Oliver studied her for a moment, as if deliberating how much to tell her. "Bolt and I are going to take a look around his house this evening. It shouldn't take long."

320

"Why?" Annie demanded. "What do you think you'll find?"

"I don't know."

"I'll come with you."

"No, Annie."

"Yes."

He smiled faintly in the shadows. "No."

Forty-five minutes later Bolt did something to the lock on the back door of Cork's small house. The door opened without a sound. "Didn't think you'd be able to convince Mrs. Rain to stay home, sir."

"Mrs. Rain is smart enough to know when she's lost an argument." Oliver glanced back over his shoulder, assuring himself that the tiny backyard was empty.

The last thing they needed now was a barking dog or a nosy neighbor. But there was no sign of either. The north-end Seattle neighborhood was quiet, almost deserted.

He and Bolt had switched from the limo to the Mercedes when they had taken Annie home in hopes of not drawing any attention to themselves out here in the suburbs.

Oliver went through the door and found himself in pitch darkness. The drapes were closed.

"No offense, sir, but I was surprised when she gave up so easily." Bolt followed Oliver through the door.

"I made it easy for her when I told her that if she insisted on coming along, I would cancel the whole project."

Annie had fumed, but she had finally surrendered to the threat. Oliver wasn't about to admit to Bolt that he was privately surprised and vastly relieved by the relatively easy victory. He probably ought to put his foot down more often with Annie, he decided.

The trouble with Annie, Oliver thought as he took out a small flashlight, was that he let her get away with murder far too frequently. Right from the beginning she had taken the initiative in their relationship. She had dictated the terms of their marriage and then she had gone on to try to dictate his whole life. She'd even issued edicts in the bedroom.

She meant well, but the bottom line was that she now thought she could talk him into anything. The realization that he was busily altering his entire world in order to please Annie sent a jolt of deep unease through him.

It dawned on Oliver that in many ways he was no longer completely in control of his life. He knew he was rapidly becoming vulnerable in a way he had never before been vulnerable. For as long as he could recall, vulnerability had always been equated with weakness in his mind. A weak man could not defend his family.

"I'll take the bedrooms," Bolt said.

"Make certain the drapes are closed in them before you use the flashlight."

Bolt made an odd rumbling noise in the darkness that might have been a laugh. "You sound like an old pro at this kind of thing, Mr. Rain."

"I've been taking lessons from my wife," Oliver muttered. "If Annie can do it, I can do it."

But he could hardly claim amateur status when it came to breaking and entering, he reminded himself grimly.

He thought about the night five years ago when he and Daniel had broken into the warehouse where

Walker Gresham had been concluding his latest gun-running deal. Technically that hadn't been an act of breaking and entering, Oliver thought. The warehouse had, after all, belonged to one of his companies. Nevertheless, he had experienced much the same sensation of heightened awareness, felt the same surge of adrenalin on that occasion that he was feeling tonight. He also felt a similar sense of wrongness.

Five years ago he and Daniel had very nearly gotten themselves killed trying this particular trick.

"Be careful, Bolt," Oliver said softly.

"All clear," Bolt said. "Drapes are pulled."

Remembering what Annie had found near the wall phone in Thorpe's cottage, Oliver checked the counter next to Cork's telephone. There were no mysterious numbers penciled onto the calendar or the pad of paper that lay there.

He opened a drawer and found nothing except some pens and a Seattle phone book. There were no personal address books or notebooks with interesting names in them.

Oliver moved slowly into the small living room. He quickly went through the contents of an end-table drawer but found nothing except a paperback thriller. He had no better luck when he joined Bolt in the second bedroom, which Cork had apparently used as an office.

"Nothing," Bolt said, closing the last drawer.

"Too much of nothing." Oliver focused the narrow beam of light on the pristine surface of Cork's desk. "I've been in Cork's office at Lyncroft a couple of times. He's the kind of manager who keeps every active file out in the open where he can see it. His desk is always a disaster area."

"Maybe his family came by and cleaned things up in here."

"I'm told the authorities didn't reach his mother and sister in Virginia until late this afternoon. They aren't even in Seattle yet. According to Cork's file, he has no relatives in the Northwest."

"That leaves another possibility," Bolt said.

"Yes." Oliver took one last look around as they worked their way back toward the kitchen. "Someone else got here first."

"Whoever it was that nudged him off that freeway?"

"If he was deliberately nudged."

"I'd say the fact that someone may have cleaned out his personal files is fairly solid evidence that Cork's accident was no accident," Bolt said.

Oliver thought about that as he and Bolt exited the way they had entered. He also thought about a few other things. He waited until they reached the car, which Bolt had parked two blocks away, before he said anything else.

"None of this makes sense." Oliver sank back into the passenger seat and gazed broodingly out the window. "The worst-case scenario here is that someone murdered Daniel Lyncroft and then tried to kill Barry Cork. But where's the motive?"

"The only motive I can see is that someone wanted Lyncroft to fail," Bolt said. "Maybe one of those California outfits."

"There's another way of looking at this," Oliver said slowly. "One we haven't considered. Someone may have killed Daniel for other reasons entirely, reasons that have nothing to do with Lyncroft." Oliver paused. "But that doesn't make sense. Daniel was not the kind of man who collected enemies."

"The fact that someone is trying to make Mrs. Rain suspicious of you doesn't figure either, sir. Why reopen the question of Lyncroft's death when everyone assumes it's an accident? And why get rid of Cork?"

"Cork may have known too much. And he was in the business of selling information. The killer might have paid Cork to get the kind of inside data he would need on Daniel's plans in order to set up the plane accident."

"Used Wally Thorpe to sabotage the plane and then decided to get rid of both Thorpe and Cork so there wouldn't be any witnesses?"

"The theory fits some of the facts," Oliver said thoughtfully.

"If that's true, the killer was home free. No one even suggested that Lyncroft was murdered. No one noticed that Thorpe was missing. And unless you make an issue of it, chances are no one will question Cork's accident. So why is someone going out of his way now to make Annie suspicious of you and thereby raise all kinds of questions?"

Oliver studied the city lights as Bolt drove back toward downtown. "If we assume that destabilizing Lyncroft Unlimited is not the goal, then we have to look for other motives."

"Daniel Lyncroft is dead. Someone may be trying to set you up as the fall guy. If he makes it work, you could conceivably wind up in prison for a very long time." Bolt turned his head briefly to glance back at Oliver. "I'd say you were a target, Mr. Rain."

Oliver was silent for a moment. "But why the convoluted approach? Why not kill me outright? Why go through the trouble of murdering Daniel Lyncroft first?"

"I don't know," Bolt admitted.

Oliver frowned. "And why risk the possibility that I won't be convicted of murder? After all, there's no evidence. Not even Daniel's body, let alone the sabotaged plane. I might have to hire some expensive lawyers if things get nasty, but there's not much chance that I'll end up doing time for the murder of Daniel Lyncroft."

"No, but the publicity would be pretty rough on the family," Bolt said softly.

"Yes." Not unlike what they had all gone through fifteen years ago when his father had walked out, Oliver acknowledged silently. Only this time the pain and humiliation the others would feel would be his fault. An intolerable thought.

"The killer may be planning to produce fake evidence," Bolt added.

"Complicated."

"Yes, sir."

"And where the hell's the motive?" Oliver muttered.

There was a long silence while Bolt mulled that over. "It's been my experience that there are usually just three basic motives for murder, Mr. Rain. Greed, passion, and revenge."

"There's no obvious financial motive," Oliver said. "That leaves passion and revenge."

"I'd say revenge is the most likely one. But who do you know who would want to get revenge on both you and Daniel Lyncroft? You didn't have much in common. The two of you didn't even move in the same circles. Your only connection to Lyncroft was a business one."

"Until recently," Oliver reminded him. "I'm married to his sister now. I've taken control of his company."

"But the two of you don't know the same people or have the same enemies," Bolt insisted. "In fact, as you pointed out, Lyncroft didn't have any enemies at all as far as we know."

"That's not entirely true," Oliver said slowly. "Daniel and I had one enemy in common."

"Who?"

"Walker Gresham." It was strange how often lately his thoughts were returning to that night in the island warehouse. "The problem is that Gresham is dead."

"Are you absolutely certain of that?"

"Yes," Oliver said, remembering the vast pool of blood on the concrete floor of the warehouse. "I'm very certain of that."

"Then that leaves us back at square one."

Annie was waiting with tea and a demand for a full accounting of the night's activities. Oliver and Bolt gave it to her. She deserved the answers, Oliver told himself. As she so often reminded him, her brother was at the heart of this. And Daniel was still at the top of Annie's list of priorities.

"It seems to me," Annie declared as she paced up and down Oliver's study, "that you're overlooking something here."

"What's that?" Oliver sipped tea and watched her as she stormed back and forth across the small room. All that feminine energy and vitality fascinated him. He could sit and watch her for hours, he thought, although if he had a choice he would rather make love to her.

And he did have the choice. She was his wife. And she said she loved him.

"You say Gresham is dead so he can't be the one

who's behind all this." Annie whipped around and started back in the opposite direction. "But what if someone else is out to avenge him?"

Oliver had his teacup half way to his mouth. He narrowed his eyes at Annie and set the cup down again very slowly. He saw Bolt frown consideringly.

"I doubt that gunrunners have the kinds of friends who would go out of their way to avenge each other," Oliver said. "Especially five years after the fact."

"Who said anything about friends? What about family?"

Oliver shook his head. "Gresham didn't have any family. There were no relatives listed in his file. No one came forward at the time of his death."

"You and your precious files." Annie walked over to the desk and poured herself some more tea. "Almost everyone has family, Oliver." She looked at him over the rim of the cup. "And we both know how far some people will go when it comes to protecting family."

Bolt nodded gravely. "She's got a point, Mr. Rain."

"You're both forgetting that Gresham died five years ago. Where has his avenger been all these years? Why did he wait until now to get even?" Oliver asked.

"Who knows?" Annie said. "Maybe whoever is doing this took five years to find out exactly what happened and who to blame." Her eyes widened. "Good grief. I just thought of something."

Bolt sat forward. "Yes, Mrs. Rain?"

Annie looked at Oliver. "Remember our wedding day?"

"Quite clearly," Oliver said dryly. "It was less than two weeks ago."

"Yes, well, remember how Barry Cork came running up to me and told me that you had very likely murdered Walker Gresham in order to get hold of a company?"

Oliver watched her steadily, but there was no sign of suspicion in her eyes, just intent concentration. "I remember."

"How did he know about Gresham?" Annie asked.

"I told you, the incident was kept quiet because I didn't want publicity. Also, it happened a long way from Seattle. But it wasn't a secret."

"Barry Cork was not in Seattle five years ago. He comes from Virginia," Annie said. "How did he learn about Gresham's death?"

"Cork was selling information to a lot of people," Bolt said. "He might have run into someone who knew something about the incident."

"Or," Annie announced triumphantly, "he might have known about it because he came out to Seattle to get revenge on the two people responsible. Maybe he took the job at Lyncroft Unlimited just so that he could get close to my brother and plot against him. And then he went after you, Oliver."

Oliver gazed at her with unwilling admiration. "An interesting theory. But it leaves open the question of who tried to kill Cork."

Bolt spoke up. "That could be an unrelated event, sir. We already know Cork was playing dangerous games. People who sell information frequently go in for other sidelines such as blackmail. Maybe one of his victims took drastic steps to silence him."

Annie nodded in agreement. "If Barry is a blackmailer, he probably has all kinds of enemies."

"This is what comes of keeping incomplete files," Oliver said. "I tried to impress upon Daniel the importance of maintaining good records on key people.

He was always far too trusting." He ignored Annie's grimace and looked at Bolt. "Pull up Gresham's old file. It will be in my personal archives. I never throw that kind of thing away."

"Naturally not," Annie murmured.

"I doubt that we'll get anything out of it," Oliver said, "but it won't hurt to see if there's any indication that Gresham might have been related to Cork."

Bolt stood, looking almost eager. "I'll get right on it."

Oliver waited until he and Annie were alone. "I'm sorry," he said quietly. "Everything we learn makes it less and less likely that Daniel's plane went down by accident."

"I know." She turned back toward the window and drew the back of her sleeve across her eyes. "But I still believe he's alive, Oliver. I'd know if he were dead." She hesitated. "Just as I'd know for certain if something ever happened to you."

Oliver could not think of anything to say to that. He got to his feet and went to her. He rested his hands on her shoulders and tugged her gently back against him.

For a long while they stood together in silence and gazed out into the blackness of the winter night.

19

Joanna, calm down, everything's going to be okay."
Annie huddled over her cup of steaming latté and
wondered if she had been wise to tell Joanna the latest
news. Not that she'd had a lot of choice in the matter,
she reminded herself. Joanna was engaged to Daniel
and carrying his baby. She had a right to know
whatever Annie and Oliver learned.

Nevertheless, Annie feared that the latest uncertain-
ties might prove to be too much for Joanna. Her future
sister-in-law looked more weary and depressed than
ever this morning.

They were seated at a tiny table in front of a roaring
fire. The old red brick walls of the café added a mel-
low, comforting feel to the high-ceilinged room. The
place hummed with the conversations of Pioneer
Square professionals and office workers on their
morning coffee break.

Coffee breaks were a serious matter in Seattle. No
one drank instant anymore. Most people were convinced that one couldn't get a good cup of coffee
outside of Seattle. It made for a booming business for
establishments such as the one in which Annie and
Joanna sat.

Joanna cast an anxious glance around the room to
make certain that no one was within hearing distance.
She leaned forward. "For God's sake, we're talking

about murder. You're telling me that someone tried to kill Daniel?"

"It's a possibility."

"But it doesn't make any sense. Who would want to kill Daniel?"

"The motive may have been revenge for something that happened five years ago." Annie quickly explained the investigation that had led to the shoot-out in the warehouse. "Daniel was the one who found the proof of Gresham's gunrunning, according to Oliver. And he was with Oliver that night when Gresham got killed."

"Daniel never said anything to me about being involved in such a dangerous matter." Joanna's voice had risen in a squeak so swiftly that it disappeared entirely on the last word.

"You didn't know him five years ago," Annie reminded her. "Still, if it makes you feel any better, he never told me about it, either. Probably a misguided masculine effort to protect the ladies from unpleasant news."

"What you're telling me," Joanna said grimly, "is that what is happening now is all Rain's fault."

Annie straightened abruptly. "I'm not saying that at all. I'm just saying there may be a connection between Daniel's disappearance and the investigation he and Oliver conducted five years ago."

"Damn it, I knew Oliver Rain was dangerous. Everyone knew it. You should never have married him, Annie. Not even to save Lyncroft Unlimited."

"Please, will you take it easy?" Annie slanted a meaningful sidelong glance at the nearest table where a couple sat sipping espresso. "Everything's under control."

"Nothing's under control. This mess is getting scarier by the minute. Annie, I think you should file for divorce."

Annie was stunned. "Why on earth would I do that now?"

"It's the only way to get rid of Rain. He scares me, Annie. He's made me nervous right from the beginning, but now he's really starting to scare me."

"Well, he doesn't scare me," Annie declared. "He's got a few personal problems, I'll admit, but he's not dangerous. At least not to me or to you or to Lyncroft Unlimited."

"Listen," Joanna said urgently, "I don't want you to take any more risks, do you understand? Something is going on here, something we don't know anything about. I think you should get out of the situation entirely and the only way to do that is to divorce Rain."

"I'm perfectly safe," Annie assured her. She put down her cup and got to her feet. "Look, I'm sorry I upset you." She belted her raincoat around her. "I just wanted to fill you in on the latest. But I don't want you to worry. Everything's under control."

"No offense, Annie, but that does not reassure me one bit." Joanna got up and reached for her trench coat, which was hanging over the back of her chair. "What are you going to do now?"

"First, I have to deliver this to a client in a law firm down the street." Annie picked up the large glass parrot that was sitting beside the table. The parrot was wrapped in plastic to protect it from the rain. "Then I'm going back to my shop. I'll call you as soon as I have more news."

Joanna touched her arm. "Annie, please, think about

what I've said. You're in over your head. I want you to divorce Rain."

Annie smiled reassuringly. "Don't you see? Oliver is not the problem. He's the solution." She tucked the glass parrot under her elbow, pulled up the hood of her raincoat, and hurried toward the door.

Half an hour later, after delivering the parrot safely to its new owner, Annie walked back into Wildest Dreams.

Sybil was waiting for her with a deeply troubled expression.

"Hi, Sybil." Annie led the way into her office. "Something wrong?"

"I have to talk to you. I heard the rumors last night at Valerie's preview. They started circulating right after you and Oliver left. Are they true?"

"Have a seat. What rumors?" Annie shook raindrops off her coat and hung it on a peacock-headed coat rack.

"You're probably wondering why I'm so concerned," Sybil said as she sat down. "After all, you're well aware that Oliver and I haven't had what you'd call a strong stepmother-stepson relationship these past few years. Nevertheless..."

Annie held up a hand as she sat down behind her desk. "Hold it. Before we get into why you're concerned about the rumors, you'd better tell me first what those rumors are."

Sybil frowned. "I'm talking about the rumors of your divorce."

Annie's mouth dropped open. "My *divorce*."

"I'll be the first to agree that Oliver can be extremely difficult."

"Wait, wait, back up a second." Annie gestured wildly to silence Sybil. "What divorce?"

"Did you think you could keep it quiet? Not likely. Annie, I know this is going to sound crazy, but I'm here to ask you to reconsider."

"Reconsider what? I'm not getting a divorce. At least not that I know of. Oliver's sneaky at times, but I'm sure he'd at least consult with me on something like this before he filed. His communication skills have improved a lot lately."

"I don't understand." Sybil eyed her closely. "You're saying the rumors are false?"

"Definitely."

"But they're all over town."

Annie chuckled. "Hardly. What you probably mean is that everyone in your small circle of friends is talking about it, but I assure you, that's a tiny part of the population of Seattle."

Sybil lifted one shoulder in a gesture that clearly indicated the rest of Seattle didn't matter. "I'm saying that nearly everyone at the Eckert Museum preview last night was talking about your divorce before the evening was over. The fact that you and Oliver left rather abruptly in the middle of things certainly fueled the gossip."

Annie groaned. "You know Oliver. He doesn't make excuses or explanations. He decided he wanted to leave, so we left. There was nothing more to it than that."

"Are you certain?" Sybil looked unconvinced. "Let's be honest here. We both know that your marriage to Oliver was based on business in the beginning. I'm well aware of the fact that Oliver wanted Lyncroft Unlimited very badly."

"He did?"

"Of course he did. Everyone knows it."

Annie recalled Oliver's comment on how unimportant Lyncroft Unlimited was in the grand scheme of his investments. A mere blip on the screen. She nibbled thoughtfully on her lower lip. "You've got it backward, Sybil. Oliver did me a favor by stepping in to save Lyncroft."

Sybil smiled wryly. "Trust Oliver to make you believe that. When you've known him as long as I have, you'll realize that Oliver doesn't do favors unless there's something in it for him. But that's beside the point now."

"I'm glad you think so."

"The point," Sybil continued forcefully, "is that Oliver has changed since he's married you. And to be perfectly blunt, we all like the change."

"We?"

"His family." Sybil raised her chin. "You're the reason he's become more understanding and sensitive lately."

"Thank you." Annie was genuinely touched.

"And we would just as soon you didn't leave him." Sybil's mouth tightened. "I think it's a sure bet that if you do, he'll go back to his old ways."

"Sybil, this is all really unnecessary. I promise you Oliver and I are not even talking about divorce."

Sybil furrowed her brow. "Then why are the rumors so strong?"

"I have no idea." Annie straightened and made a show of shuffling some papers. "Now, if that's all you're worried about, set your mind at ease. If you don't mind, I'd better get back to work. I'm trying to run a business here."

"I see." Sybil stood.

Annie immediately felt guilty for being rude. "I'm sorry, Sybil. It's just that things have been hectic lately and I'm swamped."

"It's all right." Sybil walked to the door and turned. "You're really not planning to file for divorce?"

"Not at the moment," Annie said cheerfully.

"I'd be the first to understand, of course. As I said, I won't deny Oliver is a difficult man. But you're good for him. It's probably very selfish of me and the rest of the family, but the truth is, we'd like to see the marriage work."

"I appreciate your good wishes, Sybil."

Sybil looked as if she were about to say something else, changed her mind, and walked on out the door.

Annie sat staring after her for a long time.

Later that evening Annie spooned couscous onto a large platter and ladled the piping hot vegetable stew over the top. She watched Oliver out of the corner of her eye, deliberately hoping to catch him off-guard. He was pouring wine into two glasses. She waited until he had finished one glass and was starting to fill the other.

"I wonder why the rumors are suddenly flying about our impending divorce," Annie said in a deliberately chatty tone.

The wine bottle came down on the counter with a resounding crash. Oliver spun around, his eyes cold. "What the hell are you talking about?"

Annie felt herself relax slightly deep inside. "Sybil tells me that after we left Valerie's preview last night there was a lot of gossip about us. People seemed to think we were filing for divorce."

Oliver's jaw tightened. "That's one of the reasons I don't attend that sort of thing very often. There's always a lot of stupid gossip."

"Umm."

"And it is just a lot of stupid gossip, isn't it?" Oliver asked in icy tones.

Annie smiled gently. "Believe me, Oliver, if I ever decide to file for divorce, you'll be the first to know." She paused delicately. "I assume I'd get the same courtesy?"

His expression turned fierce. "There's no reason for us to even talk about it. Things are working out just fine."

"Are they?"

He scowled at her. "What's that supposed to mean?"

"Forget it." Annie carried the couscous over to the table and set it down. "I'm just wondering where the gossip came from, that's all."

"You wondered if it started because of something I said or did?"

"Sybil said the rumors were very strong last night." Annie sat down and began to serve the meal. "It makes one ask who started them. Aren't you curious?"

"No." Oliver sat down across from her. His eyes never left her face. "People always talk. That doesn't mean you have to listen."

"I'll remember that," Annie said dryly. She forked up a bite of couscous.

Oliver reached across the table and caught hold of her hand. "Annie."

She put down her fork and met his intent eyes. "Yes?"

"If you ever have any problems with the idea of being married to me, you come to me first. Agreed?"

She carried his hand to her lips and kissed his callused palm. "Agreed."

His expression softened. "Annie..."

The kitchen phone rang. Oliver reluctantly got up to answer it.

"Hello? Yes, Bolt. What have you got?"

Annie tapped her foot impatiently under the table and watched Oliver for clues as to what Bolt was saying. It was difficult keeping track of the one-sided conversation.

"A brother?" Oliver rubbed the back of his neck. "There was nothing about any brother in Gresham's file." He paused, listening. "Right. Stay on it. Call as soon as you've got something concrete."

He hung up the phone and came back to the table.

"Well?" Annie demanded.

"Walker Gresham appears to have had a brother."

"I knew it," Annie said with satisfaction. "I knew there must be someone out there."

"Don't get excited. There's a record of the birth in Phoenix, but nothing else yet. No credit report, no voting records. Nothing."

"Maybe he's dead?"

"Bolt's leaving for Arizona in an hour. He'll check it out."

Annie felt a frisson of uneasiness go down her spine. "I don't like this, Oliver."

"Neither do I. But if it turns out that Barry Cork is Gresham's younger brother, a lot of things will be explained."

* * *

Annie was pointing out the interesting aspects of a

trompe l'oeil mirror to a doubtful client the next afternoon when the phone rang. She let Ella answer it.

"Don't you just love the way the painting on the mirror fools the eye and makes you think you're looking through an open window?" Annie admired the mirror. "Very effective and quite unique."

The client, a young man who was furnishing his first apartment, continued to look doubtful. "I don't know. It seems to me a mirror ought to act like a mirror. I mean, I want to see myself in it when I look at it. Why would I want to see some weird painting of an open window."

"Your guests will find it fascinating," Annie assured him smoothly. "It's a wonderful conversation piece. Everyone will comment on it."

"Yeah, but is it art? My girlfriend says I should get a piece of art for the hall."

"It's a bold statement of artistic whimsy," Annie said. "A one-of-a-kind piece that will spark the rest of your interior design and add interest to your hallway."

"You think so? My girlfriend warned me not to get anything tacky."

"This mirror is definitely not tacky."

"But is it art?" the young man asked again, looking more doubtful than ever.

"Excuse me, Annie," Ella interrupted. "It's Mr. Rain's secretary, Mrs. Jameson. Or rather it's her assistant."

Annie glanced at Ella in surprise. "What does she want?"

"She says she has a message from Mr. Rain. Something important has come up. He wants you to rendezvous with him at home."

"Oliver wants me to go home now?" Annie asked, startled.

Ella nodded. "She says it's important."

"Excuse me," Annie said to her client. She walked over to the counter and took the phone from Ella's hand. "This is Annie. Is something wrong?"

"Oh, no, Mrs. Rain," the woman on the other end said hastily. "I didn't mean to give that impression. Mrs. Jameson is extremely busy at the moment with a special project for Mr. Rain. She asked me to pass along the message that he'd like you to meet him at your home as soon as possible. He's on his way there now."

"All right. Thanks." Annie tossed the phone back into the cradle.

"What's wrong?" Ella asked.

"Nothing as far as I know. But I've got to run home. I'll be back as soon as I can." Annie lowered her voice. "Take care of our customer, will you?"

"My big chance," Ella murmured. "I'll see if I can unload the elephant on him."

"Tell him it's art."

Annie opened the front door of the penthouse and stepped inside. "Oliver?"

She listened intently to the silence that ensued. Apparently she had made it home before Oliver had.

She closed the door, set down her purse, and went down the hall to the study. A sense of uneasiness ruffled her nerves. The sensation was not unlike what she had experienced the afternoon she had gone to Wally Thorpe's cottage.

There was nothing wrong, she assured herself. Perhaps Oliver had turned up new information on

Daniel. Good news, she told herself optimistically. It had to be good news.

"Oliver?" Annie stuck her head around the door and saw the familiar cone of light from the halogen lamp. It illuminated a file of neatly stacked papers on the desk. The rest of the room was in darkness.

"Oliver, I'm home. Where are you?"

"I'm afraid your husband hasn't arrived yet, Mrs. Rain." Jonathan Grace stepped out of the shadows. The light from the hall glinted on the lenses of his glasses and on the gun in his hand.

Annie went numb with shock. An instant later her fingers began to tingle and burn as the adrenalin poured through her. "What are you doing here?"

"Waiting. I have waited a long time, Mrs. Rain. I think I can manage to wait a little while longer." Grace used the gun to motion her back out into the hall. "Let's go upstairs to the greenhouse, shall we?"

Annie did not budge. "Why?"

"Because it looks like an ideal place for the little domestic quarrel I have planned." Grace's smile was devoid of all emotion except grim satisfaction.

"What are you talking about?" Annie breathed in horror.

"Shall I tell you how the scene will play out? You have discovered that Rain married you solely to get control of Lyncroft Unlimited. You are hurt and humiliated. Outraged. You are planning to file for divorce immediately."

"You started those rumors of divorce."

"I had to lay the groundwork for today's activities." Grace smiled coldly. "Now, then. Rain is furious. He threatens you. Fearful of this exceedingly dangerous

342

man, Oliver Rain, a man who has killed at least once before, you, my dear, shoot him in self-defense."

"Are you crazy?" Annie demanded. "No one will ever believe that."

"Yes, they will. I have planned it all quite carefully."

"But I'll deny everything."

"I'm afraid you won't be in a position to do that," Grace said enigmatically. He glanced at the clock. "Let's be on our way. I expect Rain will be walking in the door in about an hour. I want to be ready for him."

"Someone from his office said he'd already left work for the day," Annie announced rashly.

"The person who called you to give you Rain's message was not phoning from his office. She knows nothing about any of this. Just a young street person I found who was willing to do anything for a little cash. I gave her twenty dollars to make the call to you."

"This is crazy. You can't do this. It won't work."

"It will work. Rain will have no reason to think anything's wrong when he walks in the front door. His faithful Bolt is out of town. He'll see your purse on the table and he'll know you're home."

"He'll come looking for me," Annie said slowly.

"That's right. And when he can't find you in the usual places, he will try the roof. You and I will be waiting for him."

"I'm not going anywhere," Annie stated.

Grace did not say a word. Instead he took two rapid steps forward and backhanded her savagely across the face. Annie stumbled and nearly fell. She reeled out into the hall. Grace had moved so quickly, she had never even seen the blow coming.

Grace examined her critically and nodded, apparently pleased with the effect. "A few bruises will set the stage very nicely. No one will be terribly surprised to learn that Oliver Rain would use violence against his wife."

He grabbed Annie by the shoulder and propelled her toward the steps that led to the roof.

Oliver sat at his desk, willing Bolt to phone with the latest update. The last call had come two hours ago. Bolt had said he had some answers and would have more before Oliver went home for the day.

Oliver glanced impatiently at the clock. It was a quarter to six. The Lyncroft offices were empty except for a few stragglers working late.

The phone rang. Oliver snatched up the receiver. "Bolt?"

"Yes, sir. We've got a real problem here, Mr. Rain." Bolt's voice was uncharacteristically tense. "Walker Gresham's brother is named John Gresham. He was alive and doing time in a Texas prison for a variety of charges including assault when Gresham was killed. He was released on parole earlier this year."

"That explains why he didn't come looking for revenge until now."

"Yes, sir."

"That means Cork isn't the one we're after. He's been here in Seattle working for Lyncroft for the past two years, not in prison," Oliver said.

"Right. Cork isn't Gresham's brother," Bolt said ominously. "The description and photo I've got in my hand fit Jonathan Grace, right down to the glasses."

"*Grace*." Oliver's grip on the receiver tightened. "Are you certain?"

"Absolutely. It explains a lot," Bolt said. He paused briefly. "Including how he was able to get your private number."

Oliver stared at the opposite wall of his office. "Are you saying Sybil is involved in this? That she was helping him?"

"Don't know, sir." Bolt's tone was neutral. "Not necessarily. He's been sleeping with her. It would have been easy for him to get the kind of information he needed without ever letting her know what he was up to. My guess is that she's an innocent bystander."

"He used her."

"Probably used Cork, too."

Oliver frowned. "To get information such as Daniel's flight plans? That makes sense. Grace was probably the mysterious new Seattle-based client that Daniel was worried about."

"What next?" Bolt asked.

"We're in the same position we were in before in terms of evidence. We've got nothing on Grace. But at least we know who to watch and where to look now. He's bound to want to make his move soon. When he does, we'll have him."

"I'll be back in Seattle by midnight. I'll start a round-the-clock surveillance on him." Bolt promised. "What about your stepmother? Going to warn her about Grace?"

"No, that would put her in danger. Hell, she probably wouldn't believe me even if I did tell her the truth." Oliver shrugged. "Maybe she wouldn't even care."

"I disagree, sir. Annie had a point when she said

Sybil has a vested interest in your welfare. Still, it might be safer for her at this juncture if you don't alarm her. Grace might decide she's a liability if he thinks she's suspicious."

"I won't do anything until you get back. Then we'll start looking for the evidence we need," Oliver said quietly.

"That shouldn't be so difficult now that we know who and what we're looking for."

Oliver hung up the phone and dialed Annie's shop. Ella answered on the second ring.

"Ella, this is Oliver Rain. Is Annie there?"

"Uh, no." Ella sounded startled by the question.

"Has she already gone home?"

"Mr. Rain, she went home over an hour ago. To meet you, she said."

"What are you talking about?"

"She got your message," Ella said quickly. "And she went straight home to meet you. I assume that's where she is now."

Oliver forced himself to keep his voice calm. "What message?"

"The one Mrs. Jameson's assistant gave her. She said you had asked her to call Annie and have her rendezvous with you at your place ASAP. That's all I know about it, Mr. Rain."

Oliver hurled the phone into the cradle and ran for the door.

20

It required all the willpower Oliver had at his command to take the elevator to the sixth floor, get off, and go down the hall to Bolt's apartment. Every instinct in him wanted to go straight upstairs to the penthouse, throw open the door, and find Annie safe and sound. He knew she was in the building because the doorman had seen her arrive.

But logic told him he was far more likely to run straight into whoever had lured Annie back to the penthouse.

The doorman had reported no sight of anyone matching John Gresham's description entering the building, but Oliver discounted that. It would have been easy enough for Gresham to disguise himself as a delivery person or any of a number of other seemingly innocent people. Once inside the elevator he would have access to the twenty-sixth floor. He could have gotten the elevator code from Sybil. Getting into the penthouse itself probably posed no more than a minor problem for someone of Gresham's background. The security system was good, but no system was fool-proof.

Oliver unlocked Bolt's door and let himself inside. He needed information before he could plot strategy.

The apartment was in darkness. It was six o'clock and although the ferries were still loading rush-hour

347

traffic, the winter night lay heavily over the city. Oliver went to the intercom panel and systematically pressed the buttons. He listened carefully as he checked each penthouse room.

There was silence from the kitchen, study, and living room. Silence everywhere. The tension that gripped Oliver's insides went up another notch when he pressed the bedroom switch.

More silence.

Perhaps Annie wasn't up there, he thought. That speculation did nothing to lessen his dread. Maybe he was already too late. She could be hurt, perhaps dying, somewhere upstairs while he fooled around with the damn intercom buttons.

No. Oliver forced back the fear that could so easily induce panic. He had to think. He had to stay in control of himself or he would not have a ghost of a chance of taking control of the situation.

He made himself run through the train of logic he had constructed on his way here from the Lyncroft offices. It was obvious Gresham had made his move. That was the only thing that could explain the phone call Annie had received at Wildest Dreams.

That meant there were now two possibilities. Either Gresham had kidnapped Annie and taken her out of the building, a difficult project at best because of the doorman and the security cameras, or else he was upstairs with Annie now, waiting for his real target.

Oliver pressed the intercom that covered the hallways. Still nothing. His finger poised over the button marked "greenhouse." Slowly he depressed it. He sucked in his breath when he heard Annie's voice. It was sharp with indignation and accusation.

"What did you do with Wally Thorpe?" she demanded. If there was fear underlying her words, it was well concealed.

"Thorpe knew too much," Gresham replied casually. "I had made certain all along that he didn't know who he was dealing with. I handled everything by phone. But he started getting cold feet after Lyncroft's plane went down. I was afraid he might go to the authorities and confess. I had to get rid of him."

"Was that why you tried to kill Barry Cork also?" Annie asked. "Because he knew too much?"

"Cork was smarter than Thorpe. I handled him by phone, too, but he started to get suspicious. He put together enough information to try his hand at blackmail."

"So you made certain he had an accident?"

"I didn't need him any longer," Gresham said simply. "He had become a liability."

"You're a monster," Annie whispered. "You tell me you're only doing this to avenge your brother, but you're willing to kill other people in the process. How can you possibly justify that?"

Oliver winced. Annie was on the warpath.

"I don't have to justify a goddamn thing to you, lady. Now shut up."

"There's no telling what Oliver will do when he gets his hands on you," Annie said calmly. "He's a very dangerous man."

"He's a dead man. I'll know the minute he enters this place, thanks to his own fucking alarm system. Sybil explained the whole setup. Once he's inside, he's all mine. Sooner or later he'll walk into this greenhouse looking for you and when he does, you, my dear, will shoot him dead."

"Everyone who knows me will know I didn't kill him," Annie said fiercely.

"No, my dear, they won't know that. What they'll tell themselves is that hell hath no fury like that of a woman who discovers she's been married for business reasons."

"You've got it all wrong, you know." There was desperation as well as rage in Annie's voice now. "I'm the one who married Oliver for business reasons. He was doing me a favor."

"You actually believe that bullshit? Rain is a clever bastard, I'll give him that."

"He doesn't need Lyncroft Unlimited."

"He may not need it, but he sure as hell wants it. Who wouldn't? The company is hot and getting hotter."

Oliver released the intercom button. At least he knew where Gresham was holding Annie. He took off his jacket as he mentally ran through the very short list of things he knew about Jonathan Grace. It would help if he could find a weak point.

Oliver started to toss his jacket aside. He felt the weight of his reading glasses in the pocket and stopped.

Grace wore glasses. All the time, apparently. He'd had them on when he showed up at the museum preview with Sybil. Judging from the thickness of the lenses, he would be half-blind without them.

Oliver hurled the jacket over a chair and removed his tie. It wasn't much on which to base a strategy, but it was all he had.

He took the elevator to the twenty-sixth floor. When he got off, he went swiftly past the penthouse, down to the end of the short, private hall. He stopped in front of the door that opened onto the emergency stairwell. He opened it soundlessly.

He took the concrete stairs to the roof two at a time. At the top, he eased the door open and stepped outside. The stairwell exit was concealed behind the looming structure that housed the building's elevator machinery.

The eerie blue-green glow from the greenhouse lit up a large portion of the roof. Oliver could see the outlines of two figures inside the glass. Annie was standing near the grotto, nearly hidden behind a row of staghorns. Grace was a few steps away from her. When he moved his arm, Oliver could see the shape of the gun in his fist.

They would not be able to see him because the rooftop outside the greenhouse was in darkness. Crouching low in order to stay in the deepest part of the shadows, Oliver made his way to the environmental control panel he used to govern the climate inside the greenhouse.

Annie was aware of more perspiration gathering on her forehead and trickling down her arms. She didn't know if it was caused by the warmth of the greenhouse or by her nerves. She watched Grace who was beginning to glance more and more frequently at his watch.

"Maybe Oliver got held up at the office," Annie suggested coolly. "No telling when he'll be home."

"Since he married you, he's always home on time. I've been keeping an eye on his movements." Grace stood where he could watch both Annie and the greenhouse door. "It's getting damn fucking hot in here."

"What do you expect? It's a greenhouse." But Annie secretly agreed with Grace. She could have sworn that it was considerably warmer now than it had been a few minutes earlier. She wondered if something had gone wrong with the heat and humidity systems.

"Damn humidity. Place is like a jungle." Grace took off his glasses and wiped the steam off of the lenses. "Rain will get here eventually. And when he does he'll walk straight into the trap the same way my brother walked into one." He put his glasses back on.

"No offense," Annie said waspishly, "but don't you think you're going a little too far to avenge this dearly beloved brother of yours? The jerk was running guns, for heavens sake. He wasn't exactly a saint."

"He was my brother," Grace snarled. "He was all the family I had." He took off his glasses again and started to wipe the lenses. "Damn humidity."

At that instant the greenhouse lights winked out. Before Annie's eyes could even begin to adjust to the sudden darkness, a hard, driving rain started to fall from the ceiling.

The amount of water coming down was astonishing. Annie realized something must have gone wrong with the system. The torrent quickly soaked her clothes and hair. It splashed down with the force of a waterfall, creating a thundering roar as it struck the graveled paths and the glass walls. The ferns rustled cheerfully beneath the deluge. Annie felt as though she really were standing in the middle of a rain forest.

"Shit." Grace cursed wildly somewhere off to Annie's right.

She realized he couldn't see her in the darkness and the driving rain would be even more disorienting for him. This was the only chance she was likely to get.

She dropped to the floor and started to crawl swiftly toward the door. She couldn't see a thing, but she knew the layout of the greenhouse well enough to head in the right direction.

"What the fuck is going on?" Grace was screaming now. "Where are you, you bitch? Get over here. I'll kill you, I swear I will."

Annie crawled faster and blundered into a metal sprayer. She pushed it aside and kept going.

"You're going to die, anyway, you stupid woman. Did you think I'd let you live? You're going to go over the edge of the roof when I'm finished with you. A suicide. You hear me? You're going to die, too."

Annie realized that the greenhouse door was open. She could feel the cold night air pouring into the miniature jungle. In the darkness she could not see Oliver, but she knew who it was who nearly tripped over her.

"Annie?" The roar of artificial rain rendered Oliver's voice almost inaudible.

"I'm okay. Oliver, be careful, he's got a gun."

"Right now I can't see him any better than he can see me," Oliver said very softly. "Go outside and turn on the lights. Right-hand side of the control panel. Remember?"

"Yes, but, Oliver..."

"Do it."

Annie responded instinctively to the command in his voice. She lurched to her feet and went through the door. Outside things were more readily visible thanks to the reflected neon glow of the nighttime sky.

She found the control panel and started pushing

and pressing switches until the lights inside the greenhouse suddenly came to life.

"Rain? It's you, isn't it?" Grace yelled. "I'm going to kill you, you bastard."

Annie whirled around and raced to the greenhouse door. She arrived just in time to see Oliver launch himself straight at Grace. Grace appeared to be trying to take aim with the gun, but he was having difficulty finding his quarry.

Annie realized with a shock that Grace had managed to jam his glasses back on his face, but they weren't doing him much good. It was obvious he couldn't see much through the water that was sheeting off the lenses. She saw him reach up with his free hand to remove the glasses again in a desperate attempt to see more clearly, but he was too late.

A shot crackled loudly above the roar of the artificial rain. Glass shattered.

Oliver hit Grace with enough force to send both of them backward into the flooded grotto.

Annie saw Oliver sit up quickly and draw back his arm for a final punch, but there was no need. Grace was lying very still against the rocks. The greenhouse rain continued to pour down relentlessly.

Oliver got slowly to his feet. He stood looking down at Gresham for a long moment and then he turned slowly toward the door where Annie stood.

"*Oliver.*" She stared at him as he walked toward her through the driving rain. "Oh, God, Oliver, I knew you would save me."

Annie hurled herself straight into his arms.

Oliver held her to him as if he would never let go.

Hours later Annie sat curled up beside Oliver on

the sofa and listened to Bolt recount the results of his investigations and the details of what John Gresham alias Jonathan Grace had told the police.

"We had it figured fairly accurately," Bolt said. "John Gresham was in prison when his brother died. The news hit him hard from all accounts. When he got out a few months ago, he went to work to find out exactly what had happened."

"It wouldn't have been all that hard for him to find out," Oliver said. "Daniel and I kept quiet about it for business reasons, but we didn't go to the lengths of actually covering up the facts. There was no need."

Bolt nodded. "Gresham set out to get revenge. Got to give him credit for doing his homework. He studied the family and the situation at Lyncroft thoroughly before he made his move. Then he chose two weak points, Sybil and Barry Cork. He used them to get the information he needed."

Annie looked up at Oliver from the curve of his arm. "Our marriage must have thrown a real glitch into his original scheme."

"Yes." Oliver tightened his arm around her. "Shortly after he met her, he learned there was no love lost between Sybil and myself. He decided she was the perfect one to take the rap for murder. Everyone would assume that she had killed me because I threatened to cut her off financially."

"And then Annie came on the scene," Bolt said. "And Gresham realized he had an even better fall guy. Or fall lady." Bolt looked at Oliver. "He figured the only reason you would have married her was to get control of Lyncroft Unlimited."

Oliver's mouth twisted. "No one gives me any credit for being a true romantic, do they?"

Annie stirred uncomfortably against him. "Be fair, Oliver. How could Gresham or anyone else know that I was the one who pushed for a marriage of convenience? Everyone assumed the idea of marriage was yours. And they also assumed you had your reasons. Business reasons."

Bolt's brows rose, but he made no comment. He closed the notebook in his hand with a snap and stuck it into his pocket. "That's about it. Cork is awake, by the way, and willing to talk."

Annie brightened. "Barry's going to be all right?"

"Looks like it."

"I'm glad." She wrinkled her nose. "I mean, the guy is a complete sleaze, but he isn't a killer. I guess Thorpe wasn't so lucky."

"No," Bolt said. "Thorpe wasn't so lucky. When Gresham confessed to the authorities two hours ago he told them where to find Thorpe's body. It's buried somewhere on Bainbridge Island."

"Poor Sybil," Annie said quietly. "She really cares about Jonathan Grace. Who's going to tell her the truth?"

"I will," Oliver said.

The telephone rang. Bolt got up to answer it.

"Rain residence." Bolt's normally blank features formed themselves into an oddly intense expression. "Visitors? Are you certain? Give me a second to turn on the video." He reached out to switch on the small screen near the phone.

Annie watched curiously as the video picture snapped into focus. She saw two people standing in the lobby talking to the doorman. One of them was Joanna.

It took her a few seconds to realize who was with

Joanna. When the image finally registered, Annie leaped to her feet.

"*Daniel!*" she yelled at the screen. "Oliver, look, it's Daniel. He's back. He's back! I knew he was safe."

"Send them up," Bolt instructed the doorman.

It was nearly four in the morning before Oliver finally got Annie to himself. He wasted no time taking her straight to bed.

He had no self-control at all the first time. Driven by a raging, ungovernable need, he laid siege to her body and stormed the soft, warm citadel. It was as if he had to assure himself in some primitive fashion that she was safe and that he still possessed her on this most fundamental of levels.

Annie did not seem to mind the hot, wild assault. She clung to him, giving herself generously, allowing him to sink deeply into her.

When Oliver drove into her one last time, shuddering with the force of his climax, Annie joined him in the shattering release. She held him close and whispered to him of her love over and over again.

Oliver collapsed along the length of her, exhausted and yet oddly refreshed. Everything was going to be all right. She was safe. She was his. She loved him.

"Did you see the look on Joanna's face?" Annie asked after a while. "She was so happy."

"You had the same look on your face," Oliver said.

"I probably did." Annie smiled in the shadows. "I told you Daniel was alive."

"Yes."

"Picked up by a foreign freighter and carried off to the next port of call. Can you believe it?"

"Yes." Oliver recalled the tale that Daniel had given them earlier.

He had gotten himself safely out of the sabotaged plane before it went under the waves. Garbed in a survival suit, he had made it to a small island with the aid of the inflatable life raft he had carried on board. But he'd had no radio, no way of calling for help.

Daniel had employed a variety of clever methods using materials from the survival suit and the life raft to stay alive. He had subsisted on fish and wild foliage for several weeks. Then he had finally gotten lucky and caught the attention of a passing cargo ship.

The freighter's captain had spoken only minimal English, but he had managed to get across the point that his schedule was more important than returning Daniel to Seattle. The ship's radios had not been functioning so Daniel had good-naturedly earned his keep working aboard ship until the freighter had docked at its next port of call. Once on solid land he had raced to the nearest phone only to find that long-distance lines were not functioning on the tiny island that week.

He found a boat charter captain who agreed to take him to a larger island where he could catch a plane. Daniel had had fifteen minutes to make a phone call before the plane left. No one had been at home at either Annie's or Joanna's apartments. Daniel had given up trying to notify them that he was safe and sound and raced for the plane instead. Nearly two months after he had gone down, Daniel finally managed to get back to Seattle.

"He looks awfully thin," Annie said, "but I expect Joanna will fatten him up."

"Yes."

Annie turned in his arms, smiling up at him. "I'm so incredibly happy, Oliver."

"I'm glad," Oliver said. He tightened his hold on her and willed himself to take the plunge. "It looks like you won't be needing me around to save Lyncroft."

"Nope. Lyncroft is safe and sound again with Daniel at the helm."

"Annie…"

"Hmm?"

"When you proposed to me, you said you would file for divorce when Daniel returned."

She went still. "Did I?"

"Yes."

"If I recall, you implied at the time that the arrangement was fine with you," she said carefully.

"It's not. I don't want a divorce."

Annie levered herself up on one elbow. Her eyes were glowing with happiness. "Are you serious?"

"Very serious." He studied her face in the shadows and saw the hope in her eyes.

Relief surged through him. She didn't want their relationship to end any more than he did, Oliver thought with satisfaction. Everything was going to be all right. Everything was under control.

Annie smiled. "Oliver, are you telling me that you want our marriage to become a real one?"

"I've told you all along that it was real."

"I know, but we both understood that it was a marriage of convenience. You married me to do me a favor. I don't want you to feel obligated to do the noble thing just because you know how I feel about you."

"I married you," Oliver said with great precision, "because I wanted you. I wanted you from the moment I saw you. If you hadn't asked me to marry you, I would eventually have proposed."

"I'm so glad." Annie threw herself across him, cradling his face between her hands. She rained passionate little kisses down across his mouth.

Oliver smiled up at her through the storm of kisses. "Does this mean you're willing to make the marriage permanent?"

"Of course it does. There's nothing I want more." Annie raised her head slightly, her mouth curving in a rueful smile. "And don't tell me you don't know it. You've known from the beginning how I feel about you."

"I knew you were attracted to me," he admitted carefully. "But I wasn't certain I could convince you to stay married to me."

She gave him her most brilliant smile. "How could you have doubted it? I love you."

"Yes." Oliver was genuinely awed. "I believe you do." He reached up, captured her face between his hands, and dragged her mouth back down to his. "Oh, God, Annie. You won't be sorry. I swear it."

"I know," she mumbled against his lips. "Oliver?"

"Hmm?" He could feel his body hardening. The urge to bury himself in Annie's sweet heat was swamping him once more.

"You do love me, don't you?" Annie snuggled closer. "I've been telling myself all along that you do, but you've never actually said the words."

Oliver froze. "Annie?"

Annie lifted herself away from him. "What is it?"

He closed his eyes briefly, struggling to find the

words. When he looked at her again he could see the intensity in her gaze. "I want you."

"I know that."

Oliver tried again. "I care for you very much."

"I know that."

"I swear on my life that I'll take care of you for the rest of my days. You can trust me."

"I know that," she said. She was beginning to sound impatient.

Oliver sat up slowly. "I'm trying to be totally honest here."

"Tell me you love me."

"You don't understand." Wearily he pushed back the covers and got to his feet. He walked slowly to the window and stood looking out at the predawn darkness. "Everything I have is yours."

"What I want is your love. I don't give a damn about anything else."

He felt a surge of familiar panic sweeping through him. "I'm trying to explain something."

"What are you trying to explain? That you think I'll make an okay wife, but that you don't actually love me?"

"Stop putting words in my mouth," he said with soft savagery. "Damn it, Annie, I won't be manipulated. Not even by you."

"You think I'm trying to manipulate you?" she demanded furiously.

It dawned on Oliver that he was rapidly losing control of the situation. He turned around and saw that Annie was kneeling proudly on the bed, her chin high, her shoulders squared. He reached out and turned on a lamp. The soft light illuminated the dangerously militant fire in her eyes.

"All right, let's both take a step back and come at this from another direction," Oliver said in what he hoped was a soothing tone.

"What other direction is there? Either you love me or you don't."

Oliver felt his temper start to fray. The chilling apprehension inside him was a shark gnawing at his vitals. Annie had been steadily nibbling away at the edges of his control since the day of their marriage. She had found his weak point. She knew where he was vulnerable. "Calm down, Annie. You're getting emotional."

"Of course I'm getting emotional. What do you expect? I'm a woman in love with a man who hasn't got the guts to tell her that he loves her. What kind of wimp are you, Oliver Rain?"

"This argument is turning ludicrous."

"Only to you." Annie scrambled across the bed and stood up to confront him. "I want a man who's brave enough to tell me he loves me. I won't settle for less."

Oliver's temper finally slipped the leash. "Damn it, don't you understand? I'm giving you all I have to give to a woman."

"Well, it's not good enough." Annie grabbed her robe off the bedpost and swirled it around herself.

Alarm streaked through Oliver. "What the hell do you think you're doing?"

"I'm leaving you." She started toward the bedroom door.

"It's four o'clock in the morning."

"A perfect time to walk out on an idiot." She was in the hall now.

Oliver went to the door and saw that she was disappearing into the bedroom she had used when she first moved into the penthouse. "Annie, come back here."

She didn't respond. Oliver heard drawers slamming. Then he heard a suitcase being snapped shut. The sounds made him clench his back teeth.

He would not walk into the bedroom and plead with her to stay. He had his pride. He was in control. He was not weak.

When Annie reappeared a short time later, she was dressed in jeans and a fuchsia pullover. She had her suitcase in her hand.

"I'll send for the rest of my things later," she said as she walked straight past Oliver toward the front door.

"You're going to regret this," Oliver warned softly.

"Is that a threat from the extremely dangerous Oliver Rain?"

"It's not a threat, Annie, it's a promise. You're going to regret this because you'll soon change your mind. Then you'll have to swallow your pride. You'll have to ask to move back in. You won't like that, Annie. Don't make it hard on yourself."

She stopped at the door, her hand on the knob. "It's not my pride that's going to go down in flames, Oliver. It's yours."

"The hell it is."

Her eyes were bright with hurt and rage. "If you want me back, you're going to have to work at it."

"Is that right? How am I supposed to do that?"

"You're going to have to tell me you love me. You're going to have to shout it from the rooftops, Oliver. I want to hear the words loud and clear. And then you'll have to beg me to come back to you."

"Annie, this is stupid."

"I couldn't agree more. Good-bye, Oliver." She opened the door and went out into the corridor. "By the way, I'm not going downstairs to Bolt's this time. I'm going to my brother's apartment."

"Thank you for telling me," he said between his teeth.

"I'm informing you so that you won't wake Bolt up trying to find out where I am. He deserves his rest. He's had a very long day." Annie started to slam the door. She paused briefly. "By the way, thank you for saving my life tonight."

Twenty minutes later Annie drove into the underground garage beneath Daniel's apartment building. She waited in the car just inside the entrance while the security gate closed behind her.

A familiar black Mercedes cruised slowly past. Annie wasn't surprised. She had been aware of the car's headlights in her rearview mirror ever since she had left Oliver's building.

What startled her was that it wasn't Bolt at the wheel. When the Mercedes moved beneath a streetlamp, she saw Oliver watching her from the driver's seat.

He drove off silently when he saw that she was safe behind the iron gates.

Annie sighed as she parked her car in one of the visitor slots. The man loved her. Why was it so hard for him to break down that last barrier and admit it, she wondered desolately.

A few minutes later Annie stepped off the elevator on her brother's floor. She leaned on his doorbell. It was a long time before Daniel appeared. He finally answered the door garbed in a pair of jeans that he had obviously stepped into in a hurry. Irritation turned to concern in his eyes as he took in the sight of her tear-splotched face.

"Annie, what's wrong? What the devil are you doing here at this hour?"

"I've left Oliver."

Joanna appeared behind Daniel, belting a white terry-cloth robe around herself. "Annie? Are you okay?"

"No," Annie said baldly. "I'm not okay." She burst into tears.

21

For the first time ever in his dealings with Sybil, Oliver felt a degree of sympathy for her that he had never expected to feel. She sat across from him in his study while he quietly told her the truth about Jonathan Grace. It was one of the most difficult things he had ever done. But she took the blow with what he had to admit was true Rain pride.

"I fell for it," Sybil said wearily. "I think that's the hardest part to accept. I believed every word Jonathan or John or whatever his name is said. How could I have been so stupid as to trust him?"

Oliver looked down at his folded hands and then raised his eyes to Sybil's. "If it makes you feel any better, I got taken in by Walker Gresham five years ago. Nearly got myself and Daniel Lyncroft killed. The Gresham brothers were expert con artists."

Sybil's smile was bitter. "Hard to believe anyone could get away with conning you. What about all those extensive files you kept on people?"

"They didn't do me much good, did they? I didn't know Walker Gresham was using my company as a cover for gunrunning until Lyncroft discovered it. And I didn't know Gresham had a brother in prison who might one day come looking for revenge."

"I guess even criminals have family ties."

366

"Apparently." Oliver sat silently for a while. "I'm sorry about this, Sybil."

"Do you know something? I believe you. You really are sorry."

"The whole damn situation was my fault. I should have researched Walker Gresham better five years ago. I should have taken more precautions."

"You know what your problem is, Oliver?"

"Annie tells me it has to do with interpersonal communication."

"I mean in addition to your communication problems," Sybil said meaningfully.

Oliver's brows rose. "I've got other problems?"

"Yes, indeed. One of your other problems is that you always take full responsibility for everything." Sybil got to her feet, adjusting her purse over her shoulder. "For the record, you're not responsible for the fact that Jonathan, or rather John Gresham, came looking for revenge. Don't blame yourself. Could have happened to anyone."

"I'll keep that in mind."

"You do that." Sybil started for the door of the study. "In the meantime, I hear you've got another serious problem on your hands. And you do have full responsibility for this one."

Oliver eyed her cautiously. "What problem is that?"

"Annie's walked out."

"News travels fast in this family," Oliver said grimly.

"Especially bad news." Sybil smiled wryly. "And I've got to tell you, Oliver, that we all consider the fact that Annie has left you extremely bad news. If you've got half the intelligence we've always credited you with, you'll do whatever you have to do to get her back."

"I owe you, Oliver."

"Forget it."

"No, I won't forget it." Daniel sat at his desk and watched Oliver prowl the office. "I don't know how to thank you for what you did."

"Thank Annie," Oliver muttered. "She's the one who came up with the idea of marrying me to save Lyncroft."

Daniel smiled. "I get the feeling that she didn't marry you just to save the company."

"The hell she didn't. She left me within hours after you showed up safe and sound. What does that tell you?"

"That you managed to piss her off."

Oliver swore under his breath. "It tells you that she thinks she doesn't need me any more. It's obvious she just married me to save Lyncroft. She used me. That's what she did. She used me."

"You're really working yourself up into a lather of self-pity over this, aren't you? I'm surprised. That's not like you, Oliver. You're usually the ice man, remember?"

"I've never been in this situation before."

"You mean you haven't met too many people who don't jump when you lay down the law. Annie's different."

"She's different all right."

"Look, I know Annie a lot better than you do," Daniel said. "She might have engineered the marriage purely for business reasons—although I doubt it. But she sure as hell didn't sleep with you for business reasons." Daniel cocked a brow. "Uh, she is sleeping with you, isn't she?"

Oliver scowled at him. "Not any more. She walked out."

"Come on, Oliver. You know that she would never have gone to bed with you if she hadn't thought she was in love with you. You're just too pissed off yourself right now to admit it."

He was right, but Oliver refused to acknowledge it aloud. That would be the first step down a very slippery slope that would end with his surrender. "Your sister used me."

"You keep saying that."

"It's true."

"You, of course, did not use her," Daniel said with suspicious blandness.

"Hell, no. You know I didn't need Lyncroft badly enough to marry her for it."

"That doesn't mean you didn't use her."

"What would I use her for?" Oliver demanded roughly.

"You told me the night of my engagement party that you had decided it was time that you got married, too. Remember?"

"I remember," Oliver said grimly.

"You said that you had liquidated most of your holdings and cleared the decks so that you'd be free to concentrate on marriage and a family. The next thing I know you're married to my sister. What am I supposed to conclude except that you decided my sister was the woman you wanted?"

"I told you, she's the one who proposed to me."

"Damn it, don't try to con me, Rain. I know you too well. We both know you would never have married Annie just to do her a favor. You'd already set your sights on her before she came to you with her offer, hadn't you?"

Oliver shrugged, refusing to respond to the goad.

"And with your usual luck, she fell right into your hands. Hell, you didn't even have to shake the branches of the tree she was sitting in, did you? You didn't have to go through the nuisance of a courtship. Talk about convenient."

Oliver gazed stolidly out the window. "Let me tell you something, Lyncroft. Your sister is the most inconvenient woman I've ever met. All I've had from Annie is trouble."

"You've had a lot more than that," Daniel said coolly.

"So? I'm married to her. Hell, I married her before I went to bed with her. How much more can you ask of a man?"

"Tell me something, if Annie is such a difficult female, why do you want her back?"

"That's my business."

Daniel pondered that for a long moment. He picked up a pen and tapped it absently on the surface of the desk. "Oliver, you've got to look at this from Annie's point of view. As far as she's concerned, she gave you her heart. What did you give her?"

Oliver's stomach muscles clenched. "I gave her everything I have to give. I told her that. If it's not enough, that's too damn bad."

"In other words, you can't or won't tell her that you love her."

Oliver spun around. "She's trying to manipulate me into saying it, and I'll be damned if I'll let her manage me any more than she already has. You don't know what I've already done because of your sister.

You don't know how many changes she's made in my life. You don't know how much she's interfered in family matters that were none of her business."

"I know Annie. If she interfered, she was only trying to help. She's good at that kind of thing."

"And that brings up another point," Oliver growled. "I won't join her tribe of wounded males. I don't need rescuing, damn it."

"So that's it," Daniel said very softly. "You've heard about Arthur Quigley and Melvin Finch?"

"Yes."

"There are a couple more like them scattered around the countryside."

"Damn."

"But they're not anything like you, Oliver. It's true Annie rescued them, but none of them ever returned the favor."

Oliver frowned. "What's that supposed to mean?"

"You, Rain, have the distinction of being the only man who's ever rescued Annie. You saved Lyncroft for her and three nights ago you saved her life in that greenhouse. In her eyes you're a hero, not another wounded bird like Quigley and Finch."

"She's not exactly acting the part of the grateful damsel."

"What can I tell you? Annie's unique. And she's got her pride, too. You, of all people, should understand pride, Rain."

"This is a waste of time." Oliver stalked to the door. "I don't know why I came here to talk to you about your sister."

"Oliver?"

"What?" Oliver opened the door.

Daniel met his eyes. "Thanks again. For everything."

"Forget it." Oliver started through the door. He paused briefly and glanced back again. "By the way, your files on employees, competitors, and investors are almost totally worthless. I couldn't find any of the information I needed in them."

Daniel grinned. "I keep files, Oliver, not security dossiers the way you used to do."

Oliver did not bother to respond to that.

Oliver walked the streets of Seattle aimlessly for over an hour. He bought coffee at a sidewalk espresso stand, watched the ferries depart from the waterfront docks, and wandered through Pioneer Square.

The lack of focused direction felt very strange. Oliver could not recall the last time he had done anything without a clear-cut purpose. He always had a goal and he was always focused on that goal.

When he finally came to a halt, he saw that he was standing in front of Wildest Dreams.

Obviously part of him had known all along where he was headed.

He felt like an idiot standing on the sidewalk outside the shop. The feeling of indecisiveness infuriated him. He was never indecisive.

The door of the shop opened. A thin, wiry man wearing a navy blue sweater over a pair of corduroy slacks nearly collided with Oliver. The man stopped and peered up at him through horn-rim glasses.

"Sorry," the man said.

Oliver shrugged, his gaze on the shop window. "Forget it."

"I know you." The man drew himself up so that he stood a little taller. "You're Rain, aren't you? Annie's husband."

Oliver glanced at him. "What of it?"

"I'm Arthur Quigley."

Oliver looked back at the window. "Is that right?"

"Right. I'm the one who gave Annie the book she said you needed," Arthur explained helpfully. "Sorry it didn't help."

Oliver took a firm grasp on his precarious temper. "Did Annie tell you that it didn't help?"

"Not in so many words, but I've just been talking to her and she tells me that she's left you, so I have to assume things didn't work out." Arthur frowned in concern. "Say, would you like to try another book? I've got quite a good selection."

"No, thank you."

"It's nothing to be ashamed of you know," Arthur said in a confidential tone. "We men aren't born knowing how to be great lovers. It's a learned skill, just like everything else."

"I'll keep that in mind," Oliver muttered.

"Sure. Let me know if you'd like to try another book." Arthur smiled. "Guess you're here to see Annie, huh?"

"Maybe."

Arthur nodded, apparently satisfied. "It's about time. She's been eating her heart out over you. I'm glad you came to your senses."

Oliver stepped around Quigley, opened the door of Wildest Dreams, and walked inside. Ella looked up from behind the counter. She scowled at him.

"What do you want?"

"I came to see my wife," Oliver said, laying plenty of emphasis on the last word.

"She's got visitors."

"Too bad." He went past her to open the door of Annie's office.

As Ella had said, Annie was not alone. Five pairs of accusing eyes turned toward him. Sybil, Heather, Valerie, Richard, and Nathan all sat, stood, or lounged around Annie's desk. Annie was in her chair, dabbing at her tear-reddened eyes with a tissue.

"What are you doing here, Oliver?" Sybil rose to her feet. Her face still showed the strain of having learned who and what Jonathan Grace really was.

"I came to see my wife. Any objections?" Oliver surveyed the faces of the rest of his family.

"If you're here to terrorize Annie, you might as well know we won't tolerate it," Valerie said.

"She's been through enough," Heather agreed.

"Heather's right." Richard eyed Oliver. "We don't want you bullying Annie."

"You've already made her cry," Nathan growled.

"I'll be okay." Annie sniffled into the tissue. "Oliver isn't going to bully me."

"Don't be too certain of that," Sybil said. "You don't know him as well as we do. Oliver will do anything to get his own way, won't you, Oliver?"

"If you don't mind," Oliver said evenly, "I would like to talk to Annie alone."

Valerie frowned. "I don't think that's such a good idea."

Nathan straightened away from the wall. "Yeah. I don't think it's such a good idea, either."

Oliver looked at each of them in turn. "What do you think I'm going to do to her?"

"Probably not what you should do," Sybil said.

Oliver's brows rose. "And just what is it you think I should do, Sybil?"

"Beg," Sybil said simply. She gave him an odd little smile. "For once in your life, Oliver Rain, it's time you learned how to ask very nicely for what you want. It's time you learned the virtues of humility."

"I wasn't aware there were any virtues in humility," Oliver said.

"Sybil's got a point," Valerie said. "It's time you learned you can't have everything you want. Not unless you learn to ask politely."

"Stop it." Annie waved the tissue about wildly. "Stop it, please, all of you. I appreciate what you're trying to do, but there's no need to attack Oliver."

"It's true," Valerie charged. "Oliver is accustomed to taking what he wants. He always gets things his own way."

"That's not true." Annie reached for another tissue and blew furiously into it. "Good heavens, Valerie, you can't possibly believe your brother has had everything he ever wanted in life. It's just the opposite."

"What are you talking about?" Heather asked, frowning.

"Don't you understand?" Annie gulped on a sob. "Oliver never got anything he really wanted. He didn't even get the career he once dreamed of pursuing."

"Annie, you're being too soft on him," Nathan said, looking uneasy.

"Oh, for heaven's sake," Annie mumbled into the damp tissue. "Don't you see? Oliver's always had to give up what he wanted in favor of what was best for the rest of you. He sacrificed everything for the sake of the family."

Valerie and the others looked at each other. Then they looked at Oliver.

It dawned on Oliver that he had just gotten very lucky. His family's attack on him had caused Annie to spring to his defense. The balance of power had just shifted subtly in his direction. If he played his cards right, he wouldn't have to expose his vulnerability. Annie and the others would never know the extent of his weakness. He wouldn't have to beg.

"I can see I'm not wanted around here," Oliver said quietly. He looked at Annie. "Good-bye, Annie. Maybe we can talk some other time."

Her red eyes widened in dismay. "Oliver, wait."

Oliver didn't wait.

"Annie, don't you dare run after him," Sybil hissed.

Oliver didn't glance back to see if Annie was indeed trying to follow. He strode quickly through the shop and let himself out the front door.

Outside he took a deep breath. Victory was within his grasp. He could sense it. All he had to do was stay in control.

Suitcase in hand, Annie got off the elevator on the penthouse floor shortly after six o'clock. She crossed the hall to lean on Oliver's doorbell.

Bolt opened the door immediately. "Good evening, Mrs. Rain."

"Hi, Bolt. Is Oliver home?"

"Yes." His gaze went to her suitcase. "I realize this is none of my business, but I'm not certain this is a good idea."

"I know. Everyone thinks I shouldn't come back to Oliver so easily. The trouble is, the rest of you don't understand him."

"If you say so." Bolt reached down to pick up her suitcase.

Annie stepped into the ebony and gold foyer and started to strip off her raincoat. "Where is he?"

"In the study."

"Thanks." Annie handed her coat over to Bolt and went purposefully down the hall to the closed door of the study.

She knocked once and opened the door.

Oliver was sitting at his desk. His expression was perfectly controlled, as usual, but the glare of the halogen lamp revealed the tension in his face. Annie could not decide if he looked triumphant or merely coldly satisfied. She smiled wryly.

"Hello, Oliver. I'm back."

"You're just in time for dinner," Oliver said quietly. He got to his feet and walked around the desk.

"Oliver, you are such an idiot at times. I know you love me, but you can't bear to let down your guard for even a minute, can you?" Annie chuckled. "You're going to infuriate me from time to time, but that's okay. I love you anyway."

"I'm glad," Oliver whispered starkly. He opened his arms.

Annie walked straight into them.

Oliver lay awake for a long while that night. Annie was sound asleep beside him. Her soft, warm body was curled trustingly into his own. She was back where she belonged, safe in his bed. He had won. Everything was under control again.

He stared into the shadows of the darkened bedroom and wondered why being completely in control no longer gave him the satisfaction it once had.

Four days later Annie returned from lunch just in

time to see a delivery van pulling away from the curb outside Wildest Dreams. She went forward eagerly in hopes that the shipment of art deco torchière lamps had arrived a few days ahead of schedule. Stanford J. Littlewood was waiting for one.

She opened the door of the shop and came to an abrupt halt. The boutique was crammed with ferns. Wildest Dreams had been turned into a jungle.

There were ferns everywhere. They filled the room until there was barely space in which to move. Maidenhairs and staghorns hung from every available hook. Pots overflowing with luxurious green fronds of every imaginable shape and size sat on the counter and on every display table. Lady ferns and sword ferns lined a narrow path that led to her office.

"What on earth?" Annie looked around for Ella. "What's going on here?"

"Beats me." Ella poked her head out from behind a magnificent billowing maidenhair. "They started arriving just after you left for lunch. They've been pouring into the shop for the past hour." She grinned. "There are a lot more in your office."

Dazed, Annie made her way slowly through the miniature rainforest. The warm, earthy scent of rich soil and lush greenery filled the air.

This was Oliver's doing, she realized in growing wonder. Joy crashed through her. He had finally found a way to tell her of his love.

And what a way it was.

Some men would have sent dozens of red roses. Oliver had sent masses and masses of beautiful ferns.

There was an odd flickering light coming from inside her office. Annie went toward it as if drawn by a magic spell. When she pushed open the door, she saw that the office was crammed with greenery.

The flickering light was coming from a garish neon sculpture that sat on the top of her desk. The brightly glowing tubes of light spelled out three simple words in a glaring shade of purple.

Annie stopped in the doorway and read the words over and over again. Tears of happiness formed in her eyes.

I love you. I love you. I love you. I love you.

"What do you think?" Oliver asked softly from the corner. "Is it art? Or is it just tacky?"

Annie looked at him. She had not dreamed she could be so happy. "Who cares? It's perfect."

Oliver started to smile. The smile turned to laughter. The laughter reached his rain-colored eyes making it easy to read the love there.

"Oh, Oliver," Annie whispered, "whoever said you had trouble communicating?"

"I want you more than I've ever wanted anything else in my whole life, Annie. Never in my wildest dreams did I ever imagine I'd be lucky enough to find you. I love you." He said the words easily, naturally, with no hesitation at all.

Annie went into his arms knowing she would hear those words from him every day for the rest of her life.